# Hidden

# Hidden

## MARIANNE CURLEY

**BLOOMSBURY**

LONDON  NEW DELHI  NEW YORK  SYDNEY

Bloomsbury Publishing, London, New Delhi, New York and Sydney

First published in Great Britain in March 2013 by Bloomsbury Publishing Plc
50 Bedford Square, London WC1B 3DP

A CIP catalogue record for this book is available from the British Library

ISBN 978 1 4088 2262 3

Typeset by Hewer Text UK Ltd, Edinburgh
Printed in Great Britain by CPI Group (UK) Ltd, Croydon CR0 4YY

1 3 5 7 9 10 8 6 4 2

www.bloomsbury.com

*To Zachary James and Josephine Anabelle:*
*angels mine*

# 1

# Ebony

Do you ever stare at your reflection and wonder who that person is looking back at you? For as long as I can remember I've felt different, at odds with myself.

I live on a farm in Cedar Oakes West where Dad breeds horses for show. Until last year I used to be home-schooled, but now I go to Cedar Oakes High in town. My next-door neighbour is Amber Lang. We're both sixteen and best friends.

I've never had any major dramas in my life, so why do I feel this deep discontentment? It's only when I'm out riding, sprinting across the plains beneath the cliffs of Mount Bungarra with the wind in my face, that I really feel like me.

Even when I started high school, I still felt disconnected. I could run faster than boys who were older than me. I could hear whispered conversations from the other side of the playing field as if I stood there too. I soon learned this was not normal.

I taught myself to conceal my differences, and so far I've avoided attention, but that's only because, except for Amber and a few girls I sit with at lunch, I keep my head down.

But there's something that's impossible to disguise – my

violet eyes. They're not as deep as purple, or as light as lavender. They're precisely midway between blue and magenta on the colour wheel.

Who has violet eyes?

Amber says I should be proud of their uniqueness because they're beautiful. How can something that makes me a freak be beautiful? It doesn't make sense.

But I tend to over-think every aspect of my life.

It doesn't help that Mum and I aren't getting along that well at the moment. She says I'm acting strangely, but I think she is. Every time I want to know something about my relatives or our family's history, which is admittedly becoming more often, she starts an argument – on purpose. She accuses me of being on a search to find myself – as if it's a bad thing. I know she's worried I'll leave the valley some day. Almost everyone does eventually.

My parents have always been overprotective. I'm not exactly housebound, but Mum doesn't like travelling, and Dad doesn't like to leave the horses.

For the first few years of my life my skin reacted to ultraviolet light and I had to stay indoors or cover up in dark clothes. I remember the little girl next door wearing pretty yellow and pink outfits, while my clothes were mostly navy blue and black tops and pants, and always with long sleeves. But by the time I was five, my skin had developed the pigment it needed and my sensitivity to light disappeared. Today, Amber says I look tanned all year round.

Anyway, that wasn't the real reason Mum's so overprotective.

My parents had wanted a big family, but Mum miscarried twice, then lost her third pregnancy during the twenty-ninth week. It took years for them to want to try again after that. Finally she found out she was pregnant – this time with twins. But something went wrong again.

Mum gave birth to a girl and a boy. The girl, of course, was me. My brother, Ben, died in his first hour of life.

I think it made them terrified of losing me. And I'm sure it's one of the reasons they wanted me to be home-schooled. Once I understood the origin of this fear I didn't pressure them again until, well, recently.

For most of my home-schooled years I dreamed of sitting in a classroom with children my own age. It wasn't boredom. I craved companionship. When I turned twelve, my parents let me ride Shadow anywhere within the boundary of our property. With hundreds of hectares to roam, I had my first taste of freedom. I would disappear for hours, exploring the woodlands and creeks on our land. And on these expeditions I would imagine myself a princess living in a world where everyone rode horses, children played on cobbled streets, and the handsomest prince in the land courted me.

Riding Shadow around the property was exhilarating at twelve and thirteen, but I'm sixteen now, and those daydreaming days are well behind me. I need to uncover the real Ebony Hawkins, the girl suffocating inside me. It's become crucial lately, for reasons hard to explain, except that . . . I'm developing in ways I don't understand and can't find in any biology books. For a start, my light brown hair, weirdly, is turning a sort of dark reddish-brown colour with gold highlights. By itself.

Anyway, back to the here and now. It's Saturday morning and I'm in the kitchen arguing with Mum about going to a club in town with Amber tonight. Mum is bringing up every reason, absurd and otherwise, why I'm not allowed to go. Dad shot away to the stables at the first hint of raised voices.

'You have to trust me, Mum.' I'm standing at the breakfast bar with the sun warming my back through the French windows behind me. I pour a cup of home-made muesli into a bowl. 'You taught me to look after myself, so why do you still worry?' I reach into the cutlery drawer for a spoon before lifting my eyes to hers. 'Unless there's something you haven't told me?' I wait, gauging her reaction.

She closes the fridge door with a jug of milk in her hand and, keeping her eyes down, walks slowly to the breakfast bar. She's taking her time to formulate a reply, which freaks me out; my imagination leaps.

'What's wrong with me, Mum?'

She looks up then, her hand freezing in mid-air. 'Nothing is wrong with you, Ebony. Why would you think that?'

I take the milk from her hand before it spills, kicking myself for asking that foolish question. There *is* something wrong with me. I feel it in my bones. It's happening *to* my bones! But I'm not ready to tackle that particular detail with Mum yet – or with myself.

'Ebony, are you all right? You've gone pale.'

'Yeah, Mum, I'm fine ... Well, actually, no, I'm not.' At

her confused frown, I explain, 'Sometimes you and Dad look at me as if I have three heads.'

She forces a laugh. 'What on earth are you talking about, darling?'

'Forget it. Just let me go tonight, Mum, please. This dance means a lot to me. Amber's going. Leah's going. Ivy and Bec are going. And you *never* let me go to stuff like this.'

'For good reasons, Ebony. The subject is now closed.'

'Oh, this one too?'

'Don't be cheeky.'

'But, Mum, Mr Lang has already agreed to drive us both ways since we all know you wouldn't let me go if one of my friends were to pick me up.'

'Are you trying to provoke an argument, dear?'

'*Me?*' I shake my head at this. I take a deep breath and count to five in my head, in an effort to tone down any attitude in my voice. 'Mum, I just want to go to a *supervised* dance for under-eighteens. What's wrong with that?'

She cups the side of my face with her hand. 'Something bad could happen when you're away from home.'

I step backwards. 'Why do you say that all the time? What were all those self-defence lessons for?'

She lifts her eyes to the ceiling and bites down on her lower lip.

'Mum? What *were* those lessons for?'

She sighs. 'Self-protection, darling, that's all.'

There's more in her eyes than she's saying, so much more that goosebumps break out across the skin of my arms. Well, if she's not prepared to tell me anything, I'll just have to find out for myself.

5

'I'm going tonight, Mum. It's all arranged,' I say.

Her eyes turn hard and she inhales through tight lips. I know this look. I *hate* this look. 'Young lady, you are *not* going anywhere tonight.'

'I *am* going! You can't stop me. I'm sixteen!'

'I can, and I will, and sixteen is still a baby.'

'Mum, really!'

She takes a deep breath. 'Ebony, calm down. Take Shadow for a ride. Cool that fiery temper of yours.'

Not hungry any more, I dump my muesli in the bin and head for the back door. But once there I stop and turn back. 'That's funny, you know.'

'What?'

'You say I have a temper, yet I don't raise my voice or argue with anyone except you. Can you tell me why that is, Mum?'

Her mouth opens and a pained look enters her eyes. She doesn't say a word but her eyes gleam with unshed tears, and my head fills with more questions.

# 2

# Jordan

It's Saturday night, the air is cold, and I'm standing outside the nightclub – Chill – in my black T-shirt, blue jeans and the brown suede jacket I picked up at the charity shop this morning. I shiver inside my jacket. I should have told Danny I'd meet him inside. My best friend, my one-and-only friend, is running late.

Which means, while I stand here watching parents dropping off their kids, my brain has time to remind me how my father is in a prison cell with seven more years to serve, and my mum is long gone from a heroin overdose.

People say it's a wonderful world. Well, from where I stand it's a load of bull. Man, this world is feral. It's cruel and unpredictable.

I've lived in more houses than I have fingers, including a six-month stint in juvenile detention for hitching a ride in a car I didn't know my mate's brother had stolen.

I was pretty much living on a day-to-day basis at the time. Then a new caseworker named Lillian Fisher took an interest in my well-being and secured a decent place for me to live, giving me hope.

Today, a few weeks after my sixteenth birthday, my life is

still going well enough, though it's anyone's guess how long this run will last. Deep inside, I know I'm a hair's breadth away from spinning out of control. When Mum died, I thought I would too. I wanted to. What does a nine-year-old do for the rest of his life without his mum? Call me morbid, a pessimist, whatever you want, but a sense of death still simmers beneath the surface, rising up on days like today.

I glance at my tattoo. It's on the inside of my left wrist – a big strong angel, his face in profile surrounded by masses of gold curls, with big white wings on broad shoulders, and in his hands a golden bow. My mother's boyfriend, Jason, a tatooist by trade, penned it for me on the day she died. He wanted me to have something lasting to remember her by. It was my first experience of real pain.

I don't recall much from that day or the months that followed. One year blurred into another and soon I had hit eleven. Social services had just placed me with an older, childless couple. When I came to the house at No. 42 Warrigal Road, there were already two other boys there – brothers: Adam and Seth Skinner. Adam was in my year at school and we hit it off instantly. His mother was in hospital with a broken heart after his dad died from a brain tumour.

Adam had an irritation in his life in the form of his little brother, Seth. I didn't mind Seth tagging along half as much as Adam did. I used to pretend they were my real brothers. I think I knew this was the closest I would come to a family of my own. Adam never understood, back then, that having a brother made the difference between being a family and being alone.

But the good times didn't last.

People say you can tell when tragedy is about to strike. You get a vibe, a sense of déjà vu, something like that. If that's true, then I'm not one of those people. If my mother had been alive, she would have said the Angel of Death walked in our shadows that day, waiting for the right moment to collect. Maybe he was following us, and we were just too excited to notice.

It was the last weekend before school started for the new year, and we were going to an abandoned mine to search for gold.

Later, what happened earned the label 'tragic accident', but no amount of apologising could undo the damage. A split-second decision turned best friends into mortal enemies and changed my life and those of the people around me for ever.

# 3

# Ebony

The nightclub fronts one of the town's busiest roads. Its black steel door sits back in a dark recessed porch, creating an air of mystery in direct contrast to the bright flashy lights of the twin cinemas across the road.

The arriving crowd spills out on to the pavement as groups gather before going inside. Traffic is heavy in both directions. Mr Lang pulls up behind a white van and waits, engine idling, while six girls jump out of the van and start preening. The girls are Year Nines from my school, all dolled up and buzzing with excitement. Their outfits are mostly short skirts, black tights and crop tops, and they're all wearing sparkly make-up.

The girls look cute; their energy is catching.

Mr Lang inches forward into the spot the white van just vacated and releases the door locks. 'I'll be back at eleven. Don't dawdle, you two. It will be bedlam driving out of here tonight.'

'Sure, Dad. Thanks for the lift,' Amber says on her way out.

Meanwhile, I shuffle over, trying to keep my skirt from riding up my legs.

'Thanks for the lift, Mr Lang.' I have one high-heel-clad foot almost to the ground when he calls my name and I answer, 'Yes, sir?'

'Young people,' he says in a philosophical tone, 'need balance in their lives. It's not all about schoolwork and chores.'

'No, sir, it's not. Thank you for taking time out to drive us tonight.'

'It's a pleasure, Ebony. I don't mind. That's not the problem.' His fingers strum a rhythm on the steering wheel. 'If you ever find you have to climb out of your bedroom window again, promise me you'll be more careful. Your mother's rose trellis might not hold up next time.'

'Ohhh.' *So he saw me!* 'You're not going to make me go home, are you, Mr Lang?'

Looking straight ahead he says, 'I've brought you here now, so, no, I won't take you back, or tell your mother I saw you.'

'Thank you so much!'

He tries not to grin. 'This one time only, you understand,' he warns.

'Yes, of course, and thank you again, Mr Lang.' If only Mum shared Mr Lang's philosophy!

'Did you leave a note, Ebony?'

'In my room. But if Mum doesn't find it, I'm sure it won't take much to figure out where I am.'

'No doubt. Well, you should get out before I change my mind,' he says.

I climb out of the vehicle in a hurry to find Amber before she walks into the club. But when both my feet are

11

on the pavement, I swing around and collide with someone standing still.

It's a boy, and I hit him so hard I send him flying across the pavement, into the brick wall, where he slides to the floor with the wind knocked out of his lungs.

*Oh, no!*

I'm at his side before he opens his eyes. 'Are you all right?' He lifts his head at the sound of my voice and his eyes flutter open. I take his hand to help him back on to his feet. Not my wisest idea. My pull is more like a yank. He springs up in one go and slams into my chest. I hear something crack.

*Oh no, no, no! Was that his rib?*

Silently he looks at me, eyes wide open now – deep, dark blue and full of amazement at my strength.

Terrified he's going to fall, I keep my arm around his waist and a firm grip of his hand, forgetting how strong my grip can be until he yanks his fingers out and shakes them with a confused expression furrowing his brow.

Embarrassed, I offer my stammered apologies. 'I'm so, so sorry, really, truly, *so* sorry. Is anything broken? Can you stand if I let you go?'

Finally he says, 'I think I can manage.'

I breathe a sigh of relief. 'Good. For a minute there . . .' I stop mid-sentence when I realise he's staring again, his eyes wide and focused directly on mine.

'Are your eyes really . . . purple?' he says.

'They're violet, actually.'

'Does anybody have violet eyes?'

'Apparently I do.'

I hastily make to move back but find his hand is now clasping mine. Maybe he's not feeling entirely stable yet. 'Did I hurt you much? I'm stronger than most . . . you know . . . *weak* . . . people.'

*Oh no! Did I just call him 'weak'?*

'Listen, I didn't mean to say you're a weak person. I'm just . . . I'm, well, er . . . worried about you. Should I call . . . ?' I pause and inhale a quick deep breath. 'OK, I'm going to stop talking now.'

He stares at me as if I've gone nuts. I can't say I blame him. 'Ummm,' he murmurs, pointing down to our feet. 'Is that your heel sticking into the space between my toes?'

I gasp, but it comes out more like a screech. 'That *is* my heel! Oh no! It's shot right through your shoe! I'm so, so, *so* sorry! Is your toe broken? Is that what I heard?'

Still gawking at me with his mouth hanging open, he finally says, 'You heard something?'

I plaster a fake smile quickly to my face. 'Maybe you should test your toes?'

He moves them quite well, considering my stiletto heel has nailed his shoe to the ground!

Annoyed with myself, and horribly embarrassed, my face undoubtedly redder than beetroot juice, I wrench my foot up to extract my shoe's ten-centimetre heel.

All the while I can't stop mumbling. 'I'm such a klutz! I'm just not used to wearing high heels. It was my friend Amber. She said I looked like a cowgirl in my riding boots . . .' I stop suddenly. Damn it, I'm rambling again! For some reason I feel the need to fill the void created by this boy's silence.

'Has anyone ever told you how captivating your voice is?'

I laugh a little. I nearly killed him and he says my voice is captivating! 'No. No one has ever told me that.'

He smiles sweetly, obviously still dazed by pain. And shock. I lean forward and whisper, 'Actually, I *never* wear heels. I'm more comfortable riding a horse ...' *Aaargh!! What am I saying?* 'Pretty soon you're going to regret that you came and stood in this spot.'

'Somehow I doubt that.'

'By the way, how is your back? You hit that wall so *hard*.' I spin around and nonchalantly try to check his spine.

He gets that *Is-she-all-there?* look again. 'You're not checking out my butt, are you?'

I shake my head so hard my clasp drops out, and my curls tumble down all the way to my waist. 'No, I swear I'm not.'

He moistens his lips with his tongue and kind of laughs. It's an unconscious act and quite sexy. 'My back's fine, although I can't say for sure about these,' he says, pointing at his toes, 'but I think they'll survive.'

'I really am sorry about your shoe.'

'It's no big deal; it's just a small hole. You can stop apologising.'

I smile at his kindness.

'Even if my toe were broken,' he adds, 'it wouldn't matter because I have another nine. Really.' He sighs then, sounding cross at himself. '*I'm* rambling now, aren't I?'

'It's your turn,' I say. Even though he's speaking now, he still has that dazed look about him. 'Are you positive you're OK? You look a little spacey. You didn't happen to hit your head?'

14

'I didn't hit my head, but you're really strong.'

Instantly my eyes flutter downwards.

He rushes to say, 'Hey, I didn't mean anything by that. It was just a surprise when you bowled me over like a steam train. *Crap.* It's my turn to apologise. I'm sorry.'

'It's OK. I *am* strong, but I know that some people find strength intimidating in a girl. So . . . um, if you don't mind, could you keep that information to yourself?'

'Absolutely! I swear, your secret is safe with me.' He puts a hand over his heart. 'I won't tell anyone, not a soul, not a —'

'Thank you.'

We both glance down and realise how close we're standing, our joined hands between us at chest height. We stay this way, still and silent, looking into each other's eyes. I feel something tangible stretch between us, and I know he's feeling this unusual connection too. I mean, if I concentrate, I can hear a person's heart beating if they're standing close enough. Right now, this boy's heart is beating very, very fast.

The link between us feels electric.

I will remember this moment. It's burning into my memory as we continue to stare at each other, until, gradually, I see something really sad inside his eyes. This dark misery wraps around me like a shroud. I feel smothered by it, as if I'm choking and can't breathe. I don't quite know what to make of it. I sense a despair inside this boy that must be hard to live with. My smile fades at this thought and I step back. It doesn't take long for embarrassment to replace the feeling of closeness.

The world shifts back into focus quickly, starting with Amber's voice calling my name. 'Ebony! What's keeping you?'

'Over here!' I call out, turning to make eye contact.

She runs over. 'You know, I thought you were behind me this whole time until I got my hand stamped and you weren't next. Are you OK? You look a bit stunned.'

'I'm fine.'

Our friend Leah comes out then. 'Hey, are you girls coming? I found a table.'

Before I realise what's happening, the two of them are leading me inside. I swing my head around to the boy standing on the pavement watching me. I smile at him and wave, promising myself that before tonight is over I will know his name and understand the reason I feel so connected to him.

# 4

# Jordan

'How's that little heart of yours thumping now, Jordy? Still marching to the beat of the pretty girl's drum?' Danny comes up to me, thoroughly amused. Obviously he saw it all.

I glare at him to no effect.

He asks, 'Do you know them?'

'Nope.'

'Not even the redhead who was fawning all over you?' He grins.

'Her hair wasn't red,' I correct in a hurry. Danny's girl fetish this month is redheads.

'It was red under the spotlight.'

'Well, not from where I was standing. Mitts off, OK?'

'OK, OK! She's not my type anyway.' He lifts his hands in the air in a gesture of peace. 'I could swear you knew them.'

'I told you already.'

'Not even the "brunette" who couldn't keep her hands off you?' In joking fashion he hikes his fingers under my jacket, running them up and down my chest. People stare. A few laugh at his tomfoolery. 'When you looked into each other's eyes, *man*, no one knew where to look.'

I shove his hands away. These days there are times I'd like

to block Danny out, press the mute button on his remote control.

'Trust me, Danny, I would have remembered *those* eyes if I'd seen them before.'

'Man . . .' He pauses, offering a moment's silence, as if the girl's eyes warrant a profound reverence. 'What do you call that colour? Purple?'

'Violet.'

'I think those girls go to our school, but I haven't seen them around any of the local haunts, so they must be hicks from the west.'

I stare at him. *That girl goes to my school?*

He thumps my chest with an open hand. 'You know – horse people.'

'You've seen them at school?'

'What's more, I think they're in our year.'

'Dude, it's the hair. That dumb rule about keeping it tied back. Girls look different with their hair down.'

That look is back in his eyes. 'So . . . did you get her number?'

'Whose number?' Since I didn't, and could kick myself for it, I decide to be vague. It's slightly less embarrassing and gives me time to think of a reply.

'The bronze hottie, the one who almost brought down a wall of the club with your spine.'

'I *tripped* and *fell* into the wall.'

He laughs. 'Jordy, I know what I saw. I'll be your witness when you sue for injury compensation.'

'Dude, thanks for your concern, but I won't be suing anyone since it was *me* who lost *my* footing. *OK?*'

He stares, lifting his dark eyebrows. 'You're touchy tonight. Did I hit a chord? Ah, yes, the chord of *love*.' He sings this last word.

'Shut up, Danny.' I change the subject from one that's making me uncomfortable to one that might make him uncomfortable. 'So what happened with Rebecca?' His girlfriend of five months.

He clicks his fingers. 'Aah, that was her name! Apparently she was only killing time until Bosko asked her out.' He gives one of his couldn't-care-less shrugs. 'You know, it's hard being this good-looking. Girls just want to hang around with me all the time. It's getting to be a chore,' he moans with appropriate melodrama, then swings an arm across my shoulders. 'Are you coming inside? The night is still young. We can find us each a hottie to take home tonight.'

I think of the brunette with the sweet voice and stunning eyes. I'm definitely going inside.

## 5

# Ebony

Numbly I go through the motions of having my hand stamped with a red elephant and, with Amber's arm hooked through mine, follow Leah into the club's interior. The soft coloured lights, the chink of glasses, the roar of voices and laughter swirl around me like a zephyr. It's exactly what I came here for – to have fun and feel the buzz of life thrumming inside me.

I stand still, close my eyes and exhale the breath I've been holding in since . . . I don't know, but it seems like for ever.

Amber squeezes my arm excitedly. 'Leah found a table on the balcony upstairs and the girls are there already.'

She means our friends Bec and Ivy, who, along with Leah, we sit with at lunch.

We wade through the crowded stairs to find the girls bunched together in a dark corner right up the back. It's a small table in a perfect location for a romantic couple wanting to avoid the spotlight, but . . .

Leah notices my grimacing look. 'Don't you like it?'

'It's a table with chairs – what's not to like?' I say, not wanting to offend her. I wonder how on earth I'm going to find my mystery boy from up here.

Leah goes down to buy drinks. Leaving Ivy and Bec to chat about their clothes, I tug on Amber's sleeve and whisper, 'Come on; let's get out of this corner.'

Standing at the top of the stairs, we spot a few people we know and a few we'd rather not, like the group of loudmouths from town who are always taking shots at us because we're into horses.

Amber rests a hand on the balcony railing but doesn't look over into the club's interior.

'Um, Amber, why are you staring at me?'

'Oh, *I'm* the one staring?'

I hate it when she answers my question with one of her own. 'I'm staring,' I explain, 'because I don't get out often and it's all so amazing, especially the chandelier. You know, it has a hundred and forty-five little bulbs. Imagine the energy it uses when it's fully turned on.' I glance at her and smile. 'You don't have to say it – I'm pathetic.'

She laughs. 'Ebony, that line's not going to work with me. I know what you're doing.'

'Yeah? What?'

'You're looking for a cute guy who walks with a limp.'

I turn back to scanning the room, keeping an eye on everyone as they first walk in. 'I suppose he's not here because he had to seek urgent medical treatment. I knew I shouldn't have worn your heels.'

She laughs. 'Blame the shoes, why don't you?' She lifts her eyebrows. 'He didn't look too injured when he held your hand against his chest. You should have seen your face!'

'I'm glad I didn't,' I mumble under my breath.

'The way that guy looked at you, there's no doubt *he*

21

will track *you* down before this night is over. Hon, I guarantee it.'

'Do you really think so?' I try to sound as if I don't care
either way, but it doesn't work. I need to see him again.

'He goes to our school, you know,' Amber remarks
casually.

My eyes swing to hers. 'He does?'

'Yeah, his name is Jordan Blake. He's the guy that always
heads for the back row and never makes eye contact. And
it's not because he's shy.' She adds this last part softly, but
before I can ask her about it Leah's back with our drinks
and we return to the table, where we plan a riding day
together during the first week of our break.

Every so often I check the faces around me, hoping to
catch sight of the boy named Jordan.

Leah and Ivy get up to dance as soon as the band starts
playing. It's a great idea. Anything to get a better vantage
point, so we head downstairs to the dance floor, where I have
so much fun I don't realise how much time is passing.

Taking a break, Amber and I go to the restroom. When
we come out to wash our hands and freshen up, I glance
into the mirror and point out that her theory seems to
be flawed. 'I'm going to find him before anything else
distracts me.'

'I'll come with you.'

'You don't have to, you know. The band will be back
soon.'

She shrugs. 'I'm all danced out.'

We walk to the door and I pull it open. 'What about the
others?'

She pulls out her mobile phone. 'I'll text Leah and tell her where we'll be.'

We wander over to the bar and I ask a barman if he's seen a boy with blue eyes, brown hair, about my height and wearing a brown suede jacket. 'He might be walking with a limp,' I add.

'Sorry,' he says, shrugging.

But while standing there a group of five or six girls rushes past. 'What's down there?' I ask the one hanging back a little.

The blonde glances up from texting. 'The rear exit.'

And the moment she says it I know Jordan Blake has passed this way. I turn and tell Amber, 'He's outside.'

'How do you know?'

I have no answer. I just feel it. 'Instinct, I suppose.'

'You want to go out in the dark on a hunch, looking for a boy you only just met?'

'Um ... yes. I need to check on his injury,' I answer with a nervous giggle.

'All right, I'm game.'

OK, who am I kidding? I quietly admit as we head for the exit. It might be the stupidest idea I've had in a while, but there's something as strong as it is strange between this boy and me, and I need to know what it is.

# 6

# Jordan

We bumped into Sophie Hunt at the door about an hour earlier, a beautiful girl with blonde hair and blue eyes and bad taste in men. She was alone – and upset – so we decided to keep her company even though we've exchanged no more than a few words since she moved to Cedar Oakes at the start of this school year. She told us she had problems with her boyfriend, Adam Skinner – see, bad taste. Danny let slip I had history with the guy, and she started pounding me for info, trying to figure out why he has suddenly become so unpredictable.

'You know, Sophie, perhaps you should start by asking Adam to explain what happened that day at the mine.'

'Don't you think I've tried? No one mentions Seth around him. Even Josh and Damien told me to leave it alone.' Her voice drops so low I strain to hear it and move my right ear closer to her mouth. 'Josh thinks Adam is worried about losing me.' She looks at me then, her big blue eyes swimming with tears.

Adam Skinner is worried about Sophie's feelings, worried she might leave him. This isn't the Skinner I know. It surprises me.

I close my eyes for a second and finally give in. But deep inside I just know that somehow, at some time, I'm going to regret this.

She gives a barman some cash and he slides two beers under the counter, then we slip outside on our own and sit on the bottom step of a small concrete deck. By the time I finish relating what happened, she's sniffing back tears and swabbing her eyes.

Leaning forward on to her knees, Sophie cups her chin in her hands and stares straight ahead into the dark alley, where the only other sound is a cat scratching at a black garbage bag.

'Are you OK?' I ask.

'No, I'm a horrible person, pressuring you into telling me this story on his brother's birthday.' She hiccups.

'You didn't know it was Seth's birthday. And at least now you understand where Adam is coming from.'

'How can you stick up for him after all he's put you through? Danny told me how, in that first year, he turned every person in this school against you, including the teachers.'

'Well, that was three years ago, and I put up with the crap he dishes out because . . .'

She squeezes my forearm. 'Don't say, because of what you did to his brother. It was an accident, Jordan. A dreadful tragedy, but it wasn't your fault.'

She's silent a moment before she says softly, 'Why couldn't he tell me himself? I would have understood. I could have been there for him instead of . . .' She glances down the dark lane with tears welling again, her tissue shredded in her hands, 'Jordan, I was so awful to him last night. I said some horrible things. He's never going to forgive me.'

'Forgiveness isn't exactly Adam's strong point. A few days' space around certain days of the year is probably good to remember.'

She starts to cry again and wipes her eyes with the last of her tissue. 'I dumped him last night.'

'The fight was that bad, eh?'

She nods.

'I've seen you two at school together. He doesn't let you out of his sight. He'll come back.'

She slides her hand in mine and gives it a friendly squeeze. 'Do you think so?' She glances up at me with her big blue eyes half obscured behind her blonde fringe. 'If only I'd met *you* on my first day.'

Her hand in mine grows uncomfortable suddenly, as if we're crossing a line. She'll be sorry she said that by tomorrow. Obviously Sophie has some thinking to do. She's hurting and vulnerable. I glance at my watch. I've been outside too long, but at least there's still time to find the girl with the violet eyes.

Sophie gets to her feet. 'I've kept you out here long enough. You should go back inside and enjoy what's left of the night.' Taking my hand again, she hauls me up. 'Besides, I realise now I have somewhere else I need to be.'

A dark figure fills the space behind her. The figure moves and two more step out of the shadows. It's Skinner with his mates Josh and Damien. The hairs on the back of my neck bristle at the look on Skinner's face.

Quickly I drop Sophie's hand. 'What is it?' she whispers, and spins around. 'Adam! It's you. Geez, you freaked me ou—' Her voice fades as she takes in his dark eyes and hostile expression.

26

'Yes, it's *Adam*,' he mocks, glaring at her.

She goes from relieved to confused and then terrified in the space of one beat. 'What's wrong, babe?'

Skinner takes her arm and flings her to Josh as if he were discarding a rotting carcass. Josh plays football for the region. I've known him since we were kids. He was one of the many who stopped associating with me after the accident. It's his loyalty that has him here now being a moron.

'Don't let her go, Josh. I'll get back to her after I deal with this scumbag.'

'Listen, mate, you're jumping to the wrong conclusion. You should trust your girlfriend. She cares for you, and that's not something you should take for granted.'

*Whack!* His right fist smashes into my jaw, knocking me to my knees.

Man, I didn't see that coming.

'*Adam!*' Sophie screams. 'What are you doing?' She struggles to escape Josh's arms but they're braced like iron bands around her waist. 'Let me go, Josh!' He doesn't respond. 'What's the matter with you? Let me go!'

He continues to stare straight ahead.

'Josh? Josh!' She catches my eye and shakes her head. She can't explain what's going on any more than I can. She tries again, 'Think about what you're doing, Josh.'

Josh tries not to look at Sophie's big pleading eyes staring up at him.

'Josh,' she pleads, 'we're friends, aren't we? I made you a chocolate cake for your birthday.'

Finally she gets through to him. 'I'm sorry, Soph, but I saw you two with my own eyes.'

'Saw *what* exactly? Jordan and I have been out here talking, that's all.'

When he doesn't answer, I yell at him, 'You saw nothing cos there was nothing to see.'

'Go on, Josh,' Skinner pipes up, keeping his eyes fixed on me as I inch my way into a better position. 'Tell her how we saw the two of them meet up at the front desk like they obviously planned, then cosy up together every chance they got. And when that wasn't enough, they came out here for privacy!'

'I came on my own!' Sophie protests. 'Jordan came with Danny Webber. They just happened to walk in at the same time as me. Adam, we didn't plan to meet, I swear!'

'Danny was your cover. And you know how I know that? You couldn't wait to sneak out the back without him.'

Sophie groans. 'It wasn't like that! I can explain everything. We'll go somewhere quiet, just the two of us. Tell this brute to let me go. And if you don't take me seriously, I'll report this to the cops.'

'Shut up, Sophie! I saw all I needed with my own eyes. Evidence doesn't come better than that.'

'But, Adam . . .' Sophie's voice softens. 'I know what happened to Seth.'

Everyone freezes. Even the cat picking at the hole in the garbage bag suddenly stops. Realising she's made a mistake, she reaches out to Skinner's other pal, Damien Hall, with her eyes, but there's no help there. He knows mentioning Skinner's brother is a forbidden topic, especially today of all days.

'You know *nothing* about my brother,' Skinner hisses, and

pointing at me says, 'You dumped me for *him*? If it were anyone else, maybe we could talk, but *him*? From now on you are nothing to me. You're dust!'

Sophie gasps. She's never seen this side to her boyfriend before and it's clearly scaring her half to death. 'How can you dismiss me as if I'm nothing after these last three months?'

He turns slowly as if he's listening, but then he raises his hand and sucks air in loudly, making a torrid hissing sound through the gap in his front teeth. 'You cheated on me with the person who destroyed my family.'

*Whack!* He slaps Sophie in the face with the open palm of his hand.

It shocks everyone.

Sophie whimpers in disbelief, 'You hit me.' She lifts a trembling hand to her cheek.

Stunned, Josh loosens his hold. Sophie breaks free and charges at Skinner with both fists flailing. 'Don't you ever! Don't you *ever* raise a hand to me again!'

Josh and Damien pull her off, leaving Skinner completely open to me for the first time and, those two momentarily occupied, I ball my right fist and jab him across the bridge of his nose.

Enraged and in pain, he grabs my arm and twists it behind my back. 'Think you can get away with that, do you? You're a weakling, a girl, a weak little girl!' He continues to yank and twist my arm. Over the top of my head he yells at Sophie, 'I don't understand why you would pick this loser.'

'Adam, *stop*! What does it take to get through to you?'

'You're a moron, Skinner,' I yell. 'Do you think Sophie will stick with you now? You just lost the best thing you've ever had when you hit her. She's not going back to you now, not ever, man.'

'Shut up, Blake!'

When this doesn't work, I try to reason with Adam's mates. 'You guys want to risk going to jail all over a misunderstanding? You're dumber than I thought!'

'Shut up!' Skinner bellows, dragging me to the brick wall, where he starts punching me in the gut and yelling at Damien to give him a hand. Damien rushes over and hauls me to my feet. Glaring at me, Skinner knees me in the back, then kicks me with his left boot.

After a few more minutes of this, Damien releases me, steps back and says to Skinner, 'Mate, I can't do this.'

I slide to the ground.

The kicking doesn't stop.

Meanwhile, Sophie is screaming. She breaks free from Josh, hollering accusations at the two friends. 'You should be stopping him before he ends up doing time for this!' They stand back but do nothing. 'You're both pathetic.'

'He tried to steal my girl. It's what he deserves,' Adam says, pointing to my beaten body sprawled on the ground.

'That's bullshit!' I tell him. 'This goes back years.'

Finally Skinner stops and stares down at me, gloating. 'You're right. I should have done this a long time ago.'

Hurting in more places than I can count, I scramble to my feet. Broken, but not dead yet, I ram my head into Skinner's gut. He doubles over, winded. Trying to keep the momentum going I ball my fist again, and connect with the underside of his chin, then again with his nose. He sinks to his hands and knees and, gasping, scuttles away like a rat.

Skinner will get his breath back in a few seconds, so time is short. I look at Josh and Damien. I don't think they will stop me if I take Sophie and run. They glance at each other with confused looks. This is more than they had bargained for.

Standing in the darkness, Skinner appears as a ghost, hunched over and breathing heavily, blood dribbling from his nose. He steps out of the shadows, eyes on fire with rage. That's when we all see the empty beer bottle in his hand. He smashes it over the banister rail, breaking off the end. Glass scatters across the concrete.

Did I say how twisted this world is?

The golden glass glistens under the light of the single globe hanging above the club's exit. I hold my hands up, palms out, as Skinner points the bottle at me and I'm thinking I'm screwed cos Skinner is out of control. I knew he would snap one day.

He's reached the point beyond reason, but I still have to try. 'Adam, listen to me, man. I'm sorry. I'm *really* sorry for what I did. We can walk away from this peacefully if you put the bottle down. At least let Sophie walk away. She has nothing to do with the real reason we're here.'

Josh stares at Skinner as if he doesn't recognise him. He's no help at all. I try to reach Skinner again. 'Dude, remember how it used to be. I loved Seth too. He was like . . . *man*, you two were my brothers! I never meant for Seth to die. If I could go back, I'd choose differently. I swear I would take his place.'

My words only enrage him more. But at least Josh

31

comes to his senses and tries to make Skinner see reason. 'Adam, come on, mate. This has gone too far,' he says. 'We were just supposed to shake him up a bit. Not this. And . . . and . . . what if they're telling the truth? You could be making a big mistake.'

'Shut up, Josh. Just *shut up!*'

Damien says, 'Mate, I can't be found here if this goes bad, and it's bad enough already. You never mentioned hurting *her!*' Glancing briefly at each other, Josh and Damien start backing away.

'Wait!' Sophie yells after them.

They don't look back.

Disgusted, Sophie yells, 'Cowards! I thought he was your friend!'

'Sophie, stay back,' I call out before she makes a rash move. Skinner's friends are gone, but that doesn't mean he's any less dangerous. 'Go around to the front and get help.'

She shakes her head. 'I'm not leaving while this maniac is aiming a broken bottle at you.'

'He needs help, Sophie. *Please*, get help.'

She scans the ground for her handbag. Running to it, she gets out her mobile phone and calls the cops.

Undaunted, Skinner blocks the stairs by moving in front of them. 'Calling the cops won't help,' he taunts. 'They won't get here fast enough to save your new boyfriend.' He turns his attention to me. 'I should *never* have let you get away with killing my brother. Consider yourself lucky I allowed you to live this long.'

The door swings open and Danny steps on to the platform. 'There you are!' Oblivious to what's unfolding before

32

him, it takes him a moment to figure out something is wrong. 'I was wondering where you two had gone.' And then, 'What's going on?' He steps down on to the top stair.

'Go back!' I take my eyes off Skinner for a second to gesture to Danny. 'Get security out here, quickly.'

But a second is all it takes for Skinner to charge. The sharp inhalation of air screeching through his front teeth is my warning, but it's not enough. He slams into my chest, plunging the jagged glass into my gut. It rips through my shirt, my skin, the muscles of my stomach and everything in its path. I drop instantly forward into his arms. Holding me up with one arm, he twists his hand, driving the glass upwards, shredding my insides as if his purpose is not to stop until he pierces my heart.

I glance up, our eyes connect, and instantly I know two things for certain. One is that I'm looking into the eyes of someone who has lost his grip on reality, and two, I'm going to die.

It occurs so quickly it starts to feel surreal, as if I'm watching it happen to someone else. Sophie and Danny reach me simultaneously, pulling Skinner off and tossing him to the ground. From there he crawls past the bags of garbage along the back wall, scrambles to his feet and disappears into the night.

Automatically my hands search for the broken bottle. They fold around the glass, still stuck in me, slippery with my blood. I look up through a growing haze, my brain registering pain from front to back, rapidly becoming excruciating. Everything that follows is a blur. I hear sirens in the distance. People are pouring out of the club, their faces curious, alarmed, horrified. Danny and Sophie support me, one on each side. I'm still clutching the bottle with Danny's hand now folded around mine. They talk over me, frantically discussing whether they should or shouldn't remove it.

A security guard takes a look. 'Don't touch it!' he orders. 'Right now it's acting as a plug. Release it, and he's gone.'

*Gone?* Dying, he means. I know that. He orders a staff member to bring a blanket, then tells Danny to lay me down. 'Flat on his back,' he says. 'Here, I'll help you.'

My mind drifts. It's a strange sensation, as if part of me is floating while the rest is heavy as mud. I get a moment of clarity. 'Where's Skinner?'

'Beats me,' Danny says, 'but the cops will find him. His life is over, man.'

*Like mine . . .* It seems an alluring thought.

*No life, no pain. Right?*

*This life was too hard anyway.*

*But it was getting better, remember? You met that girl tonight, the girl of your dreams.*

*Yeah, and now I'll never get her number . . . never get her name . . . never . . .*

I close my eyes, drifting in a fog, but Danny urges me to stay awake, his voice breaking through my thoughts. 'Don't shut those pretty blues of yours, OK? Stay with me, Jordy.'

I open them and see Sophie. 'Where is that ambulance?' She sounds scared.

There is blood everywhere, saturating my clothes, sticking to my legs, all over Danny and Sophie. She shakes her head. 'Forget the blood. They'll give you more at the hospital.'

34

I feel myself drifting once again, but then I hear Danny pleading as if from a distance, 'Stay with us, Jordan. Come on, buddy. Stay focused, man!'

Sirens bleat loudly and an ambulance reverses into the lane. Two paramedics leap out and start working on me. The urgency in their voices scares me more than the sight of all the blood. They put me on to a gurney and gingerly take over the bottle-holding. My hand slides away.

Danny and Sophie stay close as the gurney starts moving, and Danny asks, 'I can come to the hospital, right?'

I don't hear the reply because a girl steps into my line of sight and for a second there is nothing else but her. It's the girl of my dreams.

A grey haze swims before my eyes, making everything blurry, and now the girl with the violet eyes and Sophie are side by side.

Maybe my mind is playing tricks on me. I have a broken beer bottle carving up my insides; it's not outrageous to be seeing things.

They slide me into the ambulance. Danny tries to climb in after us, but the paramedic stops him. All I can do is hold on to the three stricken faces until the door closes. Then I give in to the pull of the darkening haze.

# 7

# Ebony

Kids with shocked faces fill the corridor near the exit. It doesn't take long to figure out something terrible has happened outside. I stare at the people around me but Jordan is not among them and my stomach sinks like a rock dropped into deep water.

Something is wrong.

Two security guards in their black T-shirts push past us, one carrying a blanket. Amber murmurs, 'This doesn't look good.'

'No.' There is an urgency escalating inside me now. Somehow I know Jordan Blake, the guy with the sad blue eyes, needs my help. I start pushing people out of my way, careful not to shove and possibly hurt someone.

Amber calls out, worried about what I'm doing, but I don't *know* what I'm doing!

Finally I'm outside, overlooking a chaotic scene. There are people everywhere, blue lights flashing from two police cars, another arriving with its siren blaring, and an ambulance with its rear door open wide.

When I see him, something inside me jerks and I stagger forward, stumbling down a few steps. It's Jordan, and he's dying. I know this like I know my own name. He's lying flat on the ground with the new girl from my physics class, Sophie, down on her knees on one side of him, and another boy from my year on the other. It's clear they are trying to keep him from bleeding to death, with their clenched fists pushing down on pressure points above and below a wound to his stomach. Someone has stabbed him and it doesn't look like an accident. Sophie's face is coming out in a bruise, her right cheek gleaming bright red.

A security guard moves through the crowd, ordering everyone inside. I slip around him while his back is turned.

This is my chance.

The paramedics are working fast to strap the boy to a gurney and hook up an intravenous line. His friends are now standing aside. Sophie turns and notices the gawking crowd still hanging around. 'Hey! Get lost! This isn't a freak show!' She spots me and hesitates, probably recognising me from school, or sees my concern in the anguish that must be showing in my eyes. 'Ebony, are you OK?'

'I have to talk to him.'

The gurney starts moving towards the ambulance parked a few metres away. Sophie notices, but turns to study my face again. Blood drips from her soaked hands. She doesn't know what to do with them so just holds them out in front of her. 'Are you his girlfriend?'

*Girlfriend?* How well does she know this guy if she thinks I could be his girlfriend? Apparently not well enough to know the intimate details of his life. 'Ah, no, I'm not.'

'Friend?'

'Er . . .' It takes a moment to reach for the right word. At my hesitation her eyes flare with white-hot anger.

'You don't know him at all! You're like the rest of these vultures.' She flicks her head at the crowd, holding their phones in the air, taking pictures. 'Go back inside and take the rest of these sick losers with you.'

She rushes over to the gurney and takes Jordan's hand. Unable to stop myself, and not understanding what's driving this odd, compelling urge to touch him, I run over too and grab hold of the gurney. I try to get his attention.

But he's in shock and dazed. His eyes close and open several times as he looks from one side of the gurney to the other. He's fighting to hang on to consciousness.

I don't know what's got into me, but I've got this inexplicable yearning to help him. I can see I'm adding to his confusion, but I can't stop myself.

Looking down at the injured boy I whisper, 'I can help you. You just have to let me. Do you understand what I'm saying?'

I manage to hold on to the gurney for a few more seconds before a paramedic attempts to prise my fingers away. 'Let go or I'll have you arrested!'

I step back, feeling helpless as the ambulance door closes. Blue lights flashing, the ambulance rushes away, and I'm left standing, an emptiness searing me from the inside out.

# 8

# Jordan

A woman's gravelly voice calls my name and demands I open my eyes. She sounds so much like my fifth-grade teacher Mrs Barnes, I open them right away.

'He's awake, doctor!'

A woman in a white coat bends over me and shines a pencil-thin beam into my eyes. 'Hello, Jordan. I'm Dr Beth Reinhardt.'

'Where am I?'

'You're in Cedar Oakes Regional Hospital. You have a broken beer bottle in your abdomen.' I feel my eyes start to roll up into my head. 'Stay with me, Jordan. Good. That's good. Now, listen and don't talk. You have sustained serious injuries to your liver and spleen, causing you to bleed internally. It's imperative we operate now. Do you understand, Jordan?'

I blink and she takes this for a yes. My eyes drift to my middle and she gently pushes on my shoulders. 'Don't be alarmed,' she says, her voice starting to come in fragments, 'Too deep . . . remove in surgery . . . stay with me, Jordan.'

Through the haze I hear her explain how they're going

to operate without parental permission; that it's too urgent to wait.

'Your friends Danny and Sophie —' I blink slowly to let her know I'm following — 'who managed to beat the ambulance to the hospital —' she smiles briefly — 'explained about your state guardian, Lillian Fisher. One of my staff is letting her know you're on your way to surgery now.'

As if swept up by a magical force, I feel myself lift from the darkness suddenly.

'He's stabilising,' the doctor calls out with relief in her voice. 'Let's get him down there, stat. We move on my count — one, two . . .'

And then I'm rushing along a corridor and into an elevator with hospital staff hovering around my bed. I get the sense of dropping, then the lift opens and I'm in front of a pair of wide swinging doors marked *Theatre 2*. A different crew, wearing green outfits with matching paper caps, takes over. They're chatty and make jokes and laugh. An older guy introduces himself as Dr Mac. 'We'll have you back as good as new in no time, Jordan,' he says, grinning.

I know they're just trying to put me at ease, but their breezy attitude doesn't fill me with confidence.

At least I'm feeling no pain now, so the morphine they gave me upstairs must be kicking in. I get how bad my situation is, and the nicer these people are, the more thoroughly I get how tentative my hold on life is right now.

A dude named Todd smiles and starts explaining how he's going to be my anaesthesiologist tonight. 'Now I want you to start counting down from a hundred . . .'

My lights go out at ninety-nine.

# 9

## Ebony

We stand out on the pavement while Amber calls her dad to pick us up and I try to figure out what happened tonight. I recall one other time when my hands felt overcome with a similar compulsion. I was two years old and Dad was losing his favourite mare, Lady Elsa. She was in the final stages of a difficult labour and struggling because something was stopping her foal from being born. Dad had tried everything, even turning the foal around with his hands, but Lady Elsa was exhausted, scared and panicking. I laid my little hands on the mare's belly. She calmed right away, allowing the gutsy foal to make his final push for life.

Dad had looked at me strangely for days afterwards.

My hands feel the same now. Though they look normal, they're tingling fiercely. I take a deep breath and release it slowly. 'I think I'm hyperventilating.'

Engrossed in my memory, I'm surprised to find Mr Lang pulling up at the kerb. Amber holds open the rear passenger door. 'That's nothing,' she says as I get in behind her. 'All this commotion is making you breathe faster, that's all. You'll feel better in a minute. Trust me.'

I stare out the window for the ride home. Mum and Dad

will be waiting for me, poised and ready to attack. I know the routine. They'll drill me first, then punish. They probably plan to ground me for life!

Well, tonight I have questions too important for them to brush aside with their usual tactics. Tonight I will have answers.

Tonight I will find out the truth about the crazy things happening to me.

# 10

# Jordan

I hear a gurgling, crackling noise, like a long-distance radio picking up static, and far-off, indistinct voices.

But I'm in la-la land, aren't I?

Anaesthetic is the deepest sleep you can imagine. I've been under before. Cut my arm open trying to climb through a broken window a couple of years ago. I don't know how long I've been under – time is tricky to gauge in this kind of nothingness – but I'm almost certain I shouldn't be hearing voices.

The last I remember, Todd asked me to count backwards from a hundred and I got to ninety-nine, then nothing. But now my brain is aware of stuff. I'm thinking again, and as I become more conscious, the white noise emerges as hushed whisperings of two men with a lot to say.

I get a sudden urge to open my eyes, to see the faces that belong to these strange voices, but my eyelids won't budge. It's annoying because the whispers sound like a conversation I'm not supposed to hear.

*How is the lad holding up?* This is a deep, older voice and I'm pretty sure it has nothing to do with the doctors treating me. *After searching the Earth for sixteen years, can we really* be this fortunate, my prince? My what? Did he say, 'prince'? *How sure are you that this young man is the one?*

*Isaac, you saw the illumination in the sky*, the other voice answers. It's also male, but younger, polished, every word perfectly enunciated. *Nothing shimmers as bright as the connection between a Guardian and their human charge at the time of the human's death, or, as in this situation, his near-death. It's what alerts the Guardian to act fast.*

*And so the race with the Death Watchers begins. At least they're not here yet*, the older voice says.

Yet? What's that supposed to mean?

*It is a good sign for the lad*, it goes on.

Phew! Well, that's a relief!

*This is the break we need*, the younger one says. *We have almost found her. She's here, Isaac, hidden somewhere in this valley, cleverly concealed by those mountains we flew over.*

Flew? *Flew?*

*How were we to know the Dark Prince would select a valley so close to a Crossing guarded by* our own *people? It seemed the most unlikely choice.*

OK, I heard *that*. He said 'Dark Prince'! Someone tell me what's going on!

*Two more years and she would be lost to me, Isaac.*

*But she's not lost, my prince. She's finally within our reach.*

*And this boy is our key to finding her. Now that the bond has formed, she will feel drawn to the boy, and he to her. She will sense his needs, and her instincts will compel her to be near him.*

They go quiet. Good. I get a chance to try to figure out what's going on. Who or what do these voices belong to? They sound like . . . Nah! No way, man, that's impossible.

I've gotta be dreaming.

*Oh no!* the older voice suddenly gasps. *What's happening, my prince? Can you see inside his body?*

The young one doesn't answer right away, like he's too upset or something. *I wasn't expecting this*, he says. *I thought he reached the medical facility in time. Their connection didn't reveal this, so it must have occurred afterwards.*

*Is it certain then?*

Is *what* certain? I wish they could hear me like I hear them!

*Unfortunately for the boy, his fate is sealed. If he is to survive, I will have to assist in his repair.*

*This is a travesty! What happened, Thane?*

*I see it now. The surgeon nicked a vital artery in his spleen. They won't find the source of this new bleed without the wisdom of a post-mortem examination.*

*Human error from those he trusts in his time of greatest need! Is there anything more distressing?*

*Not in the mortals' world, nor ours.*

*How does his spirit appear?*

*Strong. Still fighting.*

*Remarkable. But I suppose it won't be long then.*

*I'm afraid it will be very soon, Isaac.*

*How long before the Death Watchers arrive?*

The 'Death Watchers' are coming *here*? What is this bullshit?

*We'd better call for assistance.* His voice sounds urgent. *Quickly, Isaac. They must be intercepted.*

Suddenly as if my eyes are wide open, I can see Dr Mac leaning over me with two metal plates attached to coils in

45

his hands. He yells, 'Stand back, everyone. On my count. Three ... two ...'

Ohhh, *man*! Don't tell me ...

My chest lurches violently.

Damn, it's true. I knew my life sucked, but still, I wasn't expecting this.

# 11

# Ebony

It's midnight by the time Mr Lang turns into my driveway, and just as I knew they would be, my parents are waiting up with lights on upstairs and down.

My mother is making a point.

I thank Mr Lang and tell Amber I'll catch up with her tomorrow. They drive off and I walk to the veranda. Here I pause, glance up at the stars and drag in a deep settling breath of crisp air. Only then do I open the front door.

Mum and Dad are sitting in their favourite couches watching late-night television. Before they start drilling me, I switch off the television and sit on the low table facing them. 'We need to talk,' I say. I apologise for my childish behaviour, and I really mean it. It was wrong to worry them like that, especially knowing how concerned Mum is whenever I leave the house.

Through tight lips Mum says, 'Firstly, since you appear to be home safely, I will accept your apology.'

It's more than I expect and I'm both relieved and grateful. 'Dad –' I turn to my father – 'do you forgive me too?'

'Of course, Ebony; you're my baby girl.'

I jump across the small space between us and give him a hug. On the way back I catch the look he exchanges with Mum. Hmm, no wonder that was easy; something's going on.

As I sit on the sofa opposite them, Mum crosses her legs. 'Now, darling, your father and I had a talk tonight and, well, we decided we will forgo punishment *this* time.'

Now I *know* something has happened. 'What's going on, Mum? Dad?'

'Nothing!' she snaps. She scans my clothes, notices the red smudges at my middle and her eyes almost pop out. 'Is that ... Ebony, is that *blood* on your shirt?'

I groan inside, and reluctantly explain, talking it down as much as I can. 'There was a stabbing in the alley at the back of the club. A boy from school was taken to hospital.'

'You didn't have anything to do with it, did you? *Did* you?' She examines my face.

'Mum, it was all over by the time I got out there.'

'How did you get blood on your shirt?' Dad asks.

*Breathe*, I remind myself. 'I must have rubbed against the gurney as the paramedics slid him into the ambulance.'

Mum gasps, covering her open mouth with her hand. 'You were *that* close?'

'I wasn't involved in the stabbing. OK?'

'Don't use that tone with me, young lady.'

'Ebony, what happened?'

'A lot happened tonight, Dad. We have to talk. I want you tell me everything you know.'

'About what?' Mum snaps.

'About me. Let's start with the day I was born.'

They glance at each other, and when they return their attention to me, though they're trying to conceal their nervousness, their eyes are still wider than usual, their pupils dilated. They look scared.

*Scared?* But I'm their daughter! It shouldn't be hard to explain how I came into the world. Should it?

They have to know how important this is to me.

What don't I know?

Mum returns to her couch, so I move to the coffee table, where I can see both their faces. 'You told me Ben was my twin who died soon after we were born. But I need to know – was Ben really my brother?'

Dad gulps hard while Mum laughs, the sound too high-pitched. She's nervous, and . . . well, I keep picking up guilty impressions. 'What's got into you tonight, darling? It's the stabbing, isn't it? It's shaken you up.'

'It's not the stabbing, Mum.' She's trying to sidetrack me again, push me into losing my temper so our discussion will fall apart, she'll start crying and, like usual, I'll get no expla-nation. 'This is what you always do. You play diversionary games so you end up telling me nothing.'

They remain silent.

'Please answer my question.'

They stare at me with their mouths both clamped shut.

'One of you, answer the damn question!'

They avoid looking at each other. They stare straight ahead, Dad over my left shoulder, Mum over my right.

*Arrrgh, this is pathetic!*

'I'm sorry, parents, if my question is a little difficult. Let me help you. It requires a yes or no answer.'

'You don't have to be sarcastic,' Mum says. 'We understand the question well enough.'

'Then what's the problem? But, please, the truth. Was Ben really my brother?'

Suddenly Dad opens his mouth, but before a word comes out Mum yells at him, 'John, stop! What do you think you're doing?'

Dad sighs. 'It's time, Heather. Our girl needs to know. We can't leave her in the dark any longer.'

'But we have to,' she hisses, giving him a warning glare colder than an arctic snowdrift.

'Dad.' I wait until he looks at me. 'Mum's scaring me. What's going on?'

He peers at her earnestly and Mum's lips turn white as she presses them together. But then she sighs and nods. She reaches out to me. I take her hand and notice it is trembling.

'Your birth didn't exactly occur the way we've led you to believe,' Dad says finally.

I pull my hand out of Mum's even though she's tightening her grasp. I don't want to be touching her when she finally reveals the truth.

'Ebony,' she whispers in a shaky voice, 'I was never pregnant with twins. I was . . . never pregnant with you.'

And as I sit back and brace myself, a minuscule part of me, the part that always knew I wasn't a Hawkins, is sighing with relief.

'Why would you tell me I was a twin? Why couldn't you tell me that you'd adopted me? Heaps of people adopt kids. You may not have heard,' I mutter sarcastically, 'apparently it's less damaging to our psyche if we're raised knowing the truth.'

Dad's eyes turn sad as he rests them on me. 'We had no choice, darling.'

I don't accept his excuse. 'Everyone has a choice.'

Mum says, 'You're right, and we chose to protect you.'

'Protect me from what? The big, bad bogeyman?'

Mum closes her eyes against my hostility. I glance at her and wait, but inside I'm so rattled I could scream. 'It was in the contract we signed.'

'An adoption agreement?'

'Sort of,' she says slowly.

Dad says, 'We were warned off telling you the truth.'

'So, I'm a black-market baby? Is this what you're saying?'

They deny the accusation emphatically.

My mother told me once that people lie because the truth is too ugly to bear. She was probably referring to this truth, this lie. I wonder how ugly this is going to get. It's obvious, though, what happened. 'You bought me after you lost your own baby.'

Mum starts to cry. 'He told us that if we told you the truth, his people would come and take you away, and we would be punished for breaching the contract.'

'Along with our neighbours in the valley,' Dad says, adding to my confusion.

Mum whispers, 'We were scared. Surely you can understand that.'

'Someone blackmailed you into silence! What happened to your brains? This man didn't want you to expose his crime so he could go on selling more stolen babies.' I pause to let this sink into their heads – and mine.

*Mum and Dad are not my real parents.*

'I . . . I promise you both right now, nothing is going to happen to me, or the neighbours, just because you're finally telling me the truth. But you're going to have to tell me *everything*.'

In a sad voice Dad says, 'A strange man came to our door unexpectedly. He was tall, impeccably dressed in a black suit with a matching long coat and a smart black fedora.'

'His name was Zavier. He was extremely good-looking with an unusual accent.'

'He claimed he lived just outside the valley, in a cottage by the Windhaven River. He said he travelled a lot and was hardly ever home.'

Mum says, 'He came to our house the night of the day we buried Ben, the day after he was born. We were still in shock.'

Dad jumps in. 'It had poured with rain all day, but Zavier didn't have a drop of water on him, not even a speck of mud on his shoes.'

Mum flicks a sharp look at Dad. 'You're scaring her.'

Dad leans forward and touches my knee. 'Are you sure you want to hear this?'

'Yes. As long as it's the truth, I want to hear it. I *have* to.'

Dad explains, 'Zavier carried a cane basket in his hand.'

'A Moses basket,' Mum throws in. 'It had a baby in it.'

'The infant was wrapped in a black blanket,' Dad continues, 'which I thought was somewhat odd.'

'Oh, that's the part you think is odd?'

They both give me an exasperated look. I tell Dad to keep going.

'He didn't show you to us at first, but you kept making little gurgling sounds and we knew a real baby was in our house.'

'It was an amazing feeling,' Mum interjects.

'Zavier explained that his work kept him away from home too much to take care of a baby.'

Mum takes up the story again. 'His sister had recently come to live with him after the situation at her home became difficult.'

I sit quietly riveted to the story of a young pregnant girl, rejected by her parents, who gave birth in her brother's house, dying later that night from an unexpected haemorrhage.

Mum touches my arm. 'You were three days old when he brought you to us.'

I gasp, my mouth falling open. 'So my birth date is incorrect.'

Dad says, 'By two days, but we had no choice. He insisted that was the birth date we give you.'

Questions hammer away at my brain. Didn't this man Zavier have other family he could turn to for help, like a grandmother, an aunt or someone? Why did he give his sister's baby to complete strangers to raise? Where was the baby's father in all of this?

Mum explains, 'You have to understand, darling, this man was . . . intimidating.'

I shake my head, unable to imagine my parents, especially my mother, who is strong and even outspoken at times, being too scared to ask such fundamental questions as what happened to the father.

'Did you even ask about the father? Weren't you worried he might turn up one day to claim custody?'

Dad answers, 'Zavier assured us his sister had had no further contact with the father, who was only seventeen at the time. So you see, sweetheart, your biological . . . *that man* . . . doesn't know you exist.'

Their story keeps growing stranger. I brace myself as Dad continues, 'Zavier said he heard of our loss and it occurred to him that, if we were willing, we could come to an arrangement for his newborn niece.'

'He was quick to point out there were conditions,' adds Mum, 'and that we would have to sign a contract for the adoption.'

'What conditions?' My voice suddenly sounds tinny. I could do with a glass of water but don't want to leave the room in case they stop talking.

'He said that we must keep the name your mother had given you.'

'*Ebony*,' I whisper.

'And that you must never see a doctor, but since you're always so healthy that hasn't been an issue. Anyway, darling,' she says a little too casually, 'they were more like incentives than conditions. And there was no way we could say no once we'd seen you.' She lifts her gaze over my head and a dreamy look enters her eyes.

Dad goes on to explain what Mum doesn't. 'Zavier promised that as long as we raised you as our own flesh and blood we would prosper. And so that we wouldn't stand out in the community, consistent rain, profitable crops and good fortune would befall everyone in the valley.'

*Who has the power to promise something like that?*

I stare at them with scepticism and a fair measure of disgust. 'You decided to keep me because you were promised I would be some kind of lucky charm for the valley? As if that could even be possible? What about the non-belief system by which you raised me?'

'Don't put it like that, Ebony,' Mum scolds, and mutters, 'You're too intelligent for your own good.'

Dad explains. 'Banks were foreclosing on properties that had been in the families of this community for generations. Everyone was suffering livestock losses and declining incomes. The longest drought in living memory ensured no one could even grow a cash crop to tide them over. Everyone's dams and all the creeks were bone dry.' He takes a breath. 'Zavier promised that your birth had broken the drought. He was very convincing. He assured us rain would follow at regular intervals for as long as you ...'

'As long as I what, Dad?'

He glances at Mum as if asking her permission. With her eyes still wider than usual, and looking at me as if she's scared I'm about to bolt for the door, she takes over: 'As long as you never leave the valley. He insisted that on no account could we take you beyond the valley's boundaries before your eighteenth birthday. It didn't seem like such a big demand at the time, when you were so small.'

'Now I'm nearing eighteen and you're worried about something.'

Neither answers. Neither looks me in the eye.

'I'm curious, Mum ... Dad. If I didn't stay, would the bubonic plague be unleashed across the valley?'

They're unhappy with my sarcasm, and for a few moments we just sit and look anywhere around the room except at each other. 'I can't believe you two actually believed the baloney coming out of that man's mouth.'

'Darling, we had just buried a child – a little boy I held in my arms for less than an hour. I felt his heart beat rapidly against my chest as he struggled to live. His blue eyes looked at me as if he understood our time together would be brief. And then, just like that, his heart stopped.' She takes a breath, her eyes swimming with tears. 'The following day a man offered us an orphaned baby girl. And yes, it was unusual and highly suspicious. We didn't know why he chose us. But at the time we didn't care. And we didn't ask questions in case it made him change his mind.' Mum reaches across and takes my hand. 'Darling, you were our miracle baby.'

I can see how, in their dark distress, they would willingly swallow the story the stranger told them, but something isn't adding up. 'What are you leaving out?'

They look uneasy and Dad says, 'What are you talking about, love?'

'Well, for starters, we're atheists. We don't believe in miracles, so how can you refer to me as your "miracle baby"?'

They glance at each other like high-school kids caught making out behind the toilet block. Mum looks away first, leaving it up to Dad to explain. 'It's just an expression for something difficult to explain in the logical sense.'

'An odd expression for an atheist, Dad,' I insist.

'I suppose, but you did bring us good luck. We prospered,

just like everyone else has around here, from the very day you came into our lives.'

I look around at our modest home, with the same furniture that's been here all my childhood, but decide not to ask what they did with their bounty. 'Do you have any names other than "Zavier"? It would give me a starting point.'

'Starting point?'

'I promise you both it won't change our relationship, but you know me. You raised me to accept nothing less than facts substantiated by a second source.'

Dad jumps back in his seat crying out, 'No, Ebony, you mustn't!'

Mum begins to wail with her hands covering her eyes. She's actually wailing!

Stunned by their reactions, I wait until they calm down. Mum collects herself first. 'I knew this would happen,' she says, still sniffling. 'I knew it!'

'Will one of you please tell me what just happened?'

'I think we've told you enough for one night,' Dad says, his voice unusually authoritative.

Mum blows her nose on a tissue, but the tears keep coming, quietly trickling from her eyes. I hate seeing her so upset. My intention is to uncover the truth, not to hurt my parents. I go and sit on the arm of her chair and hold her. 'Don't cry, Mum. Nothing is going to change.'

She forces a smile, the remainder of the truth lingering unsaid between us.

Suddenly Dad offers some advice. 'If you plan to track this man down, Ebony, you should be very careful. He emanated what I can only describe as —'

'John!'

'It's all right, Mum. You don't have to shelter me any more. I'm sure Dad's description is spot on. After all, my "uncle" is a criminal. And whether he is or isn't my biological uncle, Mr Zavier buys and sells babies, while palming off sob stories to infertile, grief-stricken couples. He may even kidnap the infants himself! How much did he want for me?'

By their outraged reactions, I take it I came free. But nothing in this world is free. There was a price on my head all right. Mum and Dad probably just haven't paid it yet.

# 12

# Jordan

I'm on the operating table, plugged into machines beeping like the cockpit of a plane about to crash, while around me doctors and nurses are in a frenzy of activity.

Can someone please tell me what's going on?

*Stay calm, Jordan, it's almost over*, the younger, soothing voice says close to my ear.

Meanwhile, in my other ear, the older voice says, *Ah, so you can hear us now, lad.*

*You'll understand soon*, the soothing voice says. *You'll have many questions, Jordan, but I'm afraid we will only have time to answer a few, so please choose carefully.*

Right. Sure. Easy.

*There's just something we must do first. Ready?*

Well, actually –

*Now!*

Suddenly two sets of strong arms wrap around me. I want to object to what feels like an invasion of privacy. Some answers first would be polite, answers the younger voice promised.

He reads my thoughts. *Trust us, Jordan, you can ask questions soon.*

'Trust you? But who are you?' I'm surprised to hear my own voice working.

*Keep still, lad. We're not going to harm you.*

Since we're communicating now, maybe I'll get my answers sooner. 'What's going on here?'

*Hold on, Jordan. Your soul is almost free.*

'Free? I don't feel . . . Did you say my . . . ?'

The arms start pulling me out of my body, but a sticky film blocks my exit. My head pushes against it.

*Hold still, Jordan. You're almost through the membrane.*

The 'membrane' breaks, dissolving around me, and suddenly I can move and see everything really clearly, clearer than . . . I don't know, but clearer than before.

What's left of the membrane turns into a blue gas that drifts up to the ceiling, where it disintegrates into millions of bubbles. And suddenly I *am* 'free' and it's awesome! If not for the arms holding me, I reckon I could fly straight out of this room.

*Stop squirming, lad!* the older voice snaps. *If you should slip from our grasp . . . This is serious, young man. You don't −*

*Now is not the time to test your new-found agility, Jordan,* the younger voice smoothly interrupts. *If you slip away from us here, we would find it difficult to return you to your body in due time.*

A chill slithers down my back. I'm not in my body? So where is my . . . ? I glance down and see it − my *real, living, breathing* body − lying on the operating table in the centre of the theatre, with lights blazing over it and doctors and nurses going nuts around it.

And then, *Whoahh!* My body lifts off the table as

high-voltage electricity jolts into my chest. I don't feel anything, but it looks terrible. And that's when I get it – my body isn't living and breathing.

I'm not breathing!

The two sets of smooth, strong arms glide me to the other side of the room, where the three of us stand back and watch. My body is a mess, spread across the operating table with tubes to my face, and my torso completely ripped open, and at least half my guts hanging out. Blood is everywhere, sprayed across the doctors and nurses from head to foot.

I can't watch any more.

I turn my head and see the younger of the two. The first thing I notice is his blue eyes. I have blue eyes too, but these are nothing like mine. Man, they're so intense they're practically blinding. Imagine a paint palette, then mix electric blue and indigo together with a touch of ice, and you still wouldn't be close.

He lets me stare as I try to figure him out. His hair is long and yellow-blond. He wears it partly loose, partly braided, but mostly tied together at the base of his neck with a string of crimson and gold threads.

The other dude is the one with the older voice, but it's weird because his darker skin is just as flawless and young-looking as the other one's warm-ivory skin. Even his silver-grey eyes are similar in intensity, though not quite as potent. He has long hair too – must be the fashion wherever these two come from. This one's hair is bright copper and tied with a white silk cord. They're wearing similar clothes – quality suits with T-shirts underneath.

It's clear they don't belong here. Not in this room. Not in this time. Not in this world!

The thing is, from the moment they pulled my soul from my body I've been experiencing everything astronomically fast. I'm noticing details in fractions of seconds, as if my powers of observation have multiplied a thousandfold. And it's amazing!

*Listen to me, Jordan, I need you to focus*, the blond one says, turning me to face him with his hands on my shoulders, pumping waves of calmness into me. *My name is Nathaneal, but you can call me Thane if you like.* He nods at his companion. *This is Isaac.*

Isaac grins and nods. *In case you haven't worked it out yet, lad, Nathaneal and I are angels.*

'What? Like angels from heaven?'

*Not quite.*

'So, what are you saying? There is no heaven?'

*All the mortal religions try hard to explain this, but the human mind can't comprehend the complexities of the afterlife and, unfortunately, I don't have time to go into details now. But, briefly, there are four dimensions: Earth, the mortal realm; Skade; the human concept of hell; Avena, where angels live; and Peridis, the destiny of the human soul, which equates to the mortal conception of heaven.*

*Are you following, lad?* Isaac asks.

I nod at Isaac. 'Trying.'

*We don't normally appear physically until the moment of transference when the Guardian ensures the soul of their charge emerges safely.*

My mother believed in angels, said she had talked to one named Solomon ever since she was a little girl. I thought it was a bedtime story.

I would have thought with my 'troubled' history and everything, it wouldn't be angels from Avena coming for me, but something darker.

'You saw dark angels, lad?' Isaac asks, in his speaking voice.

'Nah, I don't think so, but I heard you two talking before you pulled me out of my body.'

They exchange a glance over the top of my head but don't say anything.

'If I had seen dark angels, would they have taken me to Skade?'

'They're called Death Watchers, lad – dark angels who live in Skade, and whose job it is to encourage the dying to choose their world.'

Nathaneal runs a hand through his hair and takes a breath. 'Jordan, we are running out of time – you don't have long in this in-between state.'

'So talk to me.'

'I need your help, as long as you're willing.'

For all his polite asking, I don't see how I have a choice. I wonder what he'd say if I declined.

The two glance at each other again. 'You always have a choice,' Nathaneal says. 'Free Will is one of Avena's strictest codes. However, it's beneficial to know that many times the best choice proves to be the one first declined.'

On the operating table, the doctor gives my body another electric shock. 'Aw, man, is my life really over?'

'That depends, Jordan.'

'Oh, *really*? Is there ever a straight answer from you guys?'

The two look at each other and frown.

Nathaneal sighs and says, 'Angels are not men and are not guided by men's rulings.'

'Wait . . . I know what this is – a dream brought on by the anaesthetic drugs.'

Nathaneal swings around in front of me, opening his arm in a wide arc. 'I'll have to show you something,' he says, 'to make this more real for you.'

Before my eyes an image appears of a world with a shimmering pink-blue ocean under a lilac sky that sparkles so brightly I wince until my eyes adjust. He pulls at the image with his hand and it zooms in to reveal a breathtaking landscape of purple and blue mountain ranges. I see cliffs thousands of metres deep as if I'm flying closely over them, and waterfalls of staggering proportions tumbling into fast-flowing rivers. We follow one through a forest of horizontal trees with iridescent crimson leaves, and on into a vast plain covered in shades of purple and blue grass, where herds of animals I've never seen the likes of graze together.

Suddenly I'm back standing between the angels and pointing at the image, speechless.

'Yes,' Nathaneal says. 'Avena.'

'It's brilliant, man.'

Another wide sweep of his arm makes it disappear, and I mumble, 'I must be hallucinating.' It's the only sane conclusion. 'When do I wake up?'

'You are awake, Jordan,' Nathaneal says.

'Then what am I doing here? What do you want from me?'

'Sixteen years ago an angel named Ebrielle was born in one of those forests I showed you on Avena.' He stops and his eyes look glassy and pained. 'At the precise moment of her birth, a force of dark angels swooped down and annihilated our protection forces, kidnapping the infant. Ebrielle is still missing and we have until her eighteenth birthday to find her and return her home. We have tracked her to Earth, where we believe a human family is raising her as their own daughter, keeping her unaware of her true identity.'

'And I'm supposed to find this girl?'

He nods. 'Yes'.

'Sixteen years is a long time. How do you know she's still alive?'

The corners of his mouth twitch and turn up. 'Angels are immortal, Jordan. Our bodies can be maimed, we feel pain and take time to heal, similar to the human vessel, except faster, but we don't grow old and die.'

I point to my body on the operating table with my guts spilled out all over it. 'With eight billion people to pick from, couldn't you find someone better equipped, like a karate champion or an Olympic wrestler, or a marathon runner, rather than someone who's just been killed?'

'You will do nicely.'

Should I be flattered or suspicious? Normally I doubt everything so I don't think I should change now. 'Why me?'

Nathaneal glances down briefly. Usually this means someone is lying, but with this guy, though I don't really know him, I'm guessing he's just leaving something out. There's stuff he doesn't want me to know. He laughs a little, and I remember how he's aware of everything I'm thinking. 'Just be straight with me, dude, and we'll get on fine.'

'You and Ebrielle were born at the exact same moment,

making her your Guardian Angel and linking you together through the Guardian bond for all your mortal existence.'

'Get out of here!'

'Isaac and I have searched the Earth since her abduction without success, until tonight, as you drew close to dying, your Guardian bond lit up the skies like a beacon.'

'No shit.'

'Will you help me find her, Jordan?' His intense eyes grow even more intense as he waits for my decision. Realising how they're making me uncomfortable, he closes them and blinks, turning to watch my physical body thrashing about under the hands of the doctor trying to revive me.

'Why did she get stashed on Earth in the first place?'

'Her abductors are from Skade, where the air is too toxic to raise children.'

'What's with having to turn eighteen?'

Isaac, who's keeping watch over my physical body, flicks a look at me over his shoulder. 'Believe it or not, lad, even the Dark Prince has rules, all part of a treaty negotiated a couple of thousand years ago.'

Nathaneal explains, 'Eighteen is the age when an angel is considered mature and can . . .' he takes a deep breath, as if his next words are going to hurt – 'join lawfully with another.'

'Oh. Ohh! So they can have sex . . . ual relations. So what do you want from me?'

Just as he's about to explain, Isaac interrupts. 'The doctor is about to call it.'

'Call what?' I ask.

'Your death,' he says without blinking.

'We're out of time,' Nathaneal announces. 'Jordan, listen to me. You do not have to die today if you agree to help me find Ebrielle.'

'And if I don't agree?'

'We leave.' He points to the doctor who's stopped everything and is staring up at the clock on the wall with a look of death on his own face.

'Wait!' I recall the stunning landscape he showed me. 'My life wasn't all peachy, you know. You gotta understand, my life sucked. Why would I *want* to return?'

'What if I said you would return to a far better life this time around?'

'Can you assure me of that?'

'Once we find Ebrielle and she returns to Avena, you will have a Guardian Angel. Trust me; your life will improve dramatically.'

'You sound so sure, but, dude, how can I trust someone I only just met?' I take a breath quickly. 'I suppose life wasn't too bad when it was going all right, but . . . How would I know what to do? Where to look?'

'I will be with you every step.'

I stare hard at the tall stranger before me. He says he's an angel. I suppose he is. And if anyone has a trustworthy face, it's this one, but what would I be getting myself into? 'You said *every* step?'

'You have my word.'

I remind myself how this could all be a reaction to the anaesthetic and these two 'angels' could be figments of my imagination. 'This is a dream, right? I'm doped up on morphine and having a crazy hallucination.'

'If that is the case, why not give me your promise?'
Nathaneal shrugs.

'If you guys are real, will I wake to find I've sold you my soul?'

'Free Will is the governing law of Avena.'

'You call this "Free Will"? Dude, this is an ambush.'

'I'll come to your room while you're still in hospital, and you'll remember everything and know this was real.'

'How long will it take to find this girl and get my new life?'

'Hurry and make a decision, lad,' Isaac calls out. 'I've stalled for as long as I can. Your doctor fears brain damage.'

'Assure Dr Mac that won't happen.'

Isaac gives Nathaneal a look that says, 'What do you think I've been doing for the last twenty-six minutes?'

'Quickly, Jordan, yes or no?'

'Will there be danger?'

'Yes.'

'Could I die for real?'

'The destiny of your species is to die.'

Isaac shakes his head. 'He's pulling away from me!'

'My second life will be better, right?'

'I promise you, yes.'

Is he telling me the whole truth?

'What is your answer, Jordan?'

'What do you think, Thane? Of course it's *yes*.'

# 13

# Ebony

On Monday morning I wake at dawn with a dream lingering in my subconscious. It's a dream I've had several times recently, in which I can just make out a beautiful white house shimmering on the edges of my peripheral vision.

Shaking off the dream, I dress quickly, pack a small lunch, saddle up Shadow and ride over to the Langs'.

'Today, my beautiful friend —' I lean forward to pat Shadow's elegant neck and whisper in his ear — 'you will have a chance to stretch your long Arabian legs and we will fly together as if you have wings.'

Usually I enjoy the ride down the Langs' long driveway. In autumn it's especially lovely, with the changing colours of the liquidambar and golden ash trees lining both sides, but today I'm keen to start on our trip. It's a substantial distance, but with Amber for company the journey won't seem half as long.

We meet outside her front gates and put Shadow and her horse, Pandora, into a steady canter along Gunalda Road.

'It's pretty sad what happened to those best friends,' Amber says as she tries to get at an itch under her helmet. 'Their story has been the hot topic in chat rooms ever since.'

'They were best friends?'

'Years ago,' she confirms. 'Way before you started.'

'There must be more to it. Adam Skinner stabbing anybody is beyond me. He has everything going for him.'

'I know! He topped our grade two years running and he's planning to study law and become a solicitor like his mother and stepfather.'

I nod because I know this too, from Careers Day last year when Mrs Skinner-Holmes gave a talk.

Turning west on to North-West Highway One, the traffic increases, so we ride single file. We pull in at an off-road amenities park later in the morning. Truck drivers often stop to catch a nap here, but now it's quiet.

'How much further?' Amber asks as she rummages around in her backpack for something to eat.

'According to these directions –' I bring out my map and point to a small lane near the Windhaven National Park – 'we should arrive around noon.'

'Just giving us enough time to do our business and make it home before being missed.'

It's amazing how similarly we think. Last night I told Mum I'd be out riding all day with Amber, letting her assume we would be sticking to the trails in the local forests where we usually go.

The last thing I want is to hurt my parents. If this man turns out to be a criminal, I don't want him anywhere near Mum and Dad, so if I'm going to do this, it has to be discreet.

Amber bites into a juicy red apple. 'So, what's so fascinating about this lane?'

'A house.'

'A house, huh?' She frowns, lowering her apple, then gasps suddenly, 'It's not the one in your dreams, is it?'

She should know me better than to ask such a ridiculous question. This is one area of our friendship where we agree to disagree. 'You know dreams are simply brainwaves that become active while you rest.'

'Yeah, yeah.'

'They're the body's natural way to release stress. And they're not real events or predictors of your own or someone else's future.'

She shrugs. 'Psychics and mediums would disagree with you, girlfriend.'

'Well, I disagree with psychics and mediums.'

I am dying to tell Amber everything; it would help relieve the knot in my stomach that's been tightening since we started out this morning. I'm just not sure what her reaction would be. Will she still think I'm the same person? Will she be uncomfortable around me as she wonders, as I can't seem to stop doing now, who my birth parents are, and if they're out there somewhere grieving for their missing child?

It would be great, though, to have someone to talk to and share my concerns about all this.

She notices my hesitation. 'Best friends don't keep secrets, and I can tell when you're scared, and when you're lying, hon.'

'I'm nervous, I'll grant you that, but I'm not lying. I don't lie.'

'Ah, but you're clever at omitting pertinent information when you want to keep a secret. Come on, spill. What are

71

you worried about and why are you worried about telling me?'

This is all the encouragement I need, and I tell her about my conversation with Mum and Dad on Saturday night and how I'm not their biological daughter.

'Oh, my God!' she cries out.

'So there I was, two days old and wrapped in a black cashmere blanket being handed to a grieving couple to raise, just like that.'

'Oh, my God! Oh, my God!'

'Can you say something else?'

'You're adopted,' she says, then swallows deeply. 'And all these years you had no idea?'

I shake my head a little. She covers my hand with hers on the picnic table. 'That's lousy, hon. They should have told you.'

I shrug.

'It makes no difference, just so you know.'

I smile at that, because it is good to know. 'Amber, my parents would be devastated if this information became public knowledge.'

'Of course, especially because of the way it transpired.' She squeezes my hand and catches my eye. 'I won't tell anyone. I swear.' She then gives me one of her rare and beautiful smiles. Her eyes are welling with tears. 'Could your parents get into trouble over this?'

'I don't think so. I hope not. They were thinking through a fog of emotions at the time.'

'So no one's going to take you away, are they? I mean, just let them try!'

I warm inside at her eagerness to protect me. 'No one can take me away, Amber. At my age, legally I'm allowed to live by myself if I want.'

She reaches across the timber slatted table and pats my hand. 'That's a relief, but, hey, do you think this man Zavier was telling the truth?'

To ensure we have time enough to return home before dark, I start packing up and collect Shadow and Pandora from where we left them grazing. 'That's our goal today, Am, to find something to prove I was born in his house, like he told my parents, and hopefully not find proof the house was, or even still is, being used for some baby-smuggling business.'

We swing into our saddles and set off along the highway once more.

'What if he's still living there?' Amber asks.

'He'll be in for a surprise, won't he?'

She giggles, but it gets me thinking. What if he is? He could be affiliated with a big-time crime organisation! The house is in a pretty remote area.

'Amber, you have to turn back right away. I didn't think this through. I could be putting you in danger.'

'You're not doing this on your own!' she exclaims emphatically. 'What sort of friend do you think I am?'

'This could get ugly.'

'Forget it. We stick together. Where you walk, I walk. OK?'

There's no arguing with the conviction in her voice, so I simply nod and promise myself to keep Amber out of danger.

At noon we turn off the highway into the first of a series of country roads. It's not long before my stomach flutters at my first glimpse of the Windhaven River. This river forms the border between the two council districts Windhaven and Cedar Oakes.

It's weird to think I've never been outside the valley where I was born. I must be the most sheltered sixteen-year-old that's ever lived!

And now that we're riding along the riverbank, the scenery changes dramatically from open farmland to hills of stunning pine forests. My mood soars. 'It's beautiful here,' I murmur, vowing to see more of the world once I've finished school next year.

After what seems like an age, we finally locate Willow Tree Lane and, *whoa*, it's so beautiful we both stop to stare. Lined on either side with stately poplars and scarlet oaks, this country lane has a manicured look – expensive and private. 'This is it,' I tell Amber.

She leans forward to give Pandora a 'good girl' pat. 'Nice,' she says, scrunching up her nose. 'It screams "Private property" and "Keep out", don't you think?'

Our eyes connect and we burst into giggles for no other reason than we're more than a little nervous. 'You can pull out now, Amber, and I won't blame you.'

'Not happening,' she says, and tugging on Pandora's reins she takes off, click-clacking down the brick-paved lane.

I catch up, quietly relieved not to be doing this alone. We ride side by side, content to have a few silent moments with our own thoughts. A light breeze rustles the crisp autumn leaves. The lane itself is strangely pristine, devoid of dust, debris and, amazingly, even fallen leaves. At this time of year that's majorly remarkable. I study the trees more closely. There don't appear to be any bare branches. The trees have not shed any leaves, almost as if time has caught them in a vacuum.

I should listen to myself! What am I thinking?

We stop at the end of the lane in front of a set of black iron gates with a silver letterbox built into one of the brick pillars. Engraved on the front in fancy calligraphy is a name:

*ZAVIER*

Beyond the gates a sweeping driveway curves out of view behind leafy trees and manicured gardens. An ominous chill runs down my spine as I stare through the gates. I'm not normally superstitious. I know there are no paranormal states, but I am startled by the thought that this residence is evil. It makes me want to turn Shadow around and gallop all the way home. But I'm not ready to leave yet, not without trying to get answers.

Damn it, I'm being silly. It's a flare of panic, that's all. I'll burst into a fit of laughter next. I do that when I'm nervous. I take a deep breath to pump some oxygen and sense into my brain.

A light touch on my arm makes me jump. It's only Amber. She's frowning. 'Are you all right, hon?'

I nod, not ready to speak just yet. She seems to sense this. 'We know where Mr Zavier lives now, so if you want to come back another time . . .'

'No, I want to do this now.'

Amber's blonde eyebrows lift as she forces a smile to her face. 'OK. Remember, I'm right beside you.'

We leave Shadow and Pandora tethered to the left pillar of the gate, which opens at the touch of my hand on the handle. It swings wide enough for us to walk through in single file, and closes behind us automatically.

'Neat trick,' Amber says.

'The whole place is probably electronically monitored.' I search for the eye of a surveillance camera. 'They could be watching us now, assessing whether we're undercover cops come to break up their black-market baby-napping ring.'

A paved footpath leads away from the main driveway to meander through a tall rainforest garden. The canopy grows thick and adds an ominous dimension that rekindles the chill that ran down my spine at the front gates. I start to feel breathless, the urge to run away kicking in, but finally the house swings into view.

'I thought we'd never find it,' Amber murmurs, pulling aside a moss-covered vine. She hooks her arm through mine. 'Not bad! Sandstone, right? I like the timber veranda with the white rails. It has a colonial look, don't you think?' She seems unaware that I've not spoken yet, not moved a fraction, or even taken a breath. 'Ebony?'

Unconsciously I step backwards and, taking notice of the pressure building inside my chest, I open my mouth. My breath rushes out in a gasp and Amber runs to my side. 'Ebony, what's wrong?'

'I've been here before. I don't know how I know this, I just do. And ...'

'And ...? And what?'

'It's the same house as in my dreams.' I look at her and ask, 'What does this mean, Amber? What could this mean?' I go on to answer myself. 'I have memories of being inside this house. I remember a red room with mushrooms, and fairies pointing wands at mice.' I shift my eyes from the house to her. 'How is this possible?'

She looks lost for words. 'I don't know. How could you remember it when you were so little?'

'I don't have any memory of Willow Tree Lane, the driveway or this path through the forest.'

'Do you still want go inside?'

I nod and she whispers, 'Wait here.'

She runs off around the side of the house. I don't know where she's gone, but she returns quickly, breathing fast. 'We could be lucky.'

'What's going on?'

'Well, there's no car in the garage, no clothes drying on the outside line and no pets in the yard.'

I look at her blankly. She raises both her arms. 'I don't think anyone is home.'

'Oh, OK, but we still have to be careful in case we're wrong.'

She nods and we walk up the steps of the front veranda, where I pull on an elaborate doorbell. When no one responds, Amber tries the door handle, but it seems firmly closed. She takes a step back and looks to see if there are any open windows, and I try the door handle, just to be sure. Just like the outside gates, it opens as soon as my fingers curl around it.

'That's creepy,' Amber says, both eyebrows lifting high.

I shrug. I have no idea what it means.

We walk into a pristine, white-tiled foyer, then a living room where white leather sofas sit on either side of a brick fireplace. A baby grand piano, in front of a window dressed in white curtains, completes the picture.

Beside me, Amber's mouth hangs open. I put my knuckles under it and gently push her chin up. She smiles at me and I shrug. 'We should hurry before someone returns.'

She nods and we start working the living room, checking bookcases, a bureau, an antique chest of drawers, but find nothing. In the adjacent kitchen the minimalist style continues, with spotless white cupboards and a black marble worktop clear of all appliances except for one of those automatic espresso machines. We rummage through the bathroom and laundry; even the study produces nothing. There's not even dust in this place. The man who returns here occasionally either doesn't use the facilities or is literally the cleanest person alive.

Amber moves down a hallway while I wander back into the living room to check behind paintings for a wall safe, but again I find nothing. I start to wonder if I'm going to find anything here when Amber calls out from a bedroom, 'I found something you *have* to see.'

I walk into a white room, the only furniture a wooden rocking chair, also painted white. 'What did you find?'

Her eyes roll up to the ceiling. Mine follow, wondering what on earth she's on about. I see it and gasp, inadvertently bringing my hand up to cover my open mouth.

'Well?'

I try to put words together that make sense, but no

words can make sense of this. The high ceiling is painted red, with small clusters of brown mushrooms and fairies standing around them pointing sparkling wands at inquisitive little mice.

'It's exactly how I remember it,' I whisper, 'right down to the very same shade of red sky.' It's a memory that is definitely mine. And the only way I could have imprinted it in my mind is if I was lying on my back when looking at it.

The way babies do when they lie in their cots to go to sleep.

# 14

# Jordan

Dazed and disoriented, I wake from a deep sleep with the sound of someone calling my name from a great distance. *'Jordan!* Come on, kiddo, wake up.'

It's a nurse. And each time she calls me she drags me further from the . . . *dream?* Is that what it was?

'Listen, Jordan, I know you can hear me. You've been sleeping for thirty-six hours. It's time, kiddo.'

OK, I get it. I have to check out of the dream and into reality, and this nurse is my ticket. It's lucky for me she's so persistent it's hard to resist, because resisting is something I'm usually good at.

'Hey, Jordan, I want you to come back now, please.'

That's not a nurse. That's Lillie!

'Your housemates have been asking about you. They want to visit as soon as you're well enough . . .' She pauses and I know I should say something, but her voice is so easy to listen to, and there's something else pulling my thoughts in another direction – the image of a beautiful girl with amazing violet eyes.

'You have the will to survive.' Lillie sniffs. 'You've proven it more times than any young man should have to, more times than you've been given credit for,' she tags on kindly, 'but this time you're going to have to dig deeper than ever before to show me you can breathe on your own.'

What's this? I'm not breathing on my own? I feel the bulky cylinder between my lips for the first time and begin to splutter and gag as I try to push it out.

'Hold on!' the sharper voice of the nurse wails, as she pulls the tubing out of my mouth. That feels better. I take a huge gulping breath and open my eyes.

It's worth the effort to see Lillie smiling down at me. 'Welcome back to earth, Jordan Blake.'

'Huh? What did you ...?' *Ease up, she's only joking.* So why does her reference to earth shake me up? It's the dream I had, parts of it are still so vivid, still rolling through my head like a movie I can't switch off.

The nurse takes my vitals and, while she buzzes around me, the dream spills out like a confession that has to be told. Between sucking on little chips of ice Lillie keeps popping into my mouth, I tell her as much as I can recall. Some details are fuzzy, like the angels' names, but the intensity of their eyes, and the deal I agreed to, return in perfect clarity.

Lillie is riveted. Occasionally the nurse grunts as if she's heard it all before. Her reaction is mildly comforting, but not enough to stop me freaking out.

'That dream has really shaken you up.'

I shrug my shoulders and wince as pain spears through my chest from front to back and straight down my middle.

The nurse runs over. 'Hold on, Jordan. You're recovering remarkably well. Dr Mac is extremely pleased with you, but your injuries are extensive.' She places a remote in my hand. 'Press this for pain. It's morphine.'

I toss it away and she frowns. 'It could put me back in the dream, and I don't want to go there again.'

'I'll have a word with the doctor,' she says. 'There are other painkillers that go easy on the hallucinations.' She collects her bits and pieces on a trolley and pushes it out of the room.

'Lillie, do you think it really was the morphine that gave me the dream?'

Lillie helps me sip water from a bent straw. 'It's possible. Try to put it out of your head, Jordan. Conserve your energy for getting better. Your doctor said you'll have to stay in hospital for a couple of weeks,' she says, trying to distract me by changing the subject, 'with physiotherapy for a few weeks afterwards. I've already spoken to your house-mates about covering your chores. Oh, and I'll be speaking with your principal tomorrow to organise worksheets for next semester.'

I start to tell her how unnecessary that'll be, but she shoots me down. 'Even though your internal injuries are healing remarkably fast, you may still need time off school. Don't expect to recover overnight, Jordan.' She pats my hand sympathetically while I stifle a yawn. I didn't know conversation could be so exhausting. Lillie notices and gets up to leave.

I grab her arm. 'No, don't go. It's the meds, that's all.' I don't want to sleep in case I slip back into the dream.

She unhooks my fingers from her arm and kisses my forehead lightly. 'You need your rest. I'll be back this evening.' At the door she turns. 'Now that you're awake, the police are going to want to interview you. I'll stall for as long as I can.'

'Thanks, Lillie,' I mumble, growing drowsy quickly now.

The sound of voices entering my room wakes me. For a moment I freeze, but it's soon obvious the voices don't belong to angels. And I mean that in the nicest possible way. It's Danny, and Sophie's here too.

I have no idea how long it's been since Lillie left, but I didn't return to *that* dream, and the further it slips away the easier it is to believe the drug-induced-hallucination theory.

So maybe now I can enjoy the fact that I'm alive and don't have to go on a stupid heroic quest to find a stupid abducted angel and return her to . . . What was the name the younger one had called the dimension where angels live?

*Avena.*

*Man, how quick did that come back to me?*

Shoving that thought aside, I welcome my visitors by plastering a grin on my face. 'How's it going, guys?'

'It must be the drugs,' Danny remarks drily. 'He's never this happy.'

Sophie giggles and kisses my forehead, her lips lingering a moment longer than normal for friends. But we are, of course, just friends. 'It's a relief to see you awake,' she says through glossy red lips. 'You look great, by the way.' She whispers this near enough to my ear to be just between her and me, and the shudder that courses down my spine is nobody's business.

'It's good to be alive, hey?' Danny says with a wink, and

plonks himself down in my visitor's armchair. 'Man, did you have us going for a while.'

Sitting near my feet, Sophie points at Danny with her chin. 'He was so scared you were going to die, he dragged me to the hospital chapel.'

My eyebrows shoot up. 'You *prayed*? *Dude!*'

He smirks at Sophie like an old friend. 'So what?'

Having Sophie here reminds me of the reason Skinner shredded my guts in the first place. 'Anyone know what's happened to –' I glance at Danny first, then Sophie. She slides off the bed and goes and studies a machine attached to a drip pumping fluids into my arm.

Danny blows out a lungful of hot air. 'The murderous coward pissed off.'

'Are you telling me the cops don't have him in custody yet?'

'They'll find him,' Sophie says. 'They won't stop until they do.' She sits on the arm of Danny's chair. 'He's a wanted criminal now.'

'They're keeping an eye on Sophie too,' Danny adds, glancing up at her. 'They think he might try to contact her.'

Sophie pulls a face, scrunching up her nose. It's a cute look I've seen her do in class a few times when she's thinking hard. 'He won't contact me because he doesn't trust me. Apparently, he never did.'

'You're better off without him, you know.'

Her eyes shoot straight to mine. 'After what he did to you, I *know* I am. How can anyone hold on to so much hatred?'

Danny says, 'He only showed you what he wanted you to

see. He kept his dark side hidden.' He pats her arm. 'Don't worry – the cops will catch him.'

'I wonder what they'll charge him with.' Her eyes mist up.

Clearly Sophie loves the guy still, and love is an emotion that can't be turned on or off at will. It's probably her first big love. 'It's all right to still love him, Sophie,' I tell her.

Danny scoffs and I glare at him to make him shut up.

'You don't have to feel bad about anything. Skinner makes his own decisions.'

'I *can't* love him any more, not after what he did to you.'

It's what she says, but her watery eyes are telling another story.

'I hope he gets charged with attempted *murder*,' Danny says.

Weirdly, I don't feel the same way. And I'm the one in the hospital bed. Skinner's anger has long roots, and I can never forget my part.

# 15

# Jordan

I don't know how Lillie manages it, but the cops don't hassle me until Saturday morning, my seventh day in hospital. Two detectives walk in, one in a brown suit, the other in grey, and pull up chairs at the side of my bed. I know then it's going to be a long session. The brown suit asks most of the questions while they both jot down notes. They want to know whether my relationship with Sophie was more than platonic. 'We weren't even friends until that night,' I explain. They can tell the questions are starting to annoy me.

'We need to hear everything you can tell us to help us make our case,' the brown suit says.

They have an eyewitness in Sophie, Adam's prints are on the bottle – what more do they need?

When the session finally draws to a close, brown suit proceeds to warn me that, even though they have every man, woman and canine on the job, they've yet to apprehend Adam Skinner.

This makes Lillie furious, especially when they say the police protection she demands for me is unwarranted but in their next breath tell me it would be best to get out of town for a couple of weeks. 'Fat chance of that happening,' I tell them, 'unless my father has a spare bunk in his cell.'

Lillie looks uncomfortable when I say this, like she's embarrassed for me. But apparently it's because she has an idea. 'Actually, sergeant, since police protection is not being offered, I might be able to organise something for Jordan myself,' she says as she leads the detectives to the door.

Adam Skinner's had it in for me for four years but I never lived in fear of him, and I'm not about to start now. When Lillie sits down in the chair next to my bed, I try to reassure her. 'I'm not worried about Skinner, Lillie.'

'We can't dismiss the possibility he might come after you, Jordan. How do you propose to defend yourself when you can hardly dress yourself yet?'

'The doctors tell me I'm doing better than they expected.'

She's nodding. 'I know, and that's great.'

'Lillie, I promise you, I *can* dress myself.'

She gives me a look I've seen her give her two-year-old nephew. She pats my hand, all motherly like. 'Everything will work out just fine, Jordan, especially since I have a surprise for you.'

'Yeah? What?'

'I'll come back tomorrow and tell you all about it.' She gets up and moves towards the door.

'Hey, can't you tell me now?'

'I still have a few things to arrange. Sleep well, Jordan. I'll see you tomorrow, bright and early.'

True to her word, Lillie arrives right at the start of visiting hours. Smiling at me, she only just sits down when Nurse

Aimee pops her head around the door. 'Papers are ready for signing, Lillie.' Glancing at me, Nurse Aimee winks and says, 'I hear you're leaving us today.'

This is news. 'Yeah?' I swing my head around to Lillie. 'Is this true? I'm going home a week earlier than expected? Aw, Lillie, this is a brilliant surprise!'

She gets up. 'Going home is not your surprise, Jordan. Sit tight, I'll be right back. But in the meantime I brought you some things from home. I thought you might want to change out of those pyjamas.' She brings in my gym bag and lifts it on to the bed before she follows Nurse Aimee out the door.

I check inside the bag to find a couple of pairs of jeans, a few T-shirts, socks, boxers, joggers, my black baseball cap, my wallet, sunglasses and, man, I don't believe it, a brand-new brown suede jacket. She didn't have to do that.

I dress slowly because, even though I'm making a remark-able recovery, I'm still in heaps of pain. Every movement smacks at my wound. When I finish, I sit in my armchair breathing hard with the effort. Moments later the door swings open and Lillie walks in again. My surprise, appar-ently, is a tall, well-built, fair-haired dude a few years older than me.

I take in his clothing: white T-shirt under a black jacket, really well-fitting across a massive chest, black jeans. It clicks and I shake my head. She's done this because she's so worried Skinner will come after me.

But, really, what was she thinking? 'Lillie, you hired me a *bodyguard*?'

Lillie's excitement dissolves. Her pink cheeks brighten to

crimson. 'Heavens, no, Jordan!' She quickly says, 'I should start at the beginning.'

The dude steps closer to where I'm sitting and his silent look says I should know him, and I should know the reason he's here. A shiver, cold as the blue ice of Antarctica, melts my spine. The long hair is gone, but the trigger is his eyes – potent as bright blue paint squeezed straight from the tube.

'Hello, Jordan,' he says, and there's no mistaking that calm voice.

'Thane.'

Lillie's excitement just falls short of clapping hands and jumping up and down. I've never seen her like this before. 'So you *do* remember each other!'

'We were . . . younger,' Nathaneal says with a wisp of a smile.

Lillie beams. 'This makes everything so much easier.'

'How do you mean, Lillie?' My voice comes out sounding as dead as my heart feels.

Nathaneal steps back and crosses his arms over his broad chest while Lillie explains, 'You don't know this, Jordan, but for the two years I've been your caseworker I've been looking for your relatives, and just when you really need family around you, I locate your cousin. Or, I should say, he locates me.'

I glance up at the stranger with my gut churning. 'Cousin, eh?' He nods. So this is how it's going to be. He nods again, just a smidgen of movement. He's hearing my thoughts. Well, that's going to have to change. He smiles and glances away.

'Nathaneal has a house up on Mount Bungarra. His property lies inside the grounds of the Holy Cross Monastery.'

I feel my eyebrows lift. *A monastery?*

His face remains expressionless as Lillie rattles on. 'He wants you to stay with him. It's a beautiful house, and your room has views over the valley.' She sighs appreciatively. 'There's everything you need for your rehabilitation, even a full gymnasium downstairs, and Nathaneal is an experienced trainer –'

'But living with monks, Lillie?'

'Brothers,' Nathaneal says. There's a difference? 'The Brothers of the Holy Cross.'

'In time,' Lillie says, 'all going well, Nathaneal will take over your guardianship and you won't be in the system any more.'

'What about school, Lillie?'

'I've arranged special dispensation for you to still attend from outside the jurisdiction, so nothing to worry about there.'

She waits expectantly for some show of enthusiasm, but when she doesn't get it, not even a smile, she puts more effort into her sell. 'This will be good for you, Jordan.'

A frown forms on her face. She can't understand my lack of interest and of course I can't explain it.

Her frown deepens as the silence lengthens. Bullshit, man, this is not Lillie's fault! She's as much a pawn in this game these 'angels' are playing as I am. There – I flick a look at Nathaneal – stick that.

I take a deep breath. 'Thank you, Lillie, for finding my . . .

*cousin.* Who would have thought I'd have a relative living so close?'

'Well,' Lillie says, patting my shoulder, 'how about that, hey?'

Fortunately she doesn't see the withering look I send my 'cousin'.

'I think Jordan may have been thinking about you unconsciously,' she tells him.

'Lillie, what are you . . . ?' But before she replies, it dawns on me. 'You mean the dream. You think my dream was about my cousin?'

As Nathaneal's eyes shift back and forth between us, Lillie forms the beginnings of an explanation, but I cut her off with a sharp look. 'Well what do you know,' I mutter with a touch of sarcasm not lost on the angel. 'I must be psychic.'

Understanding my need to change the subject, Lillie says smoothly, 'Dr Beth has given me a scrip for some painkillers for you to take home. It shouldn't take long to have it made up, but there might be a queue at the hospital pharmacy. While I attend to that, you two can reacquaint yourselves. It sounds as if it's been a while.'

She leaves and suddenly the room is silent except for the sound of a basketball thumping away in my chest. 'I didn't think you were coming.'

'I said I would.'

'Why didn't you come and see me earlier? You let me think that what happened was all a dream.'

'There's no conspiracy, Jordan. I had things to attend to that kept me busy until today.'

I give him a smirk. 'Like your haircut?'

He runs his hand around the back of his neck. 'Do you like it?'

'Nope.'

His voice grows serious. 'You have the choice of making this easy or hard.'

'I'll live my life the way I want.'

He doesn't say a word, but I know what he's thinking: I haven't done well so far. Yeah, well, is that my fault? 'What if I choose not to go with you? Are you going to kill me?'

'Angels abhor killing. But your life will be forfeit.'

'What does that mean exactly?'

'I would be unable to protect you.'

I scoff at this. 'When has any angel protected me? They never bothered to protect my mother either, by the way.'

'Let's talk about this at home.'

*Home?* 'You know, there's so much weird stuff happening at the moment, it's not a good time for me to take off on some screwy rescue mission.'

His eyes darken, his pupils dilating until they swallow all the blue, and suddenly the walls, the floor, the whole room shakes.

'What the . . . ?'

It's a display of power.

He turns his head away, closes his eyes and sighs sharply as if he's pissed at himself. When he turns back, his eyes are their usual colour and the room is still again. 'Firstly, Jordan, this is *not* a fanciful rescue mission, but I'll forgive your ignorance this once because you don't understand the angelic existence. And secondly, it's all settled with Ms

Fisher and the Department of Child Safety Services for you to recuperate at my home, under my care, on a safe and secure property.'

'If I choose to go with you, you have to stop reading my mind.'

He nods. 'I'll do better than that. I'll teach you how to protect your thoughts from everyone with mind-linking abilities.'

'OK.'

'Is there anything else you would like me to explain before we leave?'

'Ah, yep, two things.' His left eyebrow rises up into an arch. 'Are you for real?' I ask. 'I mean, is this really happening to me? And, well, I get that my life is forfeit and everything, but . . . um . . . dude, I gotta know, will I drop dead if I refuse to walk out this door with you?'

He grins. And, man, it changes him completely. He looks younger, carefree. 'I am very much real,' he says. 'And this *is* happening to you. I can't force you to do anything, but if you choose not to walk out this door with me, I don't know how long you would have, but likely not long.'

'So I could get squashed by a bus right outside this hospital.'

He doesn't answer and the silence lengthens.

'Can I still hang out with my friends?'

'Of course, but finding Ebrielle must be your main priority. It takes precedence over everything.'

Somewhat resigned to the fact that my life is about to take another turn, I look up and meet his eyes with a nod. 'All right, so where do we start?'

'In the Cedar Oakes Valley.'

'Why do you think your angel-girl is being hidden there?'

His serious frown returns. 'I've searched the Earth for sixteen years but found nothing, not even one twinkle of Ebrielle's light, before your near death alerted us. But now that I've seen this valley, I understand how he concealed her. Mountains surround it on three sides, and combined with some clever cloaking magic wielded by the darkest angel of all, her light would be impossible to pick out.'

'If you know who did it, can't you make him talk?'

'He denies involvement.'

'But you still think he did it.'

'We all do, even our High King.'

'So, dude, exactly who are you talking about?'

'He's called Prince Luca. He was once a high-ranking noble of Avena. He believed himself greater than all, greater even than the High King. A third of all the angels followed him and he fought to become High King.'

'And they lost, right?'

'Yes and no.'

'Aw, good one! What does that mean?'

'Concessions were made, a treaty signed, give and take from both sides.'

'But, dude, he was outnumbered two to one.'

'His supporters were *all* warriors.'

'So what happened?'

'He was stripped of his name and evicted, along with those who fought against the realm. He made his own kingdom in the uninhabited fourth dimension, where his followers call him king, but angels of light will never honour Prince Luca with a king's title. To us he will be known for ever as the Dark Prince.'

The door opens and Lillie timidly pokes her head around, waving a paper bag in the air. 'Your meds have arrived.'

Nathaneal pulls open the door for her. 'Thank you, Lillian. If you don't mind, Jordan and I will be leaving now.'

'All right then, and as we arranged, I'll collect the rest of Jordan's things, bring them up in a couple of days and check how everything is going.'

She comes over and hugs me. 'Take care of yourself, Jordan. I'll see you soon.' She puts the painkillers in my gym bag, has a final word with Nathaneal and leaves.

The instant the door closes behind her, Nathaneal says, 'Are you ready, Jordan?'

Put it down to my screwed-up life. I could just do with more proof, something tangible, something I can see with my own eyes. OK, I get it, *he's* proof. But he looks so . . . human.

Since he's waiting by the door, I lean down to pick up my bag. My sleeve rides up and I notice my angel tattoo. Apparently Mum was right after all.

I close my fingers around the handle and lift, only to have pain spear through my ribs and into the upper half of my chest from front to back.

This is bull! How am I supposed to find this missing angel with my insides ripped apart?

Nathaneal is beside me faster than I can blink, lifting my T-shirt. I shrink back. 'Hey, dude, if we're going to be spending serious time together, we need to set some ground rules first.'

He cracks up laughing. 'I'm sorry, Jordan, I keep forgetting how distrusting you humans are. May I?' he asks. 'I might be able to help.'

'I suppose you're going to tell me you're a doctor in your world.'

'I am, actually, though I haven't taken up my position formally yet.'

With that eyebrow of his arched up high, he stands motionless, waiting.

'OK, go ahead, but keep the touching to a minimum.'

'I'll do my best,' he says, trying not to laugh.

When he sees the red-raw, puckered-up imprint of forty-something stitches marking out a cross on the flesh of my abdomen from chest to navel, he goes quiet and shifts his eyes up to mine. Silently he places the flat of his warm hand directly over the area where the two rows of stitches meet. Almost immediately, the weirdest thing starts happening. I feel movement inside. Fluttering is the best way to describe it, like when your muscles spasm lightly. The fluttering moves along with his hand, which heats up my skin at the same time.

I close my eyes and my mind slips into a state of peacefulness. I could stay in this state all my life, except Nathaneal lifts his hand away and the feeling subsides.

'Now we can go,' he says.

Nathaneal's hand is glowing and I can't stop staring at it. It's not bright or anything, but yep, it's definitely glowing, while my stomach is still resonating. I glance down and see only a shadow of a pink cross on my chest. Even inside me feels different, as if I'm stronger somehow. I stretch my arms

96

over my head, move them in a wide arc and feel no pain. It's then I look up. 'You healed me.'

Astounded, I follow him out the door. Right now I would follow this dude absolutely anywhere.

# 16

## Ebony

I listen for sounds of Amber on horseback. She'll be on the road between our farms so she should be here in a few minutes. I still have a couple of stalls to clean, but then I'm free for the day. A good song comes on the radio – I always have music piping through the barn when I work – and when I stop to listen again she's just outside, tethering Pandora to a gatepost.

She walks in smiling and holding up a backpack bulging at the sides. 'Lunch,' she says.

'I'm almost done.'

'I'll come and help, as long as it's not shovelling dung. I've had a shower already this morning.'

'Shame,' I joke. 'I was saving that for you.'

'Forget it, hon.'

'Well ... I suppose there are some rugs that need changing.'

She grins and disappears inside the tack room. A moment later a song she loves comes on the radio and she turns the volume up.

Just as the song winds down, I hear Amber scream. I freeze with the last of the rugs in my arms, not sure what to make of it. A wolf spider is probably crawling across the tack-room wall. They always freak her out. But something in the tone makes me hurry out, locking the stall gate behind me.

As I spin around, I hear the tack-room door bang and ricochet off the wall, followed by Amber's footfalls charging down the hall.

One look at the terror in her eyes and I know something is terribly wrong. When she reaches me, I grab her shoulders and make her stand still. 'What happened?'

'The house!' she gasps, her eyes enormous. 'Ebony, your house is on fire. I saw it from the window. Hurry! I've already called for the fire brigade, but it's going to take them twenty minutes to get here because of an accident on Taylor's Bridge.'

We run outside and I stop in shock. Smoke has engulfed the top floor, where pockets of flames are breaking through the roof in a couple of places.

'Call them again! Tell them twenty minutes is too long.'

She looks at me then. 'Ebony, where are your parents?'

Breaking free from the initial shock, I start running again and shout over my shoulder, 'And call your dad.' I haven't answered Amber's question. Dad rises with the sun most mornings, but today he knew I was looking after the stables, and since there are no riding lessons on Sundays he took the opportunity to sleep in.

'Don't go in there, Ebony!' Amber calls out. The distance between us lengthens quickly as I make my legs move faster than ever, and she hollers again, 'Do you hear me, Ebony Hawkins? Don't you go inside!'

But that's exactly my intention.

The front door is locked. 'Damn it!' Remembering I exited through the kitchen this morning, I race around the back and find the doors exactly as I left them, so I slide them across and am blasted by a gush of blistering-hot wind and smoke. 'Mum! Dad! Are you in there?' I pull my jacket up over my mouth and nose and go in.

The fire is spreading fast, with curtains and some of the architraves in flames. I race upstairs to find the heat and smoke heavier at this level, so I yank my jacket right over my head and make my way practically blind to Mum and Dad's bedroom. I can't see anything through the smoke and I call out to them. Opening my mouth is a mistake. Coughing, I turn towards my bedroom, but the smoke in the hallway has intensified already. I'd be stupid to go further.

I drop down to my hands and knees and crawl to the stairwell, finding some breathable air closer to the floor. The middle two stairs are on fire. I get a sudden panicked feeling. But with no other choice, I scramble to my feet and leap.

Amazingly, I clear the stairs and land on my feet, surprising myself with how far I jump. I want to check the lounge and dining rooms before I leave, but the fire is spreading at a colossal speed.

As I gaze into the lounge the spitting, crackling and whirring sounds soar to a deafening crescendo. This fire is feeding off itself now, shifting around the living areas like a ballet dancer, leaping and twirling with a sick kind of beauty, and all I can do is turn towards the kitchen.

Behind me a hissing sound builds, setting my heart pounding. I spin around just as a massive flame with a startling blue edge roars down the stairwell with the sound of rumbling thunder. It sets the entire space ablaze in a split second.

Coughing and struggling to find breathable air, I stumble out the kitchen doors and fall straight into Amber's arms. 'Ebony! Ebony, are you all right?' Amber shakes her head, so upset she can hardly talk. 'You shouldn't have gone in there. You could have died! You scared me half to death!'

A coughing fit has me doubling over and vomiting. She groans, and when I'm done she speaks to me as if she's talking to a child. 'Come on, hon, we're too close here.'

We go around the front. Amber makes me step back another few metres. Suddenly everything seems to go still and we look at each other warily. A moment later the upstairs windows blow out across the lawn.

The force of the explosion hurls us backwards. I sit up with blurring vision and ringing in my ears. 'What was that?' I murmur. Amber's behind me, flat on her back. 'Amber! Amber? Are you all right?'

She doesn't respond. My heart feels as if a giant hand is squeezing it. 'Oh no, no, *no*!' I take her shoulders and gently shake her. 'Amber? Amber!'

Her eyes open and the tightness around my heart slowly eases. I help her sit up, then drop down beside her and hold her warm hand.

'It's spreading so *fast*!' she says. 'I just happened to be staring out the window of the tack room when I saw something odd.'

'What was it?'

'Some roof tiles were fluttering over your parents' bedroom. Then black smoke suddenly shot out, blowing a heap of them into the air.'

I peer at her. 'An explosion?'

'Uh-huh. That's what it looked like.'

As I watch fire destroy my home, wondering what might or might not have started it, a wave of helplessness hits me, quickly followed by a surge of anger. 'Where's the fire brigade? Amber, are you sure you called them? And where are your parents? Is nobody going to help us?'

Amber pats my arm. 'Mum and Dad will be here soon.'

She climbs to her feet and looks around. I follow and watch her. 'What is it?'

'I need to bring you some drinking water.' She turns to me then and gently touches my face. 'You're scorched. Your face is all red and breaking out in blisters.'

'Do you think they got out in time?'

She knows I mean my parents and her eyes drop. 'Do you think, even if they were still sleeping when the fire broke out, they would have woken with the alarms? Maybe they ran downstairs, jumped in the car and drove straight over to your place. They wouldn't have wasted time checking my bedroom, would they? They knew we were going riding . . .'

I fight back tears. 'I couldn't check my bedroom or the bathroom or . . . Amber, I missed so many spaces.'

Tears spring to her eyes.

'Oh no, don't! Please, Amber, don't cry.'

She wraps her arms around me and I draw in a deep, shuddering breath. The fire brigade are taking for ever. I listen for sounds of a siren, or wheels of a fire truck coming, but hear only the revs of a four-wheel drive accelerate so quickly out of Teralba Road it scatters loose pebbles into the paddocks on either side. 'At last!'

Amber raises her eyebrows.

'Your parents are here,' I say.

She glances at the road; seeing no sign of her parents, she looks at me quizzically. I shrug.

And then out of the blue she says softly, 'I knew you were a fast runner, but, you can run *really* fast. Did you know that?'

Just then, the Langs' big silver four-wheel drive roars into the driveway and swings on to the lawn, pulling up right beside us. They jump out and, drilling us with questions, race to the rear of their SUV and drag out two fire hoses that we quickly attach to outside faucets.

When they learn Mum and Dad are still unaccounted for, and how fast this fire has spread, they exchange a worried glance. I almost fall apart then, but the sound of two approaching fire trucks distracts me enough to hold on a little longer.

The fire fighters jump off before the trucks come to a complete stop. They quickly grasp the extent of the blaze, and before they have said a word to me, I can tell from their grave looks their arrival won't alter the outcome by much.

Two firemen quickly don breathing equipment and crawl into my house on all fours, while others connect their much more powerful hoses in place of ours. Minutes pass without word. The fire fighters inside seem to take for ever before they return and speak to the captain, who comes over. 'They found no sign of John or Heather, but some areas were impossible to check at this stage.'

Dawn Lang squeezes my shoulders while I ask about the car and if the fire fighters saw it.

'A Toyota Hilux is parked in the garage.'

'Oh. Do you know if ... um ... anyone ... ?' I have to stop to swallow.

He says, 'It was found to be unoccupied.'

This news is a significant blow. I thought for sure it wouldn't be there. Mum and Dad go on Sunday drives occasionally. Now I know they didn't make it to the car and drive to somewhere safe. I guess I just hoped ...

Sliding into a daze, wondering what could have happened to them, I walk off on my own. I don't need anyone to tell me it's too late to save my house. I can see that with my own eyes. I stand back and watch as the fire fighters do their best. Amber comes and stands as a sentinel beside me, ready to collect the pieces if this doesn't end well.

As the house burns away before my eyes, my thoughts are not of the past or what I have lost. Wood is wood after all. Houses can be rebuilt. My thoughts are on my mum and dad, hoping with all my heart that somehow, *somehow*, they managed to escape.

# 17

# Jordan

His car is a white Lamborghini.

The double-winged doors are wide but light as a feather as I get in.

'Do you like it?' he asks, grinning at me from behind the wheel.

'What do you think? Of course I like it!'

He presses the ignition switch. The controls whirr to life, purring like a kitten. He gives it a bit of oomph, and it rumbles like a mountain bear and pulls away.

In a good mood, Nathaneal looks like a teenager. I wonder how old he is.

'I'm twenty-three,' he replies, reading my thoughts.

'Isn't that young for an angel? I mean, weren't you created, like, millions of years ago, before everything?'

He glances at me, smiling. 'One of my closest friends was born several thousand years ago and doesn't look a day over twenty.'

'So, are your years the same length as human years?'

He nods. 'Our significant differences lie in our cultures. Earth is dependent on technology, whereas in Avena we rely on the natural environment and the energy we produce from within our physical bodies. We don't use machines. We don't keep clocks. We have our own inbuilt timepieces. We don't use guns or bombs and our weapons would appear rudimentary to a human, but when they are powered by our own inner forces, they are more lethal than any man-made invention.'

While he talks, my fingers run over the car's immaculate leather interior. The flashy screens and switches resemble the cockpit of a jet plane, while the charcoal-coloured upholstery with the cool, charcoal-and-white seats matches perfectly with the glossy white exterior paintwork. I sink into the sports-style contoured seat and, with my eyes closed inhale the scent of new leather.

'I'll teach you to drive it, if you like.'

My eyes snap open. 'Are you serious? You'll teach me to drive *this*?'

We're zipping through morning traffic, full-thrust mode. The throaty F1 growl turns heads on both sides of Walgett Road – girls and guys, except the blokes are looking at the car, while the girls unashamedly eye up Nathaneal.

He drives fast. I tilt my head to check the speedometer and notice it's up well in excess of a hundred.

'I kind of thought, you being an angel and everything, you might follow road rules more rigorously. What gives? Are you a rebel angel or something?'

He laughs. 'My friends and even my enemies have called me many things, but never a rebel.' Then he adds, 'I can't use my wings without attracting attention here on Earth, and driving fast helps ease the ache of inactivity.'

'Where did you get the money to buy something that moves this fast? Or am I out of line?'

'You can ask me anything, Jordan. The Brothers of the Holy Cross Monastery manage financial trusts funded from the sale of their goods and produce, and from contributions, usually in the form of bequests.'

I must be looking blank, because he says, 'You know, humans who pass away leaving something for the Brothers in their will.'

I nod.

'Well, these funds cover the costs incurred in the line of an angel's work here. But I paid for my car and my house from my own accounts, which are all legitimate, Jordan, I assure you.'

'I wasn't accusing you of anything.'

'I know.'

'So you're rich, huh? I have a wealthy cousin. Cool.' I look up as we approach the first roundabout. I expect to feel the usual gear changes slowing us down, but he doesn't change anything. 'Mate, you're not going to be able to take the curve at this ... *Whooooah!*' I grip the edges of my seat while he power-slides through the turn. As he accelerates out, thunder rumbles under my feet. 'Dude, for someone who didn't grow up surrounded by technology you're not doing too badly.'

But it's still amazing we haven't hit anything!

He smiles to himself, obviously hearing my last thought. I try to stop thinking so loudly and look out of the window instead.

It's not long before we're heading up Mountain Way. I

look at the landscape hurtling past without really seeing it. 'Man, so your house really is inside the monastery grounds. I thought you were pulling my leg.'

'I don't pull legs, Jordan.'

'Ha ha. So do I have to share a room with one?'

'With a Brother?'

I nod.

'Your new home may be inside the monastery grounds but it's nowhere near the Brothers' quarters.'

'Ohhh! That's a relief. So why do you live there?'

'The monastery grounds are much larger than you're imagining, with thousands of hectares of forest that stretch across the entire northern end of the ridge. My house is on the east side, and a river runs between it and the buildings the Brothers inhabit. I had the house constructed inside their domain for two important reasons. One is to protect Ebrielle. She will be safe to wander the grounds as she pleases while she's training.'

'And the other?'

'The house is near the Crossing.'

'Really? OK.'

'Feel better now?'

I laugh to cover my intense relief. 'More than you could know.'

He frowns and I hurry to distract him from reading my memories. 'Still, do we have to go now? I've been cooped up in a hospital bed for a whole week. I wouldn't mind catching up with some friends.'

'We don't have time for distractions, Jordan,' he answers cautiously. He's on to me; I know it. 'We need to make the most of your school break. Today you will settle into your new home. Tomorrow you will begin training in unarmed combat and I will show you the entrance to the Crossing.'

'OK.'

While looking straight ahead, he continues poking around in my head.

'Will you stop that?'

'You've been to the monastery before.'

Aw, man. I groan loudly. What's the point? Until I learn how to stop him he's going to know whatever I'm thinking! 'OK, OK. One night last month I camped outside the monastery's north boundary wall, but a couple of hours past midnight I swore I'd never return. That part of the forest is way creepy. And that's why I didn't want to go to your place. But since your house is on the east side, it should be fine, right?'

'The monastery, the grounds and the house are all protected. You have nothing to fear. Now, would you mind elaborating on "creepy"?'

I shrug and glance out the window.

'Jordan?'

'Strange things happen in that northern end of the forest. Everyone knows not to go there after dark. We shouldn't have ignored the rumours, that's all.'

'We?'

'My mate Danny. We were looking for a place to camp after a long day hiking and it seemed like a good idea at the time.'

'Even though you had heard rumours about the place?'

'Yeah, well, we thought it was just an urban legend. The escarpment there is the highest point on the ridge and has the best views over the valley. People would make the trek up there just to check out the scenery and maybe catch a sunset. Occasionally they stayed till after dark, and that's when they saw and heard things.'

'Such as?'

'Weird noises, glowing lights, rancid smells, and screaming that makes the hairs on the back of your neck stand on end.'

'When you and Danny camped up there, did you experience any of these noises, lights, smells and screaming?'

'Not really.'

'I take that to mean yes?'

'We made camp about a hundred metres from the wall, chilled out with a few beers and were just beginning to nod off, when we noticed a mist creeping in around us. It was weird, man. The smell was awful. Then we heard something cry out, a bone-chilling caw. We glanced at each other and ran to the monastery. That was weird too.' I drum my fingers on my knee.

'How so?'

'A Brother had a door open waiting for us, like he knew we were coming. We spent the night in a visitors' room and went back to collect our gear in the morning.'

Taking his eyes off the road briefly, he flicks me a troubled glance.

'Creepy, right?'

He nods. 'Did you report the incident?'

'Couldn't.'

'Why not?'

'We'd been drinking, so who was going to believe us?'

'The Brothers.'

'They told us not to concern ourselves, they would look into it. And Danny and I promised each other we wouldn't talk about it again.'

After a long moment Nathaneal says, 'Thank you for telling me. Now I have something to tell you.'

'Yeah?'

'There is a reason those rumours were started.'

I almost gasp out loud. What can this angel dude have to do with it? And then it clicks. 'It's the Crossing. You want to keep people away from the area so they don't stumble across it.'

'Or stumble across something they shouldn't.'

'That would suck.'

'Yes, it would, but what you don't know is that there are two of these Crossings that make travelling between the dimensions possible. You can think of them as portals, though what they really are is far from a portal. They are dangerous places, almost a dimension of their own, but for now it's enough for you to know that the entrance to one is here on Mount Bungarra, while the other is in Alaska. This one –' he points to the northern end of the ridge through my window, where we can just start to see glimpses of the escarpment – 'is monitored by the Brothers of the Holy Cross. It's their job. It's why they built their monastery here.'

He turns his head a moment to look directly at me, ensuring I'm following every word. 'Dark angels use the

Crossing in Alaska. That one is protected by an order of sons and daughters of dark angels that live permanently up there. But sometimes a dark angel will use this Crossing. It's one of the activities the Brothers watch for so they can warn us of impending trouble. For any number of reasons, they need to be prepared. And when it happens, whether it's one dark angel or a dozen coming through, the forest becomes active with Prince Luca's spies.'

'Spies?'

'Demons he created specifically for living and working in the Earth dimension. They're nocturnal creatures, and their screams will raise the hairs on the back of your neck, if you have any,' he adds mysteriously.

'Demons live on the ridge? Oh, man!'

'They're called Aracals. They mostly stay in the trees where you can hardly see them. Even when they come out at night, the most you should see is a glimpse of a small black animal. They're not something humans normally need worry about.'

'Great. Thanks for straightening that up for me.'

His smile is a mere tightening of his lips. 'The Brothers monitor their movements. Recently they found several small colonies lower down the mountain, and in the national parkland that surrounds the Oakes Valley. Stranger still, some are venturing out during daylight.'

'No shit! So what do they feed on, these ... Aracals?'

He gives me a quick look up and down with eyes that don't look serious for once. 'Since you're still here, apparently not you.'

*Is he joking? Of course he's joking!* He laughs a little and I

112

grizzle at his unfunny joke, 'Ha ha! Your sense of humour needs work.'

'Prince Luca isn't going to sit back and watch me swoop in and take Ebrielle home once he discovers I'm here. It's why we'll have to work fast once we find her. You'll have your work cut out.'

'What "work" exactly are you referring to? I thought you just needed my Guardian Angel radar working.'

'That part you will do instinctively.'

'And the other part?'

'It's going to be your job to convince Ebrielle to return to Avena with me.'

I stare at his profile. He doesn't flinch. He's like a statue carved from confidence rather than alabaster or marble. 'And how am I supposed to do that?'

'Once you meet her and get to know her, the words will come.'

'What if she doesn't choose to go with you or the Dark Prince? What if she wants to stay here, where she grew up?'

He nods. He's considered this possibility already, but he doesn't answer until he manoeuvres around a bus of tourists pulled over to take snapshots. 'She will never willingly choose Prince Luca.'

'Does the Dark Prince know about the Free Will thing?'

'All the dimensions abide by this law. The worst offenders are humans because they're not held account-able for these crimes. But all angels are, especially the Dark Prince, since this and other laws were part of the agreement that brought peace more than a thousand years ago.'

'OK. That helps.'

He sighs, a very strained, tense sound, and I brace myself for more bad news. 'Prince Luca is a master manipulator and we mustn't forget that,' he says. 'He may not break this law, but neither will he allow it to stand in his way. He probably has a plan already in place to circumvent it.'

'Man, I'm not in a coma and dreaming this stuff, am I?'

'You're not dreaming, Jordan.'

'Any chance I could go back and choose again?'

He pulls over suddenly. 'You need to see with your own eyes that what I'm saying is real, my friend,' he says, and hits the switch that opens both doors.

I follow him to a eucalyptus tree on the side of the road, where he points to a small furry animal curled up asleep on a branch about midway up. I try to make out what it is but come up blank.

Nathaneal flicks out his fingers and shimmering dust flies out of his hand, waking the fur-ball. It knows the dust is bad and shakes furiously, its furry cat-like ears sitting up straight on top of its possum-like head. It spots Nathaneal and snakes out black claws and screeches.

'Nice effect you have on the wildlife here.'

He sniggers. 'Watch.'

I take a step closer. But quickly step back as the little fur-ball bursts out of itself. 'Whoa!'

Right before my eyes its chubby little paws stretch, growing longer until its limbs are like a bird's wings. Meanwhile, its cute rounded snout pushes outwards to form a sharp pointed beak. It ends up part covered in glossy black feathers, part still fur. It's quite a look, as if it was in a hurry to get dressed and didn't quite finish.

I've never seen anything like it. It's almost a bird now, but with longer legs, a more slender body, larger eyes and big bright blue irises. In its near-completed transition it's dead ugly.

It squawks, its eyes focused on Nathaneal. 'It doesn't like you much.'

The hideous almost-bird tilts its head to look straight at me, and shrieks.

'Back up, buddy.'

Then, wham . . . Nathaneal takes the critter by the throat.

Dangling and squirming in the air, it tries to bite his arm. Drool forms frothy bubbles around the edges of its beak. Where its saliva drops, the grass shrivels and turns black. 'She likes firm and stringy meat like the muscles of an arm or leg. It's an easy, quick meal, with only a few layers of skin to find it.'

'She?'

'They're all female. But don't be fooled, Jordan, there isn't a feminine bone in her body. Her favourite muscle is the heart. She's been known to gnaw through the bones of the sternum to get to it.'

He releases her, and she curls into her original fur-ball shape. Using her possum-like claws, she leaps from one branch to another and scurries into the scrub.

'Man!' I'm practically speechless. 'These *things* . . . they've never actually attacked a human, have they?'

'Unfortunately, there are some known cases of human attacks. But the Aracals are observers, not fighters.'

'The Dark Prince's spies. Hey, you woke her up, and she's a spy! It won't be long before *he* knows you're here!'

Nathaneal smiles, looking too relaxed, before he says, 'This one won't be reporting anything, because I just removed all traces of us from her memory.'

'So, just how many Aracals are living here without us knowing?'

'Not as many as you're thinking, but their numbers are growing.'

Back in the car and on our way again, I hardly notice the changing scenery. Something is happening to me. I'm starting to accept there really is more to this world than I can see.

We arrive at the ancient-looking monastery. Its walls shoot up out of the cliff as if the ageing stones are part of the ridge itself, sentinels of a time in history that is long past.

Instead of driving into the parking area for visitors, Thane takes a left turn off Ridge Road and follows a dirt track around the monastery's western boundary and up into the hills where the tall pine trees grow.

A few minutes later we come to a three-metre high solid-block wall that runs alongside the road. Topped with steel mesh and barbed wire, this fence would be a challenge for a hardened criminal to cross over, but an Aracal? What about their powers?

'I'm not without powers of my own,' Thane says. 'My house and property are protected by more than bricks, mortar and wire.'

We are now close to the northern tip of the ridge, where a thousand–metre-deep gorge separates it from the next mountain range, and all the way along we follow the white block wall. 'What is this? The Great Wall of China?'

'You'll see it's a substantial property, and completely enclosed,' he says. He starts gearing down, looking for a gate. It's not easy to spot, which is the way Thane obviously wants it.

'How would I find this place in the dark? Is there a light or something?'

'A light would be too telling,' he says. 'It will just take practice. Watch for the locations of two natural markers.' He indicates a tree on our left about a hundred metres ahead, stripped bare of bark by past lightning strikes, and a boulder on the same side in the shape of a piano. He stops in front of it. 'If you pass the piano rock, you've passed the driveway. Remember that, and you'll be just fine.'

He throws the Lambo into reverse and turns into a drive-way cleverly concealed by silvery hanging vines that completely obscure a set of black iron gates. The gates open at the press of a shiny switch on the dash. When they close silently behind us, Thane draws in a deep breath and sighs contentedly.

'*Our* house is just through there.' He points to a road that cuts a path through the forest.

We follow it for what seems like ages, eventually arriving at a clearing the size of a football field with an amazing glass house in the centre, surrounded by manicured gardens and paved footpaths.

It blows me away. Built into the sloping ground there are levels going up and down all over the place and floor-to-ceiling walls of glass – tempered and non-transparent, he tells me. Holding it all together is toughened steel. The roof is in sections, with some made from the same tempered glass as the walls. They stretch across from one section to another, with each individual panel raised up higher on the outside edge, like wings. These panels give the house the look that it could take off at any moment.

After he parks in the garage, we walk out into the front yard and cross a bridge over a pond with giant floating lilies and huge silver, gold and black fish. A few steps lead up to a timber deck and the front entrance.

He opens the front door to a wide open space. Light pours through the angular glass ceiling like sun bursting through a rain cloud. One step inside and I feel as if I'm walking on sunshine. Thane tells me his idea was to build a house where Ebrielle could spend her time training in complete safety and not feel like a prisoner.

The airy feeling carries through to an open-style lounge and dining area. Everything here is restful, from the living walls of lush plants, to the trickling waterfall and the fire blazing behind the glass and sandstone block wall that divides the lounge from the dining room.

Down a flight of stairs there's a games room with a big TV, a full-size pool table and another living wall of purple flowering vines winding up a trellis to the ceiling. I can see the gymnasium down there, just like Lillie said.

This house is something else and I imagine showing Danny and Sophie and . . . and that girl from the club – if I ever get the guts to approach her at school. I have these thoughts as we pass through a kitchen that's mostly white, with marble worktops and stainless-steel appliances.

I begin to think I will like living here very much.

# 18

## Ebony

The police arrive and, while the fire crew are fighting to save as much of my house as possible, a male and a female constable ask me dozens of exasperating questions. No, I did not see my parents this morning so, no, I don't know if they left the house after I did, but they must have because they're not here now, are they?

The questions keep coming. Many are expected, like do my parents smoke? Have there been strangers hanging around? And then there are questions I don't expect, like do I get on with my parents? Had we argued in the last twenty-four hours? Were we on the verge of bankruptcy? Does Dad gamble? What insurance policies do my parents have? How much do I stand to inherit?

'We will be checking,' the dark-haired female officer declares, tapping her pen on her notebook and looking me straight in the eye.

I look her straight back. 'I don't know who benefits, but I think it's safe to assume, considering I'm their only child, the beneficiary would be me, unless Dad wanted to leave everything to the horses.' Standing close behind me, Amber snorts with laughter.

Unbelievably, the questions become even more intrusive. They want to know if my parents still love each other, if they're still intimate (as if I would know!). Standing beside me, Mr Lang notices my accelerating agitation, no doubt from the steam starting to hiss from my ears.

'For your own safety, officers, that better be it for today.'

They close their notebooks and go to talk to the fire chief.

Mr Lang asks, 'Is there someone I can call for you, Ebony?'

I shake my head. There are relatives in London on Mum's side, but she's only mentioned them once and I don't even remember their names.

Dawn comes over after talking to the lead fire fighter. She walks straight up to me and pulls me into her arms. 'You poor girl, you're coming with us. Our home is your home for as long you need or want it.' She pulls back to look into my eyes. 'Do you understand what I'm saying, Ebony?'

The kindness in Mrs Lang's eyes, golden-brown like her children's, is exactly what I need right now.

'Can Mum and Dad stay too?'

She hesitates, as if I caught her off guard.

'It won't be long before we're back on our feet. Please?'

'Of course they can!'

'They'll turn up soon,' I reassure her.

Death is final; the returning of one's body to the earth so the atoms that make us can be recycled back into the universe to start again. It's simple and beautiful, but I can't consider that concept for Mum and Dad. How can it be possible for two people to be here one moment and gone the next?

When Dad sees what's happened, he'll want to bunk down in the barn near his horses, but Mum will insist on a motel. I won't care. As long as we're together, I'll sleep under the stars.

Taking my arm Mrs Lang leads me to their four-wheel drive. 'Why don't we head over now for a strong cup of tea.' At my hesitation she adds, 'We can wait for news there, Ebony.'

'But the horses?' I glance down to the barn where Pandora remains tethered to the outer-yard gatepost, and my chest fills with the need to run to Shadow and bury my head in his striking white mane.

Amber puts her arm around me, coaxing me inside the SUV. 'The horses will be fine.'

Mr Lang says, 'I'll have my foreman help me bring them to our place right away. We have enough spare stalls. OK with you, Ebony?'

I nod. 'Thank you, Mr Lang.'

'You need to be with friends at this time, Ebony. You know we're here for you.' Across the front seat he exchanges a worried glance with his wife.

I look away from them to the house and watch as more of my home burns away. It's starting to feel surreal, like it's happening to someone else. But it *is* happening to me. That's *my* life the fire fighters are pouring water over while all I do is watch. I've never felt more helpless. My eyes burn with the effort not to cry, but I force the tears away because now is not a time to fall apart.

Later, in Amber's bathroom, I take a shower and stand still under the hot spray. The surreal feeling intensifies to the point where, if I close my eyes, I can imagine this is all a horrible dream.

A persistent knock on the door dismisses this illusion.

'Are you OK in there?' Amber pokes her head around the bathroom door. When I don't answer, she comes in, turns the taps off and holds out a robe. I step into it with mechanical movements, wondering dazedly what is happening to me.

Standing in the centre of Amber's bedroom I keep still while she wraps my hair in a towel, twisting it around my head. She then pats me dry, but when her hands near my shoulders I ensure she bypasses the patches of rough skin that have recently grown into strange little bumps there. I've been thinking I should probably see a doctor about them, but that will have to wait now.

Amber lays clothes out on her bed for me − a white T-shirt, a denim skirt, some underwear, socks and a pair of tan ankle boots. It occurs to me that I have no clothes of my own, not even a pair of socks or pants.

'You can use any of my clothes.' Amber tries to keep her voice light. 'Just think how much fun it'll be buying a whole new wardrobe.' She gasps. 'I'm sorry, hon, I didn't mean . . . It won't be fun at all.'

I blink slowly to assure her I'm not offended.

While I dress myself, Amber makes up the guest bed across the room. I've stayed in it before. It's a comforting thought in a day of trauma. Part of me wants to climb in it now, draw the curtains and turn off the lights.

When she returns, Amber leads me to the mirror on her wardrobe door. We stand side by side staring at our reflections. After a minute our eyes meet in the mirror. She's trying not to laugh. The T-shirt is too short, too clingy and gives me cleavage I had no idea I had, while her denim skirt, knee-length on her is a miniskirt on me.

'At least the boots fit,' she says, and begins to giggle.

I tug the T-shirt up to reduce the cleavage, but exposing so much midriff makes me look like a tramp.

We burst out laughing.

'When did you grow those boobs?' She shakes her head. 'And those legs! No wonder the boys at school haven't been able to take their eyes off you lately.'

'What are you talking about? What boys?'

'Let's start with Jordan Blake, and move on to the rest of the grade!'

I laugh so hard at her ridiculous statement tears roll down my face and I have to sit on the edge of her bed and clutch my stomach. At some point, the laughter changes into weeping, and then raking sobs.

Amber sits beside me passing me tissues, one after another. When I finally stop crying, my mind is clearer.

'Do you think they've turned up yet?'

She looks directly at me so I understand she's not hiding anything. 'Someone will let us know as soon as that happens. Ebony, everyone in the valley loves you.'

I close my eyes, and Mum and Dad are right there. 'Do you think it's safe to go back to the house yet?'

'Probably tomorrow.'

Unable to stop the momentum building inside me, I run over to her wardrobe and fish through hangers until I find a coat to throw over my too-small outfit. 'Amber, I'm going to search for my parents.'

'Wait!' She lunges as I head out the door, grabbing my arm. 'Ebony, how?'

'I don't know yet, but I have to do something to find them.'

'But, Eb . . .' Something in my face stops her from finishing whatever she's on the verge of saying. Instead, she runs over to her desk, collects a notebook and pen and walks out the door with me, uttering, 'We'll find your parents together.'

And I know then I have the *best* best friend in the world.

## 19

# Ebony

Amber rings every local institution from medical to recreational in Cedar Oakes, even the cafés in town that open for breakfast on a Sunday, on the off chance someone swung by and took my parents out.

But Cedar Oakes isn't a big town and it doesn't take long to run out of possibilities.

Needing air, and needing to be alone, I run down to the stables and tell Shadow everything, keeping my hand on the steadying thud of his heart. When I'm spent, I pull up a stool and sit. Occasionally I get up and take a brush to his shiny white coat, but mostly I just rest my head on his warm belly. He keeps still for me, except for the occasional glance to reassure himself that I'm all right. He knows. He understands something life-altering has happened.

Eventually Dawn and Reuben Lang come down and talk me into returning to the house. 'You should get some rest, Ebony,' Dawn coaxes. 'It's almost midnight.'

I glance up at them both. 'I'm sorry, I didn't realise it was so late.'

They walk on either side of me back up to the house, where Amber is already asleep in her bed.

'I'll sit with you,' Dawn volunteers sweetly.

'I'll be fine, I promise. I'm really tired. Please go to bed.'

She leaves, but only when Reuben pulls her away.

It's now well after midnight, all of the Lang family are sleeping, and I'm lying in bed with my eyes wide open.

Amber is snoring lightly across the other side of the room. Because she's aware of my inability to sleep in deep darkness, tonight being one of those starless, moonless nights with a storm in the air, a dull floor lamp is on.

I don't want to do anything to wake her, and yet I can't lie here a moment longer or I'll go crazy.

I get up and go to the window that looks east to the Mount Bungarra range.

The ridge is getting a real beating tonight, especially on the less populated, northern end where it's mostly forest. A bolt of horizontal lightning splits into five fingers, one of which slams into the ground, probably hitting a tree and setting it alight. At least the pouring rain will douse any fires that occur up there tonight.

If Amber was watching, she wouldn't see or hear quite so much, and I wonder if there are others with eyesight and hearing as sharp as mine. Normally I would mull over this thought for hours, but not tonight.

Unlocking the window, I slide the lower frame up halfway. The air is still, cold and moist. For some inexplicable reason I have the jitters for the people living on the mountain tonight. It's a vicious storm. Thunder pursues lightning in a tremendous rumbling stampede across the ridge. It's a disturbing display of nature's awesome power. I don't like storms. They frighten me, especially those that sweep in under the cover of darkness as if they have something to hide. On stormy nights Mum would always bring me a cup of hot chocolate, even if it was two in the morning. She knew that the first clap of thunder would wake me.

*Where are you, Mum? Where can you possibly be?*

I close the window and go back to bed. I really need to switch off, give my mind a break from this mayhem. Eventually I feel myself drifting. My eyes close and I slip into a dream where I'm wearing a long strapless gown, cinched above the waist to fall in layers of ivory silk and organza. My hair tumbles down my back and I sense the flowing dress and hair pleases someone, but the identity of this person isn't clear.

In my dream it's a dark night, lit by the soft light of a crimson moon. The field I'm running through is bathed in warm pink light. The grass itself, high as my fingertips, glistens with amber light when my fingers part the fronds. Curious, I raise my hand in front of my face. Light emanates from my entire arm, and I gasp.

It's the sound of my voice that brings him into the field. He stands watching me from the edge. Skin-tight black clothes cover a magnificent physique. Green eyes, full red lips, and hair the colour of brown sugar frames his head and shoulders.

The dream takes a curious turn when this man suddenly leaps into the air with the athleticism of a ballet dancer. Four black velvety wings emerge from his shoulders, shifting the air around him in pulsating waves, and in perfect sync with one another.

His movements, so graceful, mesmerise me. Knowing this, the winged man performs an eloquent airborne dance, drawing closer each time he circles around me until he finally touches down soundlessly at my back, so close I feel the heat from his body permeate mine. So warm it almost burnt.

He leans over me and I sense his supreme intelligence. It's a strange thought, but somehow I know it's true. This man is smarter than anyone I know, and this frightens me.

He slides an arm around my waist and sniffs me as if I am some sort of delectable prey. I instinctively stiffen and attempt to pull away, but quickly realise that to try anything against this man's wishes is pointless. I begin to tremble.

He spins me around to face him in a movement that feels as if I'm revolving on air, and I find myself gazing into his vivid green eyes, so intense yet fathomless and empty inside they shock me.

Repositioning his wings effortlessly at his back, he strokes my hair without quite touching it. His slender fingers, with unusually long nails, appear to tremble with his effort to be gentle. Confusion reigns inside me. Who is this man who is so strangely, perfectly beautiful? And why does he appear enamoured of me?

Ahh, but my heart tells me there is no love, only lust, in this strange creature.

He starts a conversation without speaking aloud; his voice simply appearing inside my head so that not only can I hear his words but I can see them and feel them as well. His voice resonates, low and rasping, sexy.

*Child, your time of maturity nears. Soon a messenger will approach you. Do not fight him. He is my trusted lieutenant on Earth and he will keep you safe.*

*Safe from what? Who are you? How will I recognise this man?*

*You will know him by looking in his eyes.*

*I'm sorry, but that's impossible.*

*You have the gift.*

I shake my head. My hair brushes against him and he breathes in sharply.

*I don't know what you're talking about,* I tell him, wishing only that I could wake up.

*Look,* he says, *into my eyes.*

I look, and suddenly feel as if I'm standing on the edge of a precipice of unfathomable depth.

*Well?* he prompts. *What do you see?*

*Nothing. And . . . everything.*

He laughs. *See?*

But my confusion only grows, and I shake my head. *See what?*

*Who I am, who you are, and who we will be together.*

*I don't see that.*

*Then you are not looking deep enough.*

*If I do what you say, I'll fall.*

*I won't let you fall.*

*I think you're evil.* I don't know where this thought comes from; it simply appears in my head with the same uncon-sciousness as blinking.

But his smile only widens; and for the first time his lips part and reveal perfect white teeth to match his perfectly chiselled face. Waves of his energy, strangely both beautiful and ugly, flow into me. I shudder and he says, *I'm building you a palace. It nears completion and when ready will contain the comforts to befit a queen.*

*Pardon me?*

*Don't be afraid. You have nothing to fear from me, my young queen.*

The lust in his eyes says differently. If he could, I think he would devour me, piece by piece, finger by finger. And yet, there is something about him, something distracting and disturbing and strangely . . . fascinating.

*When my lieutenant comes for you, go with him willingly, and for this you will be rewarded.*

Instinctively I answer, *No, I don't think that's going to happen.*

A grumbling from deep inside him sounds oddly like a beast growling. He stiffens; whether because I heard it, or at himself for not suppressing it in my presence, I don't know.

*So clever*, he murmurs as he runs his fingers along the edge of my face. I flinch at his hot touch and shudder. He fades into the night with a look of longing, his green eyes the last to disappear.

And though I feel calmer now that he's gone, I can't stop shaking.

To my relief it's Amber who's trying to wake me. When I open my eyes, her distraught face is close to mine. Seeing I'm awake, she releases my shoulders and sets me back to check me out, ensure herself I'm OK. 'I couldn't wake you! I didn't know what to think. I was about to scream out for Mum and Dad!'

She reaches out and switches my bedside lamp on before sitting back on my bed with her legs crossed, frowning. 'That must have been some nightmare. Do you want to talk about it?'

I'm not sure how to answer Amber. It was definitely a nightmare, but mixed in were intriguing portions, like the impressive-looking guy, his striking face, his wings, and the flying.

'You've had the worst day imaginable. I'm not surprised you had a nightmare. Nightmares are just dreams, and dreams are *not* real,' she says. 'At least by morning it should be nothing but a fading memory. You wait and see.'

She sighs, leans forward and takes my hands. 'And since we're wide awake, let's go raid the kitchen.'

# 20

# Jordan

I wake to the sound of a knock, in a room that doesn't look one bit familiar. It's obviously very early since the sun's rays are only just beginning to skim the valley with light. I blink hard to shift the sleep from my eyes. I'm in my new flashy bedroom in Thane's amazing glass house inside the grounds of a monastery.

My stomach grumbles. The mountain air makes me hungry. I could eat a horse, except it's too early to get up yet.

Another, louder knock has me reaching for my phone at the same time as Thane pokes his head inside my room. I jump in before he says anything. 'You gotta be joking, dude. It's barely half past five!'

He smiles. 'It's going to be a big day and I thought you might like a hearty breakfast before we begin.'

I point out the window. 'I don't count the day as started until the big yellow ball in the sky is actually *in* the sky.'

'The Brothers are up at four every day.'

'Just because I live near a bunch of Brothers doesn't mean I'll be joining their order any time soon!' I mean, really, who cares? 'There had better be bacon on the menu.'

'That I can't promise.'

'Argh! You disappoint me, Thane.'

'I apologise. Now, you'll find ample clothes for training in your wardrobe. Breakfast will be in ten minutes.'

My training clothes are a white tunic and baggy pants, while breakfast turns out to be organic fodder they probably feed their chickens! 'I gotta go shopping and get some real food,' I mutter while poking my fork through more seeds and grains than there is sand on a beach.

After breakfast we head downstairs to the gym. Built into the natural slope of the land at the rear of the house, the gym is part underground. Thane switches on the lights and the room suddenly has atmosphere. Machines, from treadmills to full bench presses, line up along the glass wall that runs along one side. There's a boxing ring in the corner with gymnastic equipment set up on the right, while in the room's centre a series of mats make a sizable training area.

'Take a look around,' Thane says.

I find a jukebox with five thousand song choices. I select some heavy metal and he laughs and says, 'Sounds like you're ready.'

We start with a forty-minute warm-up, then Thane takes me through a series of core karate lessons. I hit the machines for half an hour, then skip rope and punch the bag before we both gear up and go three rounds in the ring.

Hard to believe that only yesterday I could barely dress myself.

After a cool-down and a shower, we sit cross-legged on a mat where Thane puts me through my first set of thinking exercises. He starts with a lesson on how to clear my mind and find my inner focus, promising that as soon as I've mastered this skill he'll teach me how to block an intruder from reading my thoughts.

The day I master that lesson can't come fast enough.

After lunch we head into the village to pick up supplies. Bungarra has a quaint charm about it all year round, but when the tree-lined streets burst into their autumn colours, there's no questioning how beautiful it is. I shrug inside my jacket, yanking up the zip as the chill mountain air bites through every layer of clothing.

Thane glides into a vacant parking slot, reversing in perfectly in one go. As we stroll along the pavement towards the store, a cop car drives past.

Thane flicks them a brief glance, looking moderately interested. They pull up on the opposite side of the road, where two male cops get out and begin moving from person to person showing them a photograph.

'Someone's in trouble.'

Thane frowns. 'It's a photograph of Adam Skinner. They must be following a lead that he's up here. We'd better keep moving. Your Ms Fisher will kill me if I don't keep you safe.'

I laugh at the image that comes to mind; Lillie is a tigress when it comes to protecting her cubs. She wouldn't be happy to hear Skinner might be up this way.

As I follow Thane through the grocery-store door, our bodies trigger a bleeping sound alerting the cashier to new customers. He recognises Thane and hails him, taking him into a storage room in the rear where Thane's order is packed and set aside.

The bleeps also draw the attention of the only other

customer in the store, some dude who is standing in front of a rack of fresh-juice bottles. His hood is up and he looks dodgy. The guy senses me staring. We eyeball each other for a few seconds, standing frozen like statues.

'Adam?'

Hearing my voice makes him spring into action. He grabs a bottle, shoves it under his jacket and bolts out the door.

I run out after him. Thane is right behind me. But Skinner's head start lets him disappear into a lane. When I get there, I find it's long and narrow with lots of doorways, and he is nowhere to be seen.

Thane puts his hand on my shoulder and instantly I feel calmer.

'I can't believe it!' I shove my fists deep into the pockets of my jacket.

We start walking back to the store. 'Well, the cops are right. He *is* hiding out up here.'

'He was deciding to approach you. He has something he wants to say. But he noticed the police officers crossing the road and changed his mind.'

'Man, your mind-reading rocks.'

'It has its uses.'

'Can you teach *me* to read minds?'

He chuckles but doesn't answer.

The cops have spotted us and are making a beeline. I have to fight the instinct to run. Thane brushes my shoulder. 'You're not fourteen any more, joyriding in cars you don't own.'

I nod. These dudes are looking for Skinner, not me, not any more.

They show me the photo. Skinner is wearing an expensive black suit with a purple shirt underneath, the tips of his short hair streaked blond and pinched out as was the rage then. 'He doesn't look much like a criminal.'

The shaved-head cop smirks. 'Have you seen him? Yes or no?'

I hold the photo out at arm's length, needing a sec to make up my mind what to say. I have to decide whether to tell the cops the truth or an outright lie. The fact is Skinner tried to kill me, but there were extenuating circumstances. Lillie would tell me to take the safe route and give him up to the cops, but part of me wants to give the guy a break. He's had time to cool and think. Is he still a threat to me? I don't know, but Thane says he wants to talk.

I hand the photo back. 'Yeah, I know him from school, but we don't hang out together.'

A half-truth is better than a whole lie. Years of shifting from one home to another taught me that. Blunt denial is a red flag to adults, especially cops, but if you give them something that sounds genuine, it's usually enough to get them off your back.

Thane takes the photo and the cops switch their attention to him. 'Mr Skinner ran down this lane,' he says, pointing, then answers their unasked questions. 'A few minutes ago. He spotted you crossing the road and fled. I suggest the third door on the left, but he's moving fast.'

The cops thank him, glower at me and take off.

'What was that about?' I say.

He looks troubled but remains silent.

'I'm the one he stabbed. It was my decision to make.'

'He's struggling, Jordan. He needs to be with his family and he needs help. He won't get that on the run.'

'But his life is over if he goes to prison.'

He looks away at the sky and sighs. 'I've glimpsed inside his head. Trust me, Adam Skinner is in a prison now that's far worse.'

But to disclose his whereabouts to the cops after all I put him through – man, that doesn't sit well with me.

'That's why *I* did it,' Thane says, listening to my thoughts.

On the way back to the house, Thane drives past his driveway. He continues along the lane until it comes to an abrupt end with nothing in sight except for forest on three sides. We get out and walk through the bush to the edge of the ridge. It's a steep drop down to a gorge where a swift-flowing river runs along the basin with rocky outcrops on either side. 'Whoa!'

I try to figure out where we are exactly. It's starting to feel familiar. This is the other end of the forest where Danny and I came camping and freaked out. By day it looks harmless. I scour the trees but don't see anything unusual, not even one sleeping, shape-shifting critter.

'This way,' Thane instructs.

I follow him for what feels like ages into a thick growth area where the canopy is layers deep and the sky completely obliterated.

'Ready?' Thane asks.

'For what?'

'This,' he says, opening his hand and moving it in a wide arc.

Shimmering, flickering lights are the first clue. 'Are we at the Crossing?'

He turns me by my shoulders. 'Due north.'

I can only stare. Words just don't come at first. It's enough trying to absorb the colours of the flashing lights in the form of bursting stars surrounding a black centre large enough to fit a bus. 'So this is how you dudes come and go from Avena?'

He nods. 'It's complicated though, because it will also lead to Skade. You need to know how to navigate, and of course you need wings.'

'Oh? Why? It's just another dimension, isn't it?'

'Not exactly, Jordan. It's between dimensions. I brought you here because you need to know where this Crossing is, but you must *never* step into it.'

'Why? Because I'm human?'

'Because you can't fly.'

When we get back to the house, we go for a walk through the forest there. Thane wants to show me some strategic features set up on his property, which he's divided up into sectors for my benefit. The first is a cabin in the east sector with a safe room, then we walk to a cave in the south sector that houses the exit to one of the monastery's escape tunnels, and finally, in the north sector, a ledge at the top of a hill with extensive views.

While we walk, I get the opportunity to ask a few questions. 'Why can't I see your wings? Dude, where do you keep them?'

'There's no trick, Jordan. Our wings are simply an

extension of our skeletal structure. You can't see them because they retreat into our bodies when we have to assimilate with humans. If we didn't have to assimilate, they wouldn't retreat; it's that simple.'

We walk into a thick wooded area where gum trees tower overhead, while at eye level vines, leafy palms and ferns create a natural curtain from prying eyes, should there be any. It's here Thane stops, glances around and shrugs out of his jacket. I take it from him and stand back. He flexes his shoulders, rolls them around a couple of times as if loosening them up. My heart starts to pound at the thought of what I'm about to see. 'Hey, what about your T-shirt? Won't your wings rip it to shreds?'

'Not this one. I brought it with me from Avena. It's made from a special fibre. When my wings push on the fabric, the cells inside the fibres separate naturally, returning to form afterwards.'

As I think about this, Thane releases his wings. Whatever preconceived ideas I had just flew out the window. I never expected the silky whiteness of Thane's feathers, or the softness of his wings as they unfold like the flexing of a sail. Every feather has a coloured tip, alternating dark red and gold.

He turns and walks towards me, his wings floating behind him as they gracefully respond to his every movement. He inhales a deep breath and hangs his head back for a moment, clearly revelling in the feel of their release as if he's giving them some kind of long-awaited freedom from prison.

He comes up to me and I feel as if I should bow or drop to my knees or something. 'Dude, they're awesome!'

He smiles and reaches for his jacket. By the time it's in his hands his wings have disappeared, leaving only the sound of a soft whoosh and a slight rush of air.

'Can a human become an angel?'

'Rarely,' he says, 'but it has happened, though from memory more have become dark angels or the occasional demon.' His eyes flit sideways to me. 'Thinking about applying?'

My laugh is loud and cynical '*Me? An angel?* You've got to be kidding!'

He frowns at me. He can tell I'm mocking myself but he can't seem to grasp why. 'Care to elaborate, Jordan? Our species aren't that different.'

'Not different? Oh sure!' I watch my footing as the track grows narrow and slippery with damp leaves.

'Jordan, all I'm saying is you don't always know what you're capable of until you've tried.'

My temper erupts. 'This isn't personal, Thane. I just can't see myself as a creature of pure spirit.'

'We don't view ourselves any differently to how you humans view yourselves,' he says, his eyes flickering sideways. It's the only warning I get before he drops a heavy one on me. 'I have a question for you.'

'Sounds ominous. What is it?'

His eyes become serious as the sound of running water in the distance grows louder and my anticipation rises. 'What happened between you and your childhood friend that made him so angry, so full of hatred, that he would risk spending the rest of his life in prison to exact revenge?'

Crap! If I tell him, will he think less of me?

'Jordan, you know that won't happen.'

'It's not a pretty story, Thane.'

'I understand.'

We reach a stunning waterfall and stop.

'Don't you already know anyway?'

He's silent for a second as he watches white water swirling around partially submerged boulders below us, then turns his head to me and says, 'I'd like to hear it in your words.'

I take a deep breath and concentrate on looking at the opposite bank, hoping that what I tell Thane won't make a difference to what he thinks of me, or make him regret . . .

'Jordan, that won't happen.'

Absently I nod. Why does Adam want revenge? That's the easiest part to answer. 'He believes I killed his brother.'

## 21

## Ebony

I wake with the lingering memory of a peculiar dream and the flawless face of a winged man, but as my eyes open and my brain registers morning light, memories rush in of red flames gorging on my house, and the dream slips away.

It's Monday morning, the second week of the break, and I'm relieved that I don't have to face school for another whole week.

'Ebony, two detectives are here to talk to you,' Dawn says, stepping through Amber's bedroom door. She realises I'm just waking and murmurs, 'Oh, sorry. I thought you were awake.'

'Almost,' I whisper a little groggily. 'Did you say the police are here?'

She turns to Amber, who is already up and sitting at her desk letting down the hem of her favourite dress. 'Darling, take the detectives into the dining room, make them a cup of tea and tell them Ebony will be with them shortly.'

She hands me a bag of clothes. 'I was going to give these to charity.' I peek inside to find several pairs of boy jeans, T-shirts and jumpers, one grey, two black. 'They're mostly Luke's,' she says when I glance up. 'He grew the fastest of the boys even though he's the younger by five minutes,' she says. 'They'll probably swim on you, but the length should be good.'

I pull out the pair of dark blue jeans and the grey jumper, the least masculine of the bunch. 'Thank you.' I muster the courage to ask, 'Do they have news of Mum and Dad?'

'They haven't said anything yet, so we'll find out together.'

Dawn sits beside me at the dining table, opposite Detective Sergeant Sawyer, the older of the two, while the other officer, Detective Constable Barrett, elects to stand.

'Have you found my parents yet?'

Dawn squeezes my hand while Sergeant Sawyer, notebook in hand, absurdly flicks pages as if he needs to check his notes before answering me.

'Sergeant?' Dawn presses when neither detective volunteers an answer.

Looking up from his notebook, Sergeant Sawyer says slowly, 'It appears that shrapnel and smoke were the culpable parties in this case.'

Not sure what he means by 'culpable parties', I ask my question in another way. 'Do you know where my parents are?'

His eyes deliberately find mine. 'Miss Hawkins, we haven't been able to locate your parents. They've been missing now for twenty-four hours. Regretfully we have to assume that shrapnel and smoke from the explosion in their bedroom killed your parents. I'm very sorry for your loss.'

Silence creeps into the room with the stealth of an uninvited guest. Then, one after another, the sounds return,

144

beginning with my breathing, slowly in and out. Eventually Constable Barrett says, 'If it's any consolation, it would have been quick.'

Dawn's arm wraps around my shoulders. 'I'm sorry, Ebony.'

The sergeant says, 'It's the most likely result.'

'That's a bit vague, sir.'

Detective Barrett, says, 'The explosion caused intense heat, rapid burn and massive volumes of smoke. Nothing was found to indicate your parents survived the blast.'

'Was anything found to indicate they didn't? If what you're telling me is correct, where are their . . . remains?'

Neither officer is expecting this question. They glance at each other and consult their notes awkwardly.

The sergeant says, 'I'm afraid there were none.'

Flicking me a cautious, worried glance, Dawn asks, 'Nothing that could be tested for DNA? Fragments of bone or, um, teeth, I heard, aren't always destroyed.'

'Nothing, ma'am.'

'Sergeant, how can you confirm my parents are dead if you found nothing that proves they were in the house at the time of the fire?'

He looks to Dawn, but when she's not forthcoming turns back to me. 'Miss Hawkins, we checked transport links, hospitals, medical centres, hotels and morgues. Your parents have not run away.'

'I appreciate your thoroughness, but what about ditches, creeks or under bridges? They could have walked somewhere, dazed and confused. Who knows where they could be!'

He looks at me as he stands to leave. 'I'm sorry we had to

bring you this sad news. We have other questions, but we can leave them for another time.'

I look away, adamant they have it wrong.

There's nothing to identify because Mum and Dad were not in the house at the time of the explosion. The simplest answer is usually the correct one. It's the basic principle of science.

*So where are they? Could they have faked their own deaths? But that would mean they deliberately left me behind.* 'Oh shut up, Ebony!' I inadvertently say it out loud. Dawn and the detectives glance at me weirdly.

My parents are gone. I just turned sixteen. Parents aren't supposed to disappear when their child is still a teenager!

The officers start walking to the front door, but suddenly Sergeant Sawyer turns back. 'Miss Hawkins, do you know anyone who might want to harm your parents?'

I shake my head. 'My parents are wonderful people, everybody loves them. Who would want to harm them?'

Dawn notices I'm becoming distressed and beckons Amber over. Sitting beside me, she leans over and hugs me. 'Is there anything I can do?'

Nothing springs to mind, except ... I stand up with the intention of catching the officers before they leave. 'I'm going to file missing persons reports.'

I overhear Sergeant Sawyer talking to Dawn outside the front door, 'We've been doing some checking into the family.' The words tweak my interest. I stand still and focus on listening. 'The only child registered to John and Heather Hawkins was a boy named Ben, who lived for –' I hear paper rustling, and then – 'forty-eight minutes.'

Detective Barrett says, 'We followed this up by checking national adoption records and . . .'

Amber approaches the door and I hold my hand up to stop her. I want to hear the rest and quickly tune back in. 'Since she's in your care now, Mrs Lang, we thought you should know there are no records of Ebony Hawkins ever being adopted. We're going to have to look into why this is the case and run a nationwide missing children's search.'

'Ebony is adopted? But Heather had twins.' Dawn sounds bewildered.

It is bewildering!

'No twins were born to Mrs Heather Hawkins. There are no birth records for Ebony Hawkins,' Sergeant Sawyer insists. 'We don't know who she is, or where she comes from. But someone out there knows something, and we will continue digging until we solve this puzzle.'

# 22

# Ebony

The fire chief calls on Wednesday afternoon to say the house is safe to enter now. I decide to ride over straight away. I have to see for myself what is left of my home.

'Do you think that's a good idea, Ebony?' Dawn asks when I step out on to the back veranda to tell the family where I'm going.

Amber is sitting with her legs crossed on the lawn playing tug-of-war with Lucy, one of their three dogs. She jumps up. 'Relax, Mum, I'm going with Ebony.' She looks at me then. 'Right?'

At my hesitation she comes up to me and whispers, 'You're not going on your own and that's final.'

Quietly relieved, I give her a small smile and we head down to the stables and saddle up.

Riding Shadow goes a small way to relieve the pressure building inside my head. My whole life is in that house. Everything I own. Mum and Dad are – *were* – in that house the last time I saw them. What will I find? A clue that will tell me what happened to them?

As much as I try to prepare myself on the ride over, as soon as I'm on my front lawn looking at the blackened wreck, I understand what a futile exercise this was.

This used to be a two-storey house, but to look at it now, with most of the roof gone from the top floor, you would never know. Amber follows me as we head round the back for a look. The ground floor appears to have remained largely intact, with the kitchen managing to escape the worst of the ravaging flames. Dad's study in the south corner, the garage alongside it, and the dining room walls still stand. The flooring on the ground level has also survived, along with the living room fireplace and a few internal walls, though most of what is left looks black and ruined. Upstairs is clearly a different story. There used to be two bedrooms on either side of the staircase. From what I can see from here, still in the saddle on Shadow with Amber beside me on Pandora, my bedroom at the rear appears to have retained a few floor beams, but the fire totally annihilated Mum and Dad's room.

Watery eyes blur my vision momentarily and I sigh as an overwhelming sense of aloneness fills me.

'Hey,' Amber says as she reaches out for my hand, 'how about I check out the barn and give the horses a drink?'

I nod and blink away the tears. Trust Amber to know when I need to be alone. 'I'll be back in a while,' she says.

I climb off Shadow and nuzzle his neck before handing her the reins. Then, taking a deep breath, I walk towards the blackened remains of my front veranda.

Treading carefully over charred debris I pick my way to the lounge fireplace. I'm not sure what I'll find, if anything, but something of Mum's or Dad's, a locket or keychain, anything that was dear to them, would be good.

But I find nothing except a button-sized portion of a mangled picture frame that once held our family portrait.

Tucking the piece of metal into my jeans pocket, I make my way to the area directly below my parents' bedroom, but there's nothing but blue sky above and the blackened floor of the living room below. I then head over to the area beneath *my* bedroom. I am standing still for a moment when a nearby sound makes me think I might not be here alone. I swing my gaze outside to the barn and catch sight of Amber pouring water into a trough where she's tethered the horses.

Hmm.

I listen for a heartbeat and sure enough hear one with the slow steady pace of mine. I look around with the fleeting hope that somehow this is Mum or . . . 'Dad? Dad!'

There's no reply because the reality is my parents are not here.

I glance around at the debris, the smell of burnt timber still strong in the air.

And then a young man in an immaculate black suit and hat steps out from what's left of the stairwell. At a guess, and though his clothes say otherwise, I would put him in his early to mid-twenties. My first thought is, *What an unlikely looter.*

For a moment we simply stare at each other, until I remember this is *my* place. 'You're on private property, mister.'

'I beg your pardon,' he says politely and in a rich accent, though not one I recognise. 'I apologise for startling you, Miss Hawkins. I assure you, I am not a looter.'

Did I mention that aloud?

Though I can't be sure, I think his eyes widen, but he maintains eye contact and that's hard to do if you have something to hide.

'Do you want to tell me what you're doing here?' As he steps towards me I contain a sudden urge to run. 'That's close enough.'

He stops and raises both hands with his palms out.

The man is good-looking, though his appearance does nothing for me.

I take a quick inventory – tall, broad shoulders, nice tan with brown eyes and flawless presentation right down to his shiny black shoes.

And then it hits me, and the skin on my arms breaks out in goosebumps. This man has stood inside my home before.

'I'm very sorry for your tragic loss, Ebony.'

I consider replying but choose to watch him instead, hoping he'll squirm under my stare and start to fess up his reason for being here. But he doesn't squirm, not even slightly.

'How do you know my name?'

'That's not important.'

'How do you know what's important to me?'

'I understand how my appearance here must be confusing to you. If it helps, I knew your parents.'

'And they just happened to introduce me?'

'Something like that.'

'What if I don't believe you, Mr Zavier?'

He smiles and nods. 'Since you know who I am, then you know I am your uncle.'

'Aren't you a little young to be my uncle?'

Looking directly into my eyes, he says, 'Everyone in our family holds their age well. It must be in our genes. Tell me, Ebony, which one cracked first?'

'What are you talking about?'

'Which one of your parents told you about your birth?'

'Why do you want to know that?'

'It's important.'

'Why? Do you know where they are?'

His big brown eyes narrow and darken, and suddenly a cold breeze blows in my face and the smell of burning timber fills my senses as ash from all around me stirs and lifts into the air. 'Are you *really* my uncle?'

He nods so deeply the brim of his hat momentarily conceals his eyes. 'Indeed I am.'

'Did you have anything to do with this fire?'

He shakes his head and his eyes remain clear. 'I did not.'

'Do you know who my biological father is?'

'I'm afraid my sister kept the boy's name secret from everyone.'

'How do I know you're telling me the truth, Mr Zavier? Can you offer me any proof that your sister really was my biological mother? Would you be willing to submit to a blood test to prove it?'

'I would.'

He sounds as if he's telling the truth, but there's something not quite right about this. He told my parents that my biological mother died on his lounge floor while giving birth to me, but . . .

'This is hardly the appropriate place to hold this

conversation,' he suddenly says, his eyes drifting over my shoulder.

I look back through blackened beams and shattered windows to see Amber approaching on foot. My instincts tell me I should probably run for the nearest police station rather than find a quiet place to talk with this man. But I have questions that need answers.

I take a deep breath. My questions can't resolve themselves. 'All right. Where?'

'I have a house. You know where it is. You visited recently.'

It's an effort not to react, though my reddening face is a dead giveaway. 'Time?'

'When you are ready to know who you are,' he says ambiguously, then turns and walks away.

'Hey! How will I contact you?' I follow him into the other side of the house, but there's no sign of him. I exit through the kitchen and look for a car, but there is none.

'There you are,' Amber says after walking right through the house after me. 'What's wrong, hon? You look as if you just saw a ghost.' She gasps. 'Sorry, Ebony, I didn't mean that the way it sounded.'

'It's fine, Amber,' I reassure her, taking a final wide look around. 'But I think you might be right about that ghost.'

# 23

# Jordan

When I wake on Thursday morning, all the muscles in my body are aching. Three days of training with Thane is killing me. He insists on making the most of every waking minute of the day, with morning sessions in the gym on one machine after another, followed by twelve-kilometre runs before we even break for lunch. The afternoons are taken up with teaching me how to fight in every style known to man, from ancient grappling to modern-day cage fighting. I didn't know there were so many ways to choke a person.

It sucks because the only time I get to think about the girl with the violet eyes is in my dreams. But with school back in on Monday, I'm hoping that when I do see them again, they'll be as amazing as I remember. Maybe it's time to stop burying my head in the back row. But then I wonder if Thane's quest means I won't be going.

After dragging myself into the shower, the hot spray loosens my aching muscles and I head down to the gym, where Thane is waiting on the mats, ready to start my warm-ups. By now I know the routine and climb straight on the mini-trampoline for a light jog. 'School's back in a few days and I was wondering –'

'Of course you'll be going.' Thane answers my unasked question. 'I would have a problem with Lillie if you didn't. Besides, I'm hoping Ebrielle attends your school.'

'Dude, what makes you think that?'

'The other schools in the area are both religion-based, correct?'

'Yep. Why?'

His eyes shift to me and hold for a second as if he can't believe some of the things I say. 'She wouldn't have been sent to a religious-based school. She may not attend school at all, of course. Most likely she's being home-schooled, but we need to be thorough about this, and your school is a good place to start.'

I give my memory cells a jolt. 'She doesn't go to Cedar Oakes High.'

'How can you be so sure?'

'Ebrielle's not a name I would easily forget.'

Nathaneal shakes his head. 'I think we can assume the kidnappers changed her name.'

'OK, just tell me what to look for.'

Thane smirks. 'We may have to rely on your reaction to her.'

'Dude, I react to all pretty girls, and since she's an angel I assume she would fall in to that category.'

He glances out the window and stares across the lush green lawn to where the forest begins. This is the look that makes me think he's keeping something from me. 'What is it? Is something going to happen when I meet my Guardian Angel for the first time? Are the stars going to fall from the sky or something?'

He laughs, but his eyes remain serious. 'Humans aren't supposed to exist in the same world as their Guardian. The bond will draw you to each other, especially when you are in close physical proximity.'

'And . . . ?'

'It should be intense and memorable.'

I laugh. 'Dude, that's hardly abnormal. It's a male thing, if you know what I mean.' It's not really a question – I'm not asking about Thane's love life, though, come to think of it . . . ?

'Not open for discussion.'

'Oh come on! You're twenty-three and well-travelled, there must have been someone somewhere?'

Bringing his knees up, he wraps his arms around them and glances at me from the corner of his eye as I continue jogging lightly. 'It's different with angels because of our immortality. We have one partner for ever, almost always chosen for us by a council of extremely knowledgeable and skilled angels who can see into a couple's future. They don't make mistakes because they're thorough. They don't rush their decisions.'

'But it's *for ever*! How do you know a bunch of strangers has picked the right one?'

'This is difficult to comprehend, but once a couple has the chance to mind-link together, they can *see* their future and *feel* the truth themselves. It's the ultimate confirmation a couple can have. After that, they have no reason to doubt.'

'I can't believe these dudes never get it wrong.'

He smiles to himself in the way people do when they know stuff you could never understand. I suppose he's right. 'Well?' I lift my eyebrows. 'Have they picked anyone for *you* yet, or are you too young? I mean, when there's an eternity ahead, what's twenty-three years?'

'They have chosen someone.'

I stop jogging and just bounce. 'Really?' I can't help smiling. He's so much fun to tease. He points to the trampoline and I start jogging again. 'You have a wife back in Avena, huh?'

'We're not married yet.'

'Oh, I get it. You have to finish this quest before you settle down, stop gallivanting around the universe.'

'More or less.'

'That sucks.'

'Yes, it does.'

'Well, that's incentive to find your missing angel, if ever there was any.'

'Yes, it is. So let's get back to doing just that.'

'OK. I don't suppose Ebrielle has a birthmark?'

'The birthing chamber burned to the ground so rapidly the midwife Myrinda recalled only the infant being snatched from her arms by a monster she'd never seen before. It was most likely a disguised Prodigy.'

'A *what*?'

'Prodigies are an elite division of dark angels who are superbly trained.'

'Well, isn't that wonderful news.'

He gets my sarcasm and spits out a laugh.

I try to explain how difficult this is going to be, 'Dude, I don't think you realise how many girls go to my school. This could take time. The more identifying features you can give me, the better, you know?'

157

'Myrinda noticed a smattering of dark red hair.'

'That's a start.' Then a thought occurs to me. 'Hey, Thane, do angels resemble their parents?'

He nods and smiles with one half of his mouth. 'It's safe to assume she'll be tall with medium skin colouring like her mother.'

I laugh sarcastically.

He swings his face up to me. 'What's so amusing?'

'You've just described about half the girls at my school.'

He gets up off the mat. 'She'll have distinctive eyes.'

'Yeah? Like how? Like yours?'

He nods. 'Yes, but sapphire like her mother's, or . . . mahogany like the commander's.'

I shake my head. 'Are you sure they're not green or orange?'

He flashes me a look that says he doesn't appreciate my humour. 'She'll be intelligent with superior senses, and exceptionally athletic.'

'Good at everything possible, though probably reluctant to show it.'

He frowns at me and I explain, 'No one likes to stand out at school.'

Softly he says, 'She will be so beautiful you won't be able to take your eyes off her.'

'Not everyone sees beauty the same way.'

'Wisely spoken, Jordan, but with Ebrielle, her beauty won't be all about her physical appearance.'

'That takes time to see.'

'Not if you're observant.'

'I suppose, but . . . Are you sure you haven't seen this girl before?'

Keeping his eyes down he says, 'I see her every night in my dreams, when she tells me about her day, what she did, where she went, who she met, if she's happy.'

I stare at him. 'Man, you don't tell your fiancée back in Avena this stuff, do you?'

He laughs but doesn't answer.

'Oh, man, we have to find this girl fast.'

He looks up, frowning. 'Why do you sound so concerned suddenly? Has something just occurred to you?'

'Yep.'

'Explain.'

I step off the trampoline and shake my head because he doesn't get it. 'You're obsessed with this girl. Finding her has been your whole life and, dude, that's just unhealthy. Your fiancée must be one tolerant lady.'

Again, he doesn't answer, except for the strange little smile playing around the edge of his mouth. And I know he's not telling me something.

## 24

# Ebony

On Thursday evening, while sitting at the dinner table with Amber, Dawn and Reuben, eating vegetable lasagne, the conversation swings around to school returning on Tuesday.

'I don't want you to worry about your uniform,' Dawn says. 'I have that under control, and I've organised a new set of textbooks from the library for you. I'll pick them up when I go into town tomorrow.'

I poke my fork into a juicy zucchini. 'You guys do so much for me, like this amazing vegetarian meal when I know none of you is vegetarian, and taking me into your home, and now the uniforms and books, I really appreciate everything, but if I'm going to be staying here –' I glance up and meet each set of eyes briefly – 'I don't want anyone putting themselves out or going to extra trouble on my behalf.'

'You're no trouble at all,' Dawn says. 'We're just glad you're taking up our offer to live here. Your own room upstairs will be ready in a few days. It just needs a little tweaking.'

They all look so pleased I'm staying that tears spring to my eyes. Amber runs around the dining table and hugs me. I hug her back. But she stiffens suddenly, her fingers curling tentatively over the strange growths. For the first time since I noticed them a few weeks ago, I'd forgotten the thickening bumps on my shoulders.

'Ebony!' She pulls away and takes several steps back, her hand flying to cover her open mouth, which she promptly drops to yell, 'What's with your back? Did you get hurt during the fire?'

Dawn glances at Reuben across the table. 'Amber, what are you talking about?'

'Before you turned up, the upstairs windows blew out and –' she stops addressing her dad and looks at me – 'we hit the ground pretty hard, remember?'

'I remember you hit it harder!' I try to make light of her concern, but now Dawn and Reuben are exchanging worried glances, and I wish I could slide under the table and disappear.

'Don't forget how you came hurtling out of the kitchen,' she adds. 'Did you hurt yourself in there?'

My face fills with heat and my cheeks start burning. How could I have forgotten? What a stupid, *stupid* mistake!

But, now I think about her reaction, why is it so intense? Have the bumps grown larger suddenly? They've been tingly today, but since the fire I haven't thought about them much.

'Ebony, *please* let Mum take a look.'

'There's no need. I'm fine, Amber.' I turn and sit and pretend to eat, willing her with my eyes to do the same. 'We shouldn't let this lovely meal go cold.'

Reluctantly Amber walks back to her seat and pokes at her meal.

161

I attempt to change the subject. 'I want to talk to you about photocopying your physics notes before Tuesday. That's one class I don't want to fall behind in.'

'Of course, no problem. We'll do that tomorrow.' Her voice lowers, and she says, 'But, Ebony, your shoulder blades felt . . . l–lumpy.'

My heart cries out to her as soon as I hear the tremor in her voice.

She croaks softly, 'Lumps could mean, you know . . . a tumour or something.'

Dawn closes her fingers around her daughter's arm. 'Darling, in the last two weeks, except for Shadow, Ebony has lost everything she owns; let's give her a little break over dinner.'

I don't even know what a tumour feels like. I *really* need to take a look now. 'Um, you know, I do remember falling off Blueboy, one of the geldings Dad was training just before the fire. A python shot out in front of us and Blueboy baulked. I came off and must have grazed my shoulders, but it hardly hurt and I forgot all about it.'

Finally Amber calms down. 'Mum should definitely still look at it in case the wounds are infected.'

'No! I mean, jeez, Amber, it didn't even break the skin.' I dredge up a smile. 'It's nothing, really, but I'll check it out myself after dinner. OK?'

Reuben pats his daughter's hand. 'We've all had a lot on our minds recently; it's easy to jump to conclusions.' He smiles at her sweetly. 'I'm sure Ebony would know whether or not she needs medical attention.'

Dawn smiles in that sad way she has just for me now. 'I'm here if you need me, darling.'

We settle back at the table and, while I make an effort to eat Dawn's lovely meal, I don't seem able to swallow anything larger than a pea. It's a relief when dinner is over and I excuse myself from having dessert and practically run down the hallway to Amber's room. As soon as I'm in her bathroom, I pull off her brother's clothes and turn my back to the mirror.

'Oh! *What?*' They've grown so much bigger! But what exactly am I looking at? I stretch my arms over my back and run my fingers across the growths. They feel leathery at the base and squishy at the top. A fibre of sorts comes away in my hand. I examine it under the light. It's a white feather. *A feather? A soft downy feather!*

*How can that come out of me?*

I flex my shoulders, the feathers move, and I freeze.

A primordial urge reminds me to breathe and I gulp in a deep breath. My fingers tingle, but I ignore them. I've hyper-ventilated before. Forcing myself to breathe more slowly, I lift my eyes to my reflection. A scared person looks back with violet irises almost entirely absorbed by black pupils.

The room suddenly spins. I grab hold of the basin just as the floor begins to rumble. The vibrations quickly move to the walls. Bottles, tubes, Amber's toothbrush, just about everything sitting on a shelf or not fixed to a wall starts to shake. I latch on to the towel rail for more support. 'What's happening?' I ask myself and, while looking into my reflection, concentrate on slowing down my breathing because I know it's important not to pass out.

OK, something is happening to me that I don't under-stand. I close my eyes and continue monitoring my breathing, keeping it slow. Losing control will get me nowhere.

The shelves and everything on them stop rattling. I look around the room; everything appears normal with nothing broken. I move a few items back into their positions.

OK, whatever that was, it's over. I glance into my reflec-tion. Even my eyes have returned to normal. The wide-pupil stare is gone, and I sigh.

I angle my body like a contortionist to take one last look at my shoulders. The feathers are still there.

Revolted, I slide to the floor, hug my knees to my chest and try to figure out how I'm going to fix this. I wonder what would happen if I pulled them out? Maybe I should simply cut them off as if I were having a haircut. Or shave them off with a razor?

*What if they grow back thicker?*

What am I thinking? What if I cut them off and they can't stop bleeding?

'How can I stay here now?' I whisper to myself, feeling enormous sadness bearing down on my heart.

I take a deep breath and wipe away the self-defeating tears.

I have to go and see the man who claims to be my uncle. Maybe these things are hereditary and he can tell me about them. Some reassurance that I don't belong in a carnival sideshow right now would be welcome.

The light rapping on the bathroom door doesn't register,

but Amber's startled cry when she opens it and sees me huddled on her bathroom floor does.

'Oh my God, Ebony. Oh my *God*! Look at your back!'

I look up. 'That's what I've been doing for the last twenty minutes.'

'I'll get Mum!'

I grab her ankle and slam the bathroom door shut with my other hand. 'Don't do that, Amber.'

'But . . . Ebony, have you seen your back? Have you seen those . . . those —'

'*Feathers*, I believe, is the word you're trying to say.'

She seems put out suddenly. 'How can you be so calm?'

I get to my feet, slide into a towelling robe and point to my face. 'Do I look calm?'

She takes in my swollen red eyes and trembling mouth and yanks me into her arms. She holds me tight until my renewed sobbing eases a few minutes later.

We sit on her bed and I explain how I noticed small brown spots a few weeks ago, and how they've been growing steadily ever since. I also tell her how different I feel from everyone, how I can do stuff that just isn't normal.

She stares at me with her mouth open. 'Ebony, you need a doctor.'

'Do you believe me, Amber?'

She looks straight into my eyes. 'Every word.'

'Then why do you want me to see a doctor?'

'Not *that* kind of doctor! I mean a skin doctor.'

I swallow around the lump in my throat. It helps stop tears from flowing again. 'Amber, I can't see *any* kind of doctor, at least not yet.'

'Why not?'

'They'll want to write me up in a medical journal. There'll be endless tests and experiments. I'll have no life, no privacy. A regular doctor isn't the answer for me. One of the conditions of the adoption was that I never see a doctor. Mr Zavier told my parents I wouldn't need one, and so far I haven't. I don't get sick. If I cut myself . . .' I stop, remembering another time when my wounds healed fast. 'Or my face came too close to a flame . . .'

'You heal faster than other people do,' she says. 'Well, sweetie, you're sick now. You have feathers growing out of –'

'*Jeez*, Amber, I know!'

She looks down at her hands. 'I'm sorry, but they're not just going to disappear, are they?'

'No, and *I'm* sorry. You don't have anything to be sorry about.' I shake my head. 'I need answers. I need information on my biological family – who my mother was, and especially my father.'

'I'll help you find them.'

'Thank you.' I smile at Amber with tears welling. 'Maybe I shouldn't go back to school yet. Maybe I should leave the area.'

'And what good would that do?'

'But if anyone sees these . . .'

'No one has to. It'll be our secret.'

'You won't tell your mum or dad?'

'I promise.'

'Or the girls at school?'

'No way! We'll work out what these things on your back

are, even if we have to research every medical database in the world.'

I nod.

'You have to find out who you are,' she declares. 'And I'm going to help you.'

'Actually, Amber, I have to find out *what* I am.'

# 25

# Jordan

On Monday, after training from five in the morning until four in the afternoon, Thane is so pleased with my efforts he gives me a driving lesson in the Lambo.

It doesn't take long before I'm cruising the quiet mountain backstreets. On the way home my stomach growls. 'You know, I could do with some real food for a change.'

He shakes his head as if he can't believe I eat so much.

'Dude, school's back tomorrow.'

'I'm not sure what that has to do with eating,' he says, but he directs me into a reverse park in front of a Chinese restaurant.

On the same side but a few doors down is a small park with a toilet block at the rear. 'I just have to duck in there for a minute. I won't be long.'

I jog to the men's room and just as I'm zipping my fly back up a cold bare arm swings around my neck. 'You *gotta* be kidding.' At the same time the tip of a sharp blade pushes against my back. 'Mate, if you don't let me go, well ... suffice to say, it's not going to be your lucky day cos when we step outside ...'

He growls low and deep and with a rumble like *I'm*

irritating *him*! 'Dude, if it's money you're after, you can pull the wallet out of my back pocket.'

'Shut up, Blake, and listen. This is what we're going to do.'

'*Skinner!* Haven't the cops caught up with you yet?'

'I said shut up! And yeah, thanks for tipping them off; they're all over the mountain now.'

'I'm not alone, you know. If you keep me here too long, my, um, friend is going to come searching for me, and mate, you do not want to rile this guy up.'

'If you don't shut up, I'm going to ram this knife into your spine and finish the job I started two weeks ago.'

'What do you want? How much? There's enough in my wallet to keep you going for a few days. Take it. Just let me go and I won't tell a soul I saw you, I promise.'

'I don't remember you ever talking so much. I'm only going to tell you one more time to shut up or I *will* stick you with this knife. Understand?'

'If it's not money, what then?'

He groans, hooks his foot around the leg of a stool standing in the corner with a wastepaper basket on top, drags it over and makes me sit. Keeping one hand pressed down on my shoulder, he shifts the blade from my back to the right side of my neck. 'You dobbed me in!'

'You tried to kill me!' While I keep him talking, I try to suss out his strength. He probably hasn't been working out lately, while I have. What are my chances of wrenching that knife from his hand?

'Yeah, well, I've been thinking that maybe you were telling the truth that night.'

'You're timing is off, mate, but why the change of heart?'

He shrugs. 'Hiding out up here I've had time to think. Anyway, you don't look too badly injured.'

'I died.'

I see his face in the mirror. His eyes bug out. 'Watching you with Sophie made me so furious I wanted to kill you, but . . . Man, you're kidding me, you really died?'

'On the operating table.'

'You recovered quickly. I saw you run in here.'

'He had a little help from me,' Thane says, shoving the door open and breaking the lock in the process.

Skinner frowns but doesn't look too worried . . . yet. 'Who are you?'

'I'm the one who dobbed you in.'

'You a cop?'

Thane pats his jacket pockets with open palms. 'I'm not the police, Adam, and I'm not carrying a weapon. My name is Nathaneal, and you can think of me as Jordan's bodyguard.'

He doesn't believe him for a second and laughs so hard he takes his eyes off Thane. 'That's cute, Blake. Did you really think I would fall for that?' It's only for a second but it's a mistake he's going to regret. 'You buy your clothes from charity shops and live in a shelter for losers! Do you really expect me to –'

Thane reappears behind him. 'What were you saying, Adam?'

'Hey . . . ! How did you do that?'

The surprise works like a dream. As Skinner turns his head towards his voice, Thane snatches the knife from his hand, puts it into his back pocket while suspending him a foot-length off the floor with his other hand around his neck. 'What would you like me to do with him, Jordan?'

'What are my options?'

'Let's see.' He pauses for effect. 'I believe you have two.'

'Uh-huh?'

'The first is to break his neck and leave him here to be found, eventually.'

'*What? No! Please, no!*' Skinner pleads. 'W-what's the second option?'

Thane has no trouble keeping a straight face, but I have to glance away.

'The second option is to call the police, maintaining this position until they arrive.'

'No, don't do that, I'll suffocate! Jordan, tell him I can't breathe! There must be a third option. Listen, man, I can't get caught. If I go to jail, it'll kill my mother. She's been through so much already. It's enough I've made a mess of my life, but Mum has already lost one son.' Glaring at me, he says, 'Thanks to *him*. He ruined our family.' He shifts his eyes back to Thane. 'Don't let this freak be the reason she loses another son.'

For a heartbeat there is only silence. 'Let him go, Thane.'

But he doesn't. 'Jordan, how can I release Adam when his heart is filled with anger and hatred? Have you ever thought perhaps it isn't all directed at you?'

Skinner mutters, 'Who *is* this guy?'

'Jordan, I want you to think about what happened that day.'

'I already told you everything.'

Skinner tries to break free but groans at the futility of

171

even trying. 'I don't know who you are, but don't listen to Blake's lies. I can tell you exactly how it went down that day. The water kept rising around us so fast it formed a whirlpool. *He* got himself out first and tied the only rope we had left around a tree. When he returned, Seth was on one side and I was on the other of a wide tunnel and the water was coming in fast.'

He tries again to squirm out of Thane's hold, but finally seems to accept the futility of his efforts. 'Did he explain how the waters rose so fast there was only time to save one of us? And even though I was screaming at him to save Seth, he threw the rope to me? To me!'

'Which you took gratefully, of course,' Thane suggests in his placid voice. 'What would have been the point of both of you dying and leaving your mother with no children?'

'Exactly! I had no choice but to accept the rope. The water was already up to my chest.'

'And where was the water up to on Seth?' Thane asks.

He doesn't answer. I see his lips press together like he's trying to keep words in. 'It was up to his neck,' he says, closing his eyes. When he opens them, he seems to have his energy for lying back. 'That's why I got angry. I could easily have hung on until he'd pulled Seth out. I was twice Seth's size and I could ... swim.'

Still holding Skinner up by the throat with his legs dangling in the air, but somehow not causing him any harm, Thane looks at me and asks, 'Is that how it happened, Jordan?'

I glance up at Skinner. 'He adored you. You were his superhero.'

Skinner's eyes close tight as if he's trying to block out an image that won't go away.

'We got to a dead end. It was odd, coming across a wall like that with a bolted door. We knew from the old library maps that this tunnel went all the way to a pond where the last of the big hauls of gold had come from. Adam kicked the door in frustration. That's where he wanted to go. Some dust fell on our heads and Seth freaked out, but the door moved on its rusted hinges and Adam got inspired.'

I take a deep breath as the memories keep rolling and I see Seth's scared eyes and feel his fingers digging into my arms.

'Did the door give out eventually, Jordan?' Thane asks.

'Nope. The whole wall collapsed. And Adam was so excited he nearly wet himself.' I flick the guy a glance but can't look at him right now. 'At this point Seth was beyond freaking out and I'd had enough. The dust was making us all cough. I took Seth's hand and started making my way back. I didn't know if Adam was following or not and I didn't care. But we didn't get far before we heard the sound of rushing water in the distance growing louder really fast. And we knew, without saying a word to each other, why they put that wall there. The pond that was a hundred years old had turned into a lake.'

Skinner sighs and closes his eyes.

'Seth kept falling over so I hoisted him on to my back and we ran for our lives. It was uphill all the way, but the lower tunnels filled first, which bought us time. When we finally got to the entrance, the water flooded in and the force behind it made a whirlpool. It was crazy and happening so fast we couldn't think. It was as if we were in the bottom of a well. To make the situation worse, we couldn't find the ladder we'd used to get down there. It probably got washed away. There was an iron bar loosely attached to the wall. Seth clung to it, trembling. Whimpering.'

My mouth is arid, but, man, I have to finish. 'I made him promise not to let go of the bar, and I scrambled over the top. If I'd been any shorter, I wouldn't have made it. I glanced back and saw that Adam had lost his footing. He went under for a few seconds and shot back up in a panic. When he found his feet again, the water was chest high and he was on the opposite side to Seth with a whirlpool swirling between them.'

I walk up to Adam and lock my eyes on to his. 'I was a scrawny kid. I knew I couldn't haul them in on my own, so I tied my rope to the nearest tree. I had only enough length to throw it to one of them. By this time the water was high and strong and dragging them both down. Seth had gone quiet. His eyes were trained on Adam, while Adam was screaming out, "He's a good swimmer, he'll be all right. Throw the rope to me. Throw the rope to *me!*"'

I poke my finger into Adam's chest. 'I remember you said, "Rescue me, and together we'll pull Seth out."'

I look across at Thane because I need him to believe I'm telling the truth. 'I threw the rope to Adam, but by the time we turned around to pull Seth out he was gone. I tied the rope around my waist and jumped in. I looked until they wouldn't let me look any more. They found his body when they drained the mine, I don't know when.'

'The next day,' Adam says.

Thane lowers Skinner to the ground and then on to the stool, where Adam drops his chin to his chest and mumbles, 'I thought I was going to die.' He looks up and tears are running down his face. 'I lied to everyone. At some point I started to believe the lies. But the truth was Seth couldn't swim. I saw the look in his eyes. He couldn't understand why I said he could. I'll have to live with that look for the rest of my life. I'd do anything to make it go away.'

He makes a choked sobbing sound as he turns his gaze on me. 'I had to believe it was you who made the wrong choice. I couldn't look Mum in the eye and tell her it was me. *I* was supposed to look after him!'

Thane hands me his mobile phone. 'Call the police.'

I glance at Skinner as I make the call; two local cops arrive a few minutes later. As they lead him out in handcuffs, I grab his arm. 'I really am very sorry, Adam.'

He stares straight at me, nods and says, 'I know. I am too. But all the apologies in the world can't bring my brother back.'

## 26

# Ebony

On the following Monday when Amber and I are enjoying a final morning lazing in bed, Dawn comes and sits on the edge of my bed with a cup of chamomile tea. 'I thought we might have a chat,' she says, 'about school.'

Across the room Amber sits straight up. 'Five nights without a nightmare!' she beams.

I smile back. Only Amber can truly understand how relieved I am.

'So are you coming to school tomorrow?' she asks.

'That's what I want to talk about,' Dawn says as she takes my hand and pats it. 'There's no need to rush, Ebony. Would you like a few days off? Mr Pritchard will understand. Everyone will understand. And when you return, the school counsellor would like you to schedule some visits with her.'

I groan silently. I don't need a counsellor because my parents aren't dead. And while taking a few days off might seem like a good idea, keeping my thoughts occupied these days is essential for my peace of mind. 'School will be good for me.'

I run my hand through my hair. I have thick hair that

grows fast, and Mum usually trims and thins it out every second Sunday. It's been four weeks since my last trim and it's becoming unruly and hard to control.

Dawn gets off the bed. 'A few of your classmates dropped in with items they thought you might need. I put them in your new bedroom. It's finished, so you can move in whenever you like.'

'Thanks, Dawn, for everything.'

She smiles at me in that special sad way. 'I'll be driving you girls into school tomorrow. And before you say anything, I won't have you getting the bus; it's not a problem.'

She heads to the door and turns. 'You'll find a uniform hanging in your wardrobe that should fit. In fact, you'll find just about everything a young lady could possibly need in your new wardrobe,' she says, revelling at the surprised look on my face.

When Dawn leaves, Amber goes to her cupboard and brings over a long length of white fabric, draping the first metre across her arm and mine. 'It's so soft.'

'Stretch cotton,' she says. 'It breathes, it won't irritate your skin, and wrapped around tightly enough –'

'It won't fall off!'

'Not a chance.'

'Comfortable. Discreet. It's brilliant.' I give her a hug.

'It's the least I can do. You've been through hell, and those weird growths are more than you need to deal with right now.' She pauses to make sure I'm looking at her and focused on what she's about to say, even though I'm sure I know already. 'Ebony, you have to see a doctor about them soon. I understand how you need time to adjust, but don't leave it too long. *Please!*'

I nod. 'I will. I promise. It's just that I've reached my trauma limit at the moment.'

'I know, so if anyone even looks like hassling you tomorrow, they're going to have to deal with me.' She thumps her fists together dramatically. 'Just let someone try to get close.'

# 27

# Jordan

I can't believe I'm going to school in a Lamborghini! Man, it's awesome. Turning up in this little beauty is definitely going to cop some looks. After all, I'm nobody, the loser who got a tattoo when he was nine, who sits in the back corner keeping his head down.

Danny is waiting for me in the car park. He's brought Sophie, and her megawatt smile lifts my mood even higher. I haven't seen her since the hospital and she looks hot in her uniform. Best of all, she seems keen to see me.

'You look fantastic,' she says, leaning forward and kissing me on the cheek.

Thane watches and looks amused in a big-brother-is-happy-for-me way. He gets out and I introduce my newfound 'cousin'.

Danny shakes Thane's hand and shifts his eyes from me to Thane and back again. 'Yeah, yeah, I can see the family resemblance.'

I avoid catching Thane's eye. I'm having a hard enough time trying not to laugh. 'You reckon?'

Sophie doesn't say anything. Her mouth is hanging open, her eyes are wide and she's blinking too fast. And then I get it – Thane looked at her.

'Hi,' Sophie says in a breathy voice followed by a spasm of giggles.

I can't believe this! Thane's not *that* good-looking. Is he?

After a brief conversation he returns to his car and half the school watches as he drives away. Only when he's completely out of sight does Sophie finally close her jaw. Dreamily she sighs. 'Where have you been hiding him?'

Her reaction shuts me down. I shake my head and start to walk off but remember something about 'my cousin' that should wipe the star-struck expression off her face. 'He's only here until he finishes a job and then he's going home to marry his fiancée.'

Her dreamy face droops.

'Yeah, they plan to have six kids.' I can't help the dig as I hurry off to homeroom, scratching my head. On my way I keep my eyes peeled for a tall redhead with mid-range skin tones and sapphire or mahogany eyes.

Suddenly I'm seeing tall redheads everywhere. How hard is it going to be to find this girl? And then I catch a glimpse of a girl about to enter a classroom up ahead who matches Thane's criteria of being on the tall side with a sun-kissed complexion and long auburn hair. She stops as if she can tell someone is watching, and I glimpse her face. Even from here, I recognise those eyes – such a beautiful violet they draw me in like nothing I've experienced before. It's the girl from the club. I still don't know her name, but I will soon. I make a mental note of the homeroom she's entering before I head for mine.

Then, as if a bucket of cold water just splashed over my head, it hits me. Stunned, and feeling ridiculous that I didn't put it together sooner, I come to a stop in the middle of the covered walkway.

Thane said I would have an intense reaction, and that's exactly what I had that night outside the club when she knocked me into the wall. *She knocked me into the wall!* Well, if I need confirmation, that's it.

The girl from the club is Thane's kidnapped angel! I've *already* met her! All I need now is a name.

This is great news for Thane, but not for me. I couldn't be more disappointed. I had every intention of finding this girl from the club today for myself. Just my luck to fall for an angel who comes from another dimension. I was so sure we were meant for each other. Now what am I going to do? And then I remember the terrible danger she's in and I thump the nearest object – a timber post – with my fist.

Danny catches up. 'Jordy, what are you doing?'

'I didn't tell you everything.'

He glances at my lightly grazed knuckles and crosses his arms over his chest. 'Obviously.'

And then I recall Thane's voice reminding me again this morning that for Ebrielle's safety I need to keep her true identity secret. 'And I still . . . *can't*.' I run down a couple of steps only to run back up. 'This is bullshit, man!'

'What are you going on about?'

I take a deep breath and pull myself together. 'It's nothing. I just thought I recognised that girl, you know, from the club.'

'Are you still thinking of *that* girl?'

I lift my right shoulder and let it drop. 'Maybe. Yep. I am.'

'Well, I can tell you something about her.' He flicks a

look at Sophie, who has stopped to chat with some friends. 'But don't let on to Sophie I told you, OK?'

'Sure, but why not?'

'All she does is talk about you, constantly asking me questions about what you like to do in your spare time, who's your favourite band, what shows you like to watch. Man, it's never-ending.'

Sophie runs up then. I can't help but smile. Her eyes dart to Danny and back again. Smart and intuitive, it won't take her long to pick up what my smile is really about. 'Why are you so cheery suddenly?' she asks. 'Did Danny tell you something he shouldn't have?'

Danny elbows me. 'Nah, he didn't tell me anything. He was just filling me in on what I missed while living up on Mount Bungarra with my cousin.'

'Oh I know!' Her eyes fling open wider than usual. 'It was horrible – that poor girl!'

I glance at Danny for an explanation.

'I was just about to tell you.'

'Tell me what?'

'It's just so sad what happened to her.'

'Well, *one* of you had better tell me.'

The morning bell rings and everyone who's still in the walkway moves to class, but I pull Sophie and Danny aside. 'Tell me about this girl.'

'Her name is Ebony Hawkins,' Sophie finally says. 'She's in two of my classes, English and physics.'

'Ebony. Ebony Hawkins,' I whisper.

'Yeah, and during the break her house burned down and both her parents were killed in the fire.'

'Are you serious? Where was Ebony?'

'She was in the barn, getting ready for a day out riding with her best friend Amber Lang. Apparently the fire fighters combed the house afterwards and couldn't find any remains. Nothing.'

'Really?' This sends my thoughts into warp drive. I have to get word to Thane quickly. I'm not sure what it all means, but it can't be good. Ebony Hawkins is definitely our missing angel Ebrielle, and it looks as if she's in a whole heap of trouble.

## 28

# Ebony

While I sit in my homeroom with Amber, waiting for everyone else to arrive, Amber sees through my attempts to remain calm. 'You know I'm only in the classroom next door until morning break.'

'I know.' I move my shoulders around just to check the stretch fabric is holding.

She whispers, 'Can't notice a thing.'

The class begins to fill and I scoot her out. 'I'll be fine. Stop worrying. I can handle myself. I really can.'

'I know,' Amber says. 'Hon, you're as strong as a mountain.'

For no logical reason her analogy fills me with a sense of pride and I smile. 'Thank you. Now – shoo, before you're late for your own class.'

My homeroom teacher, Mr Alford, says a few words on behalf of the class, but keeps his references to the fire brief. He asks if there has been any sign of my parents yet. I appreciate his sentiment and for making it clear that, as far as our class is concerned, my parents are missing.

He moves on to other items, and the morning passes similarly until the break, when a small crowd gathers at the table where I sit with my friends, who watch everyone like seasoned bodyguards. They're doing a great job, ensuring the crowd doesn't grow too large or become invasive.

Back in class I keep my head down and my mind on my work. It helps, but I'm concerned that if I lean forward too far, someone sitting behind me might notice my uniform straining against the bumps on my shoulders. Fortunately Amber's stretchy fabric remains in place. I don't know what I would do today without it.

As the final buzzer rings through all the classrooms, Sophie Hunt walks in and hands me a folded note. It's from Jordan Blake, the guy Adam Skinner stabbed. He wants to meet me in the car park this afternoon. I stare at the note for so long the words blur and the class empties.

*Dear Ebony,*
*Sorry to hear about your parents. Life sucks. Take it from some-*
*one who knows. You probably don't remember me, but we met a*
*couple of weeks ago. And you're going to think this is weird, but*
*we need to talk. There's something you have to know. Someone*
*you need to meet. After school today I'll be standing next to the*
*Lambo (a white Lamborghini – unfortunately not mine). You*
*can't miss it. Please make time to meet me. You won't regret it.*
*Yours,*
*Jordan Blake.*

I don't know what to make of it. Amber walks in, wondering why I'm still sitting in class. I tuck the note into my skirt pocket and quickly pack my bag. In a strangely disconnected state of mind, I walk out of class, hearing but not really listening to what Amber's saying.

As soon as the car park swings into view, I see Jordan Blake standing exactly where his note said, next to a brilliant-white sports car. There's a slight nod and a bit of a smile before he turns his head towards the front end of the car and talks briefly to someone sitting in the driver's seat. Still in this vague state, I don't tune in to what he tells his friend, I just watch as the friend jumps out and joins him. The tall guy lifts his head and searches for my eyes.

The joining is sudden and powerful and stronger than anything I've experienced before. I can't look elsewhere and have to stop myself from running and jumping into this stranger's arms. And he's such a beautiful stranger! Tall, with blond hair and fair skin that appears to glow softly. There's something about him that's truly ethereal.

His lips part and he whispers a word. It wafts across the empty space between us as if carried through the air on the wings of hundreds of butterflies. 'Ebrielle.'

It's a name. A name I've never heard before.

*Ebrielle. Ebrielle.* I hear the whispers all around me. It rings with familiarity, or is it the stranger's voice I recognise? I don't know what to think, but the moment is so sublime a swell of emotion rises up inside me and makes my eyes fill with moisture.

I suddenly realise I am, unintentionally, holding my breath, because as I continue to stare, transfixed to the potent azure gaze of this astonishing stranger, the earth suddenly sways and the space around me fills with bright white light.

# 29

# Jordan

She notices Thane instantly.

They stare at each other across the parking lot, neither one moving, not a muscle, except for when Thane whispers her name.

Ebony's focus is intense, solely on Thane. I doubt she's seeing anything but him; not her friend, or a car backing out of the space beside her. Certainly not me.

Suddenly all the colour drains from her face. I realise a fraction after Thane that Ebony Hawkins is passing out.

Unbelievably, Thane catches her. He moves so fast I don't see him between the moment he leaves my side and the moment he's cradling her in his arms, one big hand preventing her head from hitting the concrete.

Amber spins around, confused and panicking. She goes from surprised to hysterical in a nanosecond. 'Ebony? Oh no, what's wrong? Ebony! Can you hear me?' She looks up at Thane as if the dude who saved her friend from a smashed head or, at the least, a very bad concussion, must also know why she fainted. 'Did you see what happened?' She sees me coming and narrows her eyes. 'Why is it whenever you're around something weird happens to Ebony?'

I don't have time to figure out her bad attitude towards me, so I just shake my head as I barge past.

Thane lifts her so gently and with such care it's as though he's afraid that after all this time she might disintegrate in his arms. He heads straight for the Lambo.

A woman rushes out of a blue Mazda and steps in front of Thane, pointing back at her car. 'You can put her in the hatchback, thank you.'

Without breaking his stride, Thane drags his eyes grudgingly from Ebony's face to the woman. 'She will be more comfortable in the Lamborghini.'

'It was kind of you to help, but this girl is my responsibility.'

The look Thane sears the woman with makes her take a step back. But he calms quickly. 'Please excuse me, but I mean no harm. I would just like to talk to Ebrielle and I believe she would be more comfortable in my car.'

'That might be, but I don't know you.' She turns to her daughter with raised eyebrows. Amber shakes her head and shrugs her shoulders. 'Apparently, neither does my daughter, and if my daughter doesn't know you, young man, I guarantee that neither does the girl in your arms, whose name, by the way, is not Ebrielle.'

Sensing a fight, some lingering kids start to gather round. Amber tugs on her mother's arm. 'Mum, he saved her from cracking her skull open. We can talk details later. We don't want Ebony waking to a scene. She would hate that.'

She cares about her friend enough to defy her mother. I like that.

Thane nods gratefully and keeps moving. I lift the

188

passenger door. As he lowers Ebony into the front seat, he reclines it by a third, gently moves her hair off her face and, without taking his eyes off her, explains himself to mother and daughter. 'My name is Nathaneal. I'm a close friend of Ebony's family.' He looks up at the mum first, and then at Amber. 'I know her parents. I have information she will want to hear.'

I quickly explain, 'He's my cousin and he means her biological parents.'

Amber says, '*Really?* She'll want to meet you for sure.' Anticipating her mother's reaction, she pins her with a pleading stare. 'You don't understand, Mum, but she needs this. Trust me.'

My estimation of this girl goes up another notch.

'I don't know what you're talking about, Amber, and normally that would be all right, but my responsibility right now is to protect the daughter of my dear friends who can't be here to do so themselves. What reason is there to trust this stranger?'

'I don't have one other than my instinct, Mum.'

'When Ebony saw this young man, she fainted. How do you explain that?'

Looking straight up at Thane, Ebony's eyes flutter open and the two of them lock gazes. It's like no one else exists.

Damn, I wish she'd looked at me like that when we first met.

Mrs Lang finally gets her attention. Ebony nods at her. 'I'm all right, Dawn. Can I have a few minutes to speak with . . .'

'Nathaneal.'

189

'Well, if you're sure, Ebony. I'll wait in the car. Come over when you're ready.'

When Mrs Lang leaves, Ebony's eyes move to Thane's face again. He's still hunkered down beside her. 'Do you really know my biological parents?'

'Yes,' he answers. 'I know them both.'

She glances up at me with her eyebrows raised, as if I would know whether this dude is for real. 'Is this true? I was told my birth mother died in childbirth.'

What am I supposed to say to that? Every instinct I have tells me Thane is the genuine article. He's shown me his wings. I saw them with my own eyes. *He* is living proof.

'Every word Nathaneal tells you is the truth.'

He gives a small smile of thanks before returning his full attention to Ebony. 'I was sent by your family to find you.'

'My *family*?' She's still sceptical, but the beginning of a hopeful spark appears in her eyes. It's hard to doubt Thane when he's staring straight at you.

'Your mother is very much alive,' he tells her with a small smile breaking through. 'You have a sister who can't wait to meet you.'

'A sister?'

'Her name is Shaephira.'

Ebony frowns. Now that he's found her, he wants to tell her everything, but the more info he gives the more sceptical she's becoming.

'And your father is –'

*Slow down, Thane. Not so much so quickly. She thinks like a human.*

'Are you a private detective?' she asks.

190

He's not expecting this question and it catches him off guard. This has me wondering if he can read *her* mind. He gives a slight shake of his head and I stamp down my surprise.

Before he answers her, she's rattling off more questions. Ebony Hawkins is thinking fast. 'What sort of name is Shaephira?' And then, 'What is their family name? Are they from around here? How do you fit into all of this?'

'I know these things about your family, and about *you*,' he adds softly, 'because I was present at your birth. I was there when the attack occurred. You were abducted, Ebony, within moments of entering the world. And I've been searching for you for the last sixteen years.'

'I beg your pardon?' Ebony's voice borders on disbelief. Something Thane said isn't making sense. She glances at Amber and starts moving out of the seat. 'Now I know you're lying.' Finding Thane inadvertently blocking her exit, she says, 'Do you mind?'

Thane's mouth falls open; he looks dazed and confused. Her abject rejection is something he never considered, but this girl has her mind made up. Thane is a fraud, and that's that.

'She wants you to move,' I whisper.

He jumps up. 'Ebony, please don't go yet. I'd like to explain.'

Almost past him, she pauses, and I can tell when she gets the full impact of Thane's eyes. She sucks in her breath and her pupils dilate. 'What's to explain?' she asks carefully. 'You're too young to have been searching for sixteen years. That would have made you, what, six?'

'Seven. And I wasn't alone. I was with an experienced Sensor who taught me everything I needed to find you.'

*Uh-oh!*

'"*Sensor*"? What's that? Some kind of sniffer dog?'

'Ebrielle, I mean Ebony, I didn't mean that. We weren't *hunting*; we were searching for your light, trying to pick up your glow above the clouds.'

She blinks hard and fast. 'That's the problem, Mr . . . ?'

'Just Nathaneal. If you prefer, you can call me Thane.'

*Crap, he's rambling!*

She sighs. 'I just want to know your surname. Is that so hard?'

He flicks me a glance that tells me he's uncomfortable answering this. But he's not going to lie; I know that much.

'Well?' she persists.

'We're not allowed to disclose our family name . . . here. It can create false idolatry, cult worship . . .'

She starts to look freaked out. I gotta do something before she decides to never speak with him again.

'He's famous. He's my famous cousin.'

'Really?' Amber calls out half sceptical, half not.

'I'm not famous,' Thane says. 'It's just . . . the explanation is complex.'

Ebony starts walking towards Mrs Lang's car. Thane calls out, 'Ebrielle.' She stops, turns, and he says, 'I apologise for alarming you in any way. I would never keep information from you deliberately. If we could go somewhere private, I'll explain everything.'

'Well, Nathaneal Whoever-you-are, I don't believe you're telling me the truth because, firstly, my name is not Ebrielle.

You seem to have trouble remembering that. You won't tell me your name, and the things you say are creepy.'

The two stare at each other.

Ebony breaks the connection, but really slowly, as if pulling away is causing her physical pain. I lean my head over and whisper, 'I told you it wouldn't be easy.'

Frustration and anxiety pulse out of him in such powerful waves it takes an effort to keep from falling over. He's finally found his kidnapped angel and can do nothing but watch her walk away. The energy, or whatever it is he's inadvertently emitting, starts making the hairs on my arms stand on end. Clouds, big white puffy ones are swirling around in a circle above us at speeds too fast for clouds to move. I cough the word 'clouds' behind my hand. Thane quickly looks up, and the swirling clouds scatter.

Four black birds perched on the top rail of the car-park fence squawk loudly while looking at us. 'Birds' I cough next, but he just frowns and I gather the birds are not his doing.

'Until she believes me, I can't protect her,' he says. 'I have to earn her trust, and I have to do it quickly or she will be lost for ever.'

But convincing Ebony to trust Thane isn't going to happen today, not here. The Lang women close in around her.

Acting on impulse, and bearing in mind Ebony thinks like a human, I run out and walk backwards in front of them with my hands splayed. 'OK. OK, I admit, Thane's a bit full on, but he *is* telling you the truth.'

Mrs Lang gives me a stern, *Get-out-of-the-way* look. But

Ebony stops and, though she doesn't say a word, her eyes look tempted to hear me out. I go on. 'I remember you from the dance. We bumped into each other out the front. You were worried I'd broken a rib and my big toe.' She laughs, melting my heart all over again. 'So you remember.'

'I remember that was only the beginning of your bad night.'

I laugh and roll my eyes at the subtle way she puts it. 'I remember you out the back too. You wanted to help me.'

Her face turns red. 'I don't know what got into me that night. I don't know what I thought *I* could do to help.'

'*He* does.'

She flicks a micro-look over at Thane, who is standing by the rear of his car frowning at the four black birds perched on the fence. 'His story doesn't make sense, and withholding his surname is really weird.'

I lower my voice to a whisper. If she's an angel, she'll still hear me. 'How much of *your* life recently has made sense?'

Her eyes close for a beat and she sighs. 'What does he want?'

'A chance to explain.'

'Explain what exactly?'

'Who you are, why you've been hidden away all your life, and why the truth is still being hidden from you.'

When she doesn't say anything, I take the chance my words have touched something inside her. 'Have you still got that piece of paper?'

She pulls it from her skirt pocket and offers it to me.

'Arghhh . . .' I pat my shirt pockets, then my pants, and come up empty.

'Here.' Mrs Lang hands me a pen.

'Thanks,' I mumble, and scrawl on the note quickly. Ebony takes it and eases into the rear seat of the hatchback. Moments later they drive away.

When I return to the Lambo, Thane is ready to take off. As I fasten my seat belt, his eyes flicker to the four black birds still perched on the fence.

'Friends of yours?' I ask.

He scoffs. 'Hardly.' He turns darkened eyes on me. 'Don't you recognise them, Jordan?'

With the engine idling, I take a good look. Except for bright blue irises in round eyes that are too large for a bird their size, they're completely black, from their pointed beaks to their long glossy tail feathers. Even their clawed feet are black.

'They're Aracals.'

'Shit! D'you think they recognised you?'

'I'm not sure. I hope not. I need more time to tell Ebrielle the truth. I'm relying on you, Jordan. You have to reach her on a level she will understand, a human level.'

# 30

# Ebony

What just happened? Did I walk out of school and on to a roller coaster? How did I end up sitting inside a luxury car staring into the most amazing pair of eyes I've ever seen? Nathaneal, that was his name. We didn't talk for long, and it's just as well because the things he said didn't make any sense, and yet there is something extraordinary about this guy. He was freaky, but at the same time I couldn't take my eyes off him.

Even now, as we drive home from school, I can't stop thinking about him, and those weird things he said. I lean forward as much as my seat belt allows and lightly tap Amber's shoulder. 'Tell me I didn't really pass out.'

She swivels around in her seat. 'Honey, you sure did. But seriously, who wouldn't? Jordan's cousin is *soooo* – ' she sighs dramatically – '*intense.*'

'Is it wrong to call a man . . . ?'

When I hesitate, she sweeps in with, '*Spectacular.*'

'I wasn't thinking of that particular word, but it'll do.'

Even Dawn giggles with us. 'He was rather beautiful for a young man, wasn't he?'

Amber gasps. 'Mum!'

'Being married doesn't mean you have to give up your sight!'

We laugh and it feels good to know there can still be lightness in my life. 'Hey, um, just so you both know, I didn't faint because of what he looks like. I wouldn't want you to think I'm that lame.'

'Of course we don't!' Amber says. 'So why did you faint?'

'I'm not sure. I think I held my breath.'

'I think you felt something, a connection.'

'Isn't that what you girls said about the Blake boy?' Dawn asks.

I shrug because she's right, but there's something about Nathaneal that is different to what I sensed when I first met Jordan.

Dawn volunteers a theory. 'If he knows your biological family so well, perhaps you're related.'

'I don't think so.' I hope not! His image so easily returns to mind – tall, broad shoulders, obviously made for doing something other than carrying fainting girls, though what I can't imagine, except perhaps hard physical labour or ocean swimming. I noticed his hair too, thick and yellow–gold. He looked young enough to pass as a teenager, but with the strong, solid body of a man.

The strangest thing happened when I first saw him. Oh, I know I fainted, but just before that there was an instant when I felt as if I knew him. It was a random and bizarre thought and, since I don't do random or bizarre, I put it out of my mind.

Then he started telling me stuff that was wrong on so many levels it was impossible to believe. I would know if I had a sister, just as I knew Ben wasn't really my brother.

And he called me by a different name, a hauntingly beautiful name, but not mine.

Evidently Nathaneal is searching for someone he hasn't met, a girl about my age with questionable birth details like me, I suppose. It's just a coincidence he found me first. Obviously his research is flawed.

I kind of wish I *was* this '*Ebrielle*'. At least then I would have my questions answered, and a much larger family!

Jordan says Nathaneal can explain things in my life that are not making sense. I doubt that! But how does he even know some of my life doesn't make sense? Are they watching me? Are they having me investigated? Are the cousins stalking me? This is getting creepier by the second.

I close my eyes tightly. I need sleep.

Resting back in the seat, my shoulder bumps suddenly move in a bizarre little flutter. This hasn't happened before. It shocks me and I gasp aloud. Dawn flashes me a look in the mirror. 'Everything all right there?'

Clasping my hands together, I remember Jordan's note. He's added a mobile number with the address of a local recreation area. I read it out. 'Do you know where this is?'

'Yes. Why?'

'Would you mind dropping me off there?'

She frowns and starts to offer up a warning, but Amber jumps in and cuts her off. 'Is that where Nathaneal and Jordan want to meet you?'

'Apparently, yes.'

'Now, Ebony, you don't know these young men,' Dawn says.

'I know, but I'll be careful. I promise.'

Dawn sighs, finding my eyes in the rear-vision mirror. 'Ebony, I don't like this. I'm not leaving you there alone.'

'Dawn, I heard what those two detectives told you about my adoption not being registered. I'd really like to find out who I am before they do. I need answers more than I need protecting right now. And I promise to keep alert to any nonsense.'

'Do either of you girls think it's a little strange that someone claiming to know your family turns up just days after you inherit a million-dollar property?'

The sudden silence grows awkward quickly.

Dawn peers at her daughter and whispers, 'What did I say?'

Amber smiles at me a little sadly before explaining in hushed tones, 'For Ebony to inherit the farm, the court has to declare John and Heather legally dead.'

'But, Amber, they —' She stops and runs her fingers through her hair.

'Ebony has lodged missing persons reports. She won't inherit her property unless forensics proves her parents passed away in the fire, or declares them legally dead, which won't happen for seven years.'

Dawn sighs, capitulating. 'Phone your father and let him know we're going to be late home.'

While Dawn finds a place to turn around, I call the

number on the note. After the first ring Jordan answers. 'Hello.'

'It's Ebony. I'm on my way to that park.'

'Good. You're doing the right thing.'

'That depends on what your cousin has to tell me.'

# 31

# Ebony

The park is beautiful, cast in early twilight by towering blackbutt trees, distinctive by their trunks, charred black from past bush fires that have painted them for ever. I can't believe I've lived in the valley all my life and never seen this place. A river, low enough to step across on moss-covered rocks, meanders around fallen logs and exposed tree roots. A rickety wooden bridge, weathered grey, joins one grassy bank to the other.

Amber spots the Lamborghini under a shady willow tree by the river's edge and Dawn parks the Mazda alongside it.

'We'll be waiting right here,' she assures me.

As I start to exit, Amber squeezes my hand. 'Want me to come with you?'

I shake my head and give a grim smile. 'I won't be long.'

They're standing beside a picnic table about twenty metres down from where the cars are parked. When they see me, they move to the table and we all sit around it, with Jordan on my left, Nathaneal opposite.

'Thank you for coming, Ebony,' Nathaneal says.

He has my name correct. That's a move in the right direction.

'I'm not here to cause you harm or increase your distress. That's not my intention.'

'So why are you here? I didn't go looking for you. You sought me out. Why?'

He seems taken back by my attitude, but I don't care. In the car park I was confused, spaced out, suddenly waking up in a strange car with a gorgeous guy staring at me. My thoughts are more collected now. 'What do you want with me?'

'There are things you need to know. It's my intention to inform you of these things, and keep you safe.'

'Like what?'

'Your birth. Your family. Who you are. Where you're from.'

'Recently I learned I was adopted. Since my parents told me this, I'm pretty sure it's true. Why don't you tell me what you know, and I'll tell you whether I believe you or not.'

He shares a glance with Jordan. He doesn't understand my attitude. After the weird things he told me in the car park, he's lucky I'm meeting him at all.

He leans forward and his blue eyes peer, unblinking, into mine. I have to remind myself to breathe because this guy's eyes are truly stunning. 'You were not given up for adoption willingly, but abducted at birth from parents who love you and sent me to find you.'

'Go on.'

'You come from a place called Avena –'

'*Avena?* I've never heard of it. Is it far away?'

'It's in another –'

'Continent,' Jordan jumps in. 'Europe.'

'Where in Europe? Which country?'

'Jordan,' Nathaneal says in a tone meant to stop him, which makes me think Jordan must have just made that up, and yet, I'm more likely to believe Jordan than Nathaneal, even though I don't know why. The connection we shared outside the club felt real. It must have been, because I still feel it now.

What if Dawn is right and these two are in cahoots to steal my inheritance? Or is this some kind of elaborate joke, or a dare?

'How can you be so sure I'm the girl you're searching for? What if you're wrong? My life is chaotic right now, and yes, I have questions about my birth, or I wouldn't be sitting here with strangers, making my friends worry. Nathaneal, I need the absolute truth, backed by proof. If you can't give me that, I'm walking away. Do you understand?'

'I understand. And when you say "proof", do you mean that my word is not . . .'

'Enough? No, it's not.' I finish for him.

'So what kind of proof is enough?'

'Forensic. An item that can be tested for DNA, like a hair follicle, or something.'

Before he answers I can tell by the way he blinks that he doesn't have any. I get straight up. 'That's it then.' Without physical proof, Nathaneal has nothing to substantiate his claims. 'It seems I'm wasting both my time and yours.'

I begin walking to Dawn's car when I hear Jordan murmur sarcastically, 'That went well.'

Then Nathaneal's voice rings out: 'Have you noticed

some unusual physical changes occurring to your body recently?'

I stop. Goosebumps raise the skin on my arms and I turn around. 'What kind of changes?'

Both of them are standing now, looking at me, then Jordan whispers, 'Go easy, Thane.'

Nathaneal says, 'Protrusions of bone and muscle that feel as if they're trying to burst through the skin of your shoulder blades.'

*How could he know this?* 'What makes you think I would have something weird like that?'

I stare at Jordan for an answer. Instinctively he feels more on my level. His blue eyes – so different to Nathaneal's, much less intense – gaze into mine, and I feel his sadness again, his suffering and longing for love, to be a part of something important. 'You told me I could believe every word he says, so you two must be working together at whatever game you're playing.'

'It's not like that,' Jordan says. 'He's telling the truth. But there's a lot more you need to hear before you understand, so it's important that you listen.'

'Why? Are you going to tell me my life is in terrible danger?'

Jordan flashes Nathaneal a frustrated look, then shrugs, and Nathaneal starts to walk towards me. I hold my hand up and he stops.'

'Ebony, I'm sorry, I fear I've gone about this the wrong way. I don't mean to startle you. This must be very hard.'

He has *no* idea.

'What's happening to your body is normal for you and not to be feared,' he says.

'The one thing I know for certain, right now, is that I shouldn't have come here.'

'Ebony, you need to know more. May I approach?'

My nod is slight, and without my seeing him move, Nathaneal is suddenly in front of me. When I look up, I lose myself in his eyes. I blink quickly a few times to sever the connection. It feels like I'm one half of a magnet where Nathaneal is the other. 'What do you want from me?'

'I have a house on Mount Bungarra. Jordan lives there too. I want you to come and stay with us until you are ready to return to Avena.'

He has to be kidding. I only met him today! I get my legs moving backwards fast. 'I don't know what you're selling, or what your game is, or how you could know . . .' I draw in a deep breath. 'I don't want any part of it.'

'Ebrielle, the house is protected. You'll be safe there.'

I turn and look at Jordan. 'Keep your cousin away from me.'

'But you need to listen to him.'

'Oh, and tell him my name is *Ebony*.'

When I get back in the car, both Amber and Dawn are keen to hear everything. 'It was just more of the same they told me in the car park.' I do up my seat belt with shaking hands, then catch Dawn's eye in the mirror. 'I'm sorry I kept you waiting. Can we go home now?'

She's already started the car.

# 32

# Jordan

The sky is darkening fast. By the time we arrive home, a strange twilight has fallen.

I glance out through the glass wall at the back of the kitchen. There's an eerie pink tinge to the sky as if smoke from bush fires on the ranges is blocking the last of the day's sunlight from getting through.

'How long until dinner's ready?' I ask.

Without looking up he murmurs absently, 'About an hour.'

'Anything I can do?'

He looks up. 'Are you all right, Jordan?' he says with a teasing grin.

I pull a face. 'Dude, you're not funny.'

His grin fades, while his stare becomes more intense. 'You look tired. Why don't you catch a nap before dinner?'

He's right, so I head up to my room and take a shower. When I have finished, an overwhelming exhaustion hits me. It's so overpowering I toss off the towel and climb into bed without dressing. I roll over once and feel sleep dragging me under as if someone is pulling me into a deep dark pool by my legs.

For a moment I fight it, forcing my eyes open as I sense something is off. But the pull to sleep is too strong. Then, from the corner of my eye, I spot something move near the window. I force my eyes to remain open and raise myself up on my elbows. 'Who's there?'

There's no answer, but what starts as a shadow turns into the shape of a tall man wearing tight clothes under a billowing floor-length cloak.

Wide awake now, I scramble off the bed to the furthest part of my room and crouch on the floor behind the leg of my computer desk. I know who it must be, but why is he here in my room? He begins striding over, and with every step his shape becomes more defined, more real. Terrifying. He stops in front of me.

*Holy crap, what do I do now?*

I wrap my arms around my knees and try to stop shivering. It's not the cold air making me shake like a leaf.

*Hello, Jordan.* His deep, hypnotic voice rumbles inside my head.

I find the strength to speak only because I have to, but my mouth is drier than the desert. 'Nathaneal will b-be here any se-se-second.'

*It's not your hero I've come to see tonight.*

How can this be happening ... *here*? *To me?* 'W-w-what do you want?'

He brings me a blanket from my bed, wraps it around my shoulders as if he cares and hunkers down beside me, his bright green eyes studying my face. *Don't be afraid. I'm not going to harm you. I'm here to help you, Jordan.*

'H-help me? H-how?' I can't stop the tremor in my

voice. After all, I'm scared. I've never been more scared in my life!

*I want to make you an offer.*

'What could you possibly have that I might want?'

He laughs, not with sarcasm but amusement.

Is this the same prince who Thane said was evil? Or is this a trick, one of many Thane told me to watch for?

*You will do well in the position I have in mind for you.*

'What position? And I'm just asking, OK?'

He walks to my window and stares at the weird twilight thing going on outside. I spot my boxers on the floor and quickly slip into them.

*My deluded young friend, who says you have a choice?*

I remember something Thane said about the code of Free Will.

*Poor human boy, do you think I follow the rules? I make the rules.*

*Only in your world.* Even knowing he can read my thoughts with ease, I can't stop them.

He walks around me, inspecting me with the look of a master purchasing a slave.

*Do you know where your mother is, Jordan?* This unexpected change of tack catches me off guard.

*Your mother is my handmaiden. She makes my clothes, cleans my boots, warms my bed.*

'You're lying! My mother isn't in Skade with you. If her soul is anywhere, it would have gone straight to ... to ...' For the life of me I can't remember the name of the place human souls go. 'Peridis!' It finally comes.

*Her soul became mine the first time she stuck a needle in her arm.*

'My father made her an addict; how can you blame her for that? Shows how much you know!'

He slaps my face, sending me reeling across the room. As I lift my head off the floor, I wonder how he did that without moving his arm.

Where is Nathaneal? Can't he hear me?

One thing I know, if I give up now, Prince Luca wins and I lose. The longer I resist, the more chance Thane will hear something or come looking.

So I get to my feet, take a deep breath and look into the over-bright eyes of the darkest angel of the universe, who just happens to be in my room with an agenda that includes signing me up for a job in his kingdom.

*She left you*, he says. *A small child alone in the world. Don't you ever ask why?*

'I suppose you're going to tell me anyway.'

He smiles as if he's won a prize. *She knew you were not worth the effort.*

I didn't have Mum for long and I value every minute we shared. They're my memories, and I won't let him ruin them or take them from me.

So as difficult as it is to look into his unnatural eyes, I hold his stare. 'My mother loved me and there's nothing you can do to taint the years we had together. Wherever her soul is now won't change that.'

Surges of energy shudder through me. My hair flies up, my face quivers. I strain every muscle trying not to succumb. It might be just my stubborn pride, but I get how important it is not to give him what he wants. Whatever job he has lined up for me, I'm not going to do it.

Minutes pass, I don't know how many, but somehow I manage to keep my footing. 'Is that all you have? I mean, aren't you the meanest bad guy in the universe? You have a reputation to uphold, and I got to tell you, you're not living up to it with this drama and dribble.'

It's a mistake. His green eyes darken and suddenly turn all black.

Crap, he was just toying with me.

*Watch, little man,* he says. Images appear inside my head. It takes only a second to realise this is a mind-link and he's showing me my mother, frail and beaten, her arms wrapped around her knees, her head buried, locked inside a concrete cell.

So he really does have her. The bastard!

She hears a sound and turns her head and stares straight at me. The sadness in her eyes slams into my heart. I feel myself crumbling inside and know it's only a matter of time before my will crumbles too.

*Take her place, and I will set her free.*

I hear myself asking, 'Would she live again – with a normal beating heart?'

*You ask too much. I can't perform resurrections.*

'A life for a life, sounds fair to me.'

*Nothing is fair; I thought you'd have worked that out by now.*

I have, and he knows it. He selects the vulnerable because they're easier to control.

*If you accept my offer, I will hand Melanie's soul to her Guardian, Solomon. He will escort her to a more peaceful destination. Do we have a deal, Jordan? Yes, or no?*

'You have to free my mother first, and when Solomon confirms he has her, I'll . . . take her place.'

He looks into my eyes. *Swear it.* His eyebrows lift.

'Wait. This means I have to die, right?'

He nods.

'How . . . how will it happen? When?'

*You have wasted enough of my time with your defiance. Leave the details to me. Now swear to our arrangement. Swear it!*

'I swear!'

He smiles, and the smile is so gloating I realise my mistake an instant before he confirms it. *Poor human boy, you have so much yet to learn.*

What have I *done*?

His smile turns evil as he fades into a swirl of black smoke and disappears.

Exhausted, I close my eyes and drop into a deep sleep. When I wake, it's dark. I swing out my arm to switch on my lamp, and then pull myself into a sitting position. I'm sweating but cold.

Then it comes back to me, the full force of my . . . *dream*? I get up and check my room, switching on more lights as I look into shadowy corners, not really sure what I'm looking for. I'm still fuzzy on the details, but I notice how everything in my room is still in its place.

It seemed so real, but . . . the Dark Prince himself?

I hear Thane moving around in the kitchen and retrace my steps. I was tired and came up for a sleep. I had a shower and fell into bed. Thane is adamant the house is secure, that nothing can get in. So, what was that? Does the Dark Prince know Thane has located Ebony?

I throw on my jeans and a jumper and take the stairs two at a time, finding Thane setting out plates. When he sees me, he frowns and points to a glass of juice, freshly squeezed, of course. Keeping his eyes on me, with a flick of his head he indicates the window. 'When is bush-fire season around here?'

I down the juice in one go. 'Not for six months. We rarely have fires in the cold season.'

He studies my face. 'What happened, Jordan?'

'I, uh, think I had a bad dream.'

'*Think?*'

'I *know*, OK? It was a nightmare. Unless . . . ?'

'Unless what?'

'This house *is* protected, right? Nothing can get in; no one can break through the protective barriers. That's what you said. You weren't lying or anything, were you?'

'Of course not. What's this about, Jordan?'

I take a deep breath. 'I took a nap like you said, and . . . dreamed the Dark Prince made a deal with me for my mother's soul.'

The dinner plates slip from Thane's hands. They hit the floor and shatter, rice, veggies and shards of china spread all over the place.

'It's not possible,' he murmurs.

'Are you sure?'

The look of horror on his face says he isn't.

# 33

# Jordan

In the morning Thane tells me to stay by Ebony's side at school today, convince her to come to live with us, and to watch for anything unusual. She turns up right on the bell, and during the morning break her bodyguards – Amber, and a few of their girlfriends – keep me from getting close.

'She doesn't want to talk to you,' Amber says.

Leah, a brunette from my metal-working class, thumps me in the chest with her flat palms. 'Leave, pretty boy.'

By lunchtime I've had enough of the bodyguards and I enlist Danny's help. 'What about the blonde chick?' he asks.

'Amber? Leave her to me.'

I find Ebony sitting beside Amber at a table crowded with Year Eleven girls.

My plan is simple. When Amber looks the other way, I run in from her blind side, climb over the bench and sit between them.

It works.

'Watch it!' Amber yells. 'Hey, not you again!'

I whisper to Ebony, 'Just hear me out. Please.'

She purses her lips together while she makes her mind up. 'Can you make it quick?'

'As long as you promise to listen this time.'

She leans around the back of me to reassure Amber that she'll be all right.

'Are you sure?' Amber checks.

At Ebony's nod, Amber gives me her best death stare.

Turning my back on Amber, I finally get to ask what's going on. 'Why are you ignoring me today?'

'After meeting Nathaneal yesterday, I was so worked up that last night I thought someone was trying to get in my bedroom window.'

'What are you talking about? Did something happen? I should ring Thane, he −'

She covers my mouth. 'If I take my hand away, you have to promise not to ring your cousin.'

I nod and she eases her hand down. 'They were just birds scratching at the glass. But your cousin is seriously starting to tip me over the edge.'

I gasp. 'Did they have blue eyes?'

'Yeah. Which I thought was really weird.' She peers at me suspiciously.

'How many were there?'

'Four.'

'Oh man. They're not what they seem. Ebony, danger is coming.'

'Could you be any more dramatic?'

She's not taking me seriously. 'OK, your life is in danger, and by staying with Amber's family you're putting them in danger too. Is that dramatic enough for you?'

'We're just talking about a few birds.'

'Except these birds are not just birds. What they were doing last night was spying on you.'

'Are you out of your mind?'

'They report to the one who orchestrated your abduction. *He* made sure you were raised in the valley. Where *he* lives the air is too toxic. But now that Thane has found you, when *he* finds out *he*'s going to come and take you away again, this time for good.'

'The one you're talking about wouldn't happen to be called Zavier, would he?'

'Who? No. You haven't met this dude. Believe me, you'd know it if you did.'

She doesn't say anything for a long time.

'Ebony, Thane has information about who you really are. Will you just hear him out?'

An Aracal suddenly swoops down and perches at the top end of our wooden table. A couple of girls sitting up that end scream, and the big bird, with its oily-black feathers, sharp clawed feet, long pointed beak and bright blue irises, sort of hops down the length of the table, making a mess of all the lunches. Everyone scrabbles to stand back, and as more people spot the bird, more screams erupt. With all the commotion, the Aracal flies up and perches on a window ledge.

Amber yanks on my shoulder. 'Are you done yet?'

'You mean talking?'

'I mean scaring Ebony. She couldn't sleep last night after talking to you and your cousin.'

I tug on Ebony's arm. 'Walk with me.' She hesitates. The Aracal has thrown her. 'Please.'

She nods, giving me a small smile, and my gut quivers, just like the first time we met. If only she wasn't the angel

215

Thane is adamant she is. Ebony is a beautiful girl, and when she's cheerful it's like everyone around her gets a breath of fresh air.

We stroll to the front of the school and sit on a vacant bench outside the admin office. 'I'm sorry if I ruined your lunch,' I tell her.

'You didn't ruin anything. That bird did. They must have nests nearby they're protecting.'

'That's not what's going on here.'

She peers at me with pleading eyes. 'Can we not talk about the bird?'

To deny her would be impossible. 'OK.' Amber's angry face comes to mind. 'So what's with your friend? Why is she so aggressive towards me?'

Ebony glances down at her lap. 'Ever since the fire she's been protective, like a big sister.'

'I get it, she's a good friend, watching out for you and all that, but does she have to be so anti-me? I'm not your enemy.'

'I'll talk to her. I'll ask her to be nicer to you.'

'Well, not *too* nice, if you don't mind. I don't want her getting the wrong idea.'

She smiles. 'No, we wouldn't want that.' Drawing in a deep breath, she unwinds just a little.

'You know, under different circumstances you and I – *we* – could have been . . .' I offer her my hand.

She takes it in hers. 'I feel something too, Jordan, but I'm not sure it's what you'd like it to be.'

'What does that mean?'

'You know how I said Amber feels protective towards me

since the fire?' I nod, and she says, 'Well, that's sort of how I feel about you.'

'Protective?'

'I don't know why. It's hard to explain.'

We sit quietly for a minute before she deftly changes the subject. 'He's not really your cousin, is he?'

'Nope.'

'How long have you known him?'

'A few weeks.'

'That's all? How can you trust someone you've known for only a few weeks?'

I shrug. I don't want to tell her the whole story. She'd trust Thane even less if she knew the deal he struck with me in the operating theatre. 'Some people are like that. You only have to know Thane a short time to realise he's on the good side.'

'That might be the case, but you know how he asked me to come and live at his house?'

'Yeah, so you'll be safe. He wants to pick you up after school today.'

She glances across the paved footpath to the green fields beyond. I give her all the time she needs. It's a big decision, and she has to make the right one.

But she doesn't. I can tell before she opens her mouth that she's not coming. 'Tell him I need more time.'

'But, Ebony, this is really important. Don't you want to know the truth?'

'I do, but . . .' She shakes her head. 'Sorry, I just don't trust him.'

*No!* 'Ebony, you're making a mistake.'

'Well, it's my mistake to make.'

*Shit! She's digging her heels in.* 'So, how long does it take?'

'I beg your pardon?'

'Before you can trust someone?'

She shrugs. 'Depends on the someone, but more than twenty-four hours.'

I have to keep trying. 'Is there anything I can say or do to change your mind?'

'Not today.'

'How long do you need?'

She shrugs again. 'I don't know. At least a week. Why? Is he going somewhere?'

*No, but you might be!* How do I get through to her without freaking her out? Thane is relying on me. My own future is relying on me.

Leah and Ivy round the corner and bear down on us. Since Danny is behind the girls, we return to the table, where Ebony's friends are cleaning up after the bird trod over their food.

I spend the rest of lunch trying to convince Ebony to change her mind. I look for her between biology and maths. I sneak out early so I can be standing outside the door of her last class. I'm getting desperate and she can tell. But she still won't budge. 'Go home, Jordan. Tell Nathaneal I'll let him know when I'm ready.'

## 34

## Ebony

Jordan is persistent, like his life depends on me doing what Nathaneal wants. Strange. I don't know these two guys well enough yet, but they're certainly intriguing. I'm starting to feel a connection between my life and theirs, but that so doesn't mean I'm ready to move in with them.

If only I could talk to Mum and Dad. Every day it seems my life grows more complicated. It burns me not knowing where they are, if they're hurt, or even if they're alive any more. And lately I feel as if they've abandoned me. It's silly because, logically, I know they would be here if they could.

We're getting the bus home today since Dawn has some errands to run. I pack my bag with my homework books and hang around the seniors' lockers for Amber to turn up. I'm surprised she's not here already. She had gym last period, a class I now avoid like the plague. Running into me is like running into a wall, so they tell me. It's all part of keeping a low profile, though lately that's been impossible.

Minutes pass and I start thinking maybe I misheard and we're meeting at the bus bay just outside the school gates. The corridor is emptying out fast now, with only a straggler or two left. It's a good thing our bus is the last to arrive and the last to leave.

A senior boy from my physics class, Josh Corbin, walks up to a locker two down from mine and starts emptying it out into a gym bag. He notices I'm watching and looks across at me with a grim smile. 'Hi, Ebony,' he says, while dragging out the dregs of a locker I know is not his, but belonged to Adam Skinner, the boy who tried to kill Jordan. Finishing, he slams the locker door shut, zips the bag closed and hooks it over his muscular left shoulder. 'That's it, then. The last of Adam Skinner's belongings are now gone from Cedar Oakes High School.'

'If you're trying to draw some kind of compassionate response out of me, sorry, Josh, that's not going to happen. I hope your friend rots in a prison cell for the rest of his life.'

He leans on the locker with an amused look on his face, one dark eyebrow arched higher than the other. 'That's harsh.'

'D'you think? After what he did?'

He glances away as if he's having a moment of conscience, which he should since he was there on that night too. 'Yeah, well, he's sorry about that night. He wasn't in a good head-space. He did something stupid and now he has to live with the consequences for the rest of his life.'

'It's called justice.'

'He had a big future ahead of him that's ruined now.'

'Maybe he should have thought about that before he shoved that glass bottle into Jordan Blake and scarred him for life.'

More angry than I can remember feeling in a long time, I turn around and start walking to the exit doors.

The sounds of his heavy footsteps behind me make me groan. I speed up my walking pace, but it only makes him break into a jog. 'Hey, wait up.' He catches up at the exit doors. 'You walk fast for a girl.'

'Maybe you're not as fast a runner as you think – for a boy.'

He laughs and, annoyingly, follows me all the way outside the gates to the bus bay. It feels wrong because I know he drives a car to school. My instinct says he's following me. I look around for Amber, but still can't see her anywhere. Even the bus appears to be running late today, which is a good thing, I guess, considering Amber is too.

Beside me, not towering, but still taller by a centimetre or two, Josh clears his throat.

'Why are you hanging around me? Do you want something?'

'I'm waiting for a friend to pick me up. My car's out of action.'

'Oh. Sorry.'

A sleek silver car, low to the ground, with windows tinted so dark it's impossible to see inside, swings into the bus bay and stops in front of us. Looking uncomfortable suddenly, Josh opens the rear door. While he throws his backpack and the gym bag inside, I catch a glimpse of his friend Damien Hall sitting in the front passenger seat.

It's such a relief to see Josh get in the car that I feel lighter, like I could skip along the footpath or something just as silly. He waves as he closes the door and, feeling generous and friendly, I wave back.

But then the driver gets out and instinctively I step back.

Wearing jeans and a black pullover, this boy stands taller than Josh, with coal-black hair, grey eyes and an air of superiority. 'What are you doing here? You should be locked up.'

Adam Skinner casually glances at his watch. 'I was released into my mother's custody until the hearing,' he says. 'But don't worry, I won't be coming back to school any time soon.'

'You shouldn't be here now.' I cast a wide look over my shoulder at the school buildings, then up to the car park and back to the bus bay, but still can't see any sign of Amber. She would not have gone home without me. Something must have happened.

The bus finally arrives, pulling up right behind Skinner's car, its doors flinging open. But I'm not getting in without Amber.

'Amber's fine now,' Skinner says, revelling in the surprise on my face. He seems in no hurry to leave; nor does he look concerned someone will see him just outside the school grounds.

'What do you mean?'

'She lost her grip when climbing rope in gym class, landed hard on her right hand, tore a ligament in her wrist and had to get bandaged by the nurse. She'll be here in time to catch the bus.'

'How do you know? Were you there? Were you watching?'

He swings his head around so that he's looking directly at me. For a mere fraction of a second his irises flash with light. 'No, I wasn't there, I'm forbidden to enter school grounds, but I was the one who made her fall.'

From inside the car, sniggering noises float out the windows, and for reasons unknown, I believe Skinner when he says he made Amber fall. His eyebrows lift. 'Smart girl. But then, I knew you had to be, or why else?'

Skinner is freaking me out. I want to ask, 'Why else what?' but I'm not sure I'd like the answer. It feels as if he's reading my mind, but that's impossible. 'What's going on here?' I ask him, but he doesn't answer. I decide to direct my question to Josh, but Amber's footsteps run up behind me and I forget everything except getting on that bus before it takes off without us.

'There you are,' she calls out breathlessly, running out the gate and over to where I'm standing between the bus and the silver car. Her right wrist is wrapped in a white bandage. 'Thank God – I thought you might have gone home with Jordan and his cousin.'

She arrives in a flurry and immediately begins dragging me towards the open bus doors, then notices the boy next to me. 'Oh, sorry, I didn't know you were talking to *Adam Skinner*!' Her eyes widen at me and she whispers, 'What are you doing, hon?'

'Hello, Amber, nice to see you too. How's that wrist doing? Nasty fall you had. You're lucky you didn't hurt more than just your hand.'

'OK, thanks,' she says with eyes still wider than normal. Pinching me, she adds, 'Our bus isn't going to wait much longer.'

'I'm just glad you made it,' I whisper. 'Let's go home.'

As I start to turn to leave, Skinner wraps his long fingers around my arm. They feel cold through my sleeve, almost

223

unnaturally so. 'I know this is none of my business, but, um, I heard you're spending a lot of time with Jordan Blake.'

I'm on the defensive instantly. 'Why is that any concern of yours? He stopped being your business when you tried to murder him.'

'Jordan and I go back a long way. He's a good guy at heart, a really good bloke, but he's keeping bad company these days.'

'Is this your idea of a warning?'

'When I was locked up, I heard some things about this so-called cousin of his.'

I want to ignore him. Every bone in my body urges me to shut my ears and keep walking. But I stop, promising myself it's just for a moment. 'What things?'

'He's not what he appears. He's dangerous. Be careful around him.'

'Why should I believe you?' I ask, peeling his fingers from my arm. 'You tried to kill Jordan. It stands to reason you would hate his cousin too.'

His voice turns hard and his fingers close around my arm again, and no matter how much I try, I can't force them off. 'That's your prerogative,' he says. 'Just don't let the cousin get too close to you. He's bad news.'

He finally releases my arm and Amber and I climb on board the bus just as it starts to inch forward. Relieved, we plonk ourselves down beside each other. My encounter with Adam Skinner has left a bitter taste in my mouth.

And I can't stop rubbing my arm where his fingers closed around it. Though they were cold, my arm feels hot where he touched it. I lift my shirtsleeve and stifle a gasp at the five-finger burn mark that's already starting to heal itself.

All the way home I try not to think about my encounter with Skinner or his dire warning to stay away from Nathaneal. He admitted to making Amber fall and causing her torn ligament. But no one could do that. I glance at my burn once more. No one should be able to do that either.

# 35

# Jordan

Thane doesn't take the news well. When I get home, I go straight up to my room to give him time to chill and work out his next move. He calls me down when dinner is ready and hands me a plate of dry seeds and salad veggies doused in a vinegary-smelling dressing.

'You've outdone yourself tonight, dude,' I murmur to myself, not caring how easily he hears everything. 'But, *man*, I can't believe I'm supposed to eat this! Ahaaa! I get it.' I point the plate at him. 'This is punishment, right?'

He ignores my question in favour of one of his own, 'Jordan, did you try −'

But I cut him off, 'Dude, I tried everything! She's just not ready to move in with you!' I shrug. 'I'm disappointed too. The quality of my future life depends on helping you get your angel home, so why wouldn't I try my hardest?'

'I'm not questioning your loyalty, Jordan.'

'I'll work on her every day at school. I promise. You can reassure your fiancée it won't be long before she has you home for good.'

He looks uncomfortable. 'About that . . .'

I throw up my hand. 'I know, I know, you don't like to talk about your private life. Relax.'

But then Thane, with his fork midway between his plate and his mouth, tilts his head to the side, frowning. I know this look: he's picking up a distant sound, trying to figure it out. He gets up and walks straight out the front door. I follow and find him looking up at the northern sky.

'What is it? Can you hear something?'

He says, 'Birds.'

'Birds? Like more Aracals?'

'No, real birds.' He points towards the horizon. 'You should be able to see them soon.'

'The birds?'

'Yes, Jordan. Many thousands of them.'

'You're kidding!'

'I assure you, I'm not kidding.'

The sky is darkening and the first stars will be showing soon.

He goes still, like unbelievably, supernaturally still. A stricken look spreads across his face like a passing shadow, his eyes are wider, his mouth slightly agape.

'Dude, you're scaring me. What is it?'

He doesn't answer, and that's when I see them – thousands and thousands of birds. I get a shiver as I watch the sky disappear behind a vast blanket of beating wings.

'Why are they heading towards Antarctica with autumn only just started?'

He doesn't respond. Then one blink and he's gone. I catch a glimpse of him passing through the front door. I run after him but he's already at the top of the stairs. 'Hey! What's going on? You're scaring me again.'

'We have to bring Ebony here.'

'Thane, she won't come.'

'No, I mean to the monastery.'

I groan. She's going to want to go there about as much as she wants to come here.

'There's a chapel, safe within the barrier walls, where I'll be able to perform a ritual that will protect her mind from the Dark Prince. He mustn't be allowed to have free rein over her thoughts as he did with yours last night when he came into your dream.'

'What makes you think he's going to try that on Ebony tonight?'

'Jordan, the Dark Prince is here on Earth. His physical presence is the reason the birds are fleeing.'

*The Crossing in Alaska!*

He nods and tosses me his mobile phone. 'Call Ebony and tell her we'll pick her up in twenty minutes.'

'What if she doesn't want to come?'

'Tell her to look outside – but *not* to go outside, and to lock all windows and doors.'

Mr Lang answers the phone, and when I ask to speak with Ebony there's a distinct hesitation. 'It's important, Mr Lang. *Really* important.'

He asks me to wait. Meanwhile, Thane is back, wearing his long black coat and carrying an overnight bag. He has my jacket in his free hand. He passes it to me and I slide it on as I follow him through the house to the garage.

I cover the mouthpiece as something occurs to me. 'Are

you sure we'll be safe on the road with the Dark Prince heading over here?'

'No, Jordan, we will not be safe. He knows I'm here. No doubt he has known from the moment Ebony's body came into contact with mine. He's coming for her and he won't be alone.'

'How long before he reaches the valley?'

'I don't know precisely, but soon, I think.'

'This is shit! How are we going to stop him? What if he gets to Ebony's place before we do?'

'Stay calm, Jordan. From here in we need help.' His eyes darken. 'But leave that to me; I'll organise it.'

Shivers barrel down my spine.

I wave the phone in the air to let him know she hasn't picked up yet. 'This prince doesn't follow the rules, he told me that himself, so what's to stop him taking Ebony tonight?'

At the garage door he stops and turns. 'That would be us, Jordan – you and me. We'll stop him.'

From somewhere distant I hear a female voice calling me. I quickly lift the phone to my ear. 'Hello?'

'You called *me*,' Ebony says. 'What's going on?'

'Hey, Ebony, um, you're going to have to come with us tonight.'

'I beg your pardon?'

'To the Holy Cross Monastery.'

'*Whaaaat?*'

I cover the mouthpiece. 'She thinks you're insane.'

About to get into the Lambo, he looks up at me with eyes that can't believe she's not complying without question.

'She's not cooperating. What do I do now?'

He holds his hand out for the phone just as the doorbell rings. Pointing to the phone, he says, 'Tell her the Lang family will be safe tonight *only* if she is with us.' Then he runs to the front door in a swish of movement.

I tell her while racing after him. 'We'll pick you up in twenty minutes. OK?'

'Has this got anything to do with the birds?'

'You've seen them, huh?'

'It's a little hard not to. Half the sky is black with them, and it's all over the news. Dawn is trying to call her church but can't get through. She thinks it's the end of the world.'

Thane is already at the front door when he hears Ebony talking about Amber's mother's concerns. He glances at me and shakes his head.

'Ebony, Thane says it's not the end of the world.'

'Does he know something?'

'Tell her I will explain everything once she's inside the walls of the monastery and I have made her safe.'

'Come on, Thane. She's going to have to give the Langs something.'

With an exasperated glare at me he opens the door. On the front porch are five angels. I know they're angels, not because I recognise Isaac among the three males, his long bright copper hair slicked back into a ponytail, and not because they're all as tall and lean and ripped as Thane, including the two females. Not even because the five of them are glowing like blowtorches. But because when he sees them, Thane's grave expression softens – with relief.

230

'What took you so long?' he says, stepping back to allow them in.

The first one resembles Thane so strongly he's gotta be his brother. They embrace like brothers too. 'You told us not to come under any circumstances unless you called. And you didn't call until, well, we just heard you, but we were already on the way. The Brothers alerted us as soon as the birds hit the radars in the monastery watchtower.' He motions to the two sports cars outside, a red Ferrari and silver Porsche. 'Call it instinct, brother, but we anticipated you might need to move fast.'

'You anticipated correctly.'

'It's good to see you, Thane. It's been too long.'

Thane takes the phone from my hand while he leads the angels into the lounge room. Isaac comes straight over to me and shakes my hand. He winks and makes a clucking sound in his mouth. 'Good to see you too, Jordan. You're looking well.' He points to the towering brunette beside him, her hair pulled up into a high ponytail which hangs so far down her back she could probably sit on it. 'This is my wife, Shaephira.'

*Ebony's sister.*

'Call me Shae,' she says, pinning me with eyes of deep, vivid sapphire.

Thane has his phone to his ear as he strides across the room. Meanwhile, Isaac introduces me to the other three. The light-haired one, Thane's brother, is Gabriel. I wonder fleetingly if he cut his hair short to blend in too. He nods, 'It's in the job criteria.' Shaking my hand, he says, 'My little brother says you're the one that found her.'

'Ah, yeah, sort of. She kind of walked into me one night, sent me flying into a wall.'

'That's my sister,' Shae says.

Isaac introduces Michael next. There's something about this one that sets him apart. It might be the way he stands back from the rest, observing the scene rather than being in it, or his ancient-Greek look, with jutting brow, square chin and dimple. But I think it's more his golden appearance. His skin is a warm honey colour, his blazing eyes caramel, and his shoulder-length ginger hair a mass of corkscrew curls.

'Hello, Jordan,' he says, with warmth I'm not expecting from someone who resembles a gold statue. 'I've been hearing good things about you.'

I glance at Thane, still trying to convince Ebony. What has he been telling his friends about me?

'He says you will become an angel one day?'

Posed as a question, they wait for my answer. '*What?* Thane said *that?*'

'As if *he* could qualify,' says the fifth angel, the female I haven't met yet. She steps around Michael and ... *Whoa*, what a crowd-stopper, with waves of shimmering black hair rolling down her long back, spectacular turquoise eyes and a sensational body. 'He's scrawny and short.'

The other angels glare at her as if they're shocked but not really surprised. Shae looks disgusted. 'He's young, Jez, and human. They take longer to grow.' Shae flicks her finger through the hair at the back of my head. 'I see potential.'

'Take a good look, Shae,' the crowd-stopper says. 'His physique is all wrong. He'll never fill out. He's weak.'

Her movements are as fluid as liquid metal. Mercury comes to mind, probably because it will kill you if you ingest enough of it. I try to pull my eyes away from her supermodel body, clad in a low-cut silver top with matching figure-hugging jacket and black pants that could pass as skin, though it's an effort. She flicks her head, releasing an intoxicating scent that makes my head spin.

'Roll it back, Jez,' Shae says sternly. 'We can see he's no match for you.'

She would be no match for anyone except a mercury-inhaling sadist, I can't help thinking.

Isaac, Gabriel and Michael burst out laughing. Shae smiles, while Jez glowers at me. They can all hear my thoughts. I try to block them like Thane's been teaching me, but these dudes are too good. My walls are like water to them; they pass right through.

Brilliant.

Isaac slaps his palm down on my shoulder. 'Don't under-estimate this one, Jez. What he lacks in size he makes up for in courage.'

'Courage or stupidity – there's a fine line between them,' she slings back with a stinging glare directed between my eyes like an arrow.

Thane returns, pocketing the phone, and glances at his friend, the majestic, golden Michael. On his way he passes the crowd-stopper, acknowledging her with a slight nod. 'Good of you to come, Jez.'

Contrarily, she looks as if she could have him for dinner.

'Uh-hum.' Isaac clears his throat, reminding me to watch

my thoughts. I promptly nod. I'm going to go nuts, but I promise to try.

'How bad is it, Michael?' Thane asks.

'He entered through the northern Crossing at midnight Eastern Standard Time, heading due south. He crossed the equator at 1800 hours, bringing six Prodigies with him.'

'Only six?' I ask. Six sets of astonishingly intense eyes swing to me. 'I mean, he has an army at his disposal, yet he only brings six soldiers?'

Thane says, 'Earth belongs to humans. Imagine the chaos if he brought an entire battalion? He's here tonight to collect one angel, not start a war of cosmic proportions.'

'If he brought a battalion,' Michael explains, 'I would bring an army of equal strength. And between our two sides we would annihilate every living being in just a few days.'

'Six Prodigies aren't going to be a pushover,' Shae explains for my benefit. 'They're fighting machines with no goal in life except to serve their king, and they never pull back.'

She brushes Thane's forearm, wrapping her fingers around it. 'Where is my sister? Do you have her in a secure place yet?'

He lays his palm over her hand and looks into her face. When neither speaks, I gather they're mind-linking. Their private chat pisses Jez off big time; her turquoise irises begin to shrink into black.

Sensing someone watching her, or maybe hearing my thoughts, it takes only a momentary distraction to bring her powers back under control. Jez flashes me a fierce look that has shivers tripping down my spine.

Thankfully, Thane starts explaining how Ebrielle goes by

234

Ebony here, which gets her attention. 'She knows nothing about our world, can't yet accept she's one of us.' He looks directly at Shae. 'I'm asking you all not to speak to Ebony on any subject without running it past me first.'

He glances at me then. 'Except for you, Jordan. You're going to be Ebony's source of information.'

I nod and he says, 'We need to leave now. Any other questions will have to wait.'

'How do you want to do this?' Gabriel asks.

Thane draws a breath as he thinks. 'Michael, you will come with me.'

This makes sense since he can call on his army for reinforcements in a hurry if needed.

'Isaac and Shae, you take the lead car.'

Shae's eyes narrow at Thane. She's clearly upset at not being in the car with her sister. A silent communication passes between them before Thane says, 'Trust me, Shae. Your emotions will overwhelm her. She's not ready for you yet.'

Isaac takes his wife's hand, leans in as if to whisper something, and though they exchange no words, she nods and sighs resignedly.

Gabriel glances at Jez, 'Looks like we're bringing up the rear, my lady.'

'Story of my life,' she mutters acidly. No one pays attention.

'What about me, Thane?' I ask.

Six sets of impressive eyes zoom in on me again; I feel like a fly in a room full of bees. 'You will sit behind me,' Thane says. 'Your presence will keep Ebony calm.'

Four angels dart outside while I run through the house to the garage without a hope of keeping up with Michael and Thane. They're in the car with the engine idling when I get there. On the road we hit a hundred in four seconds, the darkening landscape whipping past.

'What did you tell Ebony?' I ask Thane.

Concentrating on driving very fast, he says, 'The truth.'

'What truth would that be?'

He flicks me a look. I should give him the benefit. He doesn't lie. 'The one who arranged her kidnapping is coming with six highly trained soldiers to collect her. And if she doesn't allow us to protect her, she will never see her friends or her beloved horse again, or find out what happened to her adoptive parents.'

'Did she freak out?'

'She warned me.'

Beside me, the golden angel laughs. 'She warned *you*?'

'She said there are three people ready to lay their lives down to stop me from taking her.'

Michael's humour dies on his face. 'They may just have to.'

Thane catches his eye in the mirror. 'There'll be no need for violence on the Lang property,' he says. 'They are honourable people. With no thought for themselves they came to Ebony's aid, providing her with reassurance and a caring home.'

Without taking his eyes from watching the darkness, Michael comments, 'The High King is just. They will be aptly rewarded when their time is upon them.' His eyes flicker to Thane. 'So how will we approach them?'

'With as much truth as they can comprehend in the shortest time possible.'

'While you negotiate, I'll secure a perimeter,' Michael advises.

My mouth goes dry suddenly. 'Are you saying Prince Luca could be here already?'

'He is here,' Michael says, his eyes darting from one side of the car to the other. 'Watching. Waiting.'

'For what?'

'An opportunity. For the instant we drop our guard.'

'That'll be me.' My gut clenches. I've been stuffing up all my life. It's like my legacy or something.

Thane finds my eyes in the mirror. 'Stay calm, Jordan; just focus on your task.'

'Keeping Ebony calm and feeding her information – I got it.'

'You'll be fine. It's time to trust me, to really trust me.'

Our convoy must make quite a sight driving down Mountain Way, all three cars travelling close and at speeds far in excess of the speed limit.

Just as Ebony said, Amber and her parents are standing across their front door with Ebony nowhere in sight. When they see the angels take up positions around the house, keeping watch of the darkness, they exchange looks, their eyes wide with fear.

Thane is out in a flash, but he waits at my door so we can approach the Langs together.

My steps are slower than Thane would like, slower than *I* would like, but he doesn't rush me; he's in my head so he knows I'm freaking out.

'Steady, Jordan.' He stays close, his hand on my shoulder. He acknowledges someone behind us. I flick a look. It's Michael, returning from setting up the perimeter already.

On the porch, Amber surveys me with a black scowl. One day I'll ask what her problem is, but not when I'm petrified of Prince Luca and his six specially trained soldiers lurking in the dark somewhere, watching, waiting for that moment when one of us –

'Jordan.' Thane shakes his head.

OK, OK. *Focus, Jordan, focus.*

Thane introduces himself in his calm, soothing voice, explaining how he and his team are angels who have come to protect Ebony from a dangerous dark angel named Luca. 'I need to take Ebony to the Monastery of the Holy Cross, where she'll be safe while I perform an ancient ritual on her to protect her from the manipulations and influences of this evil dark prince.'

Amber's parents both stare at him as if he's a ghost.

'I promise Ebony safe passage,' he adds, 'and will return her soon after dawn.'

Watching the angels running from post to post faster than humanly possible, the family can see that to call the police would be pointless. They're not stupid, they're just stunned.

'We always knew Ebony was special,' Mr Lang says, and glancing at his wife, they nod at each other. 'We won't stop her.'

Thane nods deeply. 'Thank you.'

In the distance a dog howls like a wolf, then makes a shrill whimpering sound as if begging for its life. It's so eerie, shivers rip up my spine.

Michael takes off with the speed and silence of the super-natural. One blink and he's gone.

*Is it him?* Is he *that* close?

Movement on the perimeter draws all our attention to where Jez and Michael come together whispering.

'What is it?' Mr Lang asks.

Thane tilts his head a moment, then his face drops. 'I'm sorry,' he says. 'It seems one of your dogs inadvertently crossed his path.'

Mrs Lang and Amber gasp, while from the dark interior of their house Ebony's husky voice rings out, 'No, *no*, please don't let the dogs get hurt.'

'Are our animals in danger tonight?' Mr Lang asks.

'Prince Luca has one purpose tonight, to take Ebony away with him, but anyone who attempts to stop him will assuredly be slaughtered. Your horses are safe inside their stalls. Keep your barn locked and any other animals you may have secured within.'

I gulp deeply and notice Amber's eyes bugging out like golf balls. They flicker into the darkness before settling on me. 'Is Jordan safe?'

Everyone looks at me. 'Not as long as he's standing out here.'

Then Ebony's voice calls out, 'How do I know *you* people aren't the ones killing the dog and scaring us half to death?'

Thane glances at me, and for the first time desperation appears in his eyes, so I step between Amber and her mum, find Ebony in the shadows and take her hands in mine. They're ice cold. 'Ebony, you need to come with us. We don't have time to argue about this. I'll be beside you all the way, I promise.'

She groans and Amber spins around and quickly jumps in. 'Honey, you don't have —'

I grab Amber's arm before she can finish. 'Yes, she does. And if you're really her friend, you will support her leaving with us right now.'

Her eyes flit to Thane, to Michael, to the cars, to the darkness. She bites down on her lower lip, tugging it into her mouth, and finally nods. 'OK, but she makes her own mind up.'

'I don't want to put these good people in danger,' Ebony says in a rush, 'but I don't trust what's going on here. Jordan, do you know what this looks like to me?'

I let her hands go and lift mine into the air, both palms facing upwards. 'That a whole bunch of angels are trying to keep you safe?'

She gives me a long look. She wants to think I'm joking, but my serious face is confusing her. 'That Nathaneal couldn't talk me into going with him, so he brought in reinforcements to scare the crap out of me. And it's working.'

'Ebony, this danger is real.'

She breathes in deeply. 'Jordan, I don't believe in what Nathaneal is selling, but I sure get the part where he wants me to leave everyone I love and everything I know. Mum and Dad will come home one day to find I walked out on them. I can't do that. I have to be here for them. They're all I have. Do you know what I'm saying?'

'More than you realise.'

'What's that supposed to mean?'

'I'd give anything to see my mum again. She died when

I was nine. And I never knew my father. He's been in prison for most of my life. Without parents I was made a state ward. Trusting strangers, normal or weird ones, is never easy. I had to do it because I didn't have a choice. You do. Just make sure you're not basing your decision on fear. You look freaked out. I don't blame you, but don't let it take control of your logical thinking processes up here.' I point to her head.

'I saw Adam Skinner today.'

'*What?*'

'He told me not to trust Nathaneal.'

'It's bullshit! *He's* bullshit! Don't listen to him, Ebony. He's . . . he's . . . an idiot. He's the one who's bad news. OK?'

She nods, looking tired, and I say, 'If you come with us, I'll be with you all the time. I won't leave your side. I promise.'

She nods and gives Amber a hug. 'Are you sure, hon?' Amber checks.

Ebony sends Thane a dirty look. 'Apparently, if I stay here tonight I endanger the people I care about.' As she says this, they maintain eye contact and her lower lip trembles. Thane's eyes blaze at her with such intensity it takes her a moment before she can pull her eyes off him. 'It seems I don't have a choice,' she tells the Langs.

Thane starts to say something, but she blows him off, being careful not to catch his eye this time. 'Forget it. I'm coming. You don't have to convince me any more.'

Thane gives the Lang family a curt nod and closes his big arms around Ebony, dwarfing her as he draws her into the protection of his chest.

Michael falls in on her other side, his eyes darting in all directions until they reach the passenger side, where they form a wall for Ebony to ease into the car safely.

The next thing I know Isaac is beside me with his arm around my shoulder, his wife on my other side. They shield me in the same way until I'm in the Lambo too, then dash to the red Ferrari. Last to leave their posts around the house are Gabriel and Jez.

As we drive off, Thane introduces Ebony to Michael. She looks at the golden angel with startled-doe eyes. 'How do you do?' she whispers.

He glances at Thane as if seeking permission. Thane nods, and Michael murmurs to Ebony in a kind voice, 'Better than you, I would think.' Reaching for her hand, he kisses it. 'My lady, it is wonderful to be meeting you at last.' He gives her a small smile before returning to watching the darkness flit past.

Closing her mouth, she glances at Thane as she turns back. 'Who are you people? Are my parents like you? Am I . . . ?'

Thane says, 'We are angels. Your parents are angels, and, Ebony, you too are an angel.'

She sighs. 'A man named Zavier told me he was my uncle. He said his sister was my mother who died in childbirth, but he never mentioned angels or Avena, and he has a house on the outskirts of the valley. I think I was there once when I was a baby. Do either of you know this man? He was the one who arranged the adoption with my parents.'

Thane frowns and glances at Michael, communicating

with him before answering. 'We haven't heard that name before. He may have been a man hired by Prince Luca to deliver you, and to spin the story of his sister being your biological mother to fill in the gaps in an effort to prevent you from searching for your true identity. I'll have the Brothers look into it, see what they come up with.'

Looking at Thane, Ebony says, 'If – and I'm only saying *if* – I believe you, who is Prince Luca and what does he want with me?'

'He was once a royal prince of Avena by birthright, but after a failed attempt to overthrow our High King he was stripped of his rank, excommunicated from his order and banished from Avena for eternity.'

'He wouldn't happen to be a hot Adonis-looking guy with long light-brown hair and amazing intense eyes, like yours but green?'

Thane exchanges a worried glance with Michael before turning back to her. 'Have you met him?'

'I think so,' she says, alarming both angels before adding, 'in a dream a couple of weeks ago.'

I've seen this prince too, and 'hot' and 'Adonis' aren't exactly words I'd use to describe him.

'Will you tell me about this dream, Ebony?' Thane asks, his grip on the steering wheel tightening.

'There's nothing to tell, except I suppose the guy was athletic, and he could fly. He had four velvet-black wings.'

Giving Thane a moment to absorb this, I tell her about my encounter. 'If it's any comfort, Ebony, he visited me in a dream too. He didn't show me his wings, but I got to see my mother locked up in a cell.'

After a space of silence Michael asks us both if he showed us anything else. I shake my head, while Ebony frowns. 'Let's not get carried away,' she says. 'It was just a dream.'

Thane asks, 'Did he touch you, Ebony?'

She looks straight ahead. 'He ran his fingers along the edge of my face. They were so hot I screamed.'

As she says this, Thane's hands on the steering wheel tighten so hard it's a wonder the wheel doesn't snap in two.

'Easy, Thane,' Michael warns.

'Did he ask you for anything?'

She frowns, sensing this question is important, if not to her then to Thane and Michael. But then she shakes her head. 'Not that I can remember, but he kept calling me something.'

Thane looks at her and she says, 'My young queen. He said I was his ... young ... queen.'

Thane goes quiet, and a spine-chilling silence settles over us until Ebony's voice peals out with concern: 'Nathaneal, are you all right? Have I said something to upset you?'

'Careful, Thane,' Michael warns again.

'I swear –'

Michael leaps from his seat and puts a hand on Thane's shoulder. 'Pull it back, Thane.'

'As the King of all Kings is my witness –'

'Nathaneal! Stop!'

Thane's lips tremble, his whole body shudders, fingers bone-white around the steering wheel, as he fights to stay in control.

Overhead, the sky rips apart with a bolt of lightning that divides into multiple fingers streaking across the sky in all

244

directions. It ignites the night in a blaze of colour from one horizon to the other. The birds are illuminated and scatter, terrified, millions on the move. Thunder like I've never heard before rumbles for so long it will probably register on the Richter scale. Ahead in the Ferrari, Isaac swings around. Ebony glances at me with that startled-doe look. I shrug, not at all sure what's happening, or why.

What I do know is that Thane is always careful to keep his emotions under control, or bring them back under control quickly.

Now I understand why.

When all is calm again, Michael returns to his seat, and without another word goes back to watching the darkness.

Taking a deep breath Thane peers at Ebony sideways. 'How often do you need to cut your hair? Monthly? Weekly? Some of us need to trim every day.'

Too surprised to answer, she stares back at him with a puzzled look, her eyes asking how he knows. Turning to stare out of her window she peers into the darkness for a while, absently running her hand through her long hair. 'Fortnightly.'

'It's one of those quirks we have.'

'What's with the hair?' I ask.

He catches my eye in the mirror. 'An angel's hair grows particularly fast in comparison to human hair, but we have no bodily hair except for on our head and around our eyes, whereas humans have a fine coating of hair all over their body.'

Running her hand over the skin of her arm, Ebony smiles softly, pleased with his explanation. Maybe this girl should stick around; she could learn heaps about herself.

'Why me? Why did this . . . Prince Luca take me?'

Nathaneal tells her sadly, 'Many theories have been suggested, none confirmed. I won't let anything happen to you, Ebony.'

'You didn't answer my question. Tell me what *your* theory is.'

His eyes close and he sighs. He's holding back, just like he's been doing to me from the beginning. It's why I haven't been able to trust him completely. But he won't get away with holding anything back from Ebony. I can tell, and he knows it.

I watch and wait as intently as Ebony, but before he tells her he exchanges a look with Michael as if asking for his advice. Michael shrugs with his ginger eyebrows and Thane takes a deep breath. 'It's been foreseen that you will develop the ability to read souls.'

'A formidable power,' Michael chimes in. Ebony just stares from one angel to the other. 'Quite unique. And valuable. Imagine during times of war being able to pick out spies with just one look into their eyes.'

'I don't mean to be rude or insulting or . . .' Ebony says, casting a look downwards when she pauses, 'so just for argument's sake let's say I go along with the concept of everyone having a soul . . . why does it matter so much to this prince? Is being able to pick out spies worth going to all this trouble?'

Thane explains, 'Prince Luca selects his human prey by their weaknesses.'

Michael adds, 'Your ability to read souls could provide that information in an instant.'

Thane says gently, 'But why he wants you will make no difference to the outcome, because I will protect you, Ebony. I promise to keep you close by my side and perfectly safe.'

She turns immediately to me and reaches for my hand. 'You promised you would stay with me too.'

'I meant it. I won't leave you. My promise is good.'

She sighs, sounding relieved, and links her fingers through mine. 'Don't go anywhere without me, OK?'

'You got it,' I tell her; then, out of the corner of my eye, I notice Thane's brooding look.

## 36

# Ebony

We walk through a maze of paths and outer buildings until a bald man named Brother Bernard unlocks a thick steel door and we're finally inside the monastery. It's here that Michael steps aside and Nathaneal eases his hold, but keeps one strong arm still firmly wrapped around my shoulders. And it's now I get my first real look at my surroundings, mostly dimly lit corridors. Brother Bernard leads us through one after another.

Eventually we come to a white-painted room, modestly furnished with armchairs and low tables around an open fire. Although the ceiling is high and ornately decorated, it's a casual, relaxed setting. There are several lamps, no obvious windows, and a second door at the opposite end.

Gently Nathaneal removes his arm, and as I settle on the only two-seater couch, he signals Jordan to sit beside me. He understands that this boy makes me feel at ease. I feel strongly that Jordan and I belong together. Not in a boyfriend–girlfriend way though – it's a strange feeling I have for Jordan. I can't explain why or how, but I've had it since the moment we first met. I have to be near him. I'm afraid something might happen to him if I'm not.

But it's when I'm braced against Nathaneal's chest, listening to the slow beat of his heart, seemingly synchronised with mine, that I feel safe and secure and alive. It's as if every part of me that's touching a part of him awakens with a zing of electricity and a sense of awareness that leaves me breathless and invigorated at the same time.

It's Nathaneal's embrace that imbues me with the sense that I have at last found my place in this world. Not that I would tell him any of this, not while there are so many unanswered questions, so many inexplicable details.

Jordan comes at once and takes my hand. A fleeting look of pain sweeps across Nathaneal's eyes and I want to wipe it away. It hurts to see it there and I suspect I know why.

I'm developing feelings for him. No ... and this sounds crazy, but it's as if I was born in love with this guy. Is it possible to fall in love with someone before you're born? Or after knowing them only a short time?

I know, it's ridiculous. It's insane. It's something I would normally think impossible, but nothing is normal with me, and hasn't been for a long time, especially what's happening tonight. The danger is real; I see it on everyone's faces, and the birds in the sky – that doesn't happen, ever. Just thinking about them makes me shiver.

Jordan squeezes my hand. 'Are you OK, Ebony?'

'I'm not hurt, if that's what you mean.'

'Well, I can see you're not hurt.'

'I'm fine, Jordan. Don't worry. I'm just a little overwhelmed by these incredible-looking people. There's something about them, and I'm not referring only to their physical perfection – that goes without saying.'

249

'Do you mean like an aura?'

'Yeah, an aura of greatness, of drama and power.'

The rest of the angels walk in then, and the brunette makes a beeline straight for me, her sapphire eyes, ravenous in their intensity, start turning black and freakish-looking.

She's almost upon me when Nathaneal intercepts her. 'Shae, where are you going?' He pulls her aside and they argue quietly. I try to listen, but can't hear a thing. Then I notice their lips aren't moving. But they're obviously communicating. The brunette breaks the connection first and takes a deep breath.

'What's that about?'

Jordan says, 'She's just excited to meet you.'

I frown. He's not telling me everything. 'Be straight with me. I've had enough lies.'

'You're right, sorry. You're someone very special to her.'

I frown at him and he explains. 'Thane doesn't want you to be swamped with information until he thinks you can handle it, and Shae has heaps to tell you and is annoyed with him for restricting her.'

'He's protecting me?'

'You have no idea.'

Nathaneal comes over and hunkers down in front of me. And just like the first time he looked into my eyes, I feel as if I've come home, found my place in life, where I truly belong. I then have to remind myself to breathe. 'I'd like to introduce you to everyone, if you're up for it.'

He makes it sound like he's asking my permission, so I nod and try to work some moisture into my mouth. Oddly, even though she is obviously the keenest, Nathaneal doesn't start with the brunette. 'You know Michael.'

The golden man nods and gives me a small smile and a wink, then goes and stands by the door in the far wall with his arms folded across his chest and his head tilted as if he's listening for a faraway sound. I know that look because I do it myself.

Nathaneal introduces the sandy-haired man next. Laying his hands on the guy's shoulders, he shakes him and says with unmistakable pride, 'This peculiar individual is my brother Gabriel.'

Gabriel is just a bigger version of Nathaneal, but he doesn't awaken the same emotional response in me. He comes over and lifts the back of my hand to his lips.

'It's a pleasure to meet you at last, my lady.'

Watching carefully from behind, Nathaneal smirks and rolls his eyes. 'Don't be fooled by his angelic manner. He's trying – pathetically, I might add – to impress you.'

Nathaneal impresses me more. Here, among his own kind, his relaxed demeanour is so much more charming. I have to drag my eyes back to the brother in front of me.

'What my baby brother doesn't know is that I don't have to *try* to impress. It's an inherited gift that didn't pass down to Thane, I'm afraid. It's what makes him jealous of his older brothers,' he adds in a husky whisper meant to be overheard. He spins around and ruffles Nathaneal's hair.

With a glint in his eyes Nathaneal says, 'You have to claim something to restore your self-esteem since we all know, though I'm the youngest of seven, I'm also the strongest.'

Everyone is laughing except for the black-haired female with the masses of curls, who keeps giving me furtive glances with more than a little loathing tucked inside her unusual and quite exquisite turquoise eyes.

As if noticing my interest, Nathaneal introduces her next. 'This is Jezelle, trained in seven different fighting arts, and also one of our province's most esteemed healers.'

He forgets to mention how she has the uncanny ability to change the atmosphere of a room from warm to freezing without uttering a word. Dragging her dazzling eyes reluctantly away from Nathaneal, she eyes Jordan next. Noticing our clasped hands she smiles, apparently delighted at the possibility Jordan and I might be a couple. Lifting one shoulder in a dismissive gesture, she tosses her thick hair so the curls ripple down her back. Though it has no effect on me, Jordan is lost in the scent it gives off. Done with her little game of teasing the human boy, she steps back behind Nathaneal.

The last two, Isaac and Shaephira, are married. Before he introduces Shaephira, Nathaneal crouches down in front of me. 'Ebony,' he begins, and then stops. His eyes on mine feel like a caress and suddenly all I can think about is the yearning need tightening inside me and making me hungry for the taste of his mouth. I watch as he swallows deeply and with a big inhaled breath withdraws from whatever this is we're feeling. 'Shae is your sister.'

I blink several times rapidly. 'Pardon me?'

He nods.

'But . . .' I whisper, 'that can't be right. I told you that already.'

'I can't change this for you. It is what it is.'

Shae lays her hand on Nathaneal's shoulder. 'Please, Thane.'

He gives me a long, considering look, then nods at her.

Shae sits on the low table in front of me and attempts to take my hand. Instinctively I pull away. She flinches and flicks Nathaneal a hurt look. He nods encouragingly and she turns back to me.

'Nathaneal is telling you the truth,' she says. 'I am your sister. And I've been waiting a long time for this day.' She smiles tentatively. 'I wish I'd had the chance to do all those things a big sister is supposed to do for you.' Tears swell in her eyes and my heart softens towards this young woman, but in no way does this mean I'm her sibling.

'I would have helped you with your studies,' she elaborates, 'and especially with procuring your powers,' she adds. 'With all that we've heard about them –'

'Shae,' Nathaneal interrupts.

The tears begin to flow and she sniffs. 'Our parents have struggled with your absence, Ebrielle, always wondering, worrying. They still pray in the Temple every day for your safe return.' A wave of emotion radiates from her and hits me with the force of strong wind.

'Oh, for pity's sake, child,' Jezelle's husky tones ring out, 'can't you see how much damage you've caused this family already?'

'Jez!' Nathaneal snaps.

But Jez has an agenda: humiliating me, though why I have no idea. She doesn't know me, so I can't have wronged her in the past. What is her problem? It's obvious she wants Nathaneal, and since I'm the new girl, would she see me as a threat? 'Shae's willing to accept *you*,' she says, 'which is quite a generous gesture, if you ask me.'

'Which nobody is,' Isaac mutters.

'Are you incapable of feeling anything?' she harps on. 'Or is your lack of emotion because you're not really Shae's sister? Are you a fraud, Ebony Hawkins?'

Nathaneal yells, 'That's enough, Jez!'

I look up then and meet her eyes. 'Aha!' she gasps excitedly. '*She* doesn't believe she's Ebrielle herself!' She walks up to Nathaneal and says softly, 'Thane, darling, how did you get this so wrong?'

Nathaneal glowers at her. He takes a step towards her and the air around him distorts like waves of invisible plasma.

Gabriel grabs hold of his arm. 'Not worth the reprimand, Thane.' Nathaneal eventually nods, but Gabriel keeps hold of him anyway.

Jezelle flicks a hand at me as if I'm less significant than a fly. 'Seriously, does anyone really believe this girl is Ebrielle?'

Nathaneal drags air through gritted teeth, but unperturbed she continues, 'Look at her, Thane. She's weak like a human. Even her eyes lack the intensity of our species.'

Shae tilts her head for a better angle. Isaac and Gabriel check me out too. I feel like the main event at a freak show. Whatever they see, or don't see, they keep to themselves. Only Michael doesn't come over, but that could be because he doesn't want to leave the door unattended.

Nathaneal's belief in me is not enough to convince *me* though. And I can understand Jezelle's doubts. 'Jezelle is probably right, and I think you all know that I'm not this girl "Ebrielle",' I say. 'You can all go home, because that's where I'm going right now.'

My admission starts the group arguing among themselves.

Shae gets right into Jezelle's face, accusing her of exploiting my insecurities. But to my thinking, Jezelle's arguments are the more believable.

'The proof is in the eyes,' Jezelle says. 'Humans have dull, lacklustre colours. That girl's eyes tell us all we need to know.'

I slide forward on to my elbows and bury my head in my hands so I don't have to see them all looking at me.

I should be pleased of this 'proof' that I'm not one of them. So I don't understand why instead I suddenly feel bereft. Whatever the reason, I can't think clearly among the swirls and ebbs of their emotions. So when they calm down, I'm going to get up, walk outside and phone Dawn to pick me up.

As if understanding how desperate I'm feeling, Nathaneal yells at them to get out. The room falls silent and I feel the heat from their staring eyes burning through the top of my head.

I hear whispers of apologies, but Nathaneal doesn't want to hear any of them. He's too angry, and again he asks them to leave, adding, 'I need to talk to Ebony alone. We'll meet again in the chapel annex in one hour. Jez, Shae, both of you will prepare Ebony. I'll bring her to you soon. Isaac, you will escort the girls to the chapel. Gabriel, you will instruct Jordan. Michael, you will officiate.'

I feel Michael's gaze on me and I look up. 'It will be my honour, my lady,' he says.

As they begin to file out, Nathaneal pulls Michael aside. 'Nothing must go wrong now, Michael.'

'Nothing will. You have my word.'

Nathaneal holds the door open and points to Jordan. 'You need to leave too.'

'No way, dude. I told Ebony I wouldn't leave her side and I'm not going to break that promise for anything.'

In a low, implacable voice he insists. 'You will go now and you will stay close to Gabriel.'

Jordan storms out, slamming the door behind him, and the only sound I hear then, other than my own heart beating, is Nathaneal's.

He sits beside me and takes my hands gently in his. Then, tilting my chin up with his thumb, he scrutinises my face as if locking it into his memory. 'Dear, sweet Ebony, how very human you are.'

'That's what I've been trying to tell you!'

'You seem human because you were raised to believe you are, but, Ebony, you are every measure an angel – as much as I am. You just need time to assimilate into our culture, to live among us and to *feel* deep inside your heart that you belong.'

He takes a breath and smiles. My heart skitters. Can I really belong in Nathaneal's world?

'I promise,' he says, 'you will come to love Avena with every fibre of your being. Ebony, I want to be the one to take you home.'

'But my eyes – you heard what she said. It's true; they're as dull as mud.'

'Jezelle can see no one's beauty except her own, and your eyes are far from dull.'

'You people are all stunning. I'm not even pretty. I'm less than ordinary.'

'I may have to work on your eyesight first.' He smiles.

'My eyesight is fine. It's better than fine.'

'Your hearing and your memory, are they better than fine too? What about your speed? I hear you run like the wind.'

'I know what you're trying to do.'

'Is it working?'

A small smile escapes.

'And then there is the emergence of your wings.'

I glance down at my lap and, biting on my lower lip, a tear escapes and I have to wonder why? Do I *want* wings now?

'What is it?' His face clouds over with concern.

'They disappeared. I noticed last night. I was so relieved I cried, but now ...' I bite down on my lower lip again, this time to stop it trembling.

He leans so close the heat from his face warms mine. With his thumb under my chin he tilts my head, ever so gently, until I'm looking directly into his eyes. They are as true and deep and mesmerising as only the deepest part of an ocean could be, if lit by an underwater sun. 'But now?'

'I feel as though I've lost something.'

He smiles and sighs blissfully.

'Why do you sound relieved? They would have been proof.'

'It's uncomfortable to have your wings partially emerged for any extended period of time. Your need to stretch them would be like an itch you can't reach. And as for proof, if you feel the need to show the others, there may still be a mark where they emerged. If you're willing, I could take a look, or I could call Shae back. She'd be here before I ended the mind-link.'

'You don't understand. There's nothing left. Nothing. They'll think I made it up. And please don't call Shae. I've disappointed her enough already. No one will believe me now, Nathaneal, especially Jezelle.'

'Don't worry about Jez.'

'She needs proof. I understand that because it's how I operate. Without proof there is only conjecture. If I had partial wing-growth, a mark or a feather or something that might convince her, and me, but now . . .' I shrug.

He leans his forehead down to mine, almost touching. He smells amazingly of the woods and I breathe in deeply, trying to surround myself in it and forget everything else.

'Will you show me?'

I nod and he moves back while I stand and slide Amber's coat off my shoulders. Turning my back to him, I undo the top few buttons of my shirt, enough to allow my shoulders to fall bare.

His inhalation is sharp and sudden, his heart kicks into a faster beat, and when his fingertips touch my skin a shuddering wave of awareness tightens muscles in my stomach and all sorts of places. My heart beats as fast as his now, and my instincts urge me to lean backwards into him. But if I did, would he embrace me? Or would he put distance between us?

He whispers, 'Amazing.'

'What do you mean?'

'You're right, there's no indication of wing generation. Nothing at all.'

'I told you. So you see, there's no way to explain what those growths were.'

He turns me around. 'It just means you have healthy muscle and skin tissue. It's what we call a perfect healing and indicates the possibility that one of your powers is likely to be healing.'

And while he tells me this he traces my chin with his finger, moving slowly around my jaw to my lips. His light, gentle touch ignites a fire inside me that makes me alternate between shivering and feeling feverish.

But even with these escalating sensations I *have* to ask, 'Do you still believe I'm the kidnapped angel you're looking for?'

He murmurs, 'Without a doubt.'

'But how can you be so sure?'

'I just know . . .' he murmurs, touching his chest with his fist, 'in here. And I don't want you to doubt yourself any more.'

'That's not so easy for me.'

He leans down as if . . . as if he might kiss me. My mouth opens in a soft gasp and my bottom lip trembles. The heat generating between us as his mouth hovers over mine makes my temperature rise and my knees go weak. His hand plunges into my hair and I arch my neck and wait with sweet anxiousness for his mouth to press into mine.

But he doesn't do anything but sigh. 'You're sixteen.'

I open my eyes. 'Does it count that I don't care?' My voice is a whisper, husky and practically unrecognisable. 'It was just a little . . . I mean . . . you were just going to . . .'

'Kiss you.'

'Yes.'

'Nothing little about it.'

'Why did you ... not ... kiss me?'

'I've searched most of my life for you, constantly thinking of you, wondering and talking with you in my mind. And now that you're really here, I don't trust myself to stop at one.'

'So it's not that you don't find me ... attractive?'

'If only you were older and in my arms, I'd show you how attractive I find you.' He groans deep in his throat, as if in real pain, and my heart flutters. 'Why are the rules so easy to forget in *this* world?'

'You've been here so long, maybe it's just what you're used to now.'

'That holds true for you too, Ebony.'

'So how do I change?'

He murmurs, 'Give yourself permission to trust. Hopefully, after that everything will fall into place.'

'You make it sound so easy, but I'm not a person who believes easily. I was raised that way.'

'Raised that way on purpose,' he reasons.

*It's the truth!*

'Ebony, the proof is inside your heart. You only need to look.'

My mind flits to a memory I don't recognise but it leaves me with a sense of belonging that feels important. It's as if my past is a jigsaw puzzle where one vital piece is within sight and about to drop into place but I just can't quite reach it. 'Nathaneal, how is it that I know you? And ... and ... why do I feel as if I ... you ... we ... belong to each other? Where is this coming from?'

260

He smiles and laughs simultaneously, and his warm breath blows into my mouth and tastes like honey and sweet wine. '*I* belong to *you*.'

His words trigger the memory again, but it still eludes me. 'Help me, Nathaneal. Help me remember.'

'It's what you told me once.'

'I told you? I told you that *you* belong to *me*?'

His smile is sweet and arrogant and altogether far too sexy.

'Then we *have* met before.'

'We were much younger, and it wasn't face to face.' His playful smile says he's teasing me, teasing out the memory. He wants me to remember.

With this realisation my heart plummets and my newly formed hopes dissolve, because I understand now. Nathaneal's not going to come straight out and tell me where we've met before, because he *needs* me to remember.

So much for knowing in his heart! The truth is, Nathaneal is *not* sure. He has doubts too! I'm not saying he's lying; I don't think he could. He's just not admitting to himself that he doesn't positively know who I am.

# 37

# Ebony

It's the spine-tingling whistling sound that makes me look up. Jezelle and Isaac are walking on either side of me, Shae close behind, while silently in front a Brother shows us the way to the chapel.

I walk carefully through the courtyard in a long white silk dress. It's so similar to the one from my dream that when Shae and Jez first showed it to me I almost passed out. A strange coincidence? I don't know. But not as strange as what I'm suddenly seeing coming down from the sky.

The sound is that of a meteorite that's managed to pass through the earth's atmosphere, but this is no burning rock falling from the sky. Whatever this is, it's alive.

Glowing in the darkness, it drops like a rocket, a reddish haze around its lower extremities, giving the appearance of burning up.

I blink hard to clear my eyes in case this is a figment of my exhausted imagination. But I soon pick out wings, tucked in by its sides so they're difficult to make out at first. As this 'bird' rockets closer to earth, many more appear behind it, like stars bursting into life.

'Aracals,' Isaac shouts.

Shae runs up close and shields me from behind, while Isaac and Jez close the circle around me.

'Run, Brother Tim! Tell Brother Bernard to prepare a safe room,' Isaac calls to the Brother slightly ahead of us. He then turns to Shae. 'Report to the watchtower and find out what's happening. Get us numbers, whatever you can. Inform Nathaneal. Stay there until you know exactly what's coming after the Aracals. I'll meet up with you in the court-yard grounds as soon as I can.' Her face crumples. 'Right now, Ebony needs guards around her who are not emotion-ally attached. Go, Shae, we'll get Ebony inside. We will keep her safe.' When she doesn't release me, he yells, 'Go!'

Brushing her cheek against mine fleetingly, Shae takes off. Then Jez and Isaac shuck off their coats, release their wings and spin me around so fast my feet don't touch the ground. Just before their wings wrap around me from both sides, I get a glimpse of black uniforms with weap-ons hanging from belts at their waist. I peer between Jez's blue feathers and Isaac's white, and watch the first Aracal land perfectly on its feet in the centre of a raised flower bed.

I've seen these birds before, around the school. Jordan says they're spies, but this one looks more like a soldier than a spy. As with other Aracals I've seen, the eyes of this variety are still the dominant feature, too large for the head, and circular with a single black dot in the centre, but where the other ones had bright blue irises, these have orange ones that glow like solar flares.

It senses us, turns its head and looks straight at me. When our eyes connect, it shrieks like a banshee. Its wings shoot out at sharp angles like elbows with long, sharp talons at their tips.

Isaac and Jez spin me again. Their desperation shows in the speed with which they whisk me away.

'Where is this *door*?' Jez's impassioned cry scares me almost more than the creature closing on us.

A look passes between her and Isaac over my head, and the next instant Isaac is loosening his hold on me. He turns and faces off the creature.

'No!' I cry out as Jez pulls me further away. 'We can't leave Isaac to fight that thing on his own!'

'If you really are one of us, you have many battles to come, but this one isn't yours to fight.'

'But this *is* my battle.'

'You're not ready to fight demons.'

Brother Bernard, bald and barefoot in his white tunic, holds open the heavy steel door.

'Aren't you going back?' I ask Jez when the door locks behind us.

'Are you giving me orders already?'

'Yes. No. What do you mean? I just thought to help Isaac, that's all.'

'Hmm, well, Nathaneal would have my head on a platter if I left your side now.'

'Hurry, my ladies, this way.' Brother Bernard indicates we should follow him into the inner sanctum of the monastery.

But outside I hear more screeching. 'What's going on out there?'

'Aracals are attacking.'

'But I thought Aracals weren't bred for attacking.'

'It would seem that the Dark Prince has engineered stronger ones, which fight like soldiers.'

'He *made* them?'

'He likes to dabble where he shouldn't by creating his own demons. The Aracal is his most successful species so far.'

Outside, the sounds of screeching have been joined by fighting, swishing swords and bodies hitting hard surfaces. 'There are more than Aracals attacking out there now. What's happening?'

Jez receives a message. I see it in her eyes as they find their focus on me, followed by a slight nod. 'Michael's called for reinforcements from Avena.'

I'm starting to feel dazed, as if this is happening to someone else. But it is happening, and while I'm in here with Jezelle protecting me, who's looking after Jordan? Is anyone with him? I should be with him. What if he was outside when the Aracals came down?

'Where's Jordan?'

'I don't know!' I shrink back at her venomous tone. 'Listen, making you safe is my only concern right now. Someone else will be taking care of your little human boy toy.' She eyes me sideways again, her over-bright eyes lingering a smidgen too long for comfort. My skin crawls under her scrutinising gaze. 'How close are you two anyway?'

'Pardon me?'

'You know what I mean. Are you two involved?'

'Well, yes, actually, we're very close. Haven't you heard? I'm his Guardian Angel.'

After a vicious look she goes silent, and I smile just a little. We follow Brother Bernard through the chapter house

265

and adjoining dining room to a corridor lined with the Brothers' dormitories. At the end of this long passageway we stop while Brother Bernard pulls out a ring with many keys hanging from a chain around his neck. He opens the door and Nathaneal bursts through, relief flooding his eyes when he sees me. He lifts me into his arms and whisks me down a dark circular staircase as if I'm made of air. The sound of his heart beating comforts me as no words could.

'Ebony,' he says, his voice grave, 'I'm so sorry, but the unthinkable has happened. A unit of dark angels, all Prodigies, has breached the monastery's fortified walls.'

Lifting my hand, I run the backs of my fingers around his jaw. His skin is smooth and warm but he's coiled tight and tense as a rock. 'Nathaneal, I need you to listen to me.'

'Stop there. Please say no more.'

'But I have to. Don't you see that? I don't want anyone hurt because of me.' I lay my head against the comforting thud of his heart. 'It's *me* the Dark Prince wants. If I go to him willingly, will he withdraw?'

He shudders and the tremor passes through him from head to foot. 'Don't say that. Don't even entertain the thought.'

'Answer my question, Nathaneal.'

'Then ask me one I *can* answer.'

'Can the Dark Prince reach us here?'

His pause is short, possibly no more than a fraction of a second, but I hear it as if it's screaming in my head.

# 38

# Jordan

After Thane drops me in the sacristy, I check the room out for weaknesses. Lining the walls are timber shelves stacked with vestments, candles, chalices and other items the Brothers use in their services. Behind the shelves is solid brick. With no windows, it's a secure room, but nothing special. What bothers me is the lack of an exit. There's no way out except to backtrack through the church.

Thane is always saying to trust him. If anything happens to Ebony tonight, it's all on his head. I might not have angel powers, but I'll come after him all the same.

He brings Ebony and she runs straight into my arms, knocking me against the wall. *Man*, the smell of her skin is intoxicating. I hardly notice shelves digging into my spine. I hold her tight, breathing her in and stroking her hair. I don't want to let her go, not now, not ever. I love her!

Thane frowns and I quickly shift my thoughts from the pain in my heart to the Aracals that attacked us and the dark angels I saw, the Prodigies. How on earth are we going to defeat them? 'I was so worried about you,' Ebony says, pulling away to check my face for bruises. She pushes hair from my forehead and smiles with relief in her eyes.

A surge of anger spikes through me. Thane promised my life would get better, but, man, it's been anything but. And this room will be a death trap if those Prodigies break down the only door.

Thane hears them first. 'They're in.'

'How far away?' Jez asks.

It feels as if someone is strangling me from behind.

'Ground level.'

'*Shit!*'

Sounds of battle are filtering down now. How long before they're in the corridor right outside? 'What happens now? We're stuck in here, and this is supposed to be the safest place!'

Thane looks at Jez and nods at some silent communication. They get down on their haunches and start shifting a heavy chest of drawers. Ebony figures out what's happening before I do.

'I'm not going anywhere without you,' she says in a voice that sounds like her heart is breaking. The thing is, she's not looking at me when she says this. She's looking at Thane.

'I wouldn't dream of it,' Thane replies.

*Well, isn't he a fast worker!*

He glances at me, hearing my thoughts, but I'm past caring. I'm about to die anyway. *What about your fiancée back home?* I yell at him from inside my head. *Huh? What about the one you left behind?*

Jez frowns and looks between us. He's up and in my face in a split second, whispering, 'Now is not the time, Jordan. Trust me, I will explain everything when this night is past and you and Ebony are safe.'

'Didn't you get the memo?' I whisper back loudly, not caring who's listening. 'It said not to believe anything you say any more.'

Ebony frowns, her eyes flitting between us. *Argh, man*, she has enough to worry about tonight! I plaster a smile to my face. 'It's nothing, Ebony. Just a running joke we like to play.'

'Really? Well it's not very funny, Jordan.'

'I know,' I answer, keeping my eyes on Thane. 'But that's not my fault.'

Jez opens the trapdoor in the floor where the chest was and climbs feet first into the dark interior, leaving only her head and elbows out. 'I'll check it out,' she murmurs, disappearing.

Ebony moves towards Thane and he closes his arms around her, tenderly stroking her hair. It's such a natural act; it's incredible how familiar they are. When did this intimacy develop? They had, like, five minutes alone together.

What is he doing?

Love is pouring out of him like flooding summer rains. I guessed he had feelings for Ebony the time we talked in his car and he sounded obsessed with finding her. But when did he fall in love with her?

A light rap at the door has Thane moving quickly to open it. Gabriel runs in with Michael right behind him, both breathless and bloodied. 'At least twelve Prodigies have broken through our defences,' Gabriel says, while Thane moves to check on Michael, the bloodier of the two.

Gabriel glances at Ebony and nods. 'I'm sorry, my lady, we have not been able to hold them back. Our reinforcements are yet to arrive, and the Prodigies will not stop until they find you.' Turning back to Thane, he says, 'Brother, they're relentless. They're tearing the monastery apart. We thought the Aracals were all slain, then Shae messaged from the watchtower moments before another shipment started to descend. There were so many we lost count.'

Finished with Michael, Thane checks his brother's injuries. 'And our good Brothers, how are they holding up?'

'We have lost three.'

Thane winces, closing his eyes tight. 'And casualties?'

'Many.' Gabriel takes a breath. 'Thane, if they make it to the stairs . . .'

But that's just what they do only moments after Gabriel's warning. We hear them crashing through the staircase, ripping it apart, yelling out in a creepy, guttural language none of us understands. We hear the clash of steel, the sizzle of energy colliding and, most terrifying, aftershocks that make the walls shake, the room fill with dust, the floor rumble beneath our feet.

I cover my ears, slide to the floor, where I sit on my ankles. I'm shaking but I can't help it. I am more terrified than I've ever been before in my life. Ebony runs over and throws her arms around me.

'Shhh,' she soothes, cradling my head against her shoulder. 'It will be all right. You'll see.'

Michael's head tilts slightly as he receives a message. Everyone waits anxiously to hear the update. 'Our reinforcements are not here yet.'

He looks at Thane fleetingly, then lowers his eyes to Ebony. 'I'm sorry, my lady, we need to move you again.' He holds out his hand. 'You must come with us.'

When she's up, Thane pulls her into his chest and Michael holds his hand out for me. 'We will not let anything happen to you, Jordan. Tonight we are all your guardians.'

The moment he wraps his hand around mine it glows and heat enters my body, filling me with a sense of strength and courage and amazing calm. It's the most incredible, strongest sense of myself that I have ever felt. It's awesome.

He then turns to Thane. 'Jez has just let me know the tunnel is clear and she is now bringing the Porsche to the south tunnel exit, where Brother Bernard will wait to open the wall. It's all organised, but we'll have to hurry. The ritual to protect Ebony was of vital importance, but now it is more vital that we get her somewhere safe. One of us must remain here to cover our tracks.'

'I'll stay,' Gabriel volunteers. 'Isaac and Shae will need me here.'

Thane grips his arm. 'We rendezvous at my house. Good luck.'

'Go!' Gabriel urges.

As I jump down on to a cold hard floor, the trapdoor closes over our heads and plunges the four of us into darkness.

# 39

# Jordan

Jezelle drives about a kilometre before slamming into a tree. The front-passenger corner takes the full brunt, crumbling in a screaming match between metal and wood. Dazed, it takes me a few goes to punch out the airbags and remember we were heading to Thane's house when a bolt of lightning struck the roof, its dazzling blue light blinding Jez.

That's when she lost control.

The car is empty. I must be the last to get out. I try to move but find my legs pinned. I smell fumes and a knot of panic tightens in my gut.

I see Thane in the forest, caught in the car's one remaining headlight. He has Ebony in his arms, lowering her gently and checking she's all right.

'He's conscious,' Jez calls, climbing in to help with the airbags.

'Hurry, Thane,' Michael urges.

Thane moves fast. In a flash the three of them reach over the top of the crumpled front and peel bits of Porsche off my thighs, metal grinding and scrunching. I'm free at last, and Jez reaches down through the smashed windscreen and yanks me out in one go, practically dislocating my shoulder in the process.

'Go easy. I'm not made of rubber!'

Someone kicks out the headlight just as she dumps me unceremoniously beside Ebony.

Thane and Michael share whispered words. My head's not all right yet, but I hear Michael's voice, tighter and faster than usual. 'There's activity at your house too.'

'No. *No!*' Thane loses it. He smacks his palm against a thick branch, which cracks. He yanks it off and flings it into the canopy. It travels fast and high before it snares in the upper branches and gravity returns it to earth.

His frustration spent, he takes a deep breath. 'Jez, go ahead of us. You'll be faster on your own. Report any information immediately.' She prepares to take off and he grabs her arm, 'Stay out of sight.'

Michael watches her for a moment. 'She'll be all right. As soon as the reinforcements arrive, I'll dispatch a team to back her up.'

'Take enough soldiers to install a perimeter around the house.'

Michael takes off and it's just the three of us, running along the path to Thane's house, the same one Thane and I jog on every afternoon, except it looks different tonight. It *feels* different.

'Nathaneal!' Ebony hisses in warning. 'I hear something.'

Thane says, 'Keep still.'

An Aracal, unmistakable with its weird orange eyes glowing in the darkness, scours the forest for movement from the other side of the river. It spots us so quickly it must have inbuilt heat sensors.

Thane whispers, 'Run!'

Sticking to the path, he urges us to run faster, but the creature zooms around the trees, burning leaves off branches with its wings. Another, larger Aracal rockets in behind it.

Thane and Ebony sprint ahead, only to slow down until I catch up. I'm running at capacity, but they're not. I tell them to go ahead. 'I'll find somewhere to hide, a hollow log or tree trunk.'

'Don't be stupid,' Ebony cries out. 'We're not leaving you behind.'

Without warning, Nathaneal picks me up.

'This is really embarrassing,' I murmur. 'Come on, man, put me down.'

'Not leaving you behind, Jordan.'

'Well, you should. My life's one stuff-up after another. If you keep me around, chances are you'll go down with me eventually.'

'Jordan, do I *really* need to remind you of our arrangement?'

That shuts me up quick.

We set off again, but the Aracals get so close the one in front swipes at Thane's back, almost scratching the top of my head, its black talons as long as fingers. Thane groans and, with no choice but to turn and fight, he lowers me to the ground. He spins around to face the Aracals, making sure the two of us remain behind him.

Thane peels off his coat and tosses it to Ebony. He's wearing the same battle clothes as the other angels – black trousers and top with silver shoulder armour and a wide belt. I catch Ebony staring with her mouth open, her eyebrows elevated, eyes wide. She swallows and moistens her lips with her tongue. No guesses what she thinks of his look. With his glowing body giving off enough soft light to see by, he releases his wings. This is the second time I've seen them and they're still every bit as amazing, but Ebony is in awe.

We watch as he leaps into the air and grabs the two demons by their throats, smashes their heads together as he lands, then flings them into the treetops where they sizzle and burn up. Their remains dribble to the ground like heavy raindrops.

Thane spins around to check we're OK. Ebony holds out his coat. He sees she's trembling and he wraps it around her shoulders. 'Your wings are so beautiful,' she murmurs, reaching up and touching one, caressing it with her fingertips. 'You really are . . . You're an angel. You're all angels. Angels do exist.'

He smiles and looks at her as if his heart is melting. I feel like a third wheel on a bicycle. 'Yeah, well, I'm impressed too, if anyone cares,' I mutter, 'with your slick move, that is.' Imitating his move, I smash my fists together. 'Wham! That was awesome. You gotta teach me how to do that.'

'I have every intention,' Thane replies.

Just as he's about to get us running again, I spot a pair of glowing orange eyes.

'Incoming!'

But the Aracal disappears suddenly, leaving us wondering. Thane turns his own body light off and peers into the darkness. Then his eyes widen suddenly. 'Go. *Run!*' he shouts.

We don't get far before the Aracal swoops down on to Thane's back with a deafening shriek. Her wings, larger than they ought to be for her size, wrap around his arms, immobilising him, her beak tearing into his flesh. Thane gets to his feet and rams his back into a tree to try to dislodge her, but the Aracal is strong and doesn't budge.

Ebony, meanwhile, pulls down a branch and races back to attack the Aracal. She begins belting her to little effect.

'Her eyes!' Thane yells out as he stumbles around trying to throw her off. He must be in excruciating pain.

'You poke while I drag her off,' Ebony yells to me.

I grab a stick, and aim for a bull's eye first time, but as if she knows exactly what I'm about to do, the Aracal goes feral, snapping at my hands. I pull back and scour the ground for a longer stick.

'Just do it, Jordan!' Ebony yells.

Finally I lunge, stabbing the Aracal in her right eye. She screams and wails mournfully, in a way that will alert the flock to our position for sure.

But Ebony pounces, shutting the demon up with hands around her throat. Then in one wilful tug she yanks the Aracal off Thane's back. The creature's neck snaps. I hear the crack. Ebony does too and gets a sickened look on her face, then hurls the Aracal into the canopy like Thane did.

The Aracal hits a tree and drops on to a lower branch with a thud, where it ignites into a fireball and dribbles down in a rain of ash.

'Thank you,' Thane says tightly, in obvious pain as he takes a quick look at his wound. 'It's not so bad it won't heal by itself. At least she didn't break through to the marrow.'

Ebony takes a look and gasps. 'And this will heal itself?'

'It will take a few minutes.'

I find a log to sit on and wonder at the pain *I'm* suddenly feeling. It's only then I realise my hand is bleeding. Thane hears my thoughts and comes over. Getting down on his haunches, he takes a look, then, slowly, sits back on his heels. He seems concerned.

Ebony frowns at his reaction and takes a look at my wound. She studies it, then looks at my face. 'It's not as bad as Thane's, nowhere near as deep.'

I glance at the wound and shrug. 'It's just a scratch.'

Thane shakes his head.

'Nathaneal, what is it?' Ebony figures it out and grabs his hand to make him look up at her. 'What is going on? Is ... is Jordan going to die from this?'

Nathaneal swallows deeply and gets to his feet. 'It needs cleaning quickly. As a human, Jordan is vulnerable to the demon bacteria in the saliva. It needs to be cleaned out. I can't do it while I have demon saliva in my own blood.' He looks at me then, his eyes clear and intense. 'We need to get you to Jezelle.'

We start moving, but with Thane's arm still healing he can't carry me, and it's becoming difficult to stay upright. So now we're down to walking pace with the scent of my blood advertising our position.

'You're proving to be quite invincible, Jordan, so try not to worry too much.'

'I'm not immortal, Thane.'

Ebony slides in under my shoulder, lifting me off the ground, and we're running again.

## 40

## Ebony

Jordan is dying. I can feel his life force slinking away as sure as I can feel the thud of my own heart beating faster than it should. We prop him in a sitting position, supported between the wide roots of a giant fig tree. We're near Nathaneal's house, but still deep enough inside the forest not to be seen.

I don't want to leave Jordan, but Nathaneal is positive Jezelle is nearby. He needs to know what's going on and he won't leave me in the forest without protection. 'The house is just through there.' I peer through a bunch of trees, bushes, ferns and vines, finally glimpsing a portion of a structure with multiple levels, walls almost entirely of glass, and a ceiling that looks like a pair of outstretched eagle's wings illuminated by a bright full moon.

'It's beautiful,' I whisper.

He smiles and we take off. Fortunately we don't get far before Jezelle finds us, with Isaac and Shae right behind her. Shae's eyes go straight to mine. She scans me up and down, then nods, looking relieved. But there's no relief on the other two angels' faces and Jezelle starts to relate her report. 'The house is surrounded by Prodigies. Prince Luca and his two lieutenants were first, and ever since they have been arriving in pairs –'

Nathaneal looks stricken but urges her on. 'Hurry, Jez, Jordan needs your help.'

Alarm at this news has her speaking faster. 'Prince Luca is standing on your front deck as if he owns the place, but as far as I can tell he's not managed to break through your barriers to enter the house.'

'He's taunting you,' Isaac says. He appears to want to say more but a sharp look from Jezelle has him closing his mouth.

She jumps straight back in. 'He has two of his Prodigies up on the deck, one on either side of him, six are maintaining a perimeter approximately one hundred metres out from the house, with four more who have just arrived taking positions on your front lawn. What happened to Jordan? Where is he? Where do I go?'

Nathaneal directs her to the tree where we left him, briefly describing his injury. Jezelle's eyes widen as she listens. Before Nathaneal finishes she's off and running so fast she appears as a black blur disappearing into even blacker forest.

Then Shae says, 'There are Aracals on your lawn, picking out insects and worms.'

'Any word from Michael and Gabriel?'

Isaac nods. 'They're coming now with the Brothers.'

The dark angels are in black uniforms, with helmets from the eyes up and front chest armour, with swords in scabbards by their sides. They surround Nathaneal's house, just as Jezelle described, with two standing out in front and another two at the base of the deck. I'm watching them through a thatch of trees grown so close together they form a kind of screen. Seeing them sends a chill along my spine. They've come here for me, and I'm pretty sure they won't care how much blood is spilled to achieve their goal.

But does blood have to spill tonight? If I choose to go with Prince Luca, this all stops; no one has to die. But if I choose Nathaneal, or refuse to go with either, there will be a confrontation and people will die. At least three already have.

Jordan is mortally injured; what if he dies? I can't stand the thought of that! How would I live with myself knowing I could have stopped all this?

*Wise, wise girl! I applaud your rational thinking – and under such prodigious duress.*

The voice in my head is not my own. I recognise the perfectly modulated smoky tones as the voice from the dream I can't forget. The memory of the alluring winged man is still so clear I can see him now leaning over me, the intoxication of his desire in his penetrating green eyes.

*Come with me now and end the bloodshed. Choose of your own Free Will and they will not stop you. Young Prince Nathaneal doesn't love you enough to break a code. But there is no code in any universe that would stop me.*

*Why do you want me? I'm just a schoolgirl who can run fast.*

*Ah, but you have hidden talents, my lady, talents that complement mine. Your future, foretold during the formation of the stars, is to become a queen. I intend to make you Queen of*

*Skade. I will even give you a province of your own to govern one day.*

If I hadn't met Nathaneal, and if I didn't know that evil lies at this prince's core, it's possible I could fall for his hypnotic charm. But if I really am immortal, I can't think of anything more abhorrent than to spend eternity at this dark creature's side.

*I regret to advise you that I decline your invitation.*

*To govern?*

*To everything.*

*Perhaps there is room to negotiate.*

*Go on,* I say reluctantly.

His response is to laugh. *Come with me now, and, as well as no more bloodshed, I will return your parents unscathed.*

*You* took *my parents?*

*They broke their vow of silence. We had a contract which they ignored. But, just to show how generous I can be, to make up for destroying the disgusting pile of filth they called a home, not only will I release them, I will ensure their good fortune continues through to their old age.*

*Why would you burn our house down?*

*I gave them the means to make themselves wealthy so they could raise you in an environment befitting your future status, and they provided you with nothing but bare essentials while their neighbours surrounded themselves with luxuries. They also promised to keep your true origins secret, to avoid causing you undue . . . distress.*

*I was a happy child who grew up in a loving environment.*

*That much I concede, my lady.*

*How do I know you're not lying? How do I know my parents are still alive?*

281

*They're no use to me dead!*

*Your word isn't enough.*

*Come and see for yourself. I'll have them brought to the gates and give you one night together. You can tell them what a loving environment they provided for you, keeping in mind that they agreed to hand you over to my lieutenant in perfect condition on the eve of your eighteenth birthday.*

I want to deny it, but there's a ring of truth in his words.

*What if I don't come with you tonight?*

*Need you ask?* He finds my question amusing and chuckles. *Your human caretakers remain in their cells until I grow tired of their screams and incessant wailing of how unfair I am.*

*You're evil!*

*I accept your compliment with thanks, my lady. And by the way, being evil is more fun than being good. You'll grow used to it. You may surprise yourself and discover you enjoy it.*

A moment of silence feels like a blissful reprieve. I close my eyes and take a deep breath. When I open them, Michael and Gabriel have arrived with a small band of reinforcements, every one tall and incredibly beautiful, from their shimmering hair to their strong bodies in battle uniform to their slender boot-clad feet. It makes me wonder about their homeland and if it's as perfect as its inhabitants are. I wiggle my toes, recalling how uncoordinated I am. I'm nothing like these people, and yet, they're willing to spill blood to keep me safe.

I feel suddenly guilty, like I'm consorting with the enemy. If I actually chose the Dark Prince, would any of these beautiful angels know I did it to stop them being injured? Or would they think evil was at my core too?

I look for Jordan and can tell that his condition is worse. Jez is kneeling by his side.

I'm about to hurry towards them when Prince Luca's voice chimes in my head again. *I will soon walk out to the centre of this yard and wait twelve minutes as measured by the Earth's clock. And for those twelve minutes, the fate of everyone on this mountain will be in your hands.*

*If I agree to go with you, what happens then?*

*We leave immediately, and all who inhabit this mountain remain unscathed. It's your choice.*

My choice? My *choice*! To walk away from my life?

And what if he's lying about my parents?

But he's not lying. I knew they didn't die in the fire.

And then I think of Nathaneal. I love him, though I don't know how it happened, or why.

*Get out of my head!*

*A night in my arms, in the palace I built for you, my lady, and he will be nothing but a drifting memory.*

*How is it that I can speak to you in my thoughts, and . . .*

*And not him? Interesting, isn't it? You're intelligent enough to figure it out.*

*No. No! I don't belong to you.*

'Ebony? Ebony, what's wrong? Look at me, Ebony.' Nathaneal pulls me into his arms.

*It's time I make my appearance. Your choice is a simple one. We can settle this peacefully, or we can take the carnage route. Your human friend will be the first. As a matter of fact, I believe my darling Aracals have already set his spirit on a path to my gates.*

*Go to hell!*

*I like your humour. We will get along superbly.*

*I hate you!*

Jordan's feeble voice calls out from seemingly far away, 'Thane . . . Thane! What's with Ebony? There's something wrong. I feel it!'

*Skade is your true home; your birthright is to be queen. Only I can give you that. Come to me. Come, my lady. Come . . .*

I can't think clearly with that voice in my head. I need it to stop. I grab both sides of my head. 'Make it go away!'

Nathaneal realises what's happening. He pulls me up by my shoulders and shakes me. 'Ebony! *Ebony!* Don't listen to him. Block him out. Barricade your thoughts!' He groans. 'Ebony, look into my eyes.'

I look and he says, 'Find a space in your mind, make it blank and visualise a door with a lock.'

I close my eyes and nod.

'Go inside and lock the door behind you. Ebony, you can do this.'

I open my eyes and focus on his.

'Order him from your head. Order him to leave. Do it, Ebony. Do it now!'

'But he's giving me a choice.'

Michael comes and stands beside me. He says softly, 'He's playing with you, tempting you. It's how he operates. Don't listen to his poison. You have Free Will that even *he* can't take from you, but you must assert yourself. He knows you are a kind soul who cares for others, who will put the lives of others before your own. Whether you go to him or not, tonight there *will* be a confrontation. If you choose Luca, Nathaneal will never stop looking for you and there will be retribution of the kind this universe has never seen.'

'I just don't want any of you to get hurt because of me.'

'Ebony, you aren't forcing us to do anything we don't want to do. Besides, this is our job. We're the king's soldiers and Prince Luca is his enemy and therefore ours. You are one of us, and that's all that matters.'

*Come with me and I promise a thousand years of peace on the Earth.*

I return my head to Nathaneal's chest and, hearing only the beating of his heart, I visualise my secret room. I step inside it, turn around, lock the door and scream out in my thoughts, *Get out of my head, Prince Luca! This is my private space and you aren't welcome in here!*

I wait a moment, two, three, and there is nothing but silence. 'I think it's worked.'

'I knew you could do it,' Nathaneal whispers.

'You belong to me,' I murmur.

He kisses my hair. 'Yes, I do, my love. I belong to you.'

A wave of grey mist, cold and fetid, swirls towards us through the trees. I walk out to the clearing with Thane holding my hand and the others follow. We watch the mist pour out of Prince Luca's mouth. Everyone is silent. Something is about to happen.

And then he walks down the stairs and on to the lawn. The Dark Prince is taller than I recall from my dream, and thicker set around the shoulders. It could be the armour, or an illusion caused by the distortion of air around him. He looks regal in a soldier's uniform beneath a black floor-length cloak with fur-lined hood. Six soldiers move to stand behind him.

'Your time begins now,' he announces, his voice carrying like wind to everyone's ear.

Michael moves silently to stand a pace in front of me to the right. Nathaneal loosens his hand from mine, and moves to the opposite front wing position. Isaac, Shae and Gabriel take positions at my rear so that I'm now in the centre of a circle of angels.

Meanwhile, the putrid-smelling mist spreads into the forest.

I peer between my protectors for a glimpse of Jordan. I know he's nearby; I can feel him through our bond. Trying something I never imagined I would, I reach out to him with my mind. To my surprise I find him almost instantly, and it jolts me how bad his condition is. His life force is streaming out of him like wine spilling into thirsty soil.

In my mind I see him shivering and moaning incoherently between the fig tree's roots as Jezelle holds him in her arms while sitting on the moist earth. I'm shocked to see tears are cascading down her face. Sensing me, she looks up, shakes her head and murmurs, *He's failing fast and I'm doing all I can*.

I struggle to take a deep breath, releasing it in a shuddering sigh, and the mind-link disappears.

Prince Luca calls out, 'My lady, should you decide *not* to come with me, your decision will lead to many deaths in the next twenty-four hours. The mist I have released becomes active at sunrise. It will kill every child under the age of three on this mountain. These deaths, the agony their families will endure, rest on your shoulders.'

The monster! How can he do this? But the answer is simple: because he can. He can do whatever he wants.

And if I don't choose him, if I don't walk up to him, take his hand and say, 'I choose you, my lord,' I will have to live with the guilt of knowing I could have stopped it.

# 41

# Jordan

I'm dying. Again. What does this make it? Two, three times? There's one thing I gotta know before the lights switch off for good. Why is this crazy angel crying over me? I mean, literally, crying, over the top of me. The tears are dripping straight into the Aracal's bite and stinging like gnawing ants.

'Jezelle, what . . . gives with the tears?'

'Don't talk to me, human boy. Can't you see I'm busy working?'

So she's not crushed by the thought of losing me.

'Stop moving!' She sniffs. 'Can't you feel any improvement yet?'

Now that she mentions it . . . well, no, I'm still immobile, lifeless and pretty darn sure I'm about to die. After a couple more sobs she sits up and wipes her dribbling nose on her sleeve. 'How's that?'

'Well, the ants are gone.'

Keeping me on her lap, she lays her hand on my wound and rocks back and forth while humming.

A minute passes. Then another and she's still meditating. At least she's not giving up on me easily. Suddenly she gets up without warning. I roll off her lap to the dewy forest floor. 'Hey! What's with you?'

'Why don't you look at your hand and see for yourself.'

But I don't have to. There's no pain and I have energy. *Yes!* I'm not going to die today! I have more lives than a cat!

'Don't be so sure. The night is far from over yet.'

Standing about a metre away, she fiddles with her hair, puffing up her curls and making a show of looking around at the trees. Is she waiting for something? I take a stab in the dark. 'Um, hey, thanks. I owe you one.'

'You owe me your life, but all I want is one promise.'

'Since you put it that way, sure, what is it?'

'Tell no one how I disinfected your wound.'

Confused, I nod and mutter, 'You got it, but . . . how *did* you disinfect my wound?'

She mumbles a whole string of obscenities under her breath that I wouldn't utter even alone in the shower. Finally she says, 'Tears, you dumb human. Tears contain natural antibiotics.'

'Wow, man, you cried for me.' I find this suddenly amusing and a small laugh escapes.

'I should have let you die,' she murmurs acidly.

'You made yourself cry to save my life. That's awesome, Jez. No one's ever gone to such effort over me before.'

'Don't get carried away, OK?'

'Of course not, I'm just surprised at the nature of your unique healing skills.' She shrugs and I add, 'You're a healer, sworn to save lives – that's all there is to it. Right?'

She nods.

'It's not like we have anything going on between us.' She doesn't respond. 'Right?'

'Do we have an agreement, human boy?' she snaps.

'Your secret is safe with me, sister.'

She nods sharply, her wings smacking in my face as she takes off. I follow at a run, watching the direction the trees move as she flies between them. I soon find everyone at the house, the Brothers too, and other angels that must be the reinforcements.

Jezelle places herself in the circle around Ebony. 'What's going on?' I ask, coming up beside her.

She points with her chin to the lawn area where Prince Luca and six Prodigies have come out.

'Jordan, my young human friend.' Prince Luca notices me right away. His voice carries across the night air as clearly as if I was standing next to him. 'What a remarkable recovery.'

I'm not surprised. With my luck, why wouldn't he be right on my case?

'We meet face to face at last,' he says.

Eyes turn in my direction. But so far nobody suspects he's up to anything.

'I do hope we can still be friends after this.'

Uh-oh. After what? Then he's in my head, *Our meeting was so brief we didn't get a chance to debate the finer points of our arrangement. You remember, don't you, boy, where you take your mother's place in my world, and I set her free?*

He doesn't give me time to figure out what he's up to before a bolt of sheer heat spears into my chest and I can hardly breathe.

'Jordan!' I hear Thane call out.

Practically at the same time, Jezelle asks, 'Jordan, what's wrong?'

But it happens too fast. Prince Luca points his middle finger at me, curls and uncurls it. It flashes green, and before anyone moves, the Dark Prince drags me to him by whatever invisible force he speared into my chest. In a blink I'm passing everyone, half in the air, half dragging on the ground.

And the pain is excruciating.

Ebony screams, calls my name, demands someone help me, but it's already too late because here I am the next second, standing in front of Prince Luca while two Prodigies hold me upright.

*That's better*, the Dark Prince says.

'Release him!' Thane yells, his voice echoing across the ridge like thunder. 'Your business isn't with the boy.'

'You don't know much, do you?'

'What are you talking about, Luca?'

'I'm just making Ebony's decision easier for her.'

I can't see Thane, but I know he'll be frowning, suspicious, figuring it out. But Prince Luca is too fast tonight. He glances down at me. *Do your job, boy, and the pain will go away.*

I whisper hoarsely, 'What . . . do you want me . . . to do?'

*Nothing, actually.* His eyes are like the sun, so bright they hurt, but a glimpse is enough to show his hard evil core, and the pain twists as if he's turning a knife in my chest. I scream like a baby, beyond caring who hears.

But then the Dark Prince says, *Not bad, but I'm sure you can do better. Oh, and don't expect your friends to rescue you. They won't. They now have a dilemma, you or her, and, well, they don't care about you enough. They only care about their own kind.*

His men have a quiet chuckle as the prince plays with my mind. And then it hits me: he wants me to cry out so Ebony will choose to go with *him*! 'I . . . won't do it,' I hiss through my teeth.

He responds by stabbing me in the head with a spike of burning energy that arcs down the nerve line of my spine, forcing me to my knees. Gripping my head, I rock back and forth, biting down on my tongue, refusing to make a sound.

Glowering at me, he says, 'Idiot.' Then he hisses, 'No matter, it seems you have had the desired effect already – impressive.'

*Ebony.*

*She's taken the bait. I knew she couldn't resist, bound as she is to you. Well done, Jordan.*

Around me, his men stand rock still, their eyes gleaming admiration. The way they adore him sickens me.

*That's right, my future bride,* he coaxes as Ebony takes a first step towards him.

I try yelling at Ebony to go back, except I have nothing left. That last stab in my head has fried my brain. But I soon realise the closer Ebony gets, the less intense is my pain. Flicking the prince a quick look, I notice how he's riveted to Ebony's every movement, from the gentle swing of her arms to the graceful sway of her hips in the silky white dress. When she's halfway and walking among his precious Aracals, a predatory smile appears at the corners of his mouth that makes me want to slap him.

I glance at the angels and see Gabriel, Michael and Isaac holding Thane back.

Forcing my legs to move, I start walking, and by sheer willpower make my legs run. 'Ebony, Ebony, stop! What are you doing?'

She doesn't appear to see me. She's in a trance of some kind. Helpless to break through it, I run to the angels. 'Do something! Stop her, Thane!'

His eyes remain focused on Ebony's every step. 'I *tried*,' he whispers fiercely, finally glancing down at me. 'She insisted, and I can't force . . .' His words fade as he turns away from me, trembling with fear and shaking with rage.

'Michael!' I turn to the powerful golden angel as he slowly releases Thane. 'Do something! Stop her!'

I glance at Isaac and, as though ashamed to face me, he looks only at Shae, whose eyes are closed tight. She can't bear to watch. Tears stream down her face.

'What's wrong with you people? Isn't she one of your own? Or have you given up on her because of a decision *he* coerced her into making?'

Michael casts his look downward and I get it. 'But you already know that. Then, why?'

'You were hurting and she had to stop that,' Gabriel says, 'but then she asked whether, if she didn't go, he would kill you.'

'And you told her yes.'

'It's what we believe.'

'And, of course, you can't lie, even to save someone's life.'

Jezelle grabs my arm and spins me around. 'They don't have the right to stop her. And if they do, they'll be breaking our laws.'

Their emotional pain pulsates through me, so intense I can't bear to be near them. I race back to Ebony and grab her shoulders. She stops, but her eyes are looking straight through me. I shake her. 'Why are you doing this? Don't you know what it means? How would you feel never seeing any of us again? And he wants heirs, Ebony, from you!'

'I know what it means. Please, leave me, Jordan. This is best for everyone.'

She slides from my grip, and when she starts taking those final few steps the Dark Prince smiles, his eyes raking over her, and I know he's using a mind-link or something to keep her going.

I can't believe we're just going to let her go. It all comes back to Thane. He's the one person who has the capacity to stop her making the biggest mistake of her life.

I race back to him and stand with my arms crossed over my chest. 'Is it your pride? Is that it, Thane, your stupid, bloody pride?'

He stares at me blankly, his eyes red. 'What did you say, Jordan?'

'Are you through with Ebony because she's picking *him*?'

'That's outrageous. Of course not. She doesn't want *him*!'

'Did you just hear yourself? What's stopping you? And don't give me more of that "Free Will" crap. You just said she doesn't want him. Doesn't that mean she's not *really* choosing him? Dude, you're going to have to live with the knowledge that she sacrificed everything so you can all go home without a scratch on your perfect faces.'

His eyes widen and I spin around to see why. Ebony is so close now, no matter how much I beg, it's probably too late.

'You know why else she's doing this? How he got to her?' He looks at me then and I tell him, 'She hears *his* voice in her head, and not *yours*.'

'Ebony!' he calls out, his voice thundering across the field. '*Ebony, please, stop!*'

# 42

# Ebony

A sudden silence, as if everyone is holding their breath, draws me out of a strange stupor where a red haze clouds my senses. At the same time I hear a beautiful voice call to me.

'*Ebony, please, stop!*'

It's Nathaneal, his voice filled with so much passion, so much pain, I can't do anything but what he asks.

I hear him say softly, 'Michael, I have to do this. Will you support me?'

'Yes,' Michael replies without hesitation. 'It's time, Thane.'

'*No!*' Jezelle screams out. 'I do not support this foolish decision!'

I wish I knew what she's opposing.

'If you go ahead with this, Thane, everything could change. You will make us vulnerable to attack. War between the forces of light and darkness will be inevitable.'

Michael reasons, 'War has always been inevitable between us, Jez.'

She goes silent and Nathaneal says, 'Your disapproval has been noted, Jezelle. Uriel?'

One of the newly arrived angels replies, 'You have my eternal support, my prince.'

'Mine too,' another one of the reinforcements calls out, a girl.

'Thank you, Tash.'

I hear three more give their support, followed by a whirl of swirling movement crossing the lawn. And then Nathaneal is beside me, lifting me into his arms.

Prince Luca gasps, coming out of the trance he thought he still had me wrapped within. He realises his error just as Nathaneal turns to face him. 'If you value your soldiers, send them back to Skade immediately. I will give you one tenth of the time you gave Ebony to leave this world.'

Frowning, but not believing Thane has the power to follow through with his threat, Prince Luca laughs. 'You don't frighten me; you're still young. Granted, one day you could have had what it takes to be a worthy adversary. It's a pity you won't be in existence to test yourself against me then.' He notices Michael, who stopped a couple of metres back. 'Had your wings clipped, have you, Michael?'

Michael doesn't answer.

'There's always an opening for a disgraced angel of your calibre in my army. Tell you what, Michael, cross over to my side, bring Ebony with you, and I'll make you a general again.'

'I have not lost my rank, Luca. I choose to support Prince Nathaneal, and I look forward to this meeting tonight where instead of one adversary you will have two.'

Looking bored suddenly, Prince Luca turns to his left. 'Ensure Lady Ebony is taken directly to my private chambers.' And to the soldiers on his right, 'Teach this arrogant, inexperienced young angel who is the real master here.'

Nathaneal doesn't hang around a moment more. With me in his arms, he flies back to where the others stand and motions to Jordan to follow us into the forest.

Here, surrounded by tall eucalyptus trees, he sets me on my feet but doesn't let me go. 'Jordan,' he says, 'I want you to take Ebony and run deep into the forest. Head to the east-sector cabin I showed you with the safe room.'

Jordan nods. 'Don't worry. I'll protect Ebony with my life.'

'No matter what you hear, or see, no matter how terrifying, you must stay where you are. Do not return under any circumstances. I'll come find you when this is over.'

'Dude, don't worry about us, just do what you have to, and stay safe.'

Michael appears and without saying anything Nathaneal nods. He's leaving, and my heart trembles. He looks down at me, curled into his chest, and he strokes my hair. His touch sets my pulse racing.

'Come back to me,' I whisper. 'Please come back.'

He inhales a shuddering breath, tilts my face up with his thumb under my chin. His kiss is gentle and greedy, soft and fierce, everything and not enough.

Standing on my toes, I throw my arms around his neck, push my fingers into his hair to let him know how much I want him. Forgetting Michael, forgetting everything, we kiss until we are breathless.

# 43

# Jordan

I'm pretty sure Thane chose the cabin because it's the closest shelter with a safe room. But Ebony's refusing to budge
– and of course we both know I can't make her do anything
if she's not willing.

I try pleading. 'Ebony, *please*. Think of what Thane will
do to me.'

It doesn't work. She pats my shoulder as if I'm a well-
behaved dog. 'He won't do anything to you; he loves you
like a brother.'

'He loves *you* more! If something happens to you, I'm
dead. Besides, *I* don't want you getting hurt either. I kind of
love you too,' I add this last part softly.

Now she smiles as if I'm her favourite chocolate bar.
'And I love you, Jordan.'

It's hopeless. What chance would I have now? Telling her
how I feel would be a waste of time.

She edges closer to the sounds of voices ringing out.

The swish of an arrow whistling through the air has me
ducking. The battle has begun. I'm so tempted to watch,
but I gave Thane my word. 'Ebony, I promised to keep you
safe,' I say, reluctantly following her through the trees.

'Jordan, you don't understand.' She turns with her hands on her hips; her cheeks are flushed red, her violet eyes glistening under the full moon while the white dress swirls around her legs. 'This is about me. I can't just run away.'

'Oh, *I* get it, so you can run out and throw yourself at the mercy of the Dark Prince if things start looking bad for Thane.'

Her stare is fierce, so I know I'm right. 'You don't suppose Thane wanted you far away so you wouldn't do just that?'

She shrugs and continues edging closer to the battle. 'I might be able to help.'

I give it one last try. 'If Thane sees you, he might get distracted. Do you want that?'

This makes her pause. She hangs her head as she leans on a tree. 'It's dark. He won't see me.'

'Ebony!'

'I have to,' she whispers. We're close to the edge of the forest now and she starts climbing a nearby gum tree. The lowest branch is metres above the ground, but she scrambles up like a koala, turns around and gestures for me to follow.

I've climbed my fair share of trees, but Ebony is fast. She freezes suddenly as the screams of Aracals rend the air. It goes on for a long time, raising the hairs at the back of my neck. When they die down, Ebony goes back to climbing.

About a third of the way up, the house and yard come into view. Finally Ebony settles into position on a sturdy forked branch, tucking her dress in around her legs, and I squeeze in behind her.

Below, twelve of Skade's soldiers stand in squad formation facing our way, their backs to the house. Their black wings arch behind them. Prince Luca stands out in front, an aura of terror surrounding him, his double set of black wings undulating.

The angels' camp is almost directly below us. Peering sideways at Ebony, I see her eyes are focused on Thane, who's easy to pick out, standing alone and in front.

The Dark Prince lifts his arms out before him, reaching towards Thane, and flexes his fingers.

'Oh no,' Ebony whispers. 'What's he up to?'

Screams and gasps erupt from the angels below us. Ebony yelps at the same time. Fortunately I'm watching for something like this and I slap my hand over her mouth. In anguish she bites down on it, hard. But after my recent experience with an Aracal, it's nothing. Pain is what Thane is experiencing.

Prince Luca has set him alight! Flames encircle him from head to toe. He's in a fight for his life, maybe even for his immortality.

Michael and Isaac rush over to hold Gabriel back, though why they're stopping him from helping his brother I have no idea. Thane is on *fire*!

Seconds pass where no one does a thing. It's too hard to watch and too hard not to. Ebony turns her face into my chest.

I start to notice something incredible. The flames don't seem to be making contact with Thane's skin, and the reason is now becoming apparent. In the instant before the flames reached him, Thane deployed his wings, wrapping them around his body while releasing the metallic essence he once told me gives their feathers their special shine.

Doing this has provided him with precious moments to counter the flames with his own powers.

'Ebony. Ebony, look. I think it's all right.'

She allows herself a slight sideways glance.

It soon becomes evident to everyone watching that the flames are receding, leaving Thane untouched. Michael and Isaac release Gabriel, and everyone breathes again.

Ebony sits up and smiles nervously as the flames completely dissipate.

'That was awesome, Ebony. Maybe we have a chance.'

'I hope so, Jordan. I really hope so.'

Thane unfurls his wings. He's unscathed. He then releases his second set of wings and strides across the lawn, his four wings undulating like magnificent white and gold sails.

The Dark Prince can't take his eyes off Thane's wings, especially the smaller gold pair. With only a metre between them Thane stops.

'Impressive,' Prince Luca concedes. He glances at his own double set of black ones. 'Why would you have gold wings when I was born with black?' he murmurs, frowning.

If Thane knows, he's not telling.

Prince Luca waves his hand at Thane, trying to sound flippant but failing. Thane's gold wings have thrown the Dark Prince. 'This is what you thought would have me running with my tail between my legs?' he laughs, instilling his voice with a mocking tone. 'Being born with the four wings of a king doesn't automatically make you a king, whether one pair is gold, white, black or pink, Nathaneal.'

'Isn't that what *you* believed? You thought that your

double wings revealed your destiny, and that's why you fought so hard to usurp our High King.'

'The difference between us, Nathaneal, is that I was born to be king; your wings just make you a freak of your species.'

With this comment he lifts both his hands and points them towards the Brothers at the rear. Jets of blue flames shoot out from his fingers. Now he's setting the Brothers on fire! But Nathaneal throws up his own hands, stopping the flames from going past his open palms. They bounce off as if they're hitting a brick wall.

Prince Luca tries to lower his arms but finds he can't. He turns a venomous look on Thane. 'Release me!'

'Turn off the flames.'

Instead the Dark Prince yells out, 'Thorian! Ezekeal!'

Two Prodigies charge at Thane, but they bounce back as if Thane has applied a force field around himself.

Prince Luca hisses like a snake. It's a creepy sound and my skin crawls, but he calls off the flames and Thane releases his arms.

In swift retaliation, Prince Luca makes weird motions with his hands, as if he's mixing something. He starts throwing whatever it is across the yard. Once airborne they become bolts of lightning.

Screams pierce the air as they find their marks. One slices into a nearby tree with the noise of a jet fighter breaking the sound barrier. Man, it's deafening. The trunk splits in two almost all the way down.

The shockwave that follows almost unseats us both. We lock our arms around each other and our legs around the trunk as best we can until it passes.

'Holy, crap! That could have been us, Ebony. We gotta get down.'

'But it wasn't us,' she says stubbornly. Clearly she is not planning to withdraw any further yet.

Below, Jezelle is helping the injured, sending the more critical Brothers back to the monastery.

But the Dark Prince isn't finished. He bellows an order to attack, and angels from both the dark and light forces suddenly take to the air.

The opposing winged forces are an incredible sight, but it quickly turns ugly as the two sides clash. Isaac collides with a Prodigy right in front of us. They wrestle in the air, where their wings tangle and they both struggle to keep airborne. The Prodigy gets the upper hand, hurling Isaac head first towards the earth. Isaac rolls in the air, loses his equilibrium and plummets. He only just regains control in time to prevent himself smashing into the ground. I let out my breath as he starts flying upwards again. Once he's high enough he does a somersault with his knees tucked into his chest, then he straightens out, kicking both feet into the Prodigy's exposed gut.

*Boom!* The air vibrates with the collision.

It's a powerful hit, and this time the Prodigy goes down.

*Boom! Boom!* Others go down as angels pair off. Sparks from clashing swords shower down over the lawns. Small fires break out all around. It soon looks like the end of the world.

Neither side makes any significant gains because the angels are too evenly matched.

Michael sees an opportunity to bring an end to the battle

by taking out Prince Luca himself. He selects an arrow with a gold tip and carefully takes aim from across the yard. The arrow slices the air and would be a direct strike were it not for the Prodigy called Ezekeal, who dives in front of his master, taking the hit instead.

Prince Luca goes berserk. He points one of his lethal flame-throwing hands at Thane, but Thane's wings are an impenetrable barrier, so the prince shifts his attention to Gabriel and shoots out white-hot flames. He strikes Gabriel in the chest, lifting the big guy into the air, holding him there with just the force of the flames, then he flicks his wrist in a downward motion, sending Gabriel careering to the ground. Jezelle rushes to his side.

Ebony covers her face with both hands.

I tug them down gently. 'Are you OK?'

She whispers, 'I heard his spine crack, and his leg break in three places.'

'*ENOUGH!*' Thane roars. 'Withdraw now!'

'Withdraw?' Prince Luca glowers at Thane. 'I don't answer to a foolish nonentity.' He raises his hands to the stars, twirling his fingers in an anticlockwise direction. Great clouds, black as oil drawn from the bowels of the earth, gather overhead, swirling at terrifying speeds. They obliterate the moon, submerging us into an inky darkness, until electricity begins sizzling inside and the clouds start hailing lightning bolts on everyone.

Jezelle leaves Gabriel to attend to a Brother who is writhing on the grass with terrible burns. She's working hard at healing the injured, but the number is rising.

Everyone scatters except Thane. He stands straight and

still in the centre of the yard, his eyes closed as he draws on his powers. He doesn't allow anything to distract him, not even the lightning hitting the ground and erupting into fires around him.

Michael commands the remaining Brothers to withdraw into the forest and then flies through the lightning and fires to stand behind Thane. The other angels follow, also falling in behind Thane, their faces sombre because they know what's about to happen.

Thane raises his hands with his palms facing Prince Luca. The Dark Prince and his soldiers have regrouped. They appear curious to see what other powers Thane might have. One or two even laugh mockingly. Clearly they think he hasn't got anything more powerful than what he's already revealed.

It's like watching the eye of a cyclone passing directly overhead. This is the pause before the storm returns its full fury. And then a silvery wind bursts from Thane's palms.

Ebony notices what's happening before me and points to the gardens. The lawn and everything in front of Thane is drying up. The flowering shrubs around the house are shrivelling up too, as if all the moisture inside them is evaporating. Overhead, the full moon reappears, bathing everything in its bright light. I watch as the wind passes through the forest like a wave, and every tree it hits drops its leaves. The sound of thousands of dried leaves falling to the ground combined with the hissing of Thane's wind is so eerie it will probably haunt my dreams for a long time.

Ebony's eyes have turned to the Dark Prince and his soldiers. 'The Prodigies are dehydrating like the trees,' she says. 'Their flesh, muscles, organs, everything is shrinking.'

I watch, speechless, as they shrivel up, until their loose skin hangs off their bones. Their deep eye sockets look gruesome. Even their wings hang awkwardly, their feathers dry and brittle like hay. I am horrified but mesmerised as the fierce wind still pumps out of Thane's palms. His power overrides everything Prince Luca is doing to try to stop him.

One by one the Prodigies fall.

Thane knew it would come down to this. He warned Prince Luca, gave him plenty of opportunities to withdraw.

Prince Luca stares at his Prodigies, aghast. So far he's resisted the wind, but it's too powerful even for him, and everything he tries only ends up tiring him more. His resistance finally fails. Horrified, his eyes take in the shrinking flesh of his arms, first one, and then the other. He touches the shrivelling skin of his face, the loose skin hanging at his throat, and releases an ear-shattering scream.

The Dark Prince drops to his knees among the soldiers who have collapsed around him. But Prince Luca is not one to stay down. He climbs to his feet and wraps his cloak around his skeletal body. His eyes are gaping sockets in his gaunt face. He collects his weakened soldiers, helping them to stand, then turns to Thane with a dark warning in his eyes. 'You have earned yourself a victory this night.' He looks around at the devastation with something like awe. 'I underestimated your powers. But I will come back to collect my bride before she reaches her eighteenth year, that I promise. Nothing will stop me. Heed my warning, Prince Nathaneal. I don't make the same mistake twice.'

He closes his eyes, his gaunt face intense with concentration. I wonder what he's doing until I spot the slight tilt of Thane's head. Prince Luca is mind-linking. Ebony gasps. She's hearing it too. In his weak state, the Dark Prince is probably unable to select who hears and who doesn't.

'Um, Ebs, what's he saying to Nathaneal?'

She says softly, 'He's ordering him to . . .'

She stops and her face turns red.

'To what?'

'Protect my virtue.'

I glance at the two enemies facing each other, the victor and the fallen who both want the same girl – the girl who strangely shares a bond with *me*. Well, I may be just a simple human, but I'd like to see their faces if she picked me. If only she would.

But Thane's not the type to gloat over a victory, and even though he has put the Dark Prince out of action for a long time, he doesn't look happy. His face is pained as he looks around the forest. Did I say forest? There's not much left.

'I will ensure that you *never* make Ebony your bride,' Thane says. 'And I may not have permission to annihilate you completely this night, but the next time we meet I will end your free roaming of the Earth.'

'Until you become king, which will never happen, you don't have the right to break a treaty.'

'Call your Death Watchers home, Luca. Your time of gathering human souls is coming to an end.'

Under the first rays of a new dawn, with his weakened soldiers supporting each other, Prince Luca begins his long journey home.

As soon as the weary group disappears from view, Ebony looks for my hand, the one she sunk her teeth into earlier. She lifts it and gasps at the sizeable indentation her teeth made. Taking it to her mouth, she kisses the wound softly, her face wet with tears of relief, and a million other emotions, I suppose.

'You're a good friend, Jordan Blake. You're a rare breed and there should be more of you.'

'One more of *you* is all I want.'

She is surprised at the emotion in my admission and searches my face. What am I supposed to do now? Deny what my heart is saying? I can't exactly walk away or pretend I was joking. She reaches up and pats the side of my face.

Now that it's out there, I may as well give it a shot. 'There's something strong between us, Ebony. I feel it.'

'I do too,' she admits. 'When Jezelle was healing you, I "saw" you with my mind; that's how strong this bond is.'

'Don't you think there's a reason you can do that with me and not with Thane?'

She shrugs and her eyes become teary. 'There's so much I don't understand, but . . .'

'But what?'

'I love Nathaneal.'

'You hardly know him, Ebony.'

'It doesn't matter. It's as if my life began with him and ends with him. And I'm sorry if that sounds melodramatic, it's honestly how I feel.'

'What if it's a mistake, and you just got swept up by all of this?'

'It's not a mistake.'

'But how do you know?'

She shrugs and points to her heart. 'It's in here. I'm sorry, Jordan.'

'Forget it. I knew I couldn't compete with an angel. I'll just have to wait until he goes home to his fiancée.' It just comes out, and once it's out, I can't take it back.

'What did you say?'

'Nothing. Let it go.'

'Tell me. Is it true? Nathaneal has a fiancée back in Avena?'

'That's what he told me.'

'Did he tell you her name?' Her voice sounds as if it's coming from far away.

'No, only that he has to complete his quest here before he's free to marry her.'

'And that "quest" is finding me, right?'

I nod and look down. I feel awful for telling her like this, but Thane should have told her himself before he kissed her.

On the ground everyone is congratulating Thane, with embraces and pats on the back. Gabriel, walking slowly and with a limp, gives his brother a big bear hug. Jezelle throws herself into his arms with a mega-million-bucks smile.

'Is it . . . is it *her?*' Ebony asks in a husky, breaking voice.

'I don't know, Ebony.' It's the truth. 'We should get down from here now.'

'In a minute,' she says. Her bottom lip is trembling.

The last of the night's stars are giving way to a new dawn. In the yard below us Thane finds himself momentarily alone. He closes his eyes, throws his head back. He's savouring the taste of victory, and by the smile spreading across his face, that taste is pretty darn sweet.

But then he opens his eyes and spots the two of us in the tree. For a second he can't believe what he's seeing. He's shocked, but his smile is indulgent, and his expression says he should have known better than to think Ebony would run away and hide. The victory is making his thoughts more generous than they otherwise would be, I can tell. But his smile gradually dissolves and a frown takes its place.

It doesn't take a genius to figure out why.

Just one look at Ebony's devastated face.

## 44

## Ebony

Getting down the tree proves harder than climbing up. This could be because my legs feel oddly powerless, as if they don't belong to my body any more.

Jordan scoots down around me in a big rush to get away, but when we hit the ground I grab his hand.

Of course, Nathaneal is waiting at the bottom. I take a deep breath and look up to his face without connecting with his eyes. I can't do that *and* say the words I need to say. 'You were amazing out there. Thank you.'

He continues to frown at me, knowing there's more. His eyes lower to my hand holding Jordan's tight, and his frown deepens. Jordan tries to pull away, but I don't let him. He's not going anywhere. If he really loves me, as he just professed, he should be willing to hold my hand during a few difficult minutes of my life.

'You're welcome,' Nathaneal says, his eyes shifting from mine to Jordan and back again.

'I suppose you and your, um, colleagues will be leaving now,' I begin by saying.

'The others will be leaving shortly, yes, but I will be

staying. I thought you understood that I would remain here on Earth to train you.'

'But your mission is complete so I thought —'

'Ebony, what's this about?'

'I'm releasing you from the rest of your mission or quest, or whatever you call it. You found me, you eradicated the danger, and so your job here is done.'

I take a deep breath, a *very* deep breath. I can't stand to see his face racked with confusion. *I* put that look there.

But no, *he* did this to *me*, especially with that kiss!

*That kiss!*

My lips tingle with the memory. I bite down on my lower lip hard in an attempt to exchange the pleasure of that memory for pain. It works, but only after I taste blood. 'I'd only require training if I were planning to return with you. But I'm not. I'm staying here on my farm, to run it in my parents' absence. It's . . . it's . . . my obligation.'

Nathaneal looks at Jordan and says, 'Will you leave us for a moment?'

'He stays,' I say.

'Ebony, is this about what just happened? I sent you into the forest so you wouldn't see . . . to protect you —'

'It's not that. It has nothing to do with that. It's just that your job is done here, and I'm not going to live in a foreign world all by myself.'

He takes a step towards me, but I lift up my hand to stop him.

'Ebony, you would soon make friends. You have family there, and I would be by your side as much or as little as you wish.'

'I don't know how it's done in your world, but here, at least for the most part, humans have one partner for life.'

He addresses Jordan, his voice growing dark. 'What did you tell her while you were perched in your little nest together?'

It's then that Isaac, Michael and the other angels join us. Instantly they know something is wrong. The big smile on Shae's face drops. 'What's going on, Thane?' When he doesn't answer, she turns and asks me directly, 'Ebrielle, what's going on?'

'It's Ebony.'

'All right then: *Eb-o-nee*. Is that the problem, that we forget your name sometimes?'

'Of course it's not that.' I flounder as I try to explain. 'I can't just up and leave. I haven't finished school. I have a farm to run. Horses. My parents are still missing.'

Shae smiles carefully and steps closer. 'But you're one of us.'

'This is, um, happening too fast. I need time to grow used to the idea of being an ... an ... See, I can't even say the word. And the one thing that made me think maybe I am one of you has disappeared. Without wings I'll be a freak in your world.'

Shae looks at me, frowning, but what am I supposed to tell them? The guy I fell in love with strung me along with words I wanted to hear so he could finish his quest as quickly as possible and get back to his fiancée?

'And where would I live?'

'Ebony, on your return to Avena you will live in my house, of course,' Nathaneal says, his eyes meeting mine.

'I have plenty of room. You will have an entire wing to yourself.'

'Don't you think you should run that past your fiancée first?'

My question causes uproar.

Shae asks me where I heard that, and then accuses Jezelle of rumour-mongering.

Confused, I ask Jordan softly, 'What did I say?'

He shrugs, and looks away to avoid eye contact.

Nathaneal's eyes close — he's probably embarrassed at being caught out in front of his friends. When he opens them, they shimmer with self-disgust.

Well, he should be disgusted with himself!

He tries to take my hand, but I pull away and everyone falls silent. He's not going to worm his way out of this. I look directly into his eyes. 'I know you have a fiancée in Avena waiting patiently for you to complete your quest. That's why I'm setting you free from the last part of the mission, so you can return home to her.'

Gabriel limps up to his brother and pats his shoulder with an amused glint in his eye. 'You have some explaining to do, brother.'

'Whatever excuses you offer up, I'm not changing my mind,' I say. 'I may be young and naive, but I'm not stupid, and I'm not going to Avena with you.'

Shae gasps and I turn to her quickly. 'I'm sorry, Shae.'

'Don't you want to meet your family? This news will crush our parents. Don't you care?' She turns away and smothers her face in Isaac's shoulder.

'I don't mean to hurt you.'

'It's too late,' she murmurs, and the two of them leave hurriedly after embracing Nathaneal.

I know they don't understand how I feel, but since finding out about Nathaneal's fiancée, I can't bear the thought of living on Avena and seeing him with another woman, holding her, kissing her.

I catch a look between Gabriel and Michael that reeks of disappointment.

'The law of our world is that you cannot be forced,' Michael says. 'This decision is one you must make, but I beg you, Ebony, to think carefully. If and when you change your mind, you won't be able to make the Crossing on your own.

'You know you're still in grave danger here, Ebony? The Earth is Prince Luca's free hunting zone. It's part of the treaty agreed a millennium ago, with another millennium still to go before it runs its course.'

'You remain unprotected,' Gabriel chimes in.

'The ritual?' I ask.

'That's right.'

So far Jordan has remained quiet, but something makes him finally speak up. '*Man,* with all that's happened in such a short time, it's a wonder she can think straight at all. You're all being too hard on her. Ebony shouldn't leave until she's ready. But don't worry, I'll watch over her. I'll keep a close eye on her.'

Nathaneal says, 'Thank you, Jordan, but I'm not returning home until Ebony is ready. You won't have to carry the responsibility of protecting her on your own.'

I drop Jordan's hand and poke my finger in Nathaneal's chest. 'Don't you stay on my account! This world is not your home. Go back to Avena, where you have a fiancée waiting for you! Don't you think she's missing you? Haven't you stayed away long enough because of me? You would end up hating it here, and hating me because of that.'

'Ebony, I could never hate you.' He sees me frown and adds softly, 'That would be impossible.'

Michael sighs. 'Ebony, Earth is not your home either, and as for Nathaneal's fiancée, where did you hear that?'

I glance at Jordan. The angels follow my gaze and under their scrutiny he steps backwards until he hits the tree.

Jordan says he loves me. Something like hope blossoms inside me, but fear that I'm on the wrong track keeps it down. 'Jordan, did you make it up?'

'No! I swear! Thane told me about her.'

'It's true,' Nathaneal says, and my blossoms shrivel up and die. 'But she's not waiting for me at home.'

'I beg your pardon?'

Muffled laughter wafts over from the other angels. Nathaneal sends them a withering look and they stop. 'She's not waiting for me at home because she's here.'

'Your fiancée is living here? Who is it? Do I know her?'

'Ebony, I didn't want to tell you like this.'

'Like what, Nathaneal?'

'I get it!' Jordan hits himself in the forehead with the palm of his hand. 'It all fits. I'm such an idiot! Why didn't I realise sooner?' he mutters, then looks directly up at Nathaneal. 'It makes sense – why you searched the entire planet from one pole to the other to find her, and now that you have, you can't leave.'

Nathaneal stares back at Jordan without agreeing or

denying the 'accusation', if that's what it is. His narrowed eyes look as if he's trying to suss out how Jordan feels.

'Well, I don't like it,' Jordan tells him. 'In fact, I'm really pissed off . . . How do I compete with an angel? An angel Ebony happens to think is beautiful and perfect?'

I yank on his arm when I hear him say this. 'I never said those things to you.'

He shrugs. 'I know you think them because they're in your eyes every time you look at him.'

He points a finger at Nathaneal. 'I'm right, aren't I? Ebony is really –'

'If you know what's good for you, Jordan,' Nathaneal tells him, 'you'll keep this information quiet for the moment.'

Michael, Gabriel and Jezelle burst out laughing and take this moment to say their goodbyes. They each embrace Nathaneal, and wish me good luck. Jezelle apologises to Nathaneal for leaving him with a beat-up Porsche, and then they walk off through the forest, or what used to be the forest.

Meanwhile, my patience runs out. When it's just the three of us, I put my hands on my hips and stare pointedly at Nathaneal and then at Jordan. 'One of you had better tell me what's going on.'

Nathaneal seems to melt with softness when his eyes meet mine. 'Ebony, I wanted to tell you. It was just too soon.'

I squint at him, then glance at Jordan, needing some clear answers, but he just throws his hands in the air and says, 'Sorry, Ebony, but I know what's good for me.'

I stare at Nathaneal. He takes my left hand and, without

taking his eyes from mine, he kisses my wrist so lightly his lips could be mistaken for a feather. I feel tingles from his touch go all the way to my toes.

'Sweetheart, I didn't tell you because I didn't want to frighten you, and, well . . . I held out a hope that you would remember who you are.'

'Will you tell me now?'

'I would rather tell you in the comfort of my home where we don't have to concern ourselves with anyone who might be listening.'

'I need to know now, Nathaneal. My whole life has been a lie.'

'I promise to always tell you the truth.'

He brings my hands up between us, drawing me in close to his body, then leans down so that our foreheads are touching. 'In Avena, certain facets of our lives are preordained. My marriage is one of those.'

'Ohhh.'

So now I understand. It's an arranged marriage. My heart lifts a little at this news. He probably doesn't love her. The way he kissed me, he *can't* love her. I know it's me he loves now.

'Can you get out of it somehow?'

He shakes his head.

'So why are you smiling?'

'Because my fiancée is you, Ebony.'

'Me? *Me!*'

He smiles and brings his mouth so close to mine I'm tempted to forget anything else he has to say and drag his head down to kiss me.

'OK, I'm out of here,' Jordan says, sounding annoyed. 'Hand me the keys, will you, Thane. I'll give you some privacy and go collect the Lambo.'

Nathaneal digs into his pocket and throws Jordan the keys. 'Take your time.'

We watch Jordan run off through the forest, and when he's no longer in sight Nathaneal picks me up in his arms and swings me around. When he stops, but before I stop laughing, he brings his face in close, his beautiful blue eyes melding with mine, and he whispers, 'I found you at last.'

'It took you long enough.'

He laughs and I wind my fingers through his hair and pull him down to me. Against his lips I whisper, 'I'm glad you're staying.'

'The first time you were kidnapped I was too young to protect you, but that's not the case now. I promise you, Ebony, no one will separate us again.'

# 45

## Jordan

My life sucks. It always has and now it sucks even more. Thane promised it would get better once we found his kidnapped angel. But he lied. He lies all the time – by omission, of course, because angels don't lie.

Ha! Omission is more deceitful than straight-out lying, if you ask me. At least humans tell it to your face whether you like it or not.

How could he *omit* telling me his fiancée is Ebony? I mean, really, come on, man, how could he not find one lousy minute to break the news?

The thing is, I met Ebony first, and it was way before he came on the scene. I know that doesn't mean I have some kind of claim over her. It's just I knew, from the moment she rammed me into the brick wall on that night we first met, Ebony was the girl of my dreams.

'Sucks, doesn't it?'

I stop dead in my tracks. Where did that voice come from? I spin around outside the monastery's front gate where Thane's car is parked. I can't see anyone so I click the key and unlock the doors. Taking another look around, I climb in the driver's side, switch on the motor and wait for its purr to calm me.

Ready to take off, I click my seat belt. Then I catch sight of something moving in my rear-view mirror. I look over my shoulder and jump, practically hitting the roof. 'What are you doing here? How did you get in?'

'You'd be surprised at what I can do now,' Adam Skinner says, sliding into the passenger seat.

There's something weird going on here. Goose pimples break out over my arms and a shiver zings up the back of my neck.

Even his laugh is strange, changing pitch from deep to high. 'What's the matter, dude? Aren't you pleased to see me?'

Though he sounds like Skinner, there's something not right. 'Well, *dude*, what do you want?'

He stares at me with a big goofy grin on his face that's just not him. And his usual brown eyes are black. How could that happen?

'In a hurry, are we? Can't wait to watch the girl of your dreams being carried away on an angel's white wings?'

I put the Lambo into gear and take off, burning rubber. I'm not in the mood for this. 'I don't know what you're up to, but I'm about to pick Nathaneal up and he'll know just what to do with you.'

He's quiet as we reach the part of the forest devastated by recent events. 'Stop,' he says, and for no good reason I can think of, I do what he says. There's something macabre about him today. If I play nice, maybe he'll piss off quickly.

He points across the dead forest to where in the distance Thane and Ebony are lip-locked.

'You brought me here to show me them kissing?'

'We have a mutual friend.'

'We do?'

'Yes, and you know him very well.'

'Tell me what you want and get out.'

'You don't scare me, Blake.'

'Yeah? Well, you don't scare me either!'

The second I say the words I regret them. His eyes roll up so only the whites are showing, he opens his mouth and an animal's voice screams out of it, like a rampaging chimp.

'What the crap is going on with you, Skinner?'

He smiles. 'I'm a messenger.'

'If you're talking about Prince Luca, I've got nothing to fear from him for a long time. Is he your hero these days? By the way, why aren't you locked up?'

'He gave me freedom and power and many other skills that are going to come in handy during this life.'

'I hate to burst your bubble, dude, but at what cost?'

He laughs. 'That's the beauty – I don't have to answer to you or anyone any more.'

Nathaneal and Ebony start walking towards us. 'They've seen the car. You'd better go.'

'Not before I deliver my message.'

'*Arghh*, for pity's sake, man, what is it?'

Sharp pain sears my brain. I don't know how, but Skinner's doing it even though he's not moving a thing, just piercing me with his eyes, darkened to almost all black. How strong is he now? I lift my hand – about the only thing I can move. 'Enough, man.' But he doesn't stop. 'Stop! I've had enough!'

Painstakingly slowly, he withdraws. 'Remember the dream you had where you made a deal with the King of Skade?'

I take a deep breath and swallow to make my mouth work. 'How do you know about that?'

'Do you remember, Jordy? Answer the question!'

'OK! Yes, I remember! I die and he takes my soul and releases my mother's.'

'Perfect. Well, he wants you to know he's a generous king and is willing to release you from the covenant.'

'Are you serious? Wait – what about my mother?'

He nods. 'She will be released to Solomon.'

'What does he want me to do in return?'

He laughs and nods in the direction of Thane and Ebony, walking towards us with their hands clasped together. 'It's simple. Split those two asunder. Do whatever it takes.'

'Are you nuts? Look at them!'

'Prince Luca may be physically wrecked at the moment, but his mind is still working perfectly and so are his armies of angels and demons.'

'And what are you?'

'You could say I'm a friend, his Earthly representative, and, of course, the messenger. So what is your answer, Jordan? Will you do it?'

'How much time do I have to do this?'

He snorts. 'Haven't you figured it out yet? The magical number for angels, light and dark?'

'Eighteen.'

'Jackpot.'

'So I have at least a year.'

'Let me give you some advice,' he says as he casually leans into my window from the outside.

'What the . . . ?' I glance at my suddenly vacant passenger

seat and back to where he's now resting his elbows on my driver's side window. 'How did you do that?'

He simply grins. 'Don't leave it too long before you start. You don't want to die before you break them apart, or all contracts are void and your mother stays in Skade.'

'But, how will I know when . . . it's my time to . . . you know?'

'Die?'

I nod, and quickly work moisture into my mouth. 'Will I make it to eighteen?'

'I seriously have no idea. I'm just warning you. But, mate, with your luck, you should start breaking them apart today.'

# Acknowledgements

I would like to take this opportunity to thank the people who helped create this book.

Firstly, my readers: Amanda Canham for her talented insights, ideas and critiques; Danielle Curley, for her invaluable comments; and Chris Canham for his important male perspective and honesty, even though he was analysing his mother-in-law's work!

A big thank you to Ele Fountain, a brilliant editor I have been lucky to work with on all five of my books. Isabel Ford for the line-editing and I am sure a million other things, as well as everyone else in the Bloomsbury offices – London, Australia and New York – who has had a hand in bringing *Hidden* to publication. I appreciate everything you have done to make this book happen.

To my wonderful agent, Geoffrey Radford, thank you for your help and support and belief that I could come back from the brink and deliver a work to be proud of.

And to my sister Therese, your belief in this story from inception to publication was truly inspiring. We have shared blood, sweat and tears, and I love you with all my heart.

And finally the two men in my life – my husband John and son Chris, for all your uplifting and motivating conversations, thank you both.

This book
belongs to

Kristin

...a Woman After
God's Own Heart

GROWTH AND
STUDY GUIDE

# A Woman
## After
## God's Own
# Heart®

*Elizabeth George*

HARVEST HOUSE PUBLISHERS

EUGENE, OREGON

*Cover by Garborg Design Works, Minneapolis, Minnesota*

*Cover photo © Muneyuki Nishimura/Solus Photography/Veer*

## Acknowledgment

As always, thank you to my dear husband, Jim George, M.Div., Th.M., for your able assistance, guidance, suggestions, and loving encouragement on this project.

**A WOMAN AFTER GOD'S OWN HEART® GROWTH & STUDY GUIDE**
Copyright © 2001, 2006 by Elizabeth George
Published by Harvest House Publishers
Eugene, Oregon 97402
www.harvesthousepublishers.com

ISBN-13: 978-0-7369-1884-8

**Printed in the United States of America**

09 10 11 12 13 14 15 / BP-CF / 15 14 13 12 11 10 9 8 7 6 5

# Contents

# A Word of Welcome

Please let me welcome you to this fun—and stretching!—updated and expanded growth and study guide for women like you who want to live out God's priorities. And please let me commend you for taking your journey toward becoming a woman after God's own heart one step further.

## A Word of Instruction

The exercises in this study guide should be easy to follow and to work. You'll need your copy of the updated and expanded book *A Woman After God's Own Heart*®[1] and your Bible, a pen, a dictionary, and a heart ready to grow. In each lesson you'll be asked to:

- Read the corresponding chapter from *A Woman After God's Own Heart*®.

- Answer the questions designed to guide you to greater growth.

- Select a verse or two that relate to the exercises to memorize and to hide in your heart.

- Pray about and put into action the priority discussed.

- Write out a brief paragraph of how this chapter influenced your actions in choosing God's priorities.

## A Word for Your Group

Of course, you can grow (volumes!) as you work your way, alone, through these truths from God's Word and apply them to your heart and home. But I urge you to share the journey with other women. A group, no matter how small or large, offers personal care and interest. There is sharing. There are sisters-in-Christ to pray for you. There is the mutual exchange of experiences. There is accountability. And, yes, there is peer pressure...which always helps us get our lessons done! And there is sweet, sweet encouragement as together you stimulate one another to greater love and greater works of love (Hebrews 10:24).

To aid the woman who is guided by God to lead a group, I've included two sections in the back of this growth and study book:

- Discussion questions written for your group
- Instructions on how to lead a group discussion

## A Word of Encouragement

What is it worth, dear one, to have a heart and a home that honor God and are pleasing in His eyes? Is it worth spending a few minutes a day or a few hours in a week internalizing the principles found in *A Woman After God's Own Heart*® and in this growth and study guide?

What I'm offering you is the opportunity to take what you're learning to a deeper level and to work it out in your home and family, to live out what you know you want to do and be—a woman after God's own heart.

If you will use the insights, tools, and how-to's gained from the book *A Woman After God's Own Heart*® and from this study guide, by God's grace and with His help, people who know you will begin to describe *you* as a woman after God's own heart. Your ways will bring glory to Him. It's work, I know that. But it's also joy—the deep joy of knowing God's will and doing God's will. So please, enjoy the journey...for the rest of your life!

# 1

# *A Heart Devoted to God*

❀

In your personal copy of *A Woman After God's Own Heart*®,[1] read chapter 1, "A Heart Devoted to God." What meant the most to you from this chapter or offered you the greatest challenge or inspired you deeply?

*Commit myself, all that I am, all that I have to God daily. My body, health, husband, children C, M, E, home, possessions to do with as He will. Use me as you will, time, plans, purposes, desires, hopes, destinations, work out your whole will in my life @ any cost now + forever*

*Daily*

Did you enjoy observing the contrast between the two sisters, Mary and Martha? I know that carefully considering their lives touched mine (in more ways than one!). Read their story in your Bible in Luke 10:38-42. Try to imagine the scene yourself. For instance...

Where did the story take place? *Bethany*

And what was going on? *dinner, conversation in living room*

Who were the people present? *Mary, Martha, Jesus, Laz? others?*

How did Martha act...and why? *busy time*

And how did Mary act?    *sat to listen*

What were Jesus' words to Martha?    *much troubled about many thi*

And His words to Mary?

Martha was so busy doing things *for* the Lord that she failed to spend time *with* Him. Mary, however, put worship at the top of her to-do list. As a woman after God's own heart, Mary made a choice that indicated *a heart of devotion*. She knew it was important to cease her busyness, stop all activity, and set aside secondary things in order to focus wholly on the Lord. List at least five actions you can take to put worship at the top of your to-do list.

1. *1st thing time*

2. *pray + worship first*

3. *read it " to Mom*

4. *learn a verse*

5. *daily prayer of commitment*

Write out what you will do daily—just for this next week—to…

…cease your busyness,

…stop all activity, and

…set aside secondary things

in order to focus wholly on the Lord. Then give thought to this quote:

> Modern civilization is so complex as to make the devotional life all but impossible. It wears us out by multiplying distractions and beats us down by destroying our solitude, where otherwise we might drink and renew our strength before going out to face the world again.[2]

♡ Do you have a dictionary nearby? Look up the definition of the word "priority" and write it out as simply as you can here. *Something*

*1. The fact or condition of being prior precedence in time, order, importance, etc.* *that must receive attention before*
*3. Something given prior attention* *other things*

Now, purpose to choose God as your first and ultimate priority by having a daily time with Him. I've provided a "Quiet Times Calendar" at the back of the *A Woman After God's Own Heart®* book. Just fill in the squares for each day that you have a quiet time. Remember that the goal is solid lines like a thermometer—not a "morse code" measurement (dot-dot-dash) or a "measles" measurement (here a dot, there a dot)! I know you'll be blessed, just as the woman who wrote this was:

> I have been attempting to have daily quiet times for awhile now. This past week, however, I found that having to actually record the days I had my quiet time has encouraged me to be more faithful with them. Instead of brushing it aside in the morning, I chose to have it, even if it couldn't be as long as I hoped for.

♡ And while you've got the dictionary out, go ahead and look up the definition of the word "worship" and, again, write it out as simply as you can here. *reverence, devotion (admiration, intense gratitude, awe, values worthship create i. the quality, condition, or state of*

Now, make a schedule for next week that includes a scheduled "quiet time" with God in His Word and in prayer. (And don't forget—*something is better than nothing!* Aim for consistency. Begin with even a brief time each day. Great lives are made up of many "little" disciplines! Begin the "little" discipline of meeting with the Lord daily and then filling in your Quiet Times Calendar.)

♡ Another help discussed on page 21 was Proverbs 3:6. Read this verse in your Bible and write it out here. *In all my ways acknowledge him and He shall direct my paths*

Now, purpose to actively choose God and His ways at every decision, word, moment, thought, and step—today and every day of the week. This is what it means to make God your ultimate priority, to walk with Him moment by moment and step by step. Your heart's desire should be to prefer God and His ways in all things. Ask God these questions before you speak or act:

> What do You want me to say? Lord, what do You want me to do?

♡ Another valuable principle in the "Yes, But How?" section of your book was:

> Good, better, best,
> never let it rest,
> until your good is better,
> and your better best.

Can you think of any area in your life where you are consciously settling for *good* when you know that a *better* and a *best* choice are available? Make a note of it here…and then set out to make God's better way your way.

*tongue consistency*

 **Verses to Memorize**—Luke 10:42 and Proverbs 3:6. Why not hide in your own heart these verses that speak of a heart after God?

*Luke 10:42 but (only) one thing is necessary for Mary has chosen the good part, which shall not be taken away from her*

 **A Heartfelt Prayer**—Lord, just for today, help me to cultivate a hot heart by…

*remembering you*

On the following page, relate in 100 words or less one instance when you were aware that you actively chose God as a priority over something or someone else this week. Then thank God for that opportunity.

*Bible study before reading paper*
*done, not squeezed out.*

*Words from My Heart*

# 2

# *A Heart Abiding in God's Word*

In your copy of *A Woman After God's Own Heart*® read chapter 2, "A Heart Abiding in God's Word." What meant the most to you from this chapter or what offered you the greatest challenge or inspired you deeply?

*· Shipbuilders selecting tree for mast; on top of hill, clearing all trees around it → strengthened by wind + weather (roping)*

*· Iceberg; being judged by what's on top, supported by what's beneath*

*· thought of 2 hrs / day ē Lord + His word*

*· "  "  woman I'd like to be in 1 yr*

*"  "      in 10 yrs*

## Drawing Life from God's Word

"Am I flourishing or failing? Thriving or wilting? Blossoming or withering?" These are questions we would do well to ask ourselves regularly about our spiritual condition. And abiding in God's Word is one sure way to develop a root system that causes us to draw from the Lord all we need to enjoy a flourishing, thriving, blossoming life. Let's take a few minutes to learn more about roots.

♥ *Roots are unseen*—How is your "underground" life, the time you spend abiding in God's Word and prayer out of sight, alone, in secret? Before we move on, search your heart

15

and jot down a few honest answers to this all-important question.

*could be improved*

What is the first word of Psalm 1, a psalm that spends three verses describing a woman (or man) who is flourishing, thriving, and blooming? *Blessed*

How does the person of Psalm 1 approach the Word of God according to verse 2a?

*His delight is in the law of the Lord*

And what does she do (verse 2b) with what she finds in God's Word?

*in His law he meditates day + night*

Note the results listed in verse 3 that come from time spent in God's Word:

*He will be like a tree (firmly) planted by streams/canals of water, Which yields its fruit in its season + its leaf does not wither; + in whatever he does, he prospers*

Make a schedule for this week that includes a time each day to withdraw from people, projects, and pressures to spend unseen, private time alone with God, nurturing your roots with His Word and communing with Him. And don't forget to say "no" to a few "things."

> We must say "no" not only to things which are wrong and sinful, but to things pleasant, profitable, and good which would hinder and clog our grand duties and our chief work.[3]

♥ *Roots are for taking in*—Consider again my friend Karen and her time of "taking in" on pages 33-34. Are you more like the breathless, frazzled, fretting, and worrying women in that scenario—or are you more like Karen, recognizing <u>the need to slip away for a few minutes alone with the Lord when tensions mount?</u> Write down an honest answer about how you tend to handle the pressures of life. Consider, too, how those closest to you would answer this question about you!

*frazzle; need to become more calm.*

*(Fred O.B. saw me on knees in back room after I'd whizzed by him distressed*

CONTEXT W610 *help*
*afflicted,*
*famish*
*yourself*

This is a good time to look at Isaiah 58:11 in your Bible. Here God describes the blessings that will be poured out upon those who seek after God in <u>the right ways</u>. List them here:

*+ the LORD will continually guide you.*
*+ satisfy your desire in scorched places + give strength to your bones*
*+ you will be like a watered garden,*
*+ like a spring of water whose waters don't fail*

How can you remember to sink your roots down deeper to take in the "waters [that] do not fail" when life heats up?

*In its midst, go to LORD*

♥ *Roots are for storage*—When I go through tough and trying times, I try to think of every verse of Scripture that I've memorized that can help me through those trials. Do you have a reservoir of verses hidden in your heart? Can you write down two or three that you could (or do) draw upon for strength and endurance? Thank God for these gems from His Word, and don't forget to share them with others when they're in need of "a word in season" (Isaiah 50:4).

*Ps 46:1*

*Is 26:3*

*Be still + know that I am God*

*Ps 29:11 'The LORD will give strength to His people*
*           " — bless His people with peace*          *1,2 Or "may the LORD"*

*Eph 1:18*

*Cursed is the man who trusts in mankind, makes flesh his strength*
*+ whose ♡ turns away from the Lord ... as bush in desert, ... in stony wastes*
*will not see when prosperity comes*

Next look at Jeremiah 17:5-8 in your Bible. Verse 8 describes those who hope in and trust in the Lord. Jot down a few of their characteristics.

*For he will be like a tree planted by the water; That extends*
*its roots by a stream And will not fear when the heat comes; But*
*its leaves will be green, And it will not be anxious in a year of drought*
*Nor cease to yield fruit*

Then contrast the person who trusts in man versus the person who puts his hope and trust in the Lord. *(top of page)*

When we trust in the Lord instead of ourselves, "the contrast in vitality is between being like a parched dwarf juniper in the desert or a tree drawing sustenance from a stream to bear fruit."[4] Are you remembering to turn to God and His Word, to trust in Him, and enjoy the blessings of fruitbearing—even in times of drought?

♡    *Roots are for support*—Is yours a life marked by the repeated need to be constantly staked up, tied up, propped up, and straightened up, until the next wind comes along and you topple once again? If so, what will you do today to strengthen your root system in the Lord so that you can profit from the power a network of strong roots provides?

♡    A challenge was issued on page 38 to *design a personal time for drawing near to God.* Let's do that now, remembering that…

> The redeemed heart longs
> for communion with God.[5]

First, pick a time—*When* do you think you could be most consistent in having a quiet time each day? Examine your schedule and pick a time. (Don't forget to write it on your schedule!)

*or when John does errands*

Next, pick a place—*Where* do you think you could enjoy the peace and quiet you need for your "quiet" time? (Remember, a door, some privacy, and solitude help!)

*my chair*

And now, pick a plan—*What* aids or tools can make your quiet time most meaningful? Reread the suggestions on page 39 to trigger your own ideas.

*sticky notes*
*prayer notebook*
*journal*
*pen*

And now it's time to dream (see pages 39-41)! Jot down today's date and then describe the woman you desire to be spiritually in one year.

*12/25/09*
*thankful to God + others; not complaining*

Next describe the woman you desire to be spiritually ten years from now.

*His, practicing His presence; prayer warrior; winsome for Him*

*Eph 4:29 Let no unwholesome word proceed from your mouth, but only such as is good for edification according to the need of the moment so that it will give grace to those who hear. 31 Let all bitterness & wrath & anger & clamor & slander be put away from you, along with all malice.*

**Verses to Memorize**— Why not memorize the verses you selected for your answers in the "Roots are for storage" section of this growth and study guide? And, if you already know those verses by heart, select several others to memorize.

*Ps 64:10 The righteous man will be glad in the Lord & will take refuge in Him   Ps 64:10*

*Ps 16:11 In Thy presence is fulness of joy; at Thy right hand are pleasures forevermore  Ps 16:11*

*Ps 26:11-12 But as for me, I shall walk in my integrity; Redeem me & be gracious to me. My foot stands on a level place; In the congregation I shall bless the Lord.*

*Phil 1:6*

**A Heartfelt Prayer**— Lord, just for today, help me to draw near to You by...

*thanking you for your guidance   (Ps 64, this pen)*

On the following page, relate in 100 words or less one instance when you were aware that you actively chose time in God's Word as a priority over something or someone else this week. Then thank God for that opportunity.

*Today asked for guidance & help when sorely tempted by a difficult situation  Lord said in my mind Ps 64 I went ... then rejoiced, esp @ v.10*

# Words from My Heart

# 3

# A Heart Committed to Prayer

In your copy of *A Woman After God's Own Heart*®, read chapter 3, "A Heart Committed to Prayer." What meant the most to you from this chapter or offered you the greatest challenge or inspired you deeply?

*Am I helping or hindering my family, e.g. He wants to move to better provide for the family.*
*• What can I do for you today?*
*" " — to help you make better use of your time?*

Of course, Jesus Christ is the ultimate example of a Person of prayer. Read Mark 1:35 for a glimpse of Jesus at prayer. What can you learn about His prayer life?

*In the early morning, while it was still dark, Jesus got up, left, + went to a secluded place, + was praying there*

Now describe in a few words what preceded this quiet moment in verses 21-34. *Jesus taught in synagogue; ordered an unclean spirit to depart from a man (→ news spreading into all the surrounding district of Galilee) + immediately after leaving synagogue raised Peter's mom-in-law who'd been lying sick with a fever. After sunset they began bringing to Him all who were ill + were demon-possessed + the whole city had gathered by the door. + Jesus healed many who were ill ē various diseases + cast out many demons not permitting them to speak. Wow! Busy day.*

Is your head spinning? Mine is! But Jesus shows us how to handle

*[handwritten top margin: * Corrie ten Boom: "As a camel kneels before his master to have him remove his burden, so kneel & let the Master take your burden."]*

*[handwritten: Susanna Wesley "May I be incapable of rest or satisfaction of mind under a sense of Thy displeasure. Help me to clear accounts with Thee ---"]*

the "head-spinning" events of busy, hectic, challenging days. How can you follow His example today? *[handwritten: Go to my Father & to Jesus in solitude if possible, even or @ a sleeping in crowd time]*

♡ Let's review the seven blessings of prayer listed in this chapter.

**Blessing #1: A Deeper Relationship with God**—As you consider that prayer increases faith, provides a place to unload burdens, teaches us that God is always near, trains us not to panic, and changes lives, which one of these benefits would be the greatest reason for developing a heart committed to prayer at this stage of your life? Why?

*[handwritten: increases faith / trains us not to panic / changes lives / list will show how He answers — by practising His presence I will experience His peace + joy & reflect them to others, though 1st it unloads burdens (1 Pet 5:7) [1st, humble self under His mighty hand]]*

**Blessing #2: Greater Purity**—I shared with you my problem with gossip in this area of purity. Now won't you identify your particular problem area and share briefly what you plan to do about it?

*[handwritten: Complaint or criticism ∴ gratitude attitude — is it true, kind, helpful? all 3 — Confess as offense to God each time, quenching His spirit of grace — ask Him to surgically cut it out of my life]*

**Blessing #3: Confidence in Making Decisions**—Look again at the picture of Jesus at prayer in Mark 1:35. What was the result of His time in prayer in the area of <u>decision-making</u> (verses 36-39)? What difference did prayer make in the direction for His new day? And what difference might prayer make in the direction for your new days? *[handwritten: "Everyone is looking for you."]*

*[handwritten: "Let us go somewhere else to the towns nearby, so that I may preach there also; for that is what I came for. And He went into their synagogues throughout all Galilee, preaching & casting out the demons.]*

**Blessing #4: Improved Relationships** — Hear the words of this wife about an improved relationship!

> I committed to the Lord that for this day, which happened to be my husband's day off, I would not argue with him. Recently we had been going through a season that, no matter how hard we tried not to argue, it was happening anyway.
>
> I was praying that my day would be what the Lord willed it to be, and that He would be glorified, yet I had not made a specific commitment to what I could do alone to help the situation, which was part of the problem. The thought of actually committing myself to the Lord, that I would not argue even if my buttons got pushed, seemed different to me. And so I did it.
>
> Well, the situation arose, and I heard the soft voice [of God] reminding me of this commitment. I honored it, and He did too. There was no argument. Praise the Lord!

What relationship do you need to improve through prayer, and how can you begin immediately to commit to pray about that relationship? *some 1st*

**Blessing #5: Contentment** — Identify an area in your life where you struggle with finding contentment. Now look at Philippians 4:10-13. What can you learn about contentment from these words from the apostle Paul? How can you apply Paul's lessons to your own situation? *press on → lay hold of that for which also I was [not strictly perfect but] door...thing→ forth prize of the upward call*

*that I may know Him + the fellowship of His sufferings, being conformed to His death (10)*
*→ attain → resurrection from the dead (11)*
*13: ... forgetting what (lies) behind + reaching forward to what (lies) ahead of God in J (14)*

**Blessing #6: God-Confidence** — How do these scriptures increase your trust in God?

Psalm 34:9 — *34: 8 O taste + see that the Lord is good;*
*Now blessed is the man who takes refuge in Him*
*... to those who fear Him there is no want.*

Psalm 84:11 — *...Lord God is a sun + shield;*
*" gives grace + glory:*
*No good thing does He withhold from those who walk uprightly*

**Blessing #7: The Ministry of Prayer** — Edith Schaeffer stated, "Interceding for other people makes a difference in the history of other people's lives." Who are the people you can minister to through prayer, and when do you plan to begin this "ministry"? *do*
*Lonnie + Lindburgs        Bones group*
*Sue*
*Amanda*
*Jackie D + Heather H.*

As you look one more time at these seven blessings, realize that these are blessings that you, too, can know as you cultivate a heart of prayer.

♥ Read again the suggestions made in the "Yes, But How?" section for cultivating a heart committed to prayer. After writing down which one(s) you will put into practice today, read my own story: 
· *prayer log (requests + responses)*
· *set daily time to linger with the Lord*
· *pray always*
· *enjoying God's presence*
· *" faithfully for others — including enemies*
· *Take seriously the powerful privilege of the ministry of prayer*

> I know that I do a very unspiritual thing whenever I'm slipping in the discipline of daily prayer. I get out my kitchen timer, set it for five minutes, and pray, "Lord, I'm going to pray just five minutes today." Then, when the timer rings and I've prayed for the full five minutes, I give myself permission to get up from prayer and go on with my day. I don't worry about the fact that my prayer time was only five minutes long. No, I rejoice that I prayed, acknowledging once again that *something is better than nothing!* I rejoice that I've taken the first step toward rebuilding the coveted discipline of prayer.

*God is our refuge & strength,*
*a very present help in trouble*

*I will lift up my eyes to the mt*
*From whence shall a help come?*
*My help comes from the Lord,*
*Who made heaven + earth*

**Verses to Memorize**—Psalm 46:1; Psalm 121:1-2; Mark 1:35. Choose your favorite from among these verses or pick another verse that encourages your commitment to prayer.

*In the early morning, while it was still dark, Jesus got up*
*left (the house) + went away to a secluded place,*
*and was praying there*

**A Heartfelt Prayer**—Lord, just for today, help me seek You through prayer by...

*not complaining or criticizing but by giving thanks*

*"The righteous man will be glad in the Lord who is*
*always*
*and will take refuge in Him)*  *present*
*+ all the upright in heart will glory."*

On the following page, relate in 100 words or less one instance when you were aware that you actively chose time in prayer as a priority over something or someone else this week.

(And don't forget to pay attention to your Quiet Times Calendar!)

When I felt others were talking negatively about Him, so asked Lord where I could look for help
He responded "Ps. 64"        immediately comforted + relieved
I turned aside, read it, + was relieved to see the topic, then encouraged, and by the end gladdened by the last verses

# Words from My Heart

# 4

# A Heart That Obeys

In your copy of *A Woman After God's Own Heart*®, read chapter 4, "A Heart That Obeys." What meant the most to you from this chapter or offered you the greatest challenge or inspired you deeply?

*p 60 Cease the split second you think or do anything contrary to God's heart — key to training your heart to be responsive*

It's time to get out your dictionary again. This time look up the word "obedient." To crystalize its meaning in your mind and heart, write the definition out as simply as you can here.

*obeying or willing to obey; submissive*
*to carry out the instructions or orders*
*to be guided by; submit to the control of*
*[to obey one's conscience]*

In the section titled "Two Kinds of Hearts," we contrasted the disobedience of King Saul with the obedience of David. Make notes on these instances of Saul's disregard of God's commands through His prophet Samuel.

What specific instructions and promise did Samuel give to Saul in 1 Samuel 10:8?

*... go down before me to Gilgal ∧ wait 7 days | + behold, I will come down to you to offer burnt offerings + sacrifice peace " until I come to you + show you what you should do.*

29

Seven days later, what happened (see 1 Samuel 13:8-9)?

*Saul offered the burnt offering before " 's arrival*

When Samuel finally arrived and asked Saul, "What have you done?" how did Saul answer in verses 11-12? (Or, put another way, how many excuses did he give and how many different people did he blame?)

*Because I saw that the people were scattering from me, + that you (Sam.) did not come within the appointed days, + that the Philistines were assembling at Mechmash :. I said, .. Phils will come.. against me .., + I've not asked the favor of the Lord. So I forced myself + offered the burnt offering*

What was Samuel's assessment of Saul's disobedience, and what was the result (verses 13-14)? *"You've acted foolishly; you've not kept the commandment of the LORD your God, which He commanded you, for now the LORD would have established your kingdom over Israel forever But now your kingdom shall not endure. The LORD has sought out for himself a man after His own ♡, + the LORD has appointed him as ruler over His people, because you haven't kept what the LORD commanded you.*

For another look at Saul's failure to obey the Lord, look at 1 Samuel 15:1-9. What were Samuel's direct instructions to Saul (verse 3)? (If you think this command sounds harsh, look at Exodus 17:8-16.) *go + strike Amelek + utterly destroy all that he has + do not spare him; but put to death both men + women, child + infant, ox + sheep, camel + donkey*

What did Saul do (1 Samuel 15:7-9)? *the falling the people spared Agag + the best of the sheep, the oxen, the lambs, + all that was good, + were not willing to destroy them utterly; but everything despised + worthless, that they utterly destroyed.*

When Samuel arrived (verse 12) and asked Saul, "What...is this bleating of the sheep in my ears...?" (verse 14), how did Saul answer in verse 15? (Or, put another way, how many excuses did he give and how many different people did he blame this time?) *They have brought them from the Amalekites, for the people spared the best of the sheep + oxen, to sacrifice to the LORD your God; but the rest we've utterly destroyed v.21.. the people took of the choicest of the things devoted to destruction, to sacrifice to the Lord your God @ Gilgal*

Again, what was Samuel's assessment of Saul's disobedience, and what was the result (verses 21-23)? *Has the LORD as much delight in burnt offering + sacrifices as in obeying the voice of the LORD. Behold, to obey is better than sacrifice, (and) to heed than the fat of rams. For rebellion is as the sin of divination, and insubordination is as iniquity + idolatry. Because you have rejected the word of the Lord He has also rejected you from (king) King*

♥ This growth and study guide is all about becoming a woman after God's own heart. As we considered David, who was a man after God's own heart (Acts 13:22), we noted that David was willing to obey God, lived to serve God, was concerned with following God's will, was centered on God, exhibited a heart after God over the long haul, and humbly depended upon God (pages 56-58).

The fact that you are reading this book and doing this study indicates your desire for a heart that obeys. So…it's time for some honest personal application and heart searching! Can you think of any situations in your life where you are making excuses about your disobedience? Or blaming someone else for your disobedience? Or obeying God only halfway? "The heart God delights in is a heart that is compliant, cooperative, and responsive to Him and His commands, a heart that obeys." Obedience is a heart issue, so take the time to examine your life, your relationships, your marriage, and your conduct for areas of willful disobedience or halfhearted obedience.

Write out a personal prayer of commitment to make yours a walk in obedience. You may want to use a separate piece of paper.

Then set about to take the step below:

> The most difficult part of obeying God's laws is simply deciding to start now.[6]

♡ Here's a list of several proven guidelines from the "Yes, But How?" section that can help us to walk in obedience.

*Concentrate on doing what is right*—What warning does James 4:17 give? *To one who knows the right thing to do + does not do it, to him it is sin*

*Cease doing what is wrong*—What is the instruction of Proverbs 16:17? *depart from evil*
*The highway of the upright is to depart from evil; He who watches his way preserves his life.*

*Confess any wrong*—What does 1 John 1:8-9 teach us? *If we say that we have no sin, we are deceiving ourselves + the truth is not in us If we confess our sins He is faithful + Righteous to forgive us our sins + to cleanse us from all unrighteousness*

*Clear up things with others*—What does Matthew 5:23-24 exhort? *.. if you are presenting your offering @ the altar, + there remember that your brother has something against you, leave your offering there + go; 1st be reconciled to your brother, + then come + present your offering*

*Continue on as soon as possible*—What principles do Philippians 3:13-14 give us? *forgetting what (lies) behind + reaching forward to what (lies) ahead, press on toward the goal for the prize of the upward call of God in Christ Jesus.*

♡ Read 1 Peter 2:1 and begin a list of heart attitudes and behaviors that hinder growing a heart of obedience. Which, if any, are hindering the growth of your heart?
*malice*
*deceit*
*hypocrisy*
*envy*
*slander*

Read Ephesians 4:25-32 and Colossians 3:5-9 and then add to
*falsehood*
*let sun go down on anger*
*stealing*
*labor to share*
*unwholesome words*        *ungracious*        *abusive speech*
*unedifying word*
*grieve Holy Spirit*

*[handwritten top left margin:]*
bitterness
wrath
anger
clamor
slander
malice
unforgiving

*[handwritten top right margin:]*
unkind
untender-hearted
unloving
hardness of heart
sensuality
greed

your list those actions and attitudes that need pruning. Again, what do you need to prune from your heart? Be specific.

Now focus on the positive and consider cultivating what is necessary for growth. Read 1 Peter 2:2, Ephesians 4:15-32, and Colossians 3:1-17, and list those heart attitudes and behaviors that enrich your life as a Christian. What one or two areas would you like to cultivate?

*[handwritten left column:]*
- long for pure milk of the word
- speak the truth in love
  uncallous
keep seeking the things above.
Set mind on — "

*[handwritten right column:]*
edify according to need of moment, grace
Be kind, tenderhearted, forgiving
compassion, kindness, humility, gentleness
patience, bearing with — Put on love
be thankful, giving thanks thru Christ to God the Father
Let word dwell in richly, word teaching + admonishing
with all wisdom

Has this been a difficult lesson for you, dear one? It's always hard *psalms* to face our sinful failures. But take heart as you consider some of *hymns* the marvelous benefits of your obedience.

*[handwritten:]* be thankful    spiritual songs
singing & thankfulness
in your hearts to God

> Obedience keeps our relationship with God
>    open and free.
> Obedience to God is in our best interest.
> Obedience to God often keeps us from harm.
> Obedience to God is pleasing to Him.
> Obedience to God often leads to peace.[7]

*[handwritten:]* If you love me you will keep my commandments

**Verses to Memorize**—1 Samuel 15:22 and John 14:15. Add to this list any verses that encourage you to walk in greater obedience.

*[handwritten:]*
Obey the voice of the Lord
heed

Samuel said,
"Has the Lord so much delight in burnt offerings + sacrifices
As in obeying the voice of the Lord?
Behold, to obey is better than sacrifice,
(and) to heed than the fat of rams.

Col 1:11ᵇ strengthened with all power, according to His glorious might,
for the attaining of all steadfastness + patience; joyously

**A Heartfelt Prayer**—Lord, just for today, help me choose Your path of obedience by...

On the following page, relate in 100 words or less one instance when you were aware that you actively chose to walk in obedience this week. Then thank God for that opportunity and His grace to make that choice.

# Words from My Heart

# 5

# A Heart
# That Serves

In your copy of *A Woman After God's Own Heart*® read chapter 5, "A Heart That Serves." What meant the most to you from this chapter or offered you the greatest challenge or inspired you deeply?

When I teach through the marriage chapters of *A Woman After God's Own Heart*®, I always tell the women that there are four words in the Bible that define the role of a wife. Married or single, it benefits us to know these four words—first, for personal application, and second, to pass on to others who may need this information. The first word is found in Genesis 2:18: A wife is to *help* her husband. Read Genesis 2:18-25 and then read this explanation of Genesis 2:18:

> The words of this verse emphasize man's need for a companion, a helper, and an equal. He was incomplete without someone to complement him in fulfilling the task of filling, multiplying, and taking dominion over the earth. This points

to Adam's inadequacy, not Eve's insufficiency. Woman was made by God to meet man's deficiency.[8]

Now review these words from page 69 of your book:

A helper is one who shares man's responsibilities, responds to his nature with understanding and love, and wholeheartedly cooperates with him in working out the plan of God.[9]

With these Bible definitions in mind, jot down some of the ways the world's view of a woman's role in marriage differs from God's view.
*women's lib*

♡ As you can tell from the title, this chapter is about serving one another, and more specifically, about serving our husbands. And even if you're not married, a heart that serves is a reflection of Christlikeness—a quality you should desire. Write out Matthew 20:28.
*not to be served, but to serve*
*+ to give His life a ransom for many*

What is the one word that best describes the heart of this verse?
*give/serve*

And how does Jesus say this can be accomplished in verses 26 and 27?　*whoever wants to be a leader*
*must be your servant*

♡ Now that you know you're *on assignment from God to help your husband,* and now that you have an understanding of what it means to serve others, let's look at the three suggestions made for helping your husband in the "Yes, But How?" section.

1. *Make a commitment to help your husband*—I shared about the commitment I made to become a better helper to my husband. Now why don't you write out such a commitment? Be sure and keep it in your prayer journal or notebook and look at it often!

2. *Focus on your husband*—Is yours a heart that generally focuses your energy and efforts on your husband—on *his* tasks, *his* goals, *his* responsibilities—or is yours a heart that cries out, "*Me* first!"? Also, what do you plan to do, what specific actions do you plan to take, to focus on your dear husband? (You may want to draw from some of the ideas from this chapter in your book.) After you give your honest answer, read these words from another woman just like you:

> The other evening I was extremely tired and decided to relax and get a good night's rest. Well, my husband had different plans for me. After the children were put to bed, he told me he had a lot of typing to be done before the next morning. We both knew how much I dislike our particular typewriter and how tired I was (and I did complain to myself!). But then I remembered that *I am on assignment from God to help my husband* and began to work, which did not take as long as either one of us expected.

How about, just for today, putting these two questions to work for you with your husband?

—What can I do for you today?

—What can I do to help you make better use of your time today?

3. *Ask of your actions, Will this help or hinder my husband?*—Quickly look at these women in the Bible:

   • *Eve* (Genesis 3:1-6,17)—Did Eve help or hinder her husband? Why…and how?

   • *Sarah* (Genesis 16:1-4)—Did Sarah help or hinder her husband? Why…and how?

Can you pinpoint any situation in your marriage where your actions or attitudes may be hindering your husband? In light of the fact that you are *on assignment from God to help your husband,* what do you plan to do about this action or attitude?

*be thankful*

Now treat yourself to a look at Priscilla, a woman who was a partner and a complement to her husband (Acts 18:24-26). How did Priscilla help her husband?

♥ As you think of your service to your husband, why not use these questions as a checklist?

✓ Do you see yourself as a team player, free of any competitive actions, thoughts, or desires?

✓ Is your husband your primary career?

✓ Is helping your husband your heart's primary concern and the main focus of your energy?

✓ Have you committed your life and your heart to following God's plan for you, His plan that you help and not hinder your husband?

♥ One more question for those who are not married: Christlike service involves all women. How can you nurture a heart that serves those in your family, home, school, dorm, workplace, neighborhood, and church?

**Verses to Memorize**—Matthew 20:28 and Philippians 2:3-4. Add to this list any verses that encourage you to a heart of service.

 **A Heartfelt Prayer**—Lord, just for today, enable me to be a helper to my husband by... *inspiring me*

On the following page, relate in 100 words or less one instance when you were aware that you actively chose to help your husband this week. Then thank God for that opportunity and His grace to make that choice.

*wk under conviction prior to salvation*

*Words from My Heart*

# A Heart That Follows

In your copy of *A Woman After God's Own Heart*®, read chapter 6, "A Heart That Follows." What meant the most to you from this chapter or offered you the greatest challenge or inspired you deeply?

As I mentioned in the previous lesson, there are four words in the Bible that define the role of a wife. (And just so you know, we'll look at the second and third words in this exercise, and the fourth word in the next.) The first word, as we discussed in the last chapter, is—

#1. She is to *help* her husband.

Now let's look at God's second word to a wife—

#2. She is to *follow* her husband.

(Or, in other words, she is *on assignment from God to follow her*

43

*husband's leadership.*) Write out what these verses say about our submission:

Ephesians 5:22-24 — *Wives, submit to your own husbands, as to the Lord. For the husband is the head of the wife even as Christ is the head of the church, His body + is Himself its Savior. Now as the church submits to Christ, so also wives should submit in everything to their husbands*

Colossians 3:18 — *Wives, submit to your husbands, as is fitting in the Lord.*

*+ Older train younger to love their husbands + children*

Titus 2:5 — (discreet) *controlled, pure, working @ home, to be self-controlled, pure, working @ home, kind, + submissive to their own husbands, that the word of God may not be reviled*

1 Peter 3:1 (Be sure to read verses 1-6!) — *Likewise, wives, be subject to your own husbands →, even if some don't obey the word, they may be won without a word by the conduct of their wives ... respectful + pure ... gentle + quiet spirit*

Hopefully by now you've gained greater understanding into not only the fact of submission as a Christian, but also…

the *fact* of submission as a wife — "wives, submit to your own husbands"

the *who* of submission — "to your own husbands"

the *how* of submission — "as to the Lord"   *Look past husband to Him if necessary*

the *when* of submission — "in everything"

the *why* of submission — "that the word of God may not be blasphemed"   *discredited or dishonored*

And just a note: The exception to these instructions is if you are being asked to violate a teaching from God's Word (Acts 5:29). In such a situation, seek your pastor's counsel or that of another biblical counselor.

♡ *Choose a positive word of response*—Are you ready for some application? I suggested that you choose a positive word for responding to your husband. Write out the word you chose here and relate an instance when you used it. What happened? *Theasamento*

Now read this portion of a letter I received from another wife. She writes…

> …no sooner was our new baby boy (our ninth child!) born when my husband asked, "What about naming him Mark?" All I could utter was a single, positive word, as you recommend in *A Woman After God's Own Heart*. I said, "Fine!" Mark really isn't one of my top favorite names, but he sure is a top favorite baby!

*Ask of each word, act, and attitude, "Am I bending or bucking?"*—I chose this question for myself when I learned that the word *submissive* is used to describe a horse that's been tamed. My mind went wild with the image of an unsubmissive, unyielding, bucking horse (or wife, in my case!). Pinpoint a time when you chose to bend and not buck. What happened? And then read a few words from my heart to yours.

> I can't tell you how many women have written—and called—to express their thoughts and feelings about my "lamp story" on pages 83-84. As I said, Jim was honored, I grew in grace, and God "burned up that lamp and supplied another one"! I hope and pray that you have many such wonderful stories to tell of your submission, your husband's exaltation, and God's grace.

Are you ready for God's third word for a wife?

> #3. She is to *respect* her husband.

(Or, in other words, she's *on assignment from God to respect her husband*.)

In my early days of learning what submission to my husband meant and entailed, the following exercise was invaluable—a true eye-opener! So now I'm asking you to do the same exercise.

Using your dictionary, look up the following verbs (and one adverb) from The Amplified Bible's version of Ephesians 5:33: "And let the wife see that she *respects* her husband—that she *notices* him, *regards* him, *honors* him, *prefers* him, *venerates* and *esteems* him, and that she *defers* to him, and *praises* him, and *loves* and *admires* him *exceedingly*." Write out simple definitions here:

—respect

notice 1. a) to mention; refer to; comment on
    b) to review briefly
→ 2. a) to regard; observe; pay attention to
    b) to be courteous or responsive to

## RESPECT

— notice   vt 1 a) to feel or show honor or esteem for; hold in high regard
      b) " consider or treat c deference
    2 to show consideration for; avoid intruding upon or
                            interfering with
    3 to concern; relate to
                 ready +
   ✗ ≠ ignore, but let your attention be caught

— regard 1 to observe or look @ c a firm steady gaze; look @ attentively
    2 to take into account; consider
    3 [arch] to give attentive heed to or show concern for
    4 to hold in affection + respect [to regard one's friends highly]
    5 to think of in a certain light [[as to lord]]; consider
    6 to have relation to; concern, have reference to

— honor   vi 1 to look; gaze 2 to pay heed or attention
    1. to respect greatly; regard highly; esteem
    2. to show great respect or high regard for; treat c deference + courtesy

— prefer          something or
             · one's liking, opinion, etc.; like better
    3) to put before someone else in rank; promote
    4) to give preference or priority to    promote

— venerate [ of reverence has ]
to look upon with feelings of deep respect + reverence
regard as venerable (worthy of respect or reverence by
    reason of age + dignity, character, position, etc.);
revere

— esteem   to have great regard for; value highly; respect

— defer   to give in to the wish or judgment of another,
    as in showing respect; yield c courtesy (to)

— praise (to express value)
    2. to commend the worth of; express approval or
       admiration of
    3. to laud the glory of (God, etc.), as in song; glorify; extol

— love 1. a deep + tender feeling of affection for or
     attachment or devotion to a person or persons
    5. a) a strong, usually passionate affection of one person
       for another, based in part on sexual attraction
     unselfish, loyal concern for others.

—admire *1. to regard & wonder, delight, & pleased approval*
         *2 " have high regard for*

—exceedingly *extremely, to a great degree; extraordinarily*
             *to beyond the limit set by, surpass*

Now for three "words" of application:

1. *Make a commitment to reverence and respect your husband*—
Drawing from the words and definitions you looked up, write out
a brief (no more than 10 words) motto or saying that will express
an attitude of respect for your husband (for instance, "Jim's number
one!" or "Jim's the greatest!"). Then make a commitment to live
out your motto in daily praise and admiration.
*John is worthy*

2. *Treat your husband as you would Christ Himself.* How will you
do this today?  *apply above*

3. *Ask of your attitude, "Am I demonstrating respect for my husband?"*
Look again at Ephesians 5:33. Your respect for your husband
should be obvious and active and noticeable to him and to others.
How will you show your respect for him today?  *defer to him*
*Let the wife see that she respects her husband*

**Verses to Memorize** — Colossians 3:18 and 23. Add to this list any verses that encourage you to a heart of submission.

*3:23 Whatever you do, work heartily, as for the Lord + not men.*

 **A Heartfelt Prayer** — Lord, just for today, help me to respond positively to my husband by…

On the following page, relate in 100 words or less one instance when you were aware that you actively chose to submit to your husband this week. Then thank God for that opportunity and His grace to make that choice. *John's week under conviction*

# Words from My Heart

7

# A Heart That Loves,

## Part 1

 In your copy of *A Woman After God's Own Heart*®, read chapter 7, "A Heart That Loves, Part 1." What meant the most to you from this chapter or offered you the greatest challenge or inspired you deeply?

♡ What does God say about the role of a wife?

#1. She is to *help* her husband.

#2. She is to *follow* her husband.

#3. She is to *respect* her husband.

As you look back over the past few weeks, how is what you're learning about helping, following, and respecting your husband affecting your marriage?

Now let's look at God's fourth word to us as a wife:

> #4. She is to *love* her husband.

Read Titus 2:3-5. What message does God have for wives here?

As I explained, the love spoken of in Titus 2:4 is a love that cherishes, enjoys, and likes our husband—a friendship love. I also shared that friendship love with your husband begins as you make these two choices:

> *Decide to make your husband your Number One human relationship.*
>
> *Begin to choose your husband over all other human relationships.*

Look again at the treatment of these two choices in your book (see the "Yes, But How?" section) and evaluate your marriage to see if your priorities and choices are "out of whack." What did you determine? After you've written down your answer, see what this busy wife and mother discovered!

> We have two small children, a three-year-old and a seven-month-old. It is so easy because of the amount of time spent with them to unknowingly let the other areas of your life and marriage slide. I realized that I needed to regain my focus and make my husband my VIP and give him priority over our children.

Now, let's begin to go through the nine tried-and-true ways you can express your love and build a friendship with your husband.

**1. Pray for Your Husband Daily**—*Is your husband a Christian?* If so, begin to incorporate these scriptures into your prayers for him. Look at these verses in your Bible and make notes about what they teach.

- In the area of character qualities, look at

    1 Timothy 3:1-10,12-13—

    Titus 1:6-9—

- In the area of spiritual growth, look at Colossians 1:9-12—

- In the area of God's role in your husband's life, look at
  Philippians 1:6 —

*If your husband is not a Christian,* pray using these scriptures
often:

- In the area of God's role in your husband's life, look at
  1 Timothy 2:4 —

  2 Peter 3:9 —

- In the area of your role in your husband's life, look at
  1 Corinthians 7:13 —

  1 Peter 3:1-6 —

*For all wives,* in the area of your role in your husband's life, look
again at these scriptures — God's four words for wives — and
pray!

  Help him — Genesis 2:18 —

Follow him — Ephesians 5:22-24 —


Respect him — Ephesians 5:33 —


Love him — Titus 2:4 —


Minister to his physical needs —
    1 Corinthians 7:2-5 —


Proverbs 5:15-20 —


Put an asterisk beside or circle any of these areas that were new or missing from your practice and prayers for your husband. And, because we're discussing prayer, stop and discuss these matters with the Lord.

2. **Plan for Your Husband Daily** — Since you are *on assignment from God to love your husband,* try these exercises and write down what happens to your heart...and his!

— Plan a special deed of kindness for your husband each day for a week.

—Plan a special dinner for your husband next week.

—Plan a special date alone with your husband this week. (If it doesn't work out with his schedule, that's O.K. That will be another opportunity for you to pay attention to his desires and honor him. At least your heart was willing and in the right place—and that's what this study is all about!)

As we end this lesson, I can't help but encourage you by giving you one more example from another woman (and wife) after God's own heart:

My mother had just offered us a lovely expense-paid weekend away as an anniversary present. When I happily presented this idea to my husband, he became very quiet. Later as we talked about the situation, I found that my husband really did not want to go away and showed me, practically, why it was not feasible for us.

With MUCH PRAYER, I explained to my mother our appreciation of her love for us but that my husband and I were not able to accept this lovely offer. The Lord gave me the boldness to make a suggestion on what she might be able to give us, and she gratefully appreciated our truthfulness. The depth of love and communication between the family was tested, and with God's strength to obey, I believe that He was glorified through this situation.

**Verses to Memorize**—James 5:16b and 1 John 3:18. Add to this list any verses that encourage you to pray for your husband and to love him.

 **A Heartfelt Prayer**—Lord, just for today, help me show my love to my husband by…

On the following page, relate in 100 words or less one instance when you were aware that you actively chose your husband as a priority over all others this week. Then thank God for that opportunity and His grace to make that choice.

*Words from My Heart*

# 8

# A Heart That Loves,

## Part 2

In your copy of *A Woman After God's Own Heart*®, read chapter 8, "A Heart That Loves, Part 2." What meant the most to you from this chapter or offered you the greatest challenge or inspired you deeply?

♡ I hope you enjoyed looking at the first two suggestions for loving your husband that we discussed in the previous lesson — 1. *Pray for him* and 2. *Plan for him*. But there are seven more!

3. **Prepare for Your Husband Daily** — If your husband were to write an article about his homecoming, what do you think he might report? Would there be any similarities with "The Homecoming" on pages 105-06.

Why not use these preparations as a checklist for measuring

your husband's homecoming? Also look at the accompanying scriptures.

- Prepare the house—Proverbs 31:27
- Prepare your appearance—Proverbs 27:9a
- Prepare your greeting—Proverbs 12:25 and 15:30
- Set the table—Proverbs 9:2
- "The king is in the castle!"—Proverbs 31:23
- "The party!"
- Clear out all visitors
- Stay off the phone
- Prepare all the way home—Luke 6:35
- Pray all the way home—Ephesians 6:18 and 1 Thessalonians 5:17

Which of these preparations for homecoming do you need to work on?

4. **Please Your Husband**—Make a list of your husband's likes and dislikes. How can you set about to please him and honor his preferences?

5. **Protect Your Time with Your Husband**—Does your calendar reflect more time apart than together? What changes can you make in your personal schedule to enjoy more time together?

6. **Physically Love Your Husband**—Do read 1 Corinthians 7:3-5 and Proverbs 5:18-19.

7. **Positively Respond to Your Husband**—Again, what positive word of response have you chosen, and are you using it? I love this "Sure!" from one woman:

> I don't have an example of choosing my husband over something else this week, but I was able to give the positive response of "Sure, honey," when he asked for a second bowl of ice cream that his waistline did not need.

8. **Praise Your Husband**—Write down seven of your husband's qualities or personality traits that you admire and appreciate. Now, for the next week, praise him for one each day!

- •                              •
- •                              •
- •                              •
- •

9. **Pray Always**—Don't forget to lift prayers to God throughout your day for your husband and for your relationship with him as you seek to live out God's four words for wives.

You've done a good job working through these four chapters. I know, because of the mail I receive, just how hard they are for some of us! So I want to treat you to a "story from the heart" shared by a woman just like you who is seeking to be a woman after God's own heart in her marriage. Sit back, relax, and enjoy! And again I say, "Good job!"

> Eight AM Saturday morning! Thank goodness I have Saturdays to catch up on everything that didn't get done during the week and to leave a meal for the family while I'm at work tonight.
>
> "Good morning, sweetheart! Sleep well? (Now what was it we were told in that pink book to ask?) What can I do to help you best use your time today?"
>
> "What? You need to go to the nursery in Gardena and you want the kids and me to go?!!" (Quick, Shelly, think of something. You have so much to get organized before you go to work. But wait a minute. Didn't I decide to change my priorities? Remember? Dave [husband] first. Housework can wait. So what if you'll be gone until it's time to go to work? Quick, say something positive!)
>
> "Okay honey, sure, we'd all love to go!!" (What have I just done?!)
>
> P.S. The housework didn't get done. Ronald McDonald fed my family that night, but choosing to do what Dave asked was a victory for me. (I didn't say anything negative!) We were blessed with a happy time together that day!

Do you see, dear one, what our obedience to God's four words to us as wives—help, follow, respect, and love—can mean to our beloved husbands? What a gift we give to our husbands when we communicate "I love you" God's way. As we finish these lessons on being a wife after God's own heart, let's get to work showing our husbands the love that's in our hearts!

**Verses to Memorize** — Proverbs 12:4 and 1 John 3:18. Add to this list any verses that encourage you to pray for your husband and to love him.

 **A Heartfelt Prayer** — Lord, just for today, help me show my love to my husband by...

On the following page, relate in 100 words or less one instance when you were aware that you actively chose to show love to your husband this week. Then thank God for that opportunity and His grace to make that choice.

# Words from My Heart

# 9

# A Heart That Values Being a Mother

In your copy of *A Woman After God's Own Heart*®, read chapter 9, "A Heart That Values Being a Mother." What meant the most to you from this chapter or offered you the greatest challenge or inspired you deeply?

*we all stumble in many ways*

As we launch into this section on mothering, I hope you'll notice that we are moving—in order—through the priorities that God sets down for us in His Word. Of course, God is Number One, "for in Him we live and move and have our being" (Acts 17:28). Look again at Titus 2:3-5. What is the first "topic" (or priority) on the curriculum list that the older women are to teach the younger women (verse 4)? *reverent in behavior* *v5 to be self-controlled, submissive* *to love their husbands & children*

And what is the second topic (verse 4)?

65

Now that we've spent time considering our love for God and for our husbands, let's see what God's Word says about our children and the passions that reflect <u>a heart that values being a mother.</u>

### ♥ A Passion for Teaching God's Word — First make notes regarding the teaching of Proverbs 1:8 and Proverbs 6:20

*[handwritten: Prov. 1:8 — Hear, my son, your father's instruction, + forsake not your mother's teaching]*

*[handwritten: My son, keep your father's command + forsake not your mother's teaching]*

*[handwritten: v9 - Craig - let them be a garland around your neck]*

Next, look at a mother and grandmother—Eunice and Lois—who took their assignment from God to teach His Word to their young Timothy seriously. As you may know, Timothy was a coworker and personal representative of the apostle Paul to the Ephesian church. And note, too, that Timothy's father (and Eunice's husband) was probably an unbeliever (Acts 16:1).

2 Timothy 1:5 — Describe Timothy's *[handwritten: sincere]* faith and its source.

*[handwritten margin: sincere]*

*[handwritten: dwelt 1st in your grandmother Lois + your mother Eunice]*

2 Timothy 3:15 — What is one role Eunice and Lois played in Timothy's early childhood, and what did their teaching help accomplish?

*[handwritten: acquainted i the sacred writings, able to make him wise for salvation through faith in Christ Jesus.]*

As you consider these two women after God's own heart and the impact that their faithful teaching of God's Word had upon a young child, what steps (or additional steps) are you going to take to ensure that your children, too, know the Scriptures from childhood? (Remember, as a mother you are *on assignment from God to teach His Word to your children!*)

♡ **A Passion for Teaching God's Wisdom**—Not only are we to teach the actual Word of God to our children, but we are also to teach them practical, scriptural wisdom for daily life. To witness a mother involved in such teaching, look at Proverbs 31:1-9. Who is the mother? *King Lemuel's*

And who is the "pupil"? *King Lemuel*

Make a brief list of the practical areas of life covered by this faithful, passionate mother in verses 3-9. *of all the afflicted*

*5-6 women*
*wine, strong drink & lest. forget what's been decreed & pervert the rights*
*to those in bitter to those perishing*
*( forget poverty & remember their misery no more*
*8 open your mouth for the mute, for the rights of all who are destitute*
*9 — " judge righteously, defend the rights of the poor & the needy*

And what practical area of life is included in verses 10-31? *an excellent wife*

♡ *The place for teaching God's Word and wisdom*—We tend to think first of taking our children to church to be taught God's Word and wisdom (and there is certainly a place for that, as we'll soon see), but consider the "classroom scene" God describes in Deuteronomy 6:6-7: *(the world)*
*sitting in your house*
*walking by the way*
*when you lie down*
*" " rise*

Before any teaching can take place, where must the Word of God first reside? *on your ♡ v6 (v5 a favorite)*

What urgent command is given by God to parents?

*You shall teach God's word diligently to your children...*

What four scenes of daily life does God paint as the setting for teaching our children? *see p 67, next to last entry*

*Speak of the Lord in all, of His presence, care, + works*

*walk worthy*

*Xian radio messages in background*

*show need of Lord in a person's life*

*needs of others (e.g. in nursing home. Let children give with prayers.*

*Give to needy & pray with them*

*Give experience of giving door to door (serving the needy)*

What can you do to turn the daily activities of life into a classroom for teaching God's Word and wisdom? Think of as many as you can. Use an extra page of paper if you must. Then check off two or three that you can begin *today!* Oh, please don't wait another day or minute to begin this vital ministry to your dear children!

♥ **Yes, But How**

Now for some practical how-to's.

*Make some serious decisions*—Or, put another way, "Will you or won't you make a commitment to choose to teach God's Word and wisdom to your children?" Why not write such a commitment here or in your prayer journal?

*Recognize your role of teacher*—Yes, this role will be costly and sacrifices will have to be made, but as an Italian proverb says, "A teacher is like the candle, which lights others in consuming itself." *slave for ...* Do you see yourself as a teacher of God's truth to your children? *ys*

Or does the thought of teaching them about God make you feel awkward, nervous, incompetent? Or are you afraid your family will think you are "stupid," that studying the Bible is a "dumb" idea? Or do you think your little one is too little? Answer honestly about what keeps you from this duty. Each day in your prayer time, own this awesome role, ask God for His help to faithfully live it out, and just do it! Do it badly! Do it "dumbly." Do it when your kids don't care or want you to do it. But whatever you do and however you do it, *do it!*

*Consider these examples*—How did the stories of Jochebed, Hannah, and Mary encourage you in your role as a teacher of truth to your children? +

*Memorize scripture and read the Bible together*—What are you doing or could you do in this vital area of spiritual training?

*thank them for carefully following God's word.*

*Follow the model of other mothers*—Pick out several women in your church who are making strides in this area of biblical and spiritual mothering. What can you do to duplicate their efforts?

*patience, pacing*

How about one more exercise? Design a daily schedule that includes time in God's Word with your children. Then set out what you'll need (a Bible, a teen devotional, a workbook or an activity book, a little book of prayers, books about Jesus, books about Bible characters, songbooks or sing-along tapes, memory cards, etc.). Utter a prayer, and then make sure you and your precious ones keep that appointment. Write out your initial plan here.

When will we meet?

Where will we meet?

What will we do?

And for how long?

 **Verses to Memorize** — Deuteronomy 6:6-7. Add to this list any verses that encourage you in your role of teaching God's Word and wisdom to your children and grandchildren.

*+ these words that I teach you today shall be on your ♡*
*You shall teach them diligently to your children,*
*+ shall talk of them when you set in your house, + when you walk by the way,*
*+ when you lie down, + when you rise.*

 **A Heartfelt Prayer** — Lord, just for today, help me be faithful to impart Your Word and Your wisdom to my children by...

*(praying)   finding ways to thank / encourage them ī scripture*

On the following page, relate in 100 words or less one instance when you actively chose having a time with your children in God's Word as a priority over other activities. Then thank God for His grace to make that choice.

*reading proverbs with them when they might have liked doing something else ... or when I was in distress*

# Words from My Heart

# 10

# A Heart That Prays Faithfully

In your copy of *A Woman After God's Own Heart*®, read chapter 10, "A Heart That Prays Faithfully." What meant the most to you from this chapter or offered you the greatest challenge or inspired you deeply?

· praying 1 hr / day for each child  (Susanna Wesley did )
· skipping lunch to pray

I hope your heart was stirred to action as you completed our previous study about appreciating the value of being a mother. And I hope your passions—more specifically, *a passion for teaching God's Word* and *a passion for teaching God's wisdom*—grew to embrace God's assignment to teach His Word to your children. This exercise will hopefully light a fresh fire under two more passions. First...

**A Passion for Prayer**—Look at Proverbs 31:2 and write out your Bible's translation of this verse.

What are you doing, my son?
___ " ___, son of my womb?
___ " ___, son of my vows?

Now read in 1 Samuel 1:1-10 about the life of Hannah, a woman who prayed faithfully. Make a note of Hannah's problems.

*barrenness.*

What did her difficulties lead her to do in verse 10?

*pray to Lord + weep bitterly + (vow to Lord)*

Now read verses 11-20. In addition to pouring out her heart in prayer, what additional action did she take in verse 11?

*give to your servant a son, then I will give him to the LORD all the days of his life, + no razor shall touch his head*

Hannah was faithful to pray (and to vow!), and God blessed her and gave her a son, little Samuel. Read about another step of faithfulness in the life of Hannah in verses 21-28. What was that step?

*Vow: As soon as the child is weaned, I will bring him, so that he may appear in the presence of the LORD + dwell there forever.*

Next read 1 Samuel 2:1-11. According to verse 1, what did Hannah do when she delivered her small son to Eli, the priest, at the temple of the Lord, and what were her opening words (verse 2)? *pray*

*"There is none holy like the LORD; I none besides you I no rock like our God.*

Hannah's example teaches that in every event or difficulty we are to pray, focusing our heart and mind on the person and power of God, not on our circumstances. Just like Hannah, you can be confident of God's sovereign and loving control over the events of your life—and the lives of your children! As Hannah's lips reveal her heart in verses 1-10, note the content of Hannah's impassioned prayer:

*1 Sam 2:*

- **God's salvation**

  *1: My ♡ exults in the LORD*
  *" strength is exalted in the LORD*
  *" mouth derides my enemies*
  *because I rejoice in your salvation*

- **God's holiness**

  *2: ... there is none holy like the LORD*

- **God's strength**

  *2: there is no rock like our God*

- **God's knowledge**

  *3v: ... for the LORD is a God of knowledge & by him actions are weighed*

- **God's power**

  *4. the bows of the mighty are broken, but the feeble bind on strength*
  *5 ... The barren has borne 7, but she who has many children is forlorn*
  *6 ... LORD kills & brings to life, ... brings low & exalts ... not by might shall a man prevail*
  *7 ... " makes poor & makes rich; ...*
  *8 ... on the pillars of the earth he has set the world 9 ...guards... cuts off...*
  *10 ...adversaries...broken to pieces; against them he will thunder in heaven.*

- **God's judgment**

  *10: "The LORD will judge the ends of the earth ---*

How do these scenes from the life of this mother who prayed faithfully instruct and challenge you about your prayer life and speak to you as a mother?

*commit all to God*

♥ **A Passion for Godly Training**—It's one thing to talk to your children about the Lord and to talk to the Lord about your children, but there are other steps we can and must take in the area of godly training. These steps are costly and involve personal sacrifice on your part, but God's kind of training takes time and dedication. What level of commitment are you making and willing to make in these areas of godly training?

• Church attendance— *go*

• Sunday school attendance— *go*

• Church outings and camps— *go*

• Youth groups and Bible studies— *go*    *'til late teens, eased up → choice*

Exposure to God's truth and the opportunity to be with other strong believers awaits your children when you make the effort to take these steps. I have in my teaching notes a clever article titled "Generations of Excuses."[10] Take a look at this series of excuses for not getting little ones to church that spanned two generations.

### Generations of Excuses

- Our baby Timmy's birth
- Timmy's just a baby
- Timmy always catches a cold in the nursery
- Timmy's too noisy and too active
- Timmy can't get along with the other children
- the birth of Timmy's baby sister, Sally
- Sally's just a baby
- Sally always catches a cold in the nursery
- Sally's too noisy and too active
- Sally can't get along with the other children
- We're all so busy that Sunday is our only day as a family
- My husband's boss wants to golf with him on Sundays
- I work during the week and Sunday is my only day to relax
- Timmy's soccer games are on Sundays
- Timmy thinks going to youth group is dumb
- Timmy's married now, and you know how it is with newlyweds!
- Timmy's baby's birth
- Timmy's baby is too noisy, too active, might catch a cold in the nursery...

Which of these tend to be your favorite excuses for not getting your family to church?

It's God's job to work in our children's hearts and lives, but it's our job to expose them to others who will teach them the truth. Are you committed to getting your children to church so they can be exposed to the truth no matter what it costs? What would it cost you this week? †

 In chapter 2, we talked about the value of saying "no" to things that are pleasant, profitable, and good if they would hinder or clog our grand duties and our chief work. What can you say "no" to this week in order to

—spend more time in prayer for your children?    *other thoughts*

—see that your children get to church?

**Verses to Memorize**—James 5:16b (again!), Hebrews 10:25, and Proverbs 22:6. Add to this list any verses that encourage you in your role of training your children and grandchildren.

*The prayer of a righteous person has great power as it is working.*

*Heb 10:25 "...not neglecting to meet together, as is the habit of some, but encouraging one another, + all the more as you see the Day drawing near.*

*Prov. 22:6 "Train up a child in the way he should go; even when he is old he will not depart from it"*

**A Heartfelt Prayer** — Lord, just for today, help me spend extra time praying for my children's...

On the following page, relate in 100 words or less one instance when you actively chose praying for your children as a priority over other activities. Then thank God for His grace to make that choice.

*for a day or 2 in past, spent 1 hr praying for children, + at least once, 1 hr praying as much as I managed, for each.*

# Words from My Heart

# 11

# A Heart Overflowing with Motherly Affection,

## Part 1

In your copy of *A Woman After God's Own Heart*®
read chapter 11, "A Heart Overflowing with Motherly
Affection, Part 1." What meant the most to you from
this chapter or offered you the greatest challenge or
inspired you deeply?

*Give expecting nothing in return (those things may never come)*

♡ We've dealt with some pretty serious topics in this section on
mothering, haven't we? It was sobering to consider our need
to develop a passion for teaching God's Word, for wisdom, for
prayer, and for godly training. But mothering is made up of other
things as well. Look at Titus 2:4 again. Just as we're on assignment
to love our husbands with a friendship love—to like them, to
be their friend—so we are to love our children. Let's look at ten
marks of motherly affection—ten ways to live out our assignment from God to love them. We'll examine five in this chapter
and five in the next.

*• Train the young women to love their husbands + children*

*At 5: last "Oh yes... I have a mother who prays for me + pleads w the Lord every day for me. Oh what a difference it makes for me — I have a mother who prays.*

82    A WOMAN AFTER GOD'S OWN HEART GROWTH & STUDY GUIDE

1. **A Heart That Prays** — Did you enjoy the poem about a praying mother? I know it's one of my favorites. In fact, I can just about recite it from memory. Well, here's another one that is quite touching.

---

### Baby Shoes

Often tiny baby feet, tired from their play,
Kick off scuffed-up little shoes at the close of day.
And often tired mothers find them lying there,
And over them send up to God this fervent, whispered
    prayer:

"God, guide his every footstep in paths where Thou
    has stood;
God, make him brave; God, make him strong;
And please, God, make him good!"[11]

---

Now, what kind of prayers are you praying for your dear children?
Jot down a few notes of their general contents.

*We pray for the boys + their wives to be if wives there are to be*
*keep them safe, else help them to know You, love You + live for You*
*Please give them wisdom in every situation*
*Not anxious, but trusting You as they do their b...*

2. **A Heart That Provides** — Read Proverbs 31:10-31, listing the provisions this godly mother made for her family.

*works w willing hands*
*food from afar... for her household + maidens*
*clothes*
*— the teaching of kindness      not idle*

Are there any "basics" your children are missing out on at home? What

*strength + dignity*

will you do this week to remedy this situation so that yours is a
heart overflowing with motherly affection?

*→ consistency of attitude → all*

3. **A Heart That Is Happy** — I know that we've already looked at
this scripture in our study, but please write out again the teaching
of Proverbs 12:25. How can your <u>happy hear</u>t and a <u>good word</u>
minister to your family? And the opposite, how can your lack of
a happy heart and a good word affect them negatively?

*Anxiety in a man's ♡ weighs him down,*
*but a good word makes him glad.*

Now look at a few more proverbs:

Proverbs 15:13 — *Anxiety in a man's heart weighs him down*
*A glad ♡ makes a cheerful face.*
*but by sorrow of ♡ the spirit is crushed*

Proverbs 15:15 —
*All the days of the afflicted are sad, but the cheerful of ♡*
*has a continual feast*

Proverbs 17:22 —     *joyful ♡ = good medicine,*
*but a crushed spirit dries up the bones*

Does being <u>cheerful</u> and being "up" and "<u>lighting up</u>" for your
family sound unimportant? Hypocritical? Impossible? Read
on...          *no*

> When you mentioned in class this semester that we should be "up" for our family, I struggled. I wondered, "Can we really do that and be real?" And as I began to try and make the effort for my family, I discovered that, <u>with my eyes off myself</u> and <u>onto God</u>, I could. This opened me up to viewing my family differently and allowed God to show me the dream of making our home delightful. This perspective has changed *my* attitude in the day-to-day things I am doing for my family, and it has begun transforming *me!*

Why not plan to be "up" for your family today? Why not "light up" when you see them? Why not plan the "good word" you will give right now? I remember hearing writer and teacher Elisabeth Elliot share on a tape that as the homemaker, "*you* create the atmosphere of the home with *your* attitudes." And your happiness is a powerful influence!

4. **A Heart That Gives**—Closely related to a heart that is happy is a heart that gives. Look at these verses in your Bible and write out in a few words how each encourages you to nurture a heart that gives.

John 3:16— *God so loved the world → gave Jesus → not perish*

Mark 10:45— *., Son of man came not to be served but to serve*

Here are some ways you and I can be "the givers." We can give...

— a smile

— a cheerful greeting

— a hug

— a compliment

— an encouragement

— a praise

— a time

— a listening ear

— a ride

— an extra mile ·

Jot down beside each one of these evidences of motherly affection a specific effort you can make to give these priceless gifts to your children this week.

5. **A Heart of Fun**—Just for fun, consider doing one of the following this week.

— check out a riddle book from the library

— read the newspaper cartoons together with your children

— have a "tickle time"

— have a pillow fight

— go out for a "fun" time that's not connected with any errands

— ask other mothers for their "fun" ideas

Think of three or four ideas yourself and add them to this list

— *maintain cheerful trusting attitude*

—

—

—

 **Verses to Memorize**—Mark 10:45 and Proverbs 12:25. Add to this list any verses that encourage you in your role of affectionately loving your children and grandchildren.

*For even the Son of Man came not to be served but to serve + to give his life as a ransom for many*

*Anxiety in a man's heart weighs him down, but a good word makes him glad*

 **A Heartfelt Prayer**—Lord, just for today, help my heart overflow with motherly affection by... *(see above)*

On the following page, relate in 100 words or less one instance when you actively chose to give motherly affection to your children. Then thank God for His grace to make that choice.

# Words from My Heart

when Craig had car accident

" Eric came into narrow bathroom & a creature in his hand, & defenseless

2 Sam 12:16 David for Bathsheba

1 Sam 1:27 Hanna

Job 1:5 for children

1 Chron 12:11-12 D for Solomon re temple

2 Sam 7:25-28 David for

# 12

# A Heart Overflowing with Motherly Affection,

## Part 2

In your copy of *A Woman After God's Own Heart*®, read chapter 12, "A Heart Overflowing with Motherly Affection, Part 2." What meant the most to you from this chapter or offered you the greatest challenge or inspired you deeply?

I hope you enjoyed the first five "heart exercises" in the last chapter that should propel you and me further down the road to being moms whose hearts overflow with motherly affection. Are you ready for five more?

6. **A Heart That Celebrates**—Write out Matthew 5:41.

*If anyone forces you to go one mile, go with him 2 miles*

When you think of the "first mile" of your job assignment from God as a mother, what comes to mind? (Don't forget to incorporate what you've been learning in the three previous chapters.)

*Turning the mundane into a celebration*—this is one way we as mothers can go *the extra mile*. Can you think of the many mundane activities your family will face today or in the next week? Note several here, and write out a plan for making these routine events a celebration.

7. **A Heart That Gives Preferential Treatment**—Look again at Titus 2:3-5. How important do you think your children are as you consider God's words to women in this passage? *Very*

*Older women likewise → reverent in behavior, not slanderers or slaves to much wine... to teach what is good, + so train the young women to love their husbands + children, to be self-controlled, pure, working @ home, kind, + submissive to their own husbands, that the word of God may not be reviled.*

A good way to express to your children that they take priority in your heart is to practice the principle, *Don't give away to others what you have not first given away at home.* List three ways you can communicate to your children the high priority they have in your heart. What can you do to show your children that they are more important to you than other people?

8. **A Heart That Is Focused**—Look next at Matthew 6:24 and write it out here.

*No one can serve 2 masters, for either he will hate the one & love the other, or be devoted to the one & despise the other. You cannot serve God & money or possessions*

Now consider my principle *Beware of double booking*. Looking at this past week, can you pinpoint any instances where you may have tried to double book? What happened? What did you hope to accomplish when you double booked? How did it turn out? After you've written about your experience, read what another mother just like you wrote.

> Well, it finally happened! God is dealing with my telephone habits! This week we talked about not neglecting our children by double booking. With two little ones, the phone has been my line to the adult world. But when I realized the importance of my role as their mother and started to think of all the possibilities of things I could do with them to teach them, play with them, and "have a ball" as a family, the phone lost its influence in my life.
>
> Its jingling interruptions are now handled by "Igor," our prerecorded message answering machine. With Igor on duty 'round the clock now, I can answer and return calls at nap time. I know that I'm doing the right thing.

9. **A Heart That Is Present**—After reading this section of your book, were there any new issues to think about? What were they?

What are some of the activities that tend to take you away from your family and home at night?

Evaluate these activities, spend time in prayer with God about them this next week, talk these things over with your husband, and begin to make the choices that bless your family. Then… watch for the blessings!

Speaking of blessings, consider this next quality!

10. **A Heart That Is Quiet** — Write out Proverbs 31:26. What are the two "laws" that govern this godly wife and mother's speech? *She opens her mouth with wisdom,*
*& the teaching of kindness is on her tongue*

When you speak to your children or to others about them, do your words tend to match up to the biblical standard set here in Proverbs 31:26 or do you need to make some changes? Please explain.

What is the instruction to us as women in 1 Timothy 3:11? *Be dignified, not slanderers, but sober-minded, faithful in all things*

And Titus 2:3? *Be reverent in behavior, not slanderers or slaves to much wine -- teach what is good.*

And in another of my favorites, Titus 3:2.

*speak evil of no one... avoid quarreling, be gentle & show perfect courtesy toward all people*

Now, how do these exhortations regarding gossip and slander relate to us as mothers?

I hope you are at least *thinking* about ways to express your love to your dear children! None of these exercises is overwhelming, and each is lived out in the daily minutia of life. But, dear woman after God's own heart, packaged together, the many little things we do send a loud and clear message of love to every precious person under your roof, such as this woman relates.

> I know I put my children as a priority last Thursday. I began my day by asking the Lord to help me make it special for my kids and my husband. I prayed for them as often as I could throughout the day. I went grocery shopping and made a special meal and dessert for that night. We had special dishes and a candle for the setting. (Ironically, it was my husband who thought that was neat!) The Lord gave me special time and special thoughts for each of them. It truly was a blessed day in every way. Joy abounded!

**Verses to Memorize**—Matthew 6:24 and Proverbs 31:26. Add to this list any verses that encourage you in your role of affectionately loving your children and grandchildren.

*p. 90 ₂ 2 masters*
*hate ∴ love or —*
*be devoted ∴ despise*

*opens mouth ē wisdom*
*teaching of kindness*
*is on her tongue*

**A Heartfelt Prayer**—Lord, just for today, help my heart overflow with motherly affection by…

On the following page, relate in 100 words or less one instance when you actively chose to give motherly affection to your children. Then thank God for His grace to make that choice.

# Words from My Heart

# 13

# *A Heart That Makes a House a Home*

 In your copy of *A Woman After God's Own Heart*®, read Chapter 13, "A Heart That Makes a House a Home." What meant the most to you from this chapter or offered you the greatest challenge or inspired you deeply?

♡ **The Business of Building**—To gain a better understanding of what it means to make a house a home, write out Proverbs 14:1. *The wisest of women builds her house, but folly ⁓ her own hands tears it down*

—*Creating the atmosphere.* As we start, take the temperature of your own home. Share a few words that describe typical daily life under your roof.

Now look up these scriptures and check the ones that you most need to apply in order to build your home into all that you and God want it to be.

◇ Proverbs 12:25 — *Anxiety in a man's heart weighs him down but a good word makes him glad*

◇ Proverbs 15:1 — *A soft answer turns away wrath but a harsh word stirs up anger*

◇ Proverbs 15:13 — *The eyes of the LORD are in every place, keeping watch on the evil & the good*

◇ Proverbs 15:15 — *All the days of the afflicted are evil, but he who is cheerful of heart has a continual feast*

◇ Proverbs 15:18 — *A hot-tempered man stirs up strife, but he who is slow to anger quiets contention*

◇ Proverbs 16:24 — *Gracious words are like a honeycomb, sweetness to the soul & health to the body*

◇ Proverbs 31:26 — *She opens her mouth with wisdom, & the teaching of kindness is on her tongue.*

—*Building a refuge.* Just this morning an email sister sent me this quote, which she called "another spiritual nugget":

> When the pressures of the world intrude, there is no shelter like a peaceful home.

What specific steps can you take to make your home a shelter, a haven, a refuge, a retreat, a hospital for your loved ones, to build your home into what God wants it to be?

—*Avoiding the negatives.* As we took apart Proverbs 14:1, we *The wisest of women builds her house, but folly with her own hands tears it down* noted that there are (at least!) two ways a woman can put her home-building at risk. Jot down what comes to your mind in each category.

1. Active (working destruction)—

2. Passive (failing to work)—

**Yes, But How?**—You and I both want what God wants—a home that honors Him and creates for our loved ones a little bit of heaven on earth. Here are the ways to begin the building process that brings about such a "home sweet home."

—*Understand that wisdom builds.* We've talked about "wisdom" throughout this book, so I thought this would be a good place to insert a working definition of wisdom.

> *Wisdom* is the ability to use the best means at the best time to accomplish the best ends. It is not merely a matter of information or knowledge, but of skillful and practical application of the truth to the ordinary facets of life.[12]

(I have to admit, "good...better...best" immediately comes to my mind!) What do you think the key words of this definition are, and why?

Which area of this definition challenges you most? Or, put another way, do you need more knowledge, more skills, or more careful diligence to application? Share what you plan to do about any weak areas.

*tongue*

—*Decide to begin building.* We also discussed making a commitment for doing the work involved in home-building. Look at these two scriptures and write out how they apply to creating an enchanted oasis called home.

- Proverbs 31:13 — *She seeks wool + flax + works with willing hands*

- Colossians 3:23 — *Whatever you do work heartily, as for the Lord + not for men*

"Commit your works to the LORD and your thoughts [and plans] will be established" (Proverbs 16:3). Why not write out a fresh commitment right now, committing your works, thoughts, plans, and dreams about your home to the Lord and asking for His grace to enable you in your home-building endeavors?

*buttons, papers, less, words, attitude*

—*Each day do one thing to build your home.*

Look around your home (or apartment or room or half a room), inside and out. Make a list of the things that need to be added, repaired, set up, etc., so that your area is more of a refuge. Then do just one item on your list each day—or even one each week.

If you haven't already made such a list, do so now. Put it in a special place where you can look at it often. (Remember our definition of wisdom? It's not merely a matter of information or knowledge, but of skillful and practical *application* of the truth to the ordinary facets of life—like homemaking!)

*p. 95*

**Verses to Memorize**—Proverbs 14:1 and Proverbs 31:27. Add to this list any verses that encourage you in your role of homemaker.

*Prov. 31:27 She looks well to the ways of her household & does not eat the bread of idleness*

**A Heartfelt Prayer**—Lord, just for today, help me make my house a home by... *words*

On the following page, relate in 100 words or less one instance when you actively chose to work (willingly and heartily!) on your home. Then thank God for His grace to make that choice.

( How is your Quiet Times Calendar looking? Your homemaking will benefit greatly from taking care of your *spiritual* housekeeping!)

*Words from My Heart*

14

# A Heart That Watches Over the Home

*be servant of all, give honor & preference to one another Rom 12:10*

In your copy of *A Woman After God's Own Heart*®, read chapter 14, "A Heart That Watches Over the Home." What meant the most to you from this chapter or offered you the greatest challenge or inspired you deeply?

*p.200 "growing to be more like Him strengthens & fills our ♡ & empowers us to obey" wisdom for travelling life & power to do what's right (p.201)*

*Phil 4:8*

*p.204 "holiness, self control, submission, contentment / other tongue
p.206 "strength to resist temptation (Prov 31:26 "law of kindness is
p.208 think loving, positive, sweet thoughts when it comes to other people*

We ended our last lesson by memorizing Proverbs 31:27. Can you write it out from memory here as we begin to unpack its riches?  *p.99*

💜 **Watching and Working**—Let's focus on "watching" first. How was "watching" (from Proverbs 31:27) defined and described?

*she looks well to the ways of her household*

Like a shepherdess, the woman with a heart that watches over her home looks well to the "ways" or "paths" or "tracks" of her home and those who live there. What does Psalm 23:3 say about God's watchcare over your "ways" or "paths" or "tracks"?

*He restores my soul*

*He leads me in paths of righteousness for his name's sake*

Like the Lord, our Shepherd, a homemaker after God's own heart carefully notices the patterns of her home life, the general comings and goings, the habits and activities of the people at home. The Hebrew word for "ways" means "literal tracks made by constant use." They're like the footpath that cuts across a lawn due to repeated use. Would you say that you are "watching" well over your loved ones and are aware of their "ways"? Why or why not?

Are there any "ways" developing that you are not pleased with, that don't seem to honor God's standards? What can and will you do about them? *2 patience & grace address by God's help*

**Watching and Working**—Now let's look at "working." As we head into this section, I hope you know that we're not addressing working outside the home at a job. No, this has to do with the work you do *inside* the house, *at* home, the work that turns your house into a *home*. In the book I mentioned that I had gone through a Bible study on the topic of "Why Work?" Why don't we do our own study on this same question and ethic right now? Of course, we'll want to look at some wonderful proverbs! Take notes on what God teaches us about work through them.

Proverbs 10:4— a slack hand causes poverty
but the hand of the diligent makes rich

Proverbs 12:11—
Whoever works his land will have plenty of bread
but he who follows worthless pursuits lacks sense

Proverbs 14:23— In all toil there is profit,
but mere talk tends only to poverty

Proverbs 18:9— Whoever is slack in his work
is a brother to him who destroys

Proverbs 20:13— Love not sleep, lest you come to poverty;
open your eyes, + you will have plenty of bread

Proverbs 28:19— Whoever works his land will have
plenty of bread,
but he who has worthless pursuits      — ''
— of poverty

Proverbs 31:13— She seeks wool + flax,
+ works with willing hands

Proverbs 31:27— She looks well to the ways of her household
+ does not eat the bread of idleness

Now look at the picture God paints for us in Proverbs 24:30-34. What is His message? *field of sluggard* *overgrown = thorns* *vineyard of man lacking sense* *covered = nettles* *stone wall broken down*

*33 A little sleep, a little slumber, a little folding of the hands to rest.* *34 + poverty will come upon you like a robber + want like an armed man*

Just one more verse from Ecclesiastes 9:10a—
*Whatever your hand finds to do, do it with your might*

*Then I saw + considered it; I looked + received instruction* As you "sit" and "consider" and "look at" and "receive instruction" (Proverbs 24:32) from these verses that represent only a small portion of what the Bible teaches us about the benefits and how-to's of working diligently, list two or three loud messages to your heart.

Now, make a schedule for the upcoming week that incorporates some of the Bible's wise advice regarding your work habits.

♡ **Yes, But How?**—To work out your watching and working, write out again Proverbs 14:1. Let's look at some ways to follow through on God's design for us as home-builders who watch over the place and the people at home and do the work that brings God's plan to life. *The wisest of women builds her house* *but folly + her own hands tears it down*

—*Step 1: Understand that this role as helper and guard is God's plan for you.* This is a good place to consider the word "virtuous" (Proverbs 31:10). What were the components of its definition as stated on page 169?
. *moral strength, strength of character*
. *physical ability + physical prowess*

How does God's calling to be a "virtuous" woman help you to understand and embrace your God-given role as a helper to those *in* your home and a guard *over* your home?

*upright*

—*Step 2: Begin watching over your home.* Do you need to spend some time in prayer about this vital step? Do you need to ask God to help you take this step?

—*Step 3: Eliminate idleness.* I know we've spent a lot of time on the first half of Proverbs 31:27, but write out the second part again.

*+ does not eat the bread of idleness*

Can you think of three real ways you can eliminate idleness today…and in the week (and weeks!) to come?

1. *pray do*

2. *pray do schedule*

3. *rest when needed*

As we close this lesson on the loving watchcare you and I can minister to our dear families, I just can't resist sharing this short-but-to-the-point testimony from another woman after God's own heart. She's added yet another element to this three-step formula—indeed, *the* element!

> This last week I purposed to be more "domestically inclined"! It occurred to me to PRAY about my house and housework—I never had before. But what a difference! Everything gets done more efficiently when I've brought it before the Lord and when He's helping me manage IT instead of IT managing me.

 **Verses to Memorize**—Proverbs 14:23 and Proverbs 31:10. Add to this list any verses that encourage you in your role of homemaker.

 **A Heartfelt Prayer**—Lord, just for today, help me "build" my house by…

On the following page, relate in 100 words or less one instance when you actively chose to take your role as a watcher and worker seriously this week. Then thank God for His grace to make that choice.

# Words from My Heart

15

# A Heart That Creates Order from Chaos

In your copy of *A Woman After God's Own Heart*®, read chapter 15, "A Heart That Creates Order from Chaos." What meant the most to you from this chapter or offered you the greatest challenge or inspired you deeply?

 **Responsibility and Accountability**—Read 1 Timothy 5:13-14. As the apostle Paul observed the behavior of the young widows of his day, what distressing habits did he list in verse 13?

*they learn to be idlers, going about from house to house + not only idlers, but also gossips + busybodies, saying what they should not*

What did he say was "better" for these women (verse 14)?

*younger widows marry, bear children, manage their households, + give the adversary no reason for slander*

**Yes, But How?** *First, understand that home management is God's best for us*—God's desire that we build and watch over and manage a home is obviously not only "better" for us, but also "best." (We can thus be sure that those who dwell under our roof will enjoy the beauty of order versus the confusion of chaos!) What does Titus 2:3-5 have to say on this subject?

*[handwritten] Older women — likewise to be reverent in behavior, not slanders or slaves to much wine. they — to teach what is good + so train the young women to love their husbands + children; to be self-controlled, pure, working @ home, kind, + submissive to their own husbands, that the word of God may not be reviled*

*Second, decide to take home management seriously* — Knowing what God desires for you and your home — that you are *on assignment from God to manage your home* — what decisions can you make to take the management of your home more seriously?

*Third, live as though you will be accountable for the condition of your home and the use of your time* — What is the atmosphere of your home like? What can you do to make your home a place of peace and rejuvenation?

**Twelve Tips for Time Management** — Hopefully by now you've turned the level of your commitment to your home up a notch or two! Now let's look at some practical tips that will help us with our good-housekeeping chores. Write out one goal for next week in each of these areas. Then, at the end of your week, see how many you can check off as accomplished.

1. Plan in detail — My goal:

2. Deal with today—My goal:


3. Value each minute—My goal:


> ### *Just a Minute*
>
> I have only just a minute—
>     Just sixty seconds in it;
> Forced upon me—can't refuse it,
>     didn't seek it, didn't choose it.
> But it is up to me to use it.
> I must suffer if I lose it,
>     give account if I abuse it;
> Just a tiny little minute...
>     but eternity is in it![13]


4. Keep moving—My goal:


5. Develop a routine—My goal:


6. Exercise and diet—My goal:

7. Ask the "half the time" question — My goal:

8. Use a timer for everything — My goal:

9. Do the worst first — My goal:

10. Read daily on time management — My goal:

11. Say no — My goal:

> We must say "no" not only to things which are wrong and sinful, but to things pleasant, profitable, and good which would hinder and clog our grand duties and our chief work.[14]

12. Begin the night before — My goal:

**Verses to Memorize**—Psalm 90:12 and Luke 16:10. Add to this list any verses that encourage you in your role of homemaker.

*Ps 90:2    So teach us to # our days that we may get a heart of wisdom*

*Lke 16:10    One who is faithful in a very little is also faithful in much.*

 **A Heartfelt Prayer**—Lord, just for today, help me better manage my home by... *listening to You*

On the following page, relate in 100 words or less one instance when you actively chose to put your energy and efforts to work at home. Then thank God for His grace to make that choice.

# Words from My Heart

# 16

# A Heart That Weaves a Tapestry of Beauty

✿

In your copy of *A Woman After God's Own Heart*®, read chapter 16, "A Heart That Weaves a Tapestry of Beauty." What meant the most to you from this chapter or offered you the greatest challenge or inspired you deeply?

*making home first of all a center of attraction by its harmonies of peace + love, so that no discordant note may mar the music of its joy*

*faithful in little, faithful in much*

♥ **Beauty from Busyness**—As we've been moving through this book and our priorities, we've looked often at Titus 2:3-5. We learned that, after loving God with all our heart, soul, mind, and strength, we are to learn (and the older women are to teach others) how to love our *husbands* and love our *children*. Look once again at Titus 2:3-5. How does your version of the Bible state Paul's exhortation regarding your home? Write it out here. Then look at some other Bible translations of this same exhortation.

*Older women likewise are to be reverent in behavior, not slanderers or slaves to much wine.*
*They are to teach what is good, + so train the young women to love their husbands + children, To be self-controlled, pure, working at home, kind, + submissive to their own husbands, that the word of God may not be reviled*

114

💗 **Yes, But How?**—For the past three lessons we've focused on building our home and watching over our home and working on our home. We've concentrated on learning what this means and how to do it. And we've been challenged to do it better and do it faster. All summed up, these threads—the knowledge of God's truth, a right attitude in your heart, and the skills in motion—make up the beginnings of a beautiful tapestry, a tapestry called "home." Let's look at a few more threads now.

💗 *Understand the beauty and blessings of God's will for you*—As you take God's role of homemaker more seriously, not only will your home be more orderly and lovely, but there will be added spiritual blessings, as this woman shared in a letter.

> Recently I made a very important decision to be home more often! Let me share some of the many blessings I've already experienced. First, I've been able to begin practicing God's role for me as a woman and to CONSISTENTLY spend time in prayer. I've begun to realize how important my family and home are and what a ministry God has given me there. What a blessing it is to say to my son, "What can I pray about for you today?" To have him see answers to those prayers is worth any sacrifice. My husband, too, commented on how a situation at work had begun to get better because of prayer. I now realize the importance of the family and home and what God can do when we CHOOSE to allow Him to work in our home and in our lives. I now have a full-time ministry to my family.

And *you*? What blessings are you and your family beginning to reap as you understand more about God's priorities and make the choices that reflect them? As a hymn reminds us:

> "Count your blessings; Name them one by one.
> Count your many blessings; See what God hath done."

*Understand that homemaking can be learned*—I was fortunate to find sisters in Christ to help me learn a few good housekeeping tips. Do you need a little help? Some instruction from someone who's doing a good job of weaving their tapestry of beauty? Pinpoint a few areas where some assistance would be valuable.

*dealing with papers*

Now, what can you do today and in the upcoming week to move toward getting the help you need?

*try*

And one more question—Do you own a good book on home-making or know where to borrow one? Write down the titles of several helpful books here. Also ask others for their favorites.

*Guide to cleaning*

*Be home more often*—This may sound repetitious, but being at home more often is at the heart of your homemaking. The old saying "Absence makes the heart grow fonder" is *not* true when it comes to your home! Look at your calendar for last week and note these facts:

How many meetings did you have?
How many outings did you have?
How many get-togethers did you have?
How many lunches out did you have?
How many appointments did you have?

How many evenings out did you have?
How many days did you run errands?
(For some of us, we might ask, "How many
    hours was I home?")

Now that the truth is in, make a schedule for the upcoming week
that allows you to be home more often.

♡ *Organize your outings*—What does Ephesians 5:15-16 say about
time? *Look carefully then how you walk, not as unwise
but as wise, making the best use of the time,
because the days are evil*

How do you think organizing your outings will help you and
your loved ones reap more blessings in your home?

*neater, cleaner*

In my book *Beautiful in God's Eyes—The Treasures of the Proverbs 31
Woman*, I ended the chapter on Proverbs 31:27, "A Watchful Eye,"
with these words:

> I know it may not seem very inviting or sound very exciting,
> but your home is definitely the place most worthy of your
> diligent watching. In fact, home is the most important place
> in the world for you to be spending your time and investing
> your energy. Why do I say that? Because the work you do
> in "a little place" like home is eternal work, meaningful
> work, important work—when you realize that the work
> you do in your home is your supreme service to God! I
> invite you to enjoy the beauty of serving in a little place, a
> little place…like home.

### A Little Place

"Where shall I work today, dear Lord?"
And my love flowed warm and free.
He answered and said,
"See that little place?
Tend that place for Me."

I answered and said, "Oh no, not there!
No one would ever see.
No matter how well my work was done,
Not that place for me!"
His voice, when He spoke, was soft and kind,
He answered me tenderly,
"Little one, search that heart of thine,
Are you working for them or ME?
Nazareth was a little place...
So was Galilee."[15]

 **Verses to Memorize**—Proverbs 17:24 and Ephesians 5:15-16. Add to this list any verses that encourage you in your role of homemaker.

*The discerning sets his face toward wisdom, but the eyes of a fool are on the ends of the earth.*
*Look carefully then how you walk, not as unwise but as wise, making the best use of the time, because the days are evil*

 **A Heartfelt Prayer**—Lord, just for today, help me make my home a high priority by...

*diligence*

On the following page, relate in 100 words or less one instance when you actively chose to be at home. Then thank God for His grace to make that choice.

# Words from My Heart

raising the boys

# 17

# A Heart Strengthened by Spiritual Growth

In your copy of *A Woman After God's Own Heart*®, read chapter 17, "A Heart Strengthened by Spiritual Growth." What meant the most to you from this chapter or offered you the greatest challenge or inspired you deeply? *See p 200*

*growing to be more like Him strengthens & fills our hearts &*
*empowers us to obey His commands*
*p. 204 wisdom for handling life + power to do what's right*
*p. 206 strength → resist temptation*
*p. 204 holiness, self-control, submission, contentment*
*p. 208 Phil 4:8 think loving, sweet, positive thoughts when it comes to other people.*
*Proverbs 31:26 ... on her tongue is the law of kindness. Phil 2:4 look to the interest*
*Romans 12:10 give honor + preference to one another. — Esteem others more*
*of others highly than self*
*Be the servant of all*
*generous WB p.123*

We're nearing the end of our study of what the Bible says about priorities for us as women after God's own heart. Are you perhaps wondering, "But what about *me?* Where do *I* fit in all of this?" This whole book has been about others, and as we address the area of "self," I want you to know that whenever I speak of "self" I have one thing in mind, and one thing only — <u>preparing your "self" so that your life overflows in ministry into the lives of others.</u> "Self" is merely the <u>mainspring</u> to ministry. "Self" is growth — spiritual growth and personal growth — so that others are blessed by your efforts to grow. Let's consider some of the facets of spiritual growth.

**Spiritual Growth Begins in Jesus Christ**—Note the facts about eternal life found in 1 John 5:11-12.

> *to in his Son*
> *Whoever has the Son has it*
> *E.S.N.*    *not*      *not*

Now answer as honestly as you can—Do you have the Son of God? Do you have eternal life? And why do you answer in this way?    *Y*

If you cannot answer "yes," ask God to begin to move you toward a complete knowledge of Him, His Son, and your sin. You might want to write out a prayer here.

> *The ♡ of him who has understanding seeks knowledge but the mouths of fools feed on folly*

**Spiritual Growth Involves the Pursuit of Knowledge**—Look at Proverbs 15:14 in your Bible and copy it here. Don't forget to note the contrast it gives us.

What five areas would you like to begin growing in? List them and then set up your five file folders. These will now be known as your "five fat files." Congratulations on taking a crucial growth step that few ever take!

1.

2.

3.

4.

5.

 **Spiritual Growth Includes Stewardship of Your Body** —

Look at 1 Corinthians 9:27 in your Bible.

*But I disciplene my body + keep it under control,*

How did Paul treat and view his body?

*lest after preaching to others I myself should be desgraclefied*

How can a failure to discipline your body affect the quality of your life?

We mentioned both diet and exercise as areas requiring discipline. Set a goal for each for the upcoming week.

Diet —

Exercise —

**Spiritual Growth Means Becoming Like Jesus** — What is Peter's exhortation in 2 Peter 3:18?

Under "Have a Plan," I likened spiritual growth to preparing a meal for your family. Do you have such a plan for growing in knowledge? Can you share it here? For instance...

What "thing" are you doing?

And in what place?

And with what study tools?

And at what time?

Also, how does your Quiet Times Calendar look?

**Spiritual Growth Blesses Others** — Do you agree or disagree that your mind, mouth, and manners <u>can mar or minister to others,</u> and why?  Y  *they are affected*

— *Mind your mind.* How important is your thought life according to Proverbs 23:7?  *stingy*
*he is like one who is inwardly calculating*
*"Eat + drink" he says to you,*
*but his ♡ is not with you*
23:8 *you'll vomit up the morsel you've eaten*
*+ waste your pleasant words*

What does Philippians 4:8 suggest for your thought life?
Set a goal for your thoughts about others.

*(true) honorable*
*just*
*pure*
*lovely*
*commendable          worthy of praise*

—*Mind your mouth.* Look again at Proverbs 31:26. What are two
guidelines we should establish for the words we speak?

*Open mouth & wisdom*

*the teaching of kindness is on her tongue*

What are several other guidelines found in Ephesians 4:29?

*Let no corrupting talk come out of your mouths,*
*but only such as is good for building up,*
*                   as it fits the occasion, to*
*that it may give grace to those who hear*

And what ultimate guideline does the psalmist set for our
mouth (and for our mind too) in Psalm 19:14?

*Let the words of my mouth &*
*   the meditation of my heart*
*be acceptable in your sight,*
*O LORD, my rock & my redeemer*

Set a goal for your speech to and about others.

*Kind loving sweet positive &*
*edifying*
*wise*

—*Mind your manners.* Romans 12:10 gives us guidelines for the
manner in which we should treat others. What are they?

*Love one another with brotherly affection*
*Outdo one another in showing honor*

Now look at Philippians 2:3-5. What is the message of verse
3?

*Do nothing from rivalry or conceit*
*but in humility count others more significant*
*   than yourselves*

And of verse 4?

*Let each of you look not only to his own
interests, but also to the interest of others*

And of verse 5?

*Have this mind in you which was also
in Christ Jesus*

Set a goal for your manners toward others.

*considering them higher*

—*Mary and Martha.* We've already discussed these two sisters, but look again at Luke 10:38-42. How did their actions, attitudes, and words reveal what was going on in their hearts?

| | Mary | Martha |
|---|---|---|
| Mind | *sat @ Lord's feet + listened to his teachings* | *distracted ē much serving* |
| Mouth | | *"Lord do you not care that my sister has left me to serve alone? Tell her then to help me* |
| Manners | *chose the good portion which will not be taken away from her* | *· welcomed Jesus into her house* |

Again, what steps can you take to be more like Mary and less like Martha?

*rest in His love*

**Verses to Memorize**—Psalm 19:14 and 2 Peter 3:18. Add to this list any verses that encourage you in your spiritual and personal growth.

*"Let the words of my mouth + the meditations of my heart be acceptable in your sight, O LORD, my rock + my redeemer"*

*" But grow in the grace + knowledge of our Lord + Savior Jesus Christ. To Him be the glory both now + to the day of eternity"*

 **A Heartfelt Prayer**—Lord, just for today, help me grow in grace and knowledge by...

*Kind loving edification*

On the following page, relate in 100 words or less one instance when you actively chose to put a new discipline into practice. Then thank God for His grace to make that choice.

# Words from My Heart

# 18

# A Heart Enriched by Joy in the Lord

In your copy of *A Woman After God's Own Heart*®, read chapter 18, "A Heart Enriched by Joy in the Lord." What meant the most to you from this chapter or offered you the greatest challenge or inspired you deeply?

p221 *Success comes when preparation meets opportunity*

In the previous chapter, we began an exciting journey of looking at God's pattern, plan, and desire for our spiritual and personal growth. Why grow? Note how a few scriptures answer this question.

Romans 8:29 — *For those whom He foreknew He also predestined to be conformed to the image of His Son, in order that He might be the firstborn among many brothers.*

Ephesians 2:10 — *For we are His workmanship, created in CJ for good works, which God prepared beforehand, that we should walk in them.*

2 Timothy 1:9 — *God* *Who saved us + called us to a holy calling not because of our works but because of His own purpose + grace, which He gave us in CJ before the ages began*

*became partakers of the divine nature v.4*
2 Peter 1:5-8 — *For this very reason, make every effort to supplement your faith c̄ virtue (excellence), + c̄ knowledge + c̄ self-control +, steadfastness + c̄ godliness + brotherly affection + c̄ love*

As I stated before, this section on "self" is about preparing your "self" for ministry so that your life overflows naturally in ministry into the lives of others. "Self" is the mainspring to ministry. Therefore, as women after God's own heart, we must do all we can (our part) so that God can grow us into women who bless others through our¹encouragement, our ²instruction, our³help, our⁴faith, our⁵knowledge. On and on goes the list of ways we can minister to others. So let's spend some additional time considering several more facets of spiritual and personal growth.

**Spiritual Growth Is Aided by Discipleship**—Please, just one more time, read Titus 2:3-5. What are the two categories of women named in these verses?

*older women          young women*

And what is the role of each?

*ow are to teach what is good, + so train yw ε̄ be trained*

Also, make a list of the four traits that distinguish a godly older woman.

1. *reverent in behavior*
   *not slanderers*
   *"  slaves → much wine*

2.



3.



4.



Now list the curriculum these older women are to teach to the younger ones.

1. *what is good*
   *love their husbands & children*

2. *be self-controlled*

3. *pure*

4. *working @ home*

5. *kind*

6. *submissive to their own husbands*

7.

And why, according to verse 5, was it important that these attitudes be passed on?

*that the word of God may not be reviled*


Who is your older woman, and who are your younger women? Name them here, and then read from my own interactions with Christian women.

*Lita, AnnE.*

It's shocking to me to have to list my number one most-often-asked-question as, "Where are the older women?" From California to Maine, this is the cry of young Christian women. "Where are the older women?" We know from Titus 2:3-5 that

- each of us should be teaching those who are younger, and

- each of us should be learning from those who are older.

So, dear friend, wherever you live and whatever your church situation, remember these three guidelines for yourself:

1. Be sure you are growing in the Lord. Spiritual growth *now* ensures that you will always have something vital to pass on to others.

2. Don't give up in your search for an "older woman." There are numerous older women who have put their wisdom in writing. Good books abound that come from the hearts and souls and minds of a multitude of older women in the faith. Also try to attend events where older women are speaking and sharing their knowledge.

3. Realize that *you* may be one of the older women in your congregation. If so, don't resist. Embrace the reality and do all you can to serve those in your church.[16]

💚 **Spiritual Growth Is Aided by Goals** — It's true that goals provide focus, specific measurement, and encouragement. Can you write out two or three spiritual growth goals for this next week? For instance, to have your quiet time each day. To read one chapter in a meaningful book. To memorize one verse of scripture. Now, write your own goals, commit them to God, and be sure and celebrate the progress made!

1.  *tongue kind*

2.  *Bible / Precept*

3.  *Prayer*

💚 **Spiritual Growth Depends on Choices** — Everything is a choice. We choose to turn on the TV or to pick up a good book. We choose to talk on the phone or to work on a Bible study. We choose to go out to visit or shop or we choose to meet with an older woman. We choose to collapse during the baby's nap (and sometimes we need to do just that!) or to listen to a CD series or work on a correspondence course.

As you look at these examples and think about your own set of choices, do you see any patterns? Or, put another way, what choices are you consistently making? And are they the choices that lead you to spiritual growth? Take a few minutes to write out your observations. (This is an important exercise, so you may want to use an extra piece of paper.)

*Not enough specific prayer*

*thankful*
*not kōmplaining to God v others*

♡ **Spiritual Growth Requires Time**— Read again #3 on pages 39-41 in your book and the last paragraph in the Heart Response section. Isn't this what we both want as women after God's own heart? But it takes time...each day...for each year...for each decade. So, what will you do today to grow? And each day this next week? Giving these goals a time frame will put you one week down the road toward an enriched heart and an enriched life. (By the way, this is a good exercise to repeat every week!)

Day 1                    Day 5

Day 2                    Day 6

Day 3                    Day 7

Day 4

♡ **Spiritual Growth Results in Ministry**— "You cannot give away what you do not possess." We'll look more at your ministry in the next lesson, but realize for now that if you're faithful to grow, your life— by God's grace— *will* overflow in ministry to others.

♡ **Spiritual Growth: Experiencing the Joy of the Lord**— Describe a woman you know whose life seems to overflow in joy as she shares her growth in the Lord with others. How does her joy show? How is it obvious? And what does her joy do for you as God enables her to share His joy with you and others? →outreach

*Nancy D*

And how does her spiritual joy motivate you to grow in the Lord?

*His workmanship*

**Verses to Memorize**—Ephesians 2:10 and 2 Peter 1:8. Add to this list any verses that encourage you to grow in Christ.

¹faith → ²virtue → ³knowledge → ⁴self-control → ⁵steadfastness → ⁶godliness → ⁷brotherly affection → ⁸love
2 Peter 1:8 For if these qualities are yours + are increasing, they keep you from being ineffective or unfruitful in the knowledge of our Lord Jesus Christ

**A Heartfelt Prayer**—Lord, just for today, help me grow by... *steadfastness*
Bib. study + prayer 1st + always

On the following page, relate in 100 words or less one instance when you actively chose to pursue spiritual growth before participating in some other activity. Then thank God for His grace to make that choice.

# Words from My Heart

# 19

# A Heart That Shows It Cares

❦

In your copy of *A Woman After God's Own Heart®*, read chapter 19, "A Heart That Shows It Cares." What meant the most to you from this chapter or offered you the greatest challenge or inspired you deeply?

*setting prayer time & notebook*

*p 229 being confident in our prayers (if not, Satan's cause is not failing)*

*230-231 Prov 3:27 Don't withhold good from those to whom it is due, when it is in the power of your hand to do so. Words of encouragement*

*Be direct.*

*Reach out to as many sheep as you can.*

**Reflecting on God's Plan**—So far we've spent 18 chapters looking at God's Word and seeking to determine what His priorities are for us as women after His own heart. We know of God's command to love Him supremely (Luke 10:27). Beyond that we've culled through Titus 2:3-5 over and over again where the priorities of *husband*, *children*, and *home* are spelled out. And finally, we finished considering our *self*—the nurturing of our spiritual growth. And now we come, by God's grace, to the outpouring and the overflowing of all that's gone before—a life ready for rich ministry to others.

*love the Lord your God w/ all your heart & w/ all your soul & w/ all your strength & all your mind & your neighbor*

*Older women likewise are to be reverent in behavior, not slanderers or slaves to much wine (see below)*

*Titus 2: Older men are to be sober-minded, dignified, self-controlled, sound in faith, in love & in steadfastness.*

*Tit 2: 3 cont'd They are to teach what is good, & so train the young women to love their husbands & children, to be self-controlled, pure, working @ home, kind, & submissive to their own husbands, that the word of God may not be reviled.*

136

Picture again the illustration of the Seven Sacred Pools. How did this depiction of the natural order and overflow of your priorities help you understand the flow of God's plan for you? +

What adjustment or corrections do you need to make in order for this picture to become reality in your life?

*generosity & prayer discipline    not fear; Be direct*

Now that we've considered God's plan for our loved ones and the additional blessing we can be to others, let's look at ten ways we can influence the lives of others — countless others — for eternity.

1. **Learn to Reach Out** — Look at the aspects of giving or reaching out to others that are included in Luke 6:30-38. <u>In a word, what is Jesus' command (verse 30)?</u>

*Give to everyone who begs from you & from one who takes away your goods, do not demand them back*

• What is the scope (verses 30 and 35)?

*√35: But love your enemies & do good & lend, expecting nothing in return, & your reward will be great, & you will be sons of the Most High, for He is kind to the ungrateful & evil.*

• What is to be expected (verses 30 and 35)?   *nothing but being sons of the Most High*

• Who does God give to in verse 35?

*the ungrateful & the evil*

- How much are we to give (verse 38)?
  *give, & it will be given to you. Good measure, pressed down, shaken together, running over, will be put into your lap. For & the measure you use it will be measured back to you*

Now, write out any changes you need to make in your reaching out and giving to others.

2. **Learn to Look Out**—Take a quick look at Jesus' parable of "the Good Samaritan." List the variety of ways he "looked out" for the wounded man in Luke 10:25-37.
*33 had compassion*
*34 went to him*
*bound up his wounds, pouring on oil & wine*
*set him on his own animal*
*brought him to an inn & took care of him*
*35 took out a days wages & gave them to the innkeeper*
*v37 showed him mercy*
*saying, "Take care of him*
*& whatever more you spend*
*I will repay you when I*
*come back.*

How did he manifest a "bountiful eye"?
*all, esp. last*

And how was he direct when he saw a person in need?
*went to him*

What is your normal pattern when you go to church (or elsewhere)? Do you notice—even intentionally look for— those who are hurting or lost? Think this through and answer honestly. Then, once again, note any changes that you need to make. *Y*

3. **Go to Give**—Which point (be all there, live to the hilt, or divide and conquer) meant the most to you in this section, and why? *be direct meant to be not timidly hesitant ~ fearing response or reaction*

Once again, are there changes you need to make in your ministry style and heart? *not so stingy*

4. **Develop Your Prayer Life**—Did "Will" get his point across to you—that prayer involves the "Will" and is "Willful"? So…when do you pray? *Bible reading time maybe*
*e-mail reading time*
*thru day*
*in trauma*
*when something comes to mind wherever*

Where do you pray? *in chair*
*on bed*
*anywhere*

And what is your plan? *Try to find a consistent block*

 **Verses to Memorize**—Proverbs 14:1 and Proverbs 24:3. Add to this list any verses that encourage peace in your home.
*14:1 The wisest of women builds her house, but folly with her own hands tears it down*

*24:3 By wisdom a house is built, + by understanding it is established.*

**A Heartfelt Prayer**—Lord, just for today, help me create
an atmosphere of love by…

*giving grace in my attitudes & reactions*

On the following page, relate in 100 words or less one instance
when you actively chose to reach out and encourage someone.
Then thank God for His grace to make that choice.

*had studied humility & so drawn near → God,*
*-then met Cermenita & Amanda @ next church service.*
*( Had knocked on C's door & she came)*

# Words from My Heart

# 20

## A Heart That Encourages

In your copy of *A Woman After God's Own Heart*®, read chapter 20, "A Heart That Encourages." What meant the most to you from this chapter or offered you the greatest challenge or inspired you deeply?

Let's continue on with our list of ten ways we can, by God's good grace, influence the lives of others.

5. **Take Time to Be Filled**—It's true that there are skills we can develop to strengthen our ministry. What would you consider to be an area of weakness in your life, one that tends to hinder you in the area of ministry to others? *writing calling salt seeing with God's eyes*

Now list steps you can take this week to strengthen this weak area.

*write Sarah Grace Ida Ann*

6. **Memorize Scriptures of Encouragement**—Hopefully you've been faithful to memorize the scriptures suggested each week. (And when you've finished this growth and study guide, it will be fun to begin choosing your own verses!) Share an instance when you used one of your memorized scriptures from these lessons to encourage someone else.

7. **Make Phone Calls to Encourage**—Who needs your call today? Determine not to withhold that sunshine call...when it's in the power of your hand to give it (Proverbs 3:27)!

*Katrina*

8. **Write Notes of Encouragement**—And who needs your note of encouragement today? Again, don't withhold. Do it! Write it! Right now!

*to do*

9. **Encourage Others Through Three Spiritual Gifts**—I was thrilled to discover these three ministries that all Christians can have and use in the body of Christ. Read Romans 12:7-8 and then answer these questions:

Who can you *serve* today and how? (Yes, your husband and children count—indeed, they have top priority! Can you also think of others?) *Mom*

Who needs your *mercy*? *acts of mercy & cheerfulness*

And how and to whom can you *give?*

*Katrina - call*

Now be faithful to follow through on the thoughts God brought to your mind!

10. **Live Your Priorities**—As you have begun to live out God's priorities in your life and in your family, what remarks have people made concerning the differences and changes in your life?

Do you agree that living out your priorities and modeling God's plan ministers to many? Explain, please.

*living His life*

 **Verses to Memorize**—Proverbs 3:27 and 1 Corinthians 15:58. Add to this list any verses that encourage you in your ministry.

*Do not withhold good from those to whom it is due, when it is in your power to do it  Prov. 3:27*

*1 Cor 15:58 ∴ my beloved brethren, be steadfast, immovable, always abounding in the work of the Lord, knowing that in the Lord your labor is not in va*

 **A Heartfelt Prayer**—Lord, just for today, help me reach out and encourage *Mom* by...

*truth graciously + humbly expressed.*

On the following page, relate in 100 words or less one instance when you actively chose to reach out and encourage someone. Then thank God for His grace to make that choice.

# Words from My Heart

Apولec Katrina

# 21

# A Heart That Seeks First Things First

In your copy of *A Woman After God's Own Heart*®, read chapter 21, "A Heart That Seeks First Things First." What meant the most to you from this chapter or offered you the greatest challenge or inspired you deeply?

*— do what husband wants*

*— restful organized home*

🤍 **A Word About Priorities**—Did the little poem on pages 253-54 describe you, my friend? How many hats do you feel like you're trying to wear at once? List them here. Which ones are the most demanding and why?

*organize home*

*want to study, be lifted →*

*thru His word*

🤍 **A Word About Choices**—Read these quotes from your book and mark the one you like the best or that motivates you the most and tell why.

> - As now, so then.  *To shape up, shape up*
> - What you are today is what you are becoming.
> - You are today what you have been becoming.
> - (And an extra...) Each day is a little life, and our whole life is but a day repeated.

 **A Word About Others**—List the "others" (people, positions, and pastimes) in your life. Our priorities certainly don't end with the number 6! Pray first, and then try to put them in an order that honors God and reflects His values. (And don't forget to ask your husband to help you prioritize! His insights and perspectives will reveal what he is observing and thinking.)

*Word*
*Husband, mother, children*
*Precept*
*house*

**A Word About Waiting**—How are you when it comes to waiting? Do you tend to be a person who operates on impulse, makes spur-of-the-moment decisions, and swings and sways from opportunity to option? Or are you a woman who is patient, who prays, who prioritizes, and who plans? Can you give an example?  *need*

**Some Women Who Adjusted Their Priorities**—We looked at several other women in this chapter. Now, how would *your* story read? Do you think your priorities are in order? Does your husband think so? And how about your children? Be honest. And be brave enough to make some serious changes.

**Verses to Memorize**—Colossians 2:6-7 and Proverbs 8:10-11. Add to this list any verses that encourage you to make God your priority.

① ∴ as you received the Lord, so walk in Him, rooted + built up in Him + established in the faith, just as you were taught, abounding in thanksgiving.

② Take my instruction instead of silver, + knowledge rather than choice gold, for wisdom is better than jewels, + all that you desire cannot compare with her.

 **A Heartfelt Prayer**—Lord, just for today, help me choose You first by... *listening to my husband*

On the following page, relate in 100 words or less one instance when you actively chose to reach out and encourage someone. Then thank God for His grace to make that choice.

# Words from My Heart

Carmencita & Amanda

God had helped me to be humble before Him that day & when they both showed up at the chapel that day His love in me just flowed over to them helping them to feel welcomed

# 22

# *Following After God's Heart*

✤

In your copy of *A Woman After God's Own Heart*®, read chapter 22, "Following After God's Heart." What meant the most to you from this chapter or offered you the greatest challenge or inspired you deeply?

p.272 " making choices to live your priorities enables God
to make your life a work of beauty ... a woman of dis.
p.274 treat each day as if it + it alone was our "golden day" p.275
→ string of golden days → yrs ; → give back to our LORD
p.276 → unmatchable peace → each day a pearl on our strand
p.277 _____ → lifetime of living after God's own ♡

♡ **Plan Your Day**—Two sayings immediately come to my mind here!

> • If you don't plan your day, someone else will be happy to plan it for you.
>
> • God has a wonderful plan for your life...and so does everyone else!

Planning is a good first step toward practicing your priorities. So stop and plan whatever is left of your day today. Then, before you go to bed tonight, jot down those events that are already set for tomorrow—mealtimes, appointments, responsibilities. That's a good beginning on tomorrow's wonderful day.

💗 **Pray Over Your Plans and Priorities**—Continuing on with the exercise you began above (or the evening before), and using the list of God's priorities for you, pray your way through your plan, writing out your planned activities.

💗 **Schedule Your Plans and Priorities**—If planning is the *what* of your day, scheduling is the *how*. On your calendar or day-planner write down *when* you intend to follow through on each of the plans. If you're unsure how to do this, look again at the examples.

💗 **Practice Your Priorities**—Now it's time to live out your plan and practice your priorities. Just for one day, think in terms of the numbers assigned to your priorities (#1=God; #2=husband; #3=children; #4=home; #5=self; #6=ministry; #7=others). I think you'll find this numbers exercise helpful, practical, and very eye-opening!

*spiritual growth*

💗 **Acquire God's Perspective On Your Day**—Do you share my friend's perspective on your days? She definitely had honoring the Lord with each and every day in mind when she wrote...

> To treat each day as if it and it alone was our "golden day"—then what a beautiful string of golden days becoming golden years we would have to give back to our Lord!

This perspective, dear friend, is the *how* of practicing our priorities, and it's also the *why*. What changes in your perspective or attitude toward each new day do you need to make to acquire this worthy perspective? *home children?*

 **Practice, Practice, Practice**—How do you and I become women after God's own heart? By practice, practice, practice! By practicing our priorities one day at a time...for the rest of our lives. By living our lives God's way, according to God's Word. By spending our precious time, energy, and days in the pursuit of God's best. Purpose to practice...just for today, your "golden day."

*"as your days, so shall your strength be"*

**Verses to Memorize**—Deuteronomy 33:25b and Matthew 6:33. Add to this list any verses that encourage you on your journey toward becoming a woman after God's own heart.

*But seek first the kingdom of God & His righteousness + all these things shall be added to you.*

 **A Heartfelt Prayer**—Lord, just for today, help me live out this one golden day by... *balance*

On the following page, relate in 100 words or less one instance when you actively chose to practice your priorities. Then thank God for His grace to make that choice.

when someone called me on phone
& during our conversation one of my young children
(or husband) came to me, I excused myself
momentarily to give them my attention.

# Words from My Heart

# The Legacy of A Woman After God's Own Heart

In your copy of *A Woman After God's Own Heart®*, read chapter 23, "The Legacy of *A Woman After God's Own Heart*." What meant the most to you from this chapter or offered you the greatest challenge or inspired you deeply?

*a man after My own ♡, who will do My will   David   p28*

*p282 Energized & encouraged by the grace of God {i.e. focused on Him} & propelled by my ♡'s desire to love God through obedience... move forward*

*p. 283 love Him 1st & passionately, 2 d wife + mom the*
*3 growing in my knowledge of God d serve Him + His people.*

*p. 284 Try to answer those who ask for help*

♥ *Reflecting on David's heart*—In your Bible, read Paul's comments about David in Acts 13:22. What do these words report about his behavior and his heart?

*He (God) raised up David to be their King, He also testified & said "I have found David the son of Jesse, A MAN AFTER MY HEART, who will do all my will.*

Next read Acts 13:36. What do these words reveal about the way David lived his life?

*Holy*

How does this epitaph of David's life challenge you…

In your life today?

For your future days?

List several changes you need to make right away.

*all the more carefully guard attitude & tongue, ask for clear wisdom, being guided c His eye*

♡ *Reflecting on your own heart*—Jot down the lessons you learned from the stories shared by the other women after God's own heart. Jot down the category that best represents you at this time in your life.

*283 priorities guiding beacon ♡Him 1st & passionately; best possible (for me) wife & g, George 3 sentence growing in knowledge ... to ... time Help ple to his praising His all-sufficient desire & pray to have a ♡ that of ... each new or different challenge 28 & positive impact ...*

What needs to be your focus in the days to come?

*Him + His Word*
*His guidance*
*My responsibilities*

What are your concerns for yourself? *health, physical fitness*
*John Mom + family*
*sorting, straightening, mending*

—For your loved ones? *show care, meet the needs I can*
*≈ grace abounding*

—About practicing your priorities? *✓ up*

 **A Heartfelt Prayer**—Lord, just for today, help me serve
my own generation by... *doing my best*
*Maying postludes*
*flowers / baskets*

On the following page, relate in 100 words or less how your study
of becoming a woman after God's own heart has made a difference
in your life and the lives of others. Then thank God for His grace
and power to make the choices you have made along the way.

# Words from My Heart

warmth
—> make each day a pearl!

# 24

## The Legacy of Your Heart

In your copy of *A Woman After God's Own Heart*®, read chapter 24, "The Legacy of Your Heart." What meant the most to you from this chapter or offered you the greatest challenge or inspired you deeply? *p. 283 – tell God if you don't understand... ask Him for the grace + strength to trust Him, to walk by faith*

**Becoming a Woman After God's Own Heart**—Think now about the six keys to becoming a woman after God's own heart.

*Key #1: Obey God's commands*—In your Bible, read 1 Samuel 15:16-24. As you can see, Saul chose to interpret God's commands in his own way. As you think back on your study through this book and what you have been learning, share several ways or areas in which you have chosen to <u>obey God's Word</u> and His commands regardless of the cost to you. *better than sacrifice rebellion: as divination presumption: " iniquity + idolatry*

*LORD: help me not to try to fool myself or give in to myself, but to discern + wholly to Your will*

159

*Key #2: Walk in the Spirit*—Read Galatians 5:16-23, noting God's command to you (verse 16).

Why is walking in the Spirit a challenge (verse 17)?

What characterizes a life lived in the flesh (verses 19-21)?

By contrast, what characterizes a life lived in the Spirit (verses 22-23)?

How do you think walking by the Spirit makes a difference in your life? Your home? Your marriage? Your family?

*Key #3: Pray regularly*—God's Word tells us to pray faithfully, frequently, without ceasing, and in and about everything. How do you think praying regularly will help you as a woman? As a homemaker? As a wife? As a mom? As a member of your church? Name one thing you can do today to be more faithful to pray regularly. *3x/day as David*

*Key #4: Adopt a long-range view*—David died after a long and full life. As the scripture states, "After he had served his own generation by the will of God" (Acts 13:36). To serve your own generation will take a lifetime. That means you will never retire from serving God and the people He places in your life. What—and who—can you focus on today in view of your long-range assignment to be a woman after God's own heart?

*Mern + John*

*Key #5: Accept your roles*—Interact with the questions asked in your book: Do you really believe God is asking you to serve your generation...and to serve according to His will? What evidence is there that you have accepted the challenge of following after God, of living out your roles and assignments from Him?

*Key #6: Ask, "Who am I, and what is it I do?"*—Answer these questions:

Who am I? *God's child*

What is it I actually do, and what is it I should do?

*try to follow*          *follow*

**Verses Memorized**—Review the verses you have memorized through this study. Which one encourages you the most today as you seek to be a woman after God's own heart?

**A Heartfelt Prayer**—Lord, just for today, grant me the grace to pursue Key # __3__ by... *3 x / by praying*

On the following page, relate in 100 words or less how your study of becoming a woman after God's own heart has made a difference in your life and the lives of others. Then thank God for His grace and power to make the choices you have made along the way.

# Words from My Heart

# FROM MY HEART TO YOURS

If you'll remember, I mentioned in the beginning of my book that you and I were embarking on a journey—a journey of learning about God's priorities and how to practice them, a journey of discovering and implementing the disciplines that mark us out as women after God's own heart, a journey toward greater growth and ministry to others.

Well, you've obviously taken the first steps by reading *A Woman After God's Own Heart*®...and now you've taken additional steps by working through this growth and study guide to becoming a woman after God's own heart. You've definitely come a long way already, and I'm certain you're experiencing a transformed life just by your obedience to practice God's priorities for your life.

And now, dear one, as we part and continue down our paths of pursuing Him and His good, better, and best, may God give you His grace, mercy, and peace on your journey to becoming a woman after God's own heart. May He continually bring His truths and His principles to your mind. May He reveal fresh, new ways for you to follow after Him. May the evidence of your growth and your walk with the Lord sound forth the Word of the Lord (1 Thessalonians 1:8) for all to hear and behold. May your loved ones be blessed. And may you stand tall alongside the Proverbs 31 woman. May it be said of you too, "Many daughters have done well, but you excel them all" (Proverbs 31:29).

In His exceedingly great and precious love,

*Elizabeth George*

# GROUP DISCUSSION QUESTIONS

*Chapter 1—*
What are some of the things that keep you from having a daily quiet time?

What do you think are the key ingredients to a quality quiet time?

*Chapter 2—*
What could you give up in order to spend time in God's Word?

How should a deep conviction about the benefits, power, and importance of time in God's Word affect us?

*Chapter 3—*
As a group, compile and share a list of helpful hints for finding time for prayer.

As a group, compile and share a list of ideas for an exciting time of prayer. (For instance, begin your time of prayer by reading one psalm.)

*Chapter 4—*
Make up an acrostic for the word **O-B-E-Y**.

See if you can add to the list of the benefits of obedience.

*Chapter 5—*
What are some ways you have helped your husband this past week?

How can Philippians 2:3-4 apply to you as a wife in this area of serving your husband?

*Chapter 6—*
What is or has been the greatest struggle for you in the area of submission?

How have you seen God honor your obedience when you have submitted?

## Chapter 7 —

How do you make your husband feel special? Be specific.

Share how God answered one of your prayers for your husband this past week.

## Chapter 8 —

What do you do to prepare yourself for your husband's homecoming each evening (mentally, physically, and spiritually)?

What strengths do you see in your husband? Have you ever told him you are aware of these strengths and appreciate them?

## Chapter 9 —

What are some materials or exercises you have used with your children to teach them God's Word and wisdom?

What time of day works best for you and your family for focusing on God's Word, and why?

## Chapter 10 —

What are the top three prayer requests you pray for your children?

How can a "little" excuse today affect your children in a "big" way tomorrow?

## Chapter 11 —

How would you describe the general emotional tone of your home?

Which one of the five marks of motherly affection, if applied, would make the biggest difference in the general emotional tone of your home?

## Chapter 12 —

As you worked your way through the section on mothering, how is your view of your role as a mother changing?

Which one of the additional five marks of motherly affection, if applied, would make the biggest difference in the general emotional tone of your home?

**Chapter 13 —**

Share a time when you knew your home environment ministered to someone else.

Share a time when the home environment of someone else ministered to you.

**Chapter 14 —**

What are the things that tend to rob you of time from watching over your home?

How — and what — are you teaching your children about the value of hard work?

**Chapter 15 —**

Describe your week and the difference the 12 "little steps" in time management made in creating order from chaos.

What favorite time-management tip or resources can you recommend to the group?

**Chapter 16 —**

As you think about this section on the home, what new attitudes and/or disciplines have you put into practice?

Share a challenging "I will" — either from page 197-98 or from your own list — with your group.

**Chapter 17 —**

Describe an encounter you've had with a "There you are!" person.

What do you think makes someone a "There you are!" person?

*love*
*interest in others*

**Chapter 18—**

Describe a time when you had the opportunity to learn from an older woman.

What are some things you're learning that are causing your life to overflow with joy? *thankfulness*

**Chapter 19—**

Share an opportunity you had this week to reach out to someone in need.

Share an opportunity you passed up this week to reach out to someone in need.

**Chapter 20—**

Share an opportunity you passed up this week to encourage someone.

Share an opportunity you had this week to encourage someone.

**Chapter 21—**

How does the saying, "What you are today is what you are becoming" describe you?

What motivates you each new day to keep practicing your priorities?

**Chapter 22—**

How would you respnd to the thought that "every day is God's gift of a fresh, unspoiled opportunity to live according to His priorities"?

**Chapter 23—**

Spiritually speaking, how would you like to grow in the next 10 years?

What difference do you think paying attention to your priorities will make in your life and the lives of others during the next 10 years?

**Chapter 24—**

For today, answer the questions "Who am I?" and "What is it I do?"

# LEADING A BIBLE STUDY DISCUSSION GROUP

What a privilege it is to lead a Bible study! And what joy and excitement await you as you delve into the Word of God and help others discover its life-changing truths. If God has called you to lead a Bible study group, I know you'll be spending much time in prayer and planning and giving much thought to being an effective leader. I also know that taking the time to read through the following tips will help you to navigate the challenges of leading a Bible study discussion group and enjoying the effort and opportunity.

## The Leader's Roles

As a Bible study group leader, you'll find your role changing back and forth from *expert* to *cheerleader* to *lover* to *referee* during the course of a session.

Since you're the leader, group members will look to you to be the *expert* guiding them through the material. So be well prepared. In fact, be over-prepared so that you know the material better than any group member does. Start your study early in the week, and let its message simmer all week long. (You might even work several lessons ahead so that you have in mind the big picture and the overall direction of the study.) Be ready to share some additional gems that your group members wouldn't have discovered on their own. That extra insight from your study time — or that comment from a wise Bible teacher or scholar, that clever saying, that keen observation from another believer, and even an appropriate joke — adds an element of fun and keeps Bible study from becoming routine, monotonous, and dry.

Second, be ready to be the group's *cheerleader*. Your energy and enthusiasm for the task at hand can be contagious. It can also stimulate people to get more involved in their personal study as well as in the group discussion.

Third, be the *lover,* the one who shows a genuine concern for the members of the group. You're the one who will establish the atmosphere of the group. If you laugh and have fun, the group members will laugh and have fun. If you hug, they will hug. If you care, they will care. If you share, they will share. If you love, they will love. So pray every day to love the women God has placed in your group. Ask Him to show you how to love them with His love.

Finally, as the leader, you'll need to be the *referee* on occasion. That means making sure everyone has an equal opportunity to speak. That's easier to do when you operate under the assumption that every member of the group has something worthwhile to contribute. So, trusting that the Lord has taught each person during the week, act on that assumption.

Expert, cheerleader, lover, and referee—these four roles of the leader may make the task seem overwhelming. But that's not bad if it keeps you on your knees praying for your group.

## A Good Start

Beginning on time, greeting people warmly, and opening in prayer gets the study off to a good start. Know what you want to have happen during your time together and make sure those things get done. That kind of order means comfort for those involved.

Establish a format and let the group members know what that format is. People appreciate being in a Bible study that focuses on the Bible. So keep the discussion on the topic and move the group through the questions. Tangents are often hard to avoid—and even harder to rein in. So be sure to focus on the answers to questions about the specific passage at hand. After all, the purpose of the group is Bible study!

Finally, as someone has accurately observed, "Personal growth is one of the by-products of any effective small group. This growth is achieved when people are recognized and accepted by others. The more friendliness, mutual trust, respect, and warmth exhibited, the more likely that the member will find pleasure in the group, and, too, the more likely she will work hard toward the accomplishment of the group's goals. The effective leader will strive to reinforce desirable traits" (source unknown).

## A Dozen Helpful Tips

Here is a list of helpful suggestions for leading a Bible study discussion group:

1. Arrive early, ready to focus fully on others and give of yourself. If you have to do any last-minute preparation, review, re-grouping, or praying, do it in the car. Don't dash in, breathless, harried, late, still tweaking your plans.

2. Check out your meeting place in advance. Do you have everything you need—tables, enough chairs, a blackboard, hymnals if you plan to sing, coffee, etc.?

3. Greet each person warmly by name as she arrives. After all, you've been praying for these women all week long, so let each VIP know that you're glad she's arrived.

4. Use name tags for at least the first two or three weeks.

5. Start on time no matter what—even if only one person is there!

6. Develop a pleasant but firm opening statement. You might say, "This lesson was great! Let's get started so we can enjoy all of it!" or "Let's pray before we begin our lesson."

7. Read the questions, but don't hesitate to reword them on occasion. Rather than reading an entire paragraph of instructions, for instance, you might say, "Question 1 asks us to list some ways that Christ displayed humility. Lisa, please share one way Christ displayed humility."

8. Summarize or paraphrase the answers given. Doing so will keep the discussion focused on the topic; eliminate digressions; help avoid or clear up any misunderstandings of the text; and keep each group member aware of what the others are saying.

9. Keep moving and don't add any of your own questions to the discussion time. It's important to get through the study guide questions. So if a cut-and-dried answer is called for, you don't need to comment with anything other than a "thank you." But when the question asks for an opinion or an application (for instance, "How can this truth help us in our marriages?" or "How do *you* find time for your quiet time?"), let all who want to contribute.

10. Affirm each person who contributes, especially if the contribution was

very personal, painful to share, or a quiet person's rare statement. Make everyone who shares a hero by saying something like, "Thank you for sharing that insight from your own life" or, "We certainly appreciate what God has taught you. Thank you for letting us in on it."

11. Watch your watch, put a clock right in front of you, or consider using a timer. Pace the discussion so that you meet your cutoff time, especially if you want time to pray. Stop at the designated time even if you haven't finished the lesson. Remember that everyone has worked through the study once; you are simply going over it again.

12. End on time. You can only make friends with your group members by ending on time or even a little early! Besides, members of your group have the next item on their agenda to attend to—picking up children from the nursery, babysitter, or school; heading home to tend to matters there; running errands; getting to bed; or spending some time with their husbands. So let them out *on time!*

## Five Common Problems

In any group, you can anticipate certain problems. Here are some common ones that can arise, along with helpful solutions:

1. *The incomplete lesson*—Right from the start, establish the policy that if someone has not done the lesson, it is best for her not to answer the questions. But do try to include her responses to questions that ask for opinions or experiences. Everyone can share some thoughts in reply to a question like, "Reflect on what you know about both athletic and spiritual training and then share what you consider to be the essential elements of training oneself in godliness."

2. *The gossip* —The Bible clearly states that gossiping is wrong, so you don't want to allow it in your group. Set a high and strict standard by saying, "I am not comfortable with this conversation," or "We [not *you*] are gossiping, ladies. Let's move on."

3. *The talkative member*—Here are three scenarios and some possible solutions for each.

a.  The problem talker may be talking because she has done her homework and is excited about something she has to share. She may also know more about the subject than the others and, if you cut her off, the rest of the group may suffer.

SOLUTION: Respond with a comment like: "Sarah, you are making very valuable contributions. Let's see if we can get some reactions from the others," or "I know Sarah can answer this. She's really done her homework. How about some of the rest of you?"

b.  The talkative member may be talking because she has *not* done her homework and wants to contribute, but she has no boundaries.

SOLUTION: Establish at the first meeting that those who have not done the lesson do not contribute except on opinion or application questions. You may need to repeat this guideline at the beginning of each session.

c.  The talkative member may want to be heard whether or not she has anything worthwhile to contribute.

SOLUTION: After subtle reminders, be more direct, saying, "Betty, I know you would like to share your ideas, but let's give others a chance. I'll call on you later."

4. *The quiet member*—Here are two scenarios and possible solutions.

a.  The quiet member wants the floor but somehow can't get the chance to share.

SOLUTION: Clear the path for the quiet member by first watching for clues that she wants to speak (moving to the edge of her seat, looking as if she wants to speak, perhaps even starting to say something) and then saying, "Just a second. I think Chris wants to say something." Then, of course, make her a hero!

b.  The quiet member simply doesn't want the floor.

SOLUTION: "Chris, what answer do you have on question 2?" or "Chris, what do you think about...?" Usually after a shy person has contributed a few times, she will become more confident and more ready to share. Your role is to provide an opportunity where there is *no* risk of a wrong answer. But occasionally a group member will tell you that she would rather not be called on. Honor her request, but from time to time ask her privately if she feels ready to contribute to the group discussions.

In fact, give all your group members the right to pass. During your first meeting, explain that any time a group member does not care to share an answer, she may simply say, "I pass." You'll want to repeat this policy at the beginning of every group session.

5. *The wrong answer*—Never tell a group member that she has given a wrong answer, but at the same time never let a wrong answer go by.

**Solution:** Either ask if someone else has a different answer or ask additional questions that will cause the right answer to emerge. As the women get closer to the right answer, say, "We're getting warmer! Keep thinking! We're almost there!"

## Learning from Experience

Immediately after each Bible study session, evaluate the group discussion time. You may also want a member of your group (or an assistant or trainee or outside observer) to evaluate you periodically.

# NOTES

1. Elizabeth George, *A Woman After God's Own Heart* ® (Eugene, OR: Harvest House Publishers, 1997, 2006).

2. Warren Wiersbe, ed., *The Best of A. W. Tozer* (Grand Rapids, MI: Baker Book House, 1978), pp. 149-51.

3. C.A. Stoddards, source unknown.

4. John MacArthur, *The MacArthur Study Bible* (Nashville: Word Publishing, 1997), p. 1087.

5. Ibid., p. 1933.

6. Neil S. Wilson, ed., *The Handbook of Bible Application* (Wheaton, IL: Tyndale House Publishers, Inc., 1992), p. 441.

7. Ibid., pp. 441-43.

8. MacArthur, *The MacArthur Study Bible*, p. 19.

9. Charles F. Pfeiffer and Everett F. Harrison, eds., *The Wycliffe Bible Commentary* (Chicago: Moody Press, 1973), p. 5.

10. Mary Louise Kitsen, "Generations of Excuses," *Good News Broadcaster*. Used by permission.

11. Eleanor L. Doan, *The Speaker's Sourcebook*, quoting Mary Holmes from *The War Cry* (Grand Rapids, MI: Zondervan Publishing House, 1977), p. 27.

12. Sid Buzzell, gen. ed., *The Leadership Bible* (Grand Rapids, MI: Zondervan Publishing House, 1998), p. 739.

13. Doan, *The Speaker's Sourcebook*, quote by Christine Warren, p. 266.

14. C.A. Stoddards, source unknown.

15. Author unknown, cited in Elizabeth George, *Beautiful in God's Eyes—The Treasures of the Proverbs 31 Woman* (Eugene, OR: Harvest House Publishers, 1998), p. 210.

16. "Ask Elizabeth" at www.elizabethgeorge.com.

## About the Author

Elizabeth George is a bestselling author who has more than 4.8 million books in print. She is a popular speaker at Christian women's events. Her passion is to teach the Bible in a way that changes women's lives. For information about Elizabeth's speaking ministry, to sign up for her mailings, or to purchase her books visit her website:

www.ElizabethGeorge.com